Praise for Meg Benjamin's
Wedding Bell Blues

"...a good read and a great fictional world, and Meg Benjamin is a wizard at story-telling. ... My hope, as a reader, is that I won't have to wait too long for another Konigsburg adventure."
~ *Cherry Blossom, Long and Short Reviews*

"*Wedding Bell Blues* was a laugh out loud funny read with very believable, dramatic characters. I found myself not able to turn the pages fast enough to find out what happened next. It was truly a fascinating and engaging read and I want more. I am so thankful that this is only book two in the series and I can look forward to more writing that sparkles with wit and humor. ...I strongly recommend you pick up this book as it has everything—humor, drama, mystery and a whole lot of sexual tension!"
~ *Val, You Gotta Read Reviews*

"Readers will be hooked from the very first paragraph. The characters from every generation that descend upon the bride and groom are a pure delight. The family dramas going on around the wedding will keep readers laughing and engaged through every page."
~ *Amy Lignor, Romantic Times*

"How many ways can I say I love this book....WEDDING BELL BLUES is a convoluted mess of comical what if's, that did eventually happen and it was a fun read..."
~ *Erotic Horizon Recommended Read*

Look for these titles by
Meg Benjamin

Now Available:

Konigsburg, Texas Series
Venus in Blue Jeans (Book 1)
Wedding Bell Blues (Book 2)
Be My Baby (Book 3)

Wedding Bell Blues

Meg Benjamin

A SAMHAIN PUBLISHING, LTD. publication.

Samhain Publishing, Ltd.
577 Mulberry Street, Suite 1520
Macon, GA 31201
www.samhainpublishing.com

Wedding Bell Blues
Copyright © 2010 by Meg Benjamin
Print ISBN: 978-1-60504-716-4
Digital ISBN: 978-1-60504-630-3

Editing by Lindsey McGurk
Cover by Natalie Winters

First Samhain Publishing, Ltd. electronic publication: July 2009
First Samhain Publishing, Ltd. print publication: May 2010

Dedication

To Beckie and all the Kharities ladies—thanks for the read, guys. And to my terrific editor, Lindsey McGurk. And last, but definitely not least, to my guys, Bill, Josh, and Ben.

Chapter One

Blissful people made Pete Toleffson want to puke. Normally, he spent his days getting bad guys convicted and saving good people from being victimized. He considered that world to be the real world and "bliss world" to be something like a parallel universe for the clueless. Blissful people lived in la-la land. Blissful people needed to be rapped upside the head.

Which was unfortunate because his brother Cal was currently the most blissful person in Konigsburg, Texas. Well, maybe the second most, after his fiancée, Docia Kent.

Pete studied his brother as he sat smiling beside him in the booth at the Dew Drop Inn. Cal was so blissful he made Pete's teeth hurt. At least Docia hadn't come in yet. The two of them together could induce sugar shock.

Pete felt like telling them to get a room, but they already had one, or rather they had a house together on the edge of town. Pete was staying in Docia's old apartment above her bookstore in downtown Konigsburg. Of course, his residence in Docia's apartment was strictly temporary. He was only here for the wedding. After that he'd head back home to Des Moines and the real world again.

Konigsburg was closer to something out of Disney. He kept expecting to see cartoon bluebirds twittering around over Docia's head, and maybe a couple of bunnies hopping along at her feet. A far cry from the Polk County Attorney's office.

Pete took a swig of beer and ignored the urge to check his cell phone messages that he felt every time he thought about being an assistant Polk County Attorney.

Guts up, Toleffson. They'll get along without you somehow.

A buzz arose from the corner of the room behind him, accompanied by the dull *thonk* of a dart hitting the wall. Pete turned and squinted through the gloom. If he really looked hard he could just make out the target. God only knew how somebody could actually see enough to hit anything in the dim light of the Dew Drop.

For the life of him, Pete couldn't figure out why Cal was so fond of the place. The Dew Drop was a joint, a dive, a honky tonk. Hell, he'd helped to close down better places than this when he got court orders for the Des Moines vice cops.

He turned back for another swallow of beer. Across the table, Cal's friend Wonder Dentist (and what the hell kind of nickname was that?) was squinting at the far wall too. "Bullseye. Ellison's been practicing, I see."

Cal grinned at Wonder. Cal grinned at everybody. Pete wondered briefly if he ever stopped grinning these days. Maybe at night, in bed. But then, considering he shared that bed with Docia, maybe not.

Pete surveyed the Dew Drop denizens, what he could see of them. Even though the late afternoon sun had still been shining when he'd entered the bar, only a few dim beams penetrated the smeared windows at the front. The chandeliers overhead weren't much help since half of the bulbs looked to be burned out. A dive. A dump. Depressing as hell.

Pete clenched his hands on the table in front of him. He did *not* need to check his messages.

Cal raised his chin. "There she is."

Docia Kent stood framed in the doorway, red hair curling around her shoulders in tendrils, her denim shirt knotted beneath her breasts.

Pete sighed. Cal had all the luck. If he'd seen a woman like Docia Kent sitting in a dump like the Dew Drop, he'd have thrown her over his shoulder and headed for the hills, which, apparently, was more or less what Cal had done.

Docia started toward their table, trailed by a couple of other women Pete could barely see. Hard to notice other women when Docia was around. When they got closer, Pete recognized the first woman as Wonder's girlfriend, Allie Maldonado.

He'd been introduced to the other woman, and now he ransacked his memory for her name. Jane something. Okay, Janie Dupree, the assistant manager of the bookstore. Docia's maid of honor.

Pete sighed again. He was going to have to listen to wedding talk. He'd listened to wedding talk for the past two days, ever since he'd arrived in Konigsburg. Not that he begrudged Cal or Docia their wedding, but did they have to discuss it so much?

So happily?

Docia slid into the booth beside Cal while Allie slid in beside Wonder. That left Janie Dupree perching on the edge of the seat beside Wonder and Allie, given that Pete, Cal and Docia were taking up the other side. Putting three very tall people together side by side was probably not a good idea. If they'd been on a boat they'd have capsized by now.

Pete frowned. He was shoved up against the wall to make room for Cal and Docia. Did couples naturally expand to fill any extra space? Them and their stupid happiness?

"I got the cake topper," Allie cooed. "It's perfect."

Docia's eyes narrowed. "The one Janie found? Or Mama's?"

Allie chuckled. "Janie's, of course. That china bride and groom your mama wanted would have thrown the cake proportions all to hell."

Allie owned the bakery that would produce the cake for The Wedding. Somehow whenever anybody mentioned The Wedding, Pete always thought in capital letters.

"A cake topper?" Cal frowned. "What's a cake topper?"

Wonder pinched the bridge of his nose between his thumb and forefinger. "Think about it, Calthorpe. It'll come to you."

Janie Dupree smiled. "It's the thing that goes on top of the wedding cake. Flowers or hearts or bells or—"

"Twenty-inch porcelain figurines of the bride and groom." Docia sighed. "Lladro. Limited edition."

Cal blanched.

Janie leaned forward, patting his hand. "It's okay. That was Reba's idea, but I found something a lot smaller. Docia likes it."

Cal blew out a quick breath. "Good to know."

Janie Dupree had a nice smile, Pete reflected. He hadn't noticed before. Of course, he hadn't really paid much attention to her at all before. Which was probably a mistake since he was the best man and she was the maid of honor. He was probably supposed to be working with her on something. Planning stuff. Whatever the hell a best man was supposed to do.

He clenched his hands on the table again. No cell. The office could get along without him. He probably should be directing all his attention to The Wedding anyway.

Behind him he heard another muted *thonk* followed by a chorus of groans.

"So you got the topper." Janie turned to Allie. "What about the matchbooks?"

"Those too." Allie sipped the glass of wine Wonder had ordered for her. "They even managed to spell 'Docia' correctly."

Docia grinned. "'Cal' too?"

"I think so." Allie's eyes danced. "'C-a-l-e' right?"

"That's my boy." Docia patted his hand, smiling.

Pete felt slightly nauseated.

Janie Dupree blew out a quick breath. "Great! That's two more things off the list."

"You have a list?" Pete stared at her.

"Of course!" Janie's brow furrowed. "I can't keep it all in my head. Don't you have a list?"

"Not for this!" Pete grimaced. He had a list for the office. Which he'd left back in Des Moines.

"But..." The furrows in Janie's brow grew deeper. "What about the stuff you're responsible for? How do you keep track?" Her bright brown eyes studied him, her expression grave.

Pete was suddenly—uncomfortably—aware that everyone in the booth had turned his way. He shrugged. "What's there to keep track of? If Cal wants me to do anything, he can yell. I'm here to serve."

Janie's lower jaw dropped a fraction.

There was a moment of silence at the table, then Allie guffawed. "Fantastic. Have any of you males thought to check out what exactly happens at a wedding? Or were you going to wait until the day before?"

Cal looked affronted. "Hey! I've been keeping up. Docia fills me in on what's going on. I figure if I need to do anything, somebody will let me know."

"Sounds reasonable to me." Wonder took another swig from his bottle of Spaten.

Janie, Docia and Allie exchanged glances. "Testosterone gives them wedding immunity," Allie muttered.

Wonder nodded. "Good thing too. Do you really want a bunch of men trying to decide what kind of music to have at the reception? Hell, you'd probably end up with either ZZ Top or Metallica."

"Personally, I'd favor Ray Wylie Hubbard, but that's just me." Cal turned to Docia. "I'll do anything you need me to do. Don't worry about it. It's going to be the wedding to end all weddings."

"Would that it could," Wonder muttered. Allie narrowed her eyes at him.

Cal paid him no attention, keeping his gaze on Docia. "Dinner at Brenner's tonight? I know you had something you needed to talk to Lee about."

"Right." Docia leaned across him to Pete. "You want to join us? Brenner's is that restaurant we took you to the other day— Lee's the owner and chef, remember?"

"Right." Pete managed a faintly sour grin. Brenner's had the best food he'd tasted in at least five years. If he went there, he might not worry about the office anymore. On the other hand, he was so used to worrying about the office he wasn't sure he wanted to try out another mood just then. "You go on. Maybe I'll catch up with you later."

Cal grinned happily. Pete gritted his teeth.

Docia turned to the other side of the booth. "You want to come, Janie? Lee's got some new tapas to try out for the reception."

Janie shook her head. "Not tonight. Mom's waiting dinner for me."

"I'll come," Allie said, decisively. "I need to talk to Lee anyway. We have to firm up the cake logistics. You want to come, Steve?"

Beside her Wonder gulped down the last of his Spaten. "Taste testing with Lee? Any time."

Janie stood to let them slide out of the booth as Cal and Docia joined them. Cal turned back to Pete. "Come on down when you finish here."

For a moment, Pete thought he saw a flash of concern in his brother's eyes. His jaw tightened. Cal was four years younger—his little brother, no matter how tall and broad he'd turned out to be. Concern from him wasn't acceptable. "Yeah, okay," he growled. "Shouldn't take long."

Cal's brow furrowed, then he shrugged. "Okay, then, see you later."

Docia was already headed for the door, Allie at her elbow. Pete watched Cal catch up to her so that he could open the door before she got to it. She turned slightly to look back at him, her lips curving up in a faint smile as their gazes met.

Well, goddamn. He hated being jealous of his little brother.

Across the table, Janie Dupree cleared her throat.

Pete started. He hadn't noticed she was still there.

Janie gave him a smile that didn't entirely reach her eyes and wasn't nearly as charming as Docia's. "I thought maybe the two of us should touch base, just to make sure we're taking care of all the things that need to be done before the wedding."

Pete picked up his bottle of Bud, feeling a slight prickle around his conscience. "What 'things' would those be?" He took a long pull, letting lukewarm beer slide down his throat.

Janie's smile tightened to a thin line. Her eyes narrowed further. "You mean you weren't kidding? You really haven't got a clue about what you're supposed to do?"

"I know what I'm supposed to do," Pete snapped. "I'm supposed to stand next to my baby brother, carry the ring for him and stay out of the way. Like I said, if he needs anything else, he'll let me know."

Janie looked down at the table top, tapping her fingers in a tight rhythm. "Carry the ring? Do you even know what their plans are about a ring bearer? Why do I bother to ask— obviously you don't. At one point they were going to use Cal's dog."

The beer bottle almost slipped through Pete's fingers, but he managed to catch it before it hit the table top. "His dog? That rodent?"

Janie's eyes blazed. "Pep is not a rodent. He's a sweetheart. He may be a Chihuahua, but he's got the heart of a tiger."

Pete raised his hand, leaning back slightly. "Okay, okay. He's a champ. But you're telling me they're going to have the dog carry the ring instead of me?"

"They talked about it." Janie shrugged. "I think they changed their minds. The point is, you need to find that stuff out. It's your job."

Pete's shoulders tightened. His job. Actually, his job was handling a case load that would have flattened the average county attorney. His job was putting low-life assholes where they couldn't do any more damage and making sure they stayed there. His job—which he currently wasn't doing because The Wedding had demanded all his time.

"My job," he said through gritted teeth, "is to do anything Cal asks me to do and otherwise stay out of the way, like I said."

"You're not going to help at all?" Janie's hands were spread on the table in front of her. Her eyes bored into him like laser beams—he figured he should have been a pile of ashes by then.

He shrugged. "Hey, if you think something needs to be done, go to it. Doesn't look like you need any help from me. You're doing a hell of a job here, tiny."

He watched Janie Dupree's hands turn to fists. She almost looked like she might slug him. For a moment, Pete wondered if that last crack had gone too far. She wasn't all that short. Maybe five feet or so. Instead of slugging him, she pushed herself up from the booth and stood looking down at him, her lips a grim line. Then she turned and stalked toward the door.

Oh well, just another client he'd disappointed. These days that was par for the course.

Janie kicked a piece of gravel out of her path, then worried that it might have hit the parked car next to her. Damn it, she couldn't even get mad effectively.

Too bad the parked car wasn't Peter Toleffson. She could have happily bounced gravel off his butt.

Docia was Janie's best friend, and Janie didn't envy her for much—she knew just how hard Docia had worked to get where she was. But she did envy Docia's relationship with Cal Toleffson. Cal was the sweetest guy in the world. Was it too much to hope that there might be another Toleffson at home just like him?

Clearly, there wasn't.

Pete Toleffson apparently didn't understand how important The Wedding was. He wouldn't be any help. She just hoped he wouldn't be as big a pain in the ass as he was being currently.

Shaking her head, Janie turned up Bass Street, heading for her own front door. Lights burned in the windows, glowing soft against the gathering violet shadows. Twilight in Konigsburg. Always her favorite time of day. Janie paused to drink it in—the shadows, the doves calling their evening songs, the sound of children shouting a few blocks away.

A figure moved across the window, then turned to pull the

15

curtain back and stare out. Mom. Checking to see if Janie was headed up the drive. Janie began walking again, more quickly now, telling herself at the same time she wasn't that late.

Her mother opened the door as Janie climbed onto the front porch. "Just in time. I was afraid the tuna casserole would dry out, but I think I saved it."

Janie stepped inside, then walked to the kitchen where her mother fussed around the table. Tuna noodle casserole, green peas poking through the buttery crumbs sprinkled across the top. Red Jell-O salad with bananas. A bowl of creamed corn.

If she started eating at home every night, her mother could just roll her down the street to the shop in the morning.

Her mother picked up a jug of milk—whole, of course—and reached for Janie's glass. "That's okay, Mom." She grabbed her glass back and headed for the refrigerator. "I'll have tea." She lifted her pitcher of unsweetened from the refrigerator door.

Her mother sniffed. "Janie, you need your calcium."

"I know." Janie forced her lips into a bland smile. "I have my yogurt at breakfast and I eat a lot of cheese."

She sank into her chair at the table, bowing her head briefly as her mother muttered grace, then spread her napkin across her knees.

"How's the wedding coming?" her mother asked.

"Oh fine—everything's working out." Except the best man, of course. Janie chomped on a bit of tuna, ignoring the tension in her jaw.

"Are you still doing all that extra work for Docia's mother?" Her mom's eyes narrowed slightly.

"It's not that much work, Mom, really. I enjoy it. Reba says I'm her 'Konigsburg liaison'."

In fact Janie wasn't sure whose liaison she was—Reba's or Docia's. If Docia had to work directly with her mother, the wedding would probably become an alley fight. Janie functioned as a go-between to keep the two from scalping each other, plus finding cake toppers and matchbooks—duties that would drive Docia to distraction.

"I still think you should get paid for all the things you're doing." Her mother's jaw grew square. "Wedding consultants make good money, Janie."

Janie sighed. "I'm not a wedding consultant, Mom. I'm just

helping out. And I wouldn't think of letting them pay me for this. Docia's my best friend." And her boss. And the first person who had ever thought Janie had the potential to be something more than a small town Texas girl who waited on tables at the Hofbrau Haus.

As far as she was concerned, Docia deserved the wedding of the century. And she'd get it, if Janie had anything to say about it.

Her mother plopped another spoonful of creamed corn onto her plate. "I don't know why they didn't just hire someone. Lord knows the Kents could afford it!"

"Reba has all kinds of experience planning events for her foundation. She wanted to do Docia's wedding herself."

"Is Otto coming to the wedding?" Her mother kept her gaze locked on her forkful of tuna casserole, carefully avoiding Janie's glance.

"I don't know. We haven't discussed it." Janie speared a pea.

"Well." Her mother shrugged. "It would be nice for you to have someone to dance with at the reception, wouldn't it? He has been invited, hasn't he?"

"Yes, he's been invited." Docia had asked Janie specifically if she wanted Otto to come, and Janie couldn't think of any reason why not. Because she did want him there, didn't she? She did need someone to dance with. So what if Otto wasn't exactly Mr. Perfect. Janie sighed. "I'll ask him if he's coming. I don't know what his plans are."

"Are you two going out tonight?" Her mother was watching her more closely now. "I thought you had a date this evening."

"He said he might come over. If his practice doesn't run late." Janie's stomach began to curl into a ball. Talking about Otto at dinner didn't help her digestion much.

In the living room, the phone began to ring. "Oh," her mother chirped, "maybe that's Otto." She turned and headed toward the sound.

Janie pushed herself up and began carrying plates to the sink. Given the time, it probably was Otto. She just wished she felt happier about that possibility.

After his run-in with Janie Dupree, Pete headed back to his temporary home in the apartment above the bookstore, fuming. Who was she to tell him what his responsibilities were anyway? What made her the authority on all things wedding-related? Since when did the maid of honor tell the best man what to do?

He unlocked the street-level door and climbed the stairs to the apartment. It was more comfortable than his condo back in Iowa in a lot of ways. The high tin ceilings and limestone walls were picturesque as hell, and the air conditioning worked fine, a major factor, considering the August heat in Texas.

It was just sort of...empty.

To be fair, his condo in Des Moines wasn't much more lively. And on the whole Pete liked being solitary. But sometimes, usually right after he'd spent time with Cal and Docia, being on his own felt a little more bleak than usual.

He pulled his cell out of his pocket, flipping it open before he could stop himself, and checked the messages. Nothing particularly vital. Nothing he couldn't put off.

Pete sighed. Of course, he could put it off, but he wouldn't. He hit the number for Joe Bergstrom, the County Attorney. Bergstrom would still be there. The latest Mrs. Bergstrom had taken off over a year ago.

Fifteen minutes later, in the middle of a discussion of a particularly clueless assistant's chances against one of the more aggressive defense attorneys in town, Pete remembered he was supposed to meet Cal and Docia at the restaurant down the street. He cut the conversation short, promising to call back the next day, and headed back down the stairs to Brenner's.

He was halfway there before he thought about what he was wearing—jeans, boots, and a faded T-shirt that said "Lawyers Do It With Subpoenas". Probably not the kind of outfit people usually wore to an upscale tapas bar.

He could see Cal and Docia sitting at a table near the front as he pushed open the elegant glass door to the restaurant. Lee Contreras, the owner he'd met a couple of days before, raised an eyebrow at the T-shirt, but he led the way to the table without making any comments.

Cal grinned, of course. "Nice of you to drop by, bro. Of course you missed the tapas tasting."

Pete slumped into his chair. "I don't suppose they make burgers here?"

"You suppose wrong," Docia snapped. "They make a great burger." She waved a hand at a teenaged girl wearing a tuxedo shirt and black bow tie along with her black jeans. "Bring the gentleman the special burger, Donna. Can we get the order in before the kitchen closes?"

The waitress nodded. "Sure, Docia. Anything to drink, sir?"

Pete considered having another beer then decided against it. Docia already looked fairly pissed and his getting slightly shit-faced wouldn't help. "Iced tea, please."

"Coming right up." The girl grinned and flounced off toward the kitchen.

Silence stretched across the table, then Pete shrugged. "Sorry to be late. No excuse, ma'am."

Docia exhaled, shaking her head. "You're not that late, and you didn't even promise you were coming. I'm just on edge about this whole wedding thing. I'll be a good sister-in-law, honest."

She gave him a smile that started a pain somewhere around Pete's diaphragm. *God, she was gorgeous. Why didn't he have that kind of luck?* "Hey, right now you're already the best sister-in-law I've got."

Docia's forehead wrinkled slightly. "I thought Lars was married."

Cal's grin turned wry. "He is. To Sherice. Pete's trying to make a point here."

Pete picked up a spare piece of bread lying in the bread basket, dipping it in a puddle of olive oil left on Cal's plate. "I'm going to be a better best man, trust me. I just need to get the hang of it."

"A 'better best man'?" Cal raised an eyebrow. "That sounds like an old Who song."

"Hey, consider me your hired gun. Who do you want me to kill first?"

"I'll think about it."

Docia grimaced. "Several candidates leap to mind, but most of them are related to me."

The waitress set a plate with an immense burger in front of Pete. It overflowed with mushrooms and cheese and bacon—a heart attack waiting to happen. "Sorry," she mumbled. "I forgot to ask how you wanted it. Lee figured medium rare because

19

that's the best way."

"Sounds good." Pete nodded and took a bite. Salty cheese, crisp smoked bacon and perfectly sautéed mushrooms were like a taste explosion in his mouth. "Holy shit, I will never underestimate this place again, I swear."

"I'll hold you to it." Docia pushed herself back from the table. "I still need to talk to Ken about the wine. Can you two stay out of trouble for a few minutes?"

"We'll try." Cal was grinning again. Pete wanted to kick him.

The grin stayed in place as Cal watched Docia walk across the room to the bar where Ken, the sommelier and co-owner of the restaurant, was opening a bottle of wine.

When he turned back to Pete, his grin abruptly disappeared. "Okay, so are you ready to tell me about it? Why exactly did you end up in the hospital last week? How serious is it?"

Pete pinched the bridge of his nose, telling himself he didn't feel a headache coming on. "You've been talking to Dad, haven't you?"

"Lars. And don't change the subject. What's going on?"

"It was nothing." Pete crunched a perfect French fry between his front teeth. "I just blacked out for a couple of minutes at the office. The doctor gave me some pills. I'm okay."

"Lars said you fainted."

Pete's jaw tightened. "I did not faint. I've never fainted in my life. Lars is prone to exaggerate."

"Lars is a freakin' accountant."

"I'm telling you the whole thing was no big deal. The doctor gave me some blood pressure meds. And some stuff for acid reflux. That's it." The doctor had also offered him his choice of anti-anxiety drugs, which he had politely declined. Anxiety was part of the territory.

Cal shook his head. "You used to be a better liar than this. Even I know you're not giving me the whole story here."

Pete looked down at his burger, then back up to his younger brother. "It's a high stress job, Calthorpe. Par for the course. Don't worry about it. You've got enough on your plate with The Wedding."

Cal still frowned, but Docia was headed back across the

room toward them. He shook his head. "We'll talk about this more later."

"There's nothing more to talk about. I've got the meds—problem solved."

"You're my brother, Pete. That gives me the right to bug you. But for now, I'll settle for a promise."

"And that would be..."

"You're on vacation this week. No phones. No laptop. No business. Just Texas."

Pete's jaw tightened slightly. He'd already checked his e-mail twice that afternoon. Plus the call to Bergstrom that had made him late. Cal was asking him to cut off his lifeline. Going cold turkey would not be fun.

Cal narrowed his eyes. "Promise me. Okay?"

Pete sighed. "Okay. Not that I think this is any of your business, you understand."

Cal gave him a slightly smug smile, then he shrugged. "Think of it this way, starting tomorrow, we're both going to have more than enough to keep us occupied anyway."

Pete paused, holding another fry poised in front of his mouth. "What happens tomorrow?"

"Tomorrow?" Docia glanced back and forth between them as she sat again. "Well, your mother's plane gets in to San Antonio at two."

Pete leaned back in his chair, closing his eyes in anguish. "Doomed, Calthorpe. We're both doomed."

"That we are." Cal grinned again.

Chapter Two

Pete woke the next day certain that he was late for work. Judging from the sunlight pouring in his window, he'd somehow missed the alarm. His heart raced for a few moments until he remembered—he didn't have to go to work because he wasn't in Des Moines. He was in Texas being Cal's hired gun.

He flipped open his cell and checked for messages. Nothing yet. For a few moments he considered calling in to the office, just to be sure. *No, dammit, just let it go for a week.* After all, he'd promised Cal. Sort of.

His case load would be handled. The assistants were capable of doing the work, even if none of them had conviction rates in the same ballpark as his when he'd been an assistant himself. He needed some time off—that was the general consensus of everybody in the office, including Bergstrom.

Right. Tell that to Maureen Amundson, who had lost hearing in one ear and risked losing an eye for a couple of weeks before the doctors had been able to repair the damage to her cornea. Bo Amundson had been nothing if not thorough.

Pete was going to make sure Bo Amundson spent a significant portion of the rest of his life in the slammer. He'd promised Maureen. He stared at the cell phone again. Maybe he should just call the clerk to make sure that the trial date hadn't been changed.

Enough, already. Pete sighed in disgust. He was supposed to be relaxing in Texas, letting his stress levels drop out of the stratosphere, being his brother's best man. He might even take the time today to figure out what a best man was supposed to do. Must be a bestman.com somewhere.

On the other hand, he was sure his mother could tell him what a best man was supposed to do. In detail. And she undoubtedly would as soon as she saw him.

He poured himself a cup of coffee and grabbed a banana,

then climbed out onto the fire escape to eat. Docia's backyard spread out below him, a solid expanse of grass and live oaks reaching to the stone wall around the edge. Pete leaned back against the window sill, letting one foot dangle over the side of the fire escape. He had to admit, Konigsburg had its points.

The neighbor kids played touch football in their own back yard across the alley. After a few minutes Pete heard the littlest complaining about fairness in a high-pitched, grade-school voice. Another kid, clearly the big brother, grabbed the boy's shoulder, and Pete's gut clenched. Then the smaller boy was running across the yard as his big brother stepped back to pass him a bright green football.

Pete relaxed against the window sill again, listening to the sounds of cars moving along Main Street and the kids screeching in victory.

After a few minutes, he saw a woman walk down the sidewalk beside the yards, turning to wave to the children as they ran by. Pete caught a quick glimpse of her face as she turned back again—Janie Dupree.

As if she were suddenly aware of him, she looked up to the fire escape, shading her eyes with her hand. "Good morning," she called.

Pete nodded. "Hi." On an impulse, he raised his cup. "Want some coffee?"

She shook her head. "No, thanks. I've got to open the shop." She smiled uncertainly, her sunny face puckering slightly.

"I'll give you a hand." Pete pushed up from the fire escape and ducked through the window.

He heard Janie say something that sounded like "Thanks anyway," but he ignored it. How hard could opening a bookstore be? And almost by definition, he had nothing better to do. Might as well make himself useful again. It certainly beat sitting around not checking his e-mail.

Janie had unlocked the front door by the time he'd climbed down the inside stairs and walked into the shop through the storeroom. He peered around the shop space. Six-foot-high bookcases stretched toward the pressed tin ceiling overhead. "What do you need done?" he asked.

"You can move that display case." Janie nodded toward a row of shelves where a large cardboard display loaded with paperbacks nearly blocked the aisle. "Put it over there against the wall."

He hoisted the surprisingly heavy cardboard display and staggered toward the side. "Look, I think maybe we got off on the wrong foot last night." He pushed the display against the wall, then turned to look back at her, dusting his hands on his knees. "I guess I was out of line."

Janie regarded him with one raised eyebrow. "You guess?" Her lips were pursed again. She had a perfect cupid's bow mouth, a sharply angled upper lip over a full, almost pouting lower one. *Nice.*

He shrugged. "Okay, I was totally out of line. I'm sorry."

The corners of her mouth trembled, as if she was fighting a smile. Oh well, maybe he didn't deserve one. Her short, dark hair was slightly mussed from the breeze outside, falling over her eyebrows, almost like feathers. Her eyes, the same dark color as her hair, tipped up at the ends.

"Dupree." He narrowed his eyes. "From Louisiana?"

Janie nodded. "My daddy was a Cajun from Baton Rouge. Mama's from here, though, so I'm only half coonass."

Pete blinked at her, and she grinned, her full lower lip spreading deliciously.

"It's okay for me to say 'coonass', but nobody else. One of those things, you know? And by the way, my mom would die if she knew I said that to you." She turned back to the cash register, placing bills in the tray.

He nodded, only half listening. Why hadn't he noticed those eyes until now, to say nothing of those lips? Usually he was more observant than that. Was that what overwork did to you?

"My dad always called himself a coonass, though." Her smile dimmed slightly. "He was proud of it."

Pete nodded and tried to think of something halfway intelligent to say about coonasses. Fortunately for them both, his cell phone chirped before he came up with anything. He flipped it open, expecting to see the office number, only to see Cal's number instead.

"Hey, Pete!" Cal's voice sounded absurdly cheerful. Pete was willing to bet he was grinning again. "Come on over to the clinic. I need my hired gun."

Pete grunted his assent and folded the phone into his pocket. "What's the best route to Cal's clinic from here? Drive up Main?"

Janie shook her head. "You can walk it. Go up Spicewood and cut over on Berman. The clinic's on West Street."

"Okay." He wondered if he should say anything else, maybe something about Louisiana or her dad or Cajuns. Except he didn't have anything coherent to say about any of those things. "Well, see you later," he mumbled.

Janie had already turned away to greet a customer as he headed out the door.

Oh yeah, that little encounter had gone really well. Clearly, he was a regular chick magnet.

Cal's veterinary clinic was at the top of a small rise just off a shaded residential street. A large, blacktopped parking lot filled the space behind it, spilling over into the lot next door. Right now the lot was packed with pickup trucks and SUVs— apparently, the veterinary business was booming.

Pete swung through the door. At the front counter a middle-aged brunette in multicolored scrubs was taking information from a woman with a vicious-looking poodle. The dog gave him a threatening glance, growling low in its throat. He gave it a wide berth.

A large crowd, mostly female, sat in the waiting room clutching their pets, a wide variety of dogs in various shapes and sizes, most of them yapping. The women's eyes seemed to follow Pete as he walked across the room, although he had a feeling he wouldn't catch anybody looking directly at him if he turned around.

The brunette glanced up and grinned. "You've got to be Cal's brother," she said, raising her voice to be heard over the general din. "Unless there's a convention of large, hunky men in town."

Pete nodded at her. "I'll accept the large part, anyway. Pete Toleffson, best man in training." He extended a hand.

She gave it a quick shake. "Bethany Kronk. I'm actually a bridesmaid myself, bless Docia's soft heart. Cal's waiting for you in the back—through there."

Pete headed for the door, feeling several pairs of eyes boring into his back as he did. He didn't normally get this kind of reaction. Probably just curiosity about Toleffsons, or more likely about Cal and Docia.

The back of the clinic was a hall lined with doors. From

behind one, he could hear more muffled barking. Cal leaned against one of the doorjambs, watching him approach and grinning.

This whole happiness thing was really getting out of hand. Pete might have to punch him.

"Hey, bro, you got here fast!"

Pete shrugged. "What's up?"

"Got a mission for you." Cal started down the hall toward the door with the barking.

"Doing what?"

The barking grew louder as Cal opened the door. Inside, Pete saw a row of cages filled with dogs, a few barking enthusiastically as they saw people. The room was bright with sunlight, the concrete floors immaculate, everything white and gray and sterile.

Pete raised his voice to be heard over the barks. "Patients?"

Cal nodded. "Most of them. A few are being boarded. Then we've got some adoptees." He stopped in front of one cage as Pete stepped up beside him.

A dog stared back at them, silently, eyes wide. Its ears were flat against its head, tail tucked between slender legs.

"Greyhound?"

"Right."

The greyhound was an odd combination of brown and white, almost in stripes. "What's wrong with its color?"

"Nothing." Cal raised an eyebrow. "It's called brindle—they're supposed to look like that."

The dog turned wary eyes on Pete, as if he'd been judged and found wanting.

He sighed. "So what do you want me to do? Clean its cage?"

Cal shook his head, opening the cage door. The greyhound moved toward him tentatively. "She's an ex-racer. I'm adopting her. Only I can't take her home until after the honeymoon." He reached forward and rubbed the dog's ears.

"Can't she wait? You're only going to be gone a couple of weeks."

The greyhound moved into Cal's hand, letting herself be stroked. He leaned forward to murmur into the dog's ear, then turned back to Pete. "Greyhounds are sensitive. They need a lot of reassurance. Particularly ex-racers. They're not used to being outside a box."

Pete had a sudden sneaky feeling he knew what was coming. "You want me to take her back to the apartment."

Cal nodded. "You can keep each other company until the wedding—I'll find somebody else to take over until we get back from the honeymoon. If you take her home with you now, I can still be around to help out if you need it."

Pete gave the greyhound a long look. The dog stared straight ahead as Cal rubbed her ears, almost frozen in place. The Toleffsons had grown up with a succession of noisy strays who couldn't have stood that still if their lives depended on it. The greyhound looked like she'd bathed in Novocain.

Pete scratched the back of his neck. "I don't know, Cal, I'm not much of a dog man."

"Since when?" Cal narrowed his eyes. "You're the one who used to smuggle Granger into bed with him every night. Hell, you had the flea bites to prove it."

Which, of course, was how his mother had figured out who was hiding the mostly coon hound under the covers.

"Well, Granger was Granger. This one... What's her name anyway?"

Cal looked down at the greyhound's head. "Pookie's Pleasure."

There was a moment of total silence.

"You made that up," Pete snapped.

Cal shook his head. "So help me. It was the dog's racing name. Pookie was the owner's girlfriend, or anyway that's what they told me at the rescue center."

"You can't honestly expect me to call a dog 'Pookie', Calthorpe." Pete folded his arms across his chest. "It would be an offense to the memory of every dog we ever owned."

Cal shrugged. "Hey, I own a dog who was originally named Señor Pepe. Sometimes you get stuck with other people's idiocy. If you don't like the name, you can always try calling her something else. See if she answers."

The greyhound shifted her feet, then glanced up at Pete. Her eyes looked like obsidian, dark and shiny. After a moment, she reverted to frozen again.

"Why is she standing so still?"

"Greyhound stress behavior." Cal rubbed along the dog's

shoulders again. "She's frightened, but she doesn't want to show it. She's been chasing a mechanical rabbit since she was a pup, with a lot of yelling. This is probably the first time she's ever been in a relatively quiet place. Plus it's the first time she's been off a regimented schedule."

The greyhound's shoulders shuddered lightly underneath Cal's fingers. She raised her wary black eyes to Pete again, questioning.

He sighed. "Okay, I'll do it. Does she have a leash?"

Cal shook his head. "Better wait until tomorrow. The first day she's out, you'll need to stay with her all the time."

"I'm not doing anything in particular—she can hang out with me." Plus it would give him something to do besides bugging Janie Dupree.

Cal pushed himself to his feet. "Mom might not appreciate that, seeing as how we're supposed to pick her up at the airport in a couple of hours. And then take her to dinner with Docia and her mom and dad."

Pete grimaced. He would vastly prefer spending the day with a stressed-out greyhound to spending it with his mother. But he was the best man, and the best man supported the groom in his duties. All of his duties, apparently. "Okay, tomorrow it is."

Cal thumped him on the shoulder. "Thanks, bro. I knew you'd come through. Come on, I've got some greyhound pamphlets for you."

Pete closed his eyes for a moment, counting to ten. This just got better and better. "Pamphlets. Of course you have pamphlets. Lead away, Calthorpe, lead away."

Docia came into the bookstore around noon, par for the course these days. Janie was surprised she'd made it in at all, given that The Wedding was less than a week away.

She wore a pale yellow cotton dress—full skirt, halter top, very un-Docia. Janie thought she could count the number of times she'd seen Docia in a dress without running out of fingers. She was usually more a jeans-and-T-shirt kind of girl.

"What's up?" She kept her voice chipper. Docia looked like she was headed for the gallows. These days Docia looked like that a lot.

"Oh the usual. Flower arrangements. Wedding arch. And my mother-in-law-to-be, whom I've never met, is arriving in San Antonio at two." Docia took a deep breath and gave a bright, totally artificial smile to a passing customer.

"She'll love you," Janie said automatically.

"I don't know. From what Cal and Pete have said, she's sort of difficult. Love may be asking too much—I'll settle for tolerate."

Janie slid an arm around her shoulders—not the easiest thing to do since Docia was almost nine inches taller. "She'll love you, Docia. Trust me. This is all going to be terrific."

Docia sighed. "I swear, Janie, I had no idea what I was getting into when I told Mom she could run the wedding. This whole production has gotten bigger than most grand operas. Maybe we should just have hightailed it to Vegas."

"That would have broken your mama's heart." Janie picked up a stack of books from a customer and began clicking the cash register. "And mine. Besides, this way you get to meet all Cal's brothers at once."

"All of them except the oldest. Cal wouldn't invite him. I guess none of them have forgiven him for being such a bully when they were growing up."

"Pete seems...nice." Janie kept her voice neutral. Actually, Pete had seemed nicer this morning, but who knew how long that would last?

Docia smiled. "Pete's great. Once you get to know him."

Janie wasn't sure how well she wanted to get to know Pete Toleffson. Even if he had apologized this morning, he'd still been a jerk last night. On the other hand, he had great shoulders, especially in those T-shirts he usually wore.

"Oh, I meant to ask you—" Docia half-turned again, "—is Otto coming to the wedding? He hasn't RSVPed yet."

Janie yanked her unruly thoughts away from Pete Toleffson's shoulders. Otto's shoulders were equally broad and sort of her property. "Yes, I think so. I'll remind him the next time I see him."

Janie tried to remember if she'd mentioned the wedding to Otto last night. They'd gone to the movies—some comedy with a lot of men who were apparently obsessed with bodily fluids. Otto had laughed so hard he'd had to wipe away tears. Janie had dozed off about two-thirds of the way through.

"Janie, are you sure you want Otto at the wedding?" Docia's eyes were suddenly sharp.

Janie managed a slightly tight smile. "Of course. I need somebody to dance with, after all."

The bell above the door tinkled, and Docia's mother, Reba Kent, bustled into the shop. Docia groaned, softly.

Reba was wearing a sky blue tunic over white slacks, her dangling earrings jingling as she moved. "Honey babe, don't you look yummy! Come on now, we need to check on those place cards before the boys get back with Mrs. Toleffson."

Docia grabbed her purse from behind the counter and started toward the door. Just before she went out, she turned back to Janie, the corners of her mouth slipping up in a dry smile. "You know, kid, there are a lot of dance partners out there. Maybe you should think about it."

Janie watched the two Kent women sail down the street toward Reba's Mercedes. A lot of dance partners *were* out there. But sometimes she thought Docia had grabbed the last good one.

A multi-car collision on Highway 281 made Cal and Pete late in getting to the San Antonio airport, but Pete was pretty sure their mother would have found something to be unhappy about even if they'd gotten there an hour early. Mom wasn't big on traveling, no matter how good the cause. Leaving Iowa always struck her as a somewhat subversive idea, particularly leaving Iowa for Texas.

They found her sitting in a leather chair in the baggage claim area. Pete had a few moments to study her before she saw them coming. She had on one of those outfits she always wore when she traveled—mint-colored knit slacks and a long white blouse with bright green flowers, a purse the size of Dubuque slung over her shoulder. Her baggage was heaped at her feet—a series of tapestry-covered suitcases decorated with fluorescent tape so that she could find them on the baggage carousel.

She looked up then and saw them, her face slowly smoothing out of a frown into a tight smile. Pete figured she was glad to see them, sort of. Maybe.

Cal gave her a quick hug, patting her on the back. "Sorry, Mom, a wreck on the highway closed down some of the lanes, and we got held up. We tried to call your cell."

His mother waved her hand dismissively. "Oh, I never turn it on when I'm traveling. I don't want to forget to turn it off on the airplane. They make such a fuss about that."

Pete sighed. No point in explaining she was supposed to turn the phone back on again once the plane landed. He kissed her cheek dutifully. "Hi, Mom."

His mother took a quick inventory of his outfit, her smile becoming even tighter. "Well, you certainly look comfortable!"

He managed not to grimace. Cal had put on khakis and a knit shirt. Pete still wore the jeans and souvenir T-shirt from Myrtle Beach he'd put on that morning.

Call it a statement. With his mother, of course, it was more like a call to battle.

He gathered a couple of her suitcases together. "How was your flight, Mom?"

"Oh, fine. Of course, I had a middle seat. But that's all right, it all worked out. I had a nice man on the aisle to talk to. The woman in the window seat went to sleep, but I can't sleep on airplanes."

She gathered up her spring coat, which she carried even though the temperature outside hovered in the mid-nineties. Pete wondered if she didn't trust the weather forecast or if she didn't trust Texas. Probably some of both.

"Let me carry something." Cal reached over and picked up a large shopping bag.

"Well, just don't look inside," his mother cautioned. "It's your wedding gift from Aunt Roslyn. Since she can't come all the way down here herself, she sent it with me." She took up a position between the two of them as they walked out the door, looking deceptively small and vulnerable between two towering hulks.

"Aunt Roslyn didn't feel like wrapping her present?" Pete negotiated the crosswalk between taxis and shuttle buses, heading for the parking lot. "Doesn't sound like her."

"No, it's wrapped," his mother explained, "but Cal shouldn't see the present before his fiancée does. They should see it at the same time. It's a present to both of them. It wouldn't be right for him to look at it without her."

Pete debated pointing out that seeing a wrapped package before it got to Docia didn't strike him as much of a betrayal.

But what did he know? He wasn't the one getting married.

"Oh, Cal, there's another problem I needed to talk to you about." His mother's voice hadn't really changed, but Pete heard a new undertone that set the hairs on the back of his neck prickling.

Cal apparently got the same message. Pete saw his shoulders stiffen. "What's that, Mom?"

"Erik's invitation still hadn't arrived by the time I left." His mother's lips thinned in a tight smile. "Maybe you'd better send him another one. Or call him. That would be better at this point."

Cal unlocked the SUV and began lifting suitcases inside the back. "I didn't invite Erik, Mom. I haven't spoken to him in over five years. I don't see any point in asking him to my wedding."

Cal's jaw had taken on a rigid set. Pete's shoulders tensed too.

"Well, I just thought this would be a good time for the two of you to work out your differences." His mother's eyes had a hard brightness that said she wouldn't back down on this one. "It's a family occasion, after all."

Pete had a sudden memory of fourteen-year-old Erik holding eight-year-old Cal by the back of his shirt, laughing at Cal's attempts to get loose.

Twelve-year-old Pete had grabbed the first thing his hands touched and whacked Erik across the back of his head with it. Unfortunately, the first thing his hands had touched was a large plastic Easter bunny. At least the surprise had made Erik drop Cal on the lawn rather than the sidewalk. But then both Cal and Pete had collapsed, giggling at the sight of the decapitated bunny's head hanging from Erik's shoulder.

Erik hadn't seen the humor, of course. He'd beaten the crap out of them both. Typical.

Cal sighed and turned to face his mother. "Mom, we can't work out our differences. Erik's not any more interested in having a relationship with me than I am with him."

His mother's smile was gone, her lips taut. "Erik's changed. He's trying to make up for things he did when he was younger. And he's your brother. You need to give him a chance."

"Come on, Mom." Pete snapped the trunk closed. "Time to get back to Konigsburg."

His mother turned her head quickly, giving him a narrow-eyed look that would have sent him running for cover when he was ten years old. Then she sighed, moving on to her next topic. "All right, all right, let's go. How are you feeling now, Peter? Are you taking your pills like the doctor told you to? What about the stomach problems?"

Pete opened the door for her. "Yes, ma'am. I'm doing fine." Or he would be, once he got this wedding business over and got back to work.

Chapter Three

Otto arrived at seven to take Janie to dinner with Docia and Cal's families at Brenner's. Seven was around thirty minutes late, and five minutes before Janie would have been ready to go without him. She felt an emotion oddly like regret as Mom opened the front door to let him in, beaming.

She took a moment to study him. He must have showered after afternoon football practice. His short, reddish brown hair still glinted with moisture.

He might have been ten years beyond his days as the star quarterback of Konigsburg High, but Otto still looked like a football player. Janie figured he always would, even when his metabolism slowed down. His shoulders were broad, his chest rippled with muscle, his stomach was gorgeously flat.

He was maybe a hair over six feet, significantly shorter than Pete Toleffson, but Pete's arms weren't the size of tree limbs, like Otto's were. All in all, Otto did a good job of filling out his green golf shirt, his broad shoulders and chest stretching the waffled knit. His thick forearms were dusted with light brown hair that Janie happened to know also covered his impressive pecs. For all she knew, it covered more than that, but she hadn't found out yet.

The question was, did she want to?

A lot of women did. When Otto took her to the movies or to the Silver Spur to dance, hungry eyes watched him when the other girls thought she wasn't looking. Most Konigsburg females undoubtedly believed she was one lucky lady.

Janie mentally gritted her teeth. She *was* one lucky lady. Otto was a catch. They'd been dating now for almost three months, and she knew he wanted to take their relationship to the next level because he'd told her so in exactly those words.

Janie wasn't sure why she didn't quite feel like doing that. After all, the number of months for her current dry spell was now stretching into double digits.

Maybe because making out with Otto hadn't inspired much more than annoyance when he slobbered in her ear, although she'd also had a vague ache around her stomach. It could have been desire, but it could also have been the nachos they'd shared earlier.

Janie sighed. Her mother would tell her she was being silly. Her friends would tell her she was being picky. Well, some of her friends would tell her that. Janie had a feeling Docia wouldn't.

Docia had found her prince, although she'd had to put up with a lot of toads before she did. Docia's wedding was a daily reminder that princes were out there somewhere, and a daily reason not to settle for less.

"You ready to go there, sweet thing?" Otto's voice sounded like his throat had been buttered, particularly around Janie's mother.

"Yes, I am." Janie gathered her clutch bag and a butter yellow stole she'd picked up at the weaving shop downtown. Her white strapless sundress splashed with bright red poppies always made her feel perkier than usual, particularly since it didn't look like something she could wear to church on Sunday.

Otto hadn't really noticed the dress. Or anyway, he hadn't said anything about it. Maybe he wasn't into perky.

"Oh Janie, don't you look lovely." Her mother gave her a quick hug.

Well, a mother compliment was better than no compliment at all. On the other hand, her mother had said more or less the same thing when Janie had headed off to her senior prom in the Disco Drama dress that still ranked as her biggest fashion disaster.

Otto cocked an eyebrow. "Nice dress." He sounded like he'd just noticed she had clothes on.

Janie gripped her purse more tightly and headed toward Otto's glistening black monster truck. The row of chrome lights on top of the cab glittered in the setting sun.

"So are you coming to The Wedding?" she asked as she hauled herself up to the front seat. The truck's tires seemed to increase in diameter every time she climbed into the cab.

"What wedding is that?" Otto climbed up beside her easily, sliding his key into the ignition.

Janie stared at him. "Docia's wedding. Next week. She said you hadn't RSVPed."

Otto frowned slightly. "She's taking that RSVP thing seriously? I mean, hell, who knows whether they're coming or not this far in advance?"

"It's a wedding!" Janie grasped her purse tightly and worked on keeping that grating edge out of her voice. "They have to know how many people are going to be there so they can plan and order the food."

"Oh, okay, I guess." Otto shrugged, glancing sideways. "I don't think I've got anything else going on then. You want to go with me?"

"I'm Docia's maid of honor," Janie said through clenched teeth. "I'll already be there."

Otto shrugged again. "Well that makes it easier. We can hook up afterwards at the reception."

Janie smoothed out the slight marks her nails had made in the leather of her purse and worked on keeping her breathing steady. "Right. Just remember to RSVP."

"Ah, hell, sweet thing, you just tell 'em I'm coming, okay?" Otto grinned at her devilishly, raising an eyebrow. That look probably sent the cheerleading squad into double back flips.

As far as Janie could tell, nothing about her felt remotely like flipping, most certainly not her heart.

Pete changed his clothes before he headed off to dinner at Brenner's, but he told himself doing that had nothing to do with his mother. He'd put on khaki slacks and a dark blue knit shirt because Cal and Docia, not to mention Docia's folks, had gone to a lot of trouble. He was just being supportive. Changing his clothes had nothing to do with the frequent, pointed references his mother had made to his T-shirt and jeans on the unusually long ride back to Konigsburg from the airport.

Of course, his mother probably wouldn't be satisfied with anything less than a sport coat, preferably a suit and tie. Pete had no intention of putting one on, even to keep the peace.

At Brenner's, the main room glowed with the light of the setting sun while candles threw circles of warmth on each table. Lee Contreras nodded in his direction, then pointed toward a door at the side of the room. "They're in there. The private dining room."

Pete veered to the right as the door opened behind him and Docia's mother swept into the restaurant.

Pete envied Cal for a lot of things, but he didn't think Reba Kent was one of them. In fact, he found her a little scary. None of the women he knew in Iowa looked like Reba—sort of like she was outlined in neon.

At the moment, she wore a flowing, floor-length dress made out of something soft and shimmering. The dress was patterned in the kind of purple and green Pete usually associated with Mardi Gras. The multi-colored jewels that glittered at her ears were probably real, given the net worth of Reba and her husband, Billy. She was almost as tall as Docia in flats, and her high heels elevated her eyes well above Pete's shoulder.

She caught sight of him just as he turned toward the dining room door. "Why Mr. Toleffson," Reba trilled. "Looks like I'm just in time to have an escort to the dining room." She widened her large cornflower eyes and batted her eyelashes at him.

Pete hadn't gotten used to the eyelash-batting thing yet—he'd never actually seen anybody do it before, and it still made him feel vaguely under attack. But apparently Reba didn't mean anything by it. Just some kind of all-purpose, southern belle greeting. Pete extended his arm in her direction. "I'd be delighted, ma'am."

Batting her eyelashes again, Reba laid a hand on his sleeve. "Lead on, sir, lead on."

Pete took a couple of steps inside the private dining room and stopped cold. The room looked like something out of *Dallas*. Dark oak paneling stretched on three walls. The fourth was a massive fireplace made of white limestone blocks—a huge brass star hung on the front. Lush, bright red carpeting cushioned his feet. Pete felt like he should be wearing boots and muttering nasty cracks about J.R.

Some people in the room glanced up as he and Reba came in, but then turned back to their conversations. Two pairs of eyes bored into his chest, however—one pair belonged to Reba's husband, Billy Kent, who looked like he could buy and sell Pete with his pocket change. The other pair belonged to his mother.

Of the two, Mom's look was considerably more lethal.

Pete gulped, glancing at Reba's hand where it rested on his

arm. Reba batted her eyelashes again. Terrific timing. *I'm not replacing you, Mom, honest!*

Cal waved at him. Grinning, of course.

Pete steered Reba politely toward the group, then took up a neutral position between Docia and Cal while Docia busied herself introducing Reba to Mom.

"I'm so pleased to meet you," Reba gushed. "Cal's told us so much about you."

Pete watched his mother's expression become smooth. She was wearing navy blue pants and jacket with a red, white and blue silk scarf tucked into the collar. She looked a little like a senior officer on a particularly grim cruise boat.

"A pleasure," she murmured, then straightened her shoulders. "I've just been hearing all about the...ceremony from your husband here. I need to firm up the details about the rehearsal dinner before my husband gets here. I'm not sure where we should hold it. I guess this place would do."

That little pause before "ceremony" was the mark of a master, Pete decided. Mom wasn't going to say anything openly critical about Texas and/or the wedding extravaganza, but somehow he knew she'd get her point in. She'd fired her opening salvo.

"Hey, bro." Cal's voice sounded a little strained. "Did you try the dip? I think there's some pita chips to go along with it. Lee's one fantastic cook."

Mom raised an eyebrow. Pete knew that look. Amateurs. No way she was backing off yet. "I've never been to Texas before. I guess it's always this hot in the summer." She fanned her face with one hand. "But after all, the wedding will be inside, so the air conditioning will help."

"Yes, of course it will." Reba glanced pointedly at Docia. "Sweetheart, did you talk to Janie yet about the arch?"

Pete considered it a nice attempted lateral.

"Iowa is hot in August too, of course. But it's just lovely in June," Mom continued, undeterred. "That's when most of the weddings in our family have taken place, when it's still cooler in the evening. Although some have been at Christmas. That's lovely too. All the snow. I always say Christmas isn't Christmas without snow. But I suppose you do without it here."

Oh, nice one, Mom. Points for trashing the Texas summer weather, the date of the wedding and the lack of snow. Pete glanced around the room. Janie Dupree stood next to a pillar-shaped guy who was inhaling a plate of cocktail shrimp. Pete raised an eyebrow at Docia. "Who's that?"

"Who's that who?" Docia shook her head as if she was trying to clear it.

Pete took a deep breath. Mom sometimes had that effect on people. "Janie's date."

"Oh." Docia pasted on a smile again. "Otto Friedrich. He's the high school football coach. Janie said he was a star player when he went to school here."

Pete narrowed his eyes. The guy really did look like some kind of architectural feature—a solid column of muscle, his head balancing on his shoulders apparently without benefit of neck. Beside him Janie Dupree glanced up. Her gaze caught Pete's.

She was wearing an amazing dress, white with bright splashes of orange, cut low in front to show more of her bosom than he'd noticed before. Smallish but perfect. The white of the dress set off the slight olive color of her skin and her flashing dark eyes. If she'd started tangoing around the room, Pete wouldn't have been a bit surprised.

Unfortunately, Otto didn't look like much of a tangoer.

The corners of Janie's mouth stretched up in a slight, mysterious smile, and Pete experienced the first rush of arousal he'd felt in longer than he liked to consider.

One hell of a time for it to come back to life!

"Peter."

His mother's voice cut through the fog in his brain and he glanced back at her, trying not to look guilty. He had a sneaking suspicion she could see every unclean thought that had ever crossed his mind. "Yes, ma'am."

"Would you find me a drink, please?" She made it a question, but he knew there wasn't anything questionable about it. In reality she was saying, *Get your sorry ass in gear and take care of your mother.*

"Sure. What would you like? Looks like they've got some champagne over at the side there." A couple of bottles rested in silver ice buckets on a marble bar against one wall.

His mother frowned slightly. "Oh. I was thinking of a margarita."

"They don't do margaritas here, Mom. This is strictly a wine bar. It's good champagne, though." Cal's grin began to fade for one of the few times in the four days Pete had been in Konigsburg.

Mom shrugged. "Oh, well, then. Champagne. That's fine. I'll have a margarita some other time, I guess." She gave Cal a small, sad smile as she accepted yet another Texas disappointment. "Champagne will do."

Cal glanced at Pete. The grin was gone entirely. His eyes had taken on a hunted look. "It's really good champagne, Mom. Billy had Ken bring it in, and Ken knows more about wine than anyone I've ever met. He's the other owner here."

"Of course." His mother nodded. "It's a wedding. I'm sure we'll be drinking lots of champagne over the next week." She gave a tiny, almost imperceptible sigh. "Might as well start now. Go on, Peter."

Pete went, although he suspected it was a fool's errand at that point. The champagne could be Cristal and it still wouldn't be quite good enough for Mom.

Janie Dupree and her date were standing next to the bar as he reached the silver ice bucket. Pete gave her a quick grin, hoping for another of those sinful smiles. "Care for a glass of champagne while I'm pouring?"

"Yes, please." She turned to the human support beam beside her. "Otto, this is Cal's brother, Pete Toleffson. Wouldn't you like some champagne too?"

Otto extended a hand the size of a catcher's mitt. "Otto Friedrich."

Pete allowed his hand to be crushed without crushing back. He hadn't played the handshake game since the last time he'd prosecuted a corporate embezzler. "Champagne, Friedrich?"

Otto scrunched his tanned forehead in thought. "They have any beer?"

"I'll look." Pete stepped behind the bar and found a refrigerator stocked with bottles. "Here's some."

Otto stepped beside him, squinting at the contents of the refrigerator. "Hell! No Bud?"

On Otto's other side, Janie Dupree suddenly looked less than entranced, which Pete found interesting. "Doesn't look like it," he said cheerfully. "Just imports." He poured three glasses of champagne and handed one to Janie.

She took a sip, licking wine from her upper lip with a quick swipe of her tongue.

Pete suddenly forgot his mother was waiting. "So, any news on the ring bearer front?" He raised an eyebrow.

Janie shook her head. "I think Pep's out of the running. In fact, I think they're going to just have you carry it. Apparently, no kids are available."

Pete's jaw tightened. "Daisy's not coming?"

"Daisy?"

"Lars's daughter. Our niece. She's about a year old."

Janie shook her head. "Docia didn't mention it. Maybe she forgot."

Or maybe Sherice had been up to something again. "Maybe."

"Peter!" His mother's voice cut through the murmur of conversation.

Pete turned and got the full impact of her look. He felt like ducking. Busted again! He glanced down at the glass in his hand. "Oops."

Janie gave him another of her elfin grins. His groin tightened painfully.

Behind him he heard pillar man clear his throat. "Isn't your mother calling you, Toleffson?"

Pete turned slightly to glance at him. A couple of years ago, when he'd had time to go to the gym, he could have taken Otto. Now he'd probably get his ass whipped. Still—the idea had a certain appeal, particularly when he saw Otto's faintly superior smirk.

He turned back to Janie Dupree, lifting the glass of champagne. "I'd better get this to Mom." He smiled one last time and was rewarded with a quick flash of brown eyes until Otto stepped beside her.

Oh well. Pete was just passing through Konigsburg anyway.

His mother narrowed her eyes at him when he arrived at her side. "Mercy, I hope it's not too warm. You spent so much time over there."

"Talking to the maid of honor." Pete took a quick sip of champagne. "Wedding stuff."

His mother pursed her lips slightly as she sipped. "I guess

this is all right. A little flat maybe, but all right."

Pete took another sip from his own glass. Seemed bubbly enough to him. "So what's up with Daisy—isn't she coming?"

Mom shook her head. "Sherice thinks Daisy's too young to come to a wedding. She's staying with Sherice's mother."

"She didn't want to be a flower girl?" Granted, his niece was a little young, but Pete would be willing to bet she could throw handfuls of flower petals around. Although they might have a hard time getting her to stop.

"I asked Lars," Cal said, quietly. "At first, he thought it would be a good idea. Then it wasn't."

Pete's jaw tightened again. "Sherice."

"Don't start, Peter." His mother's voice was sharp. "Sherice knows her daughter better than you do."

"I doubt it," Pete muttered. At the last family picnic, he and Lars had taken turns making sure Daisy didn't fall into the lake. Sherice had been busy reading *The Star*.

"That reminds me—" Mom turned a gimlet gaze on Cal, "—what do you have Sherice doing in the wedding?"

"Doing?" Cal's brow furrowed. "Like what?"

"Well, it wouldn't be right for her to be an usher, of course, although I understand some weddings have female ushers too. I suppose she could look after the guest book."

"Actually, my cousin Deirdre is in charge of the guest book." Docia's grip on Cal's arm looked tighter than before. "Cal didn't mention that we needed to put Sherice in the wedding."

Cal was very carefully looking at the far side of the room.

"Oh." Mom took a strategic sip of champagne. "Of course, Sherice really should be a bridesmaid. Since she's Lars's wife." She raised her gaze to Docia's. "I probably shouldn't say anything, but I know her feelings were a little hurt when she wasn't asked."

Janie Dupree suddenly materialized at Docia's elbow. For a moment, Pete wondered if she'd been there all along. Nope, he would have noticed.

"The bridesmaids' dresses have all been ordered, Mrs. Toleffson." Janie smiled apologetically. "We have our final fittings this week."

Mom's lips stretched in what might have been considered a smile, if one's smile standards were modest. "Of course. I'm sure they have. It's too much trouble. Forget I said anything. It's just a shame Sherice wasn't included."

"Mom, I doubt Sherice cares one way or the other." Cal's grin had become a thin line. "It's not like the two of us are all that close."

Mom put her glass down. "Cal, it's not a matter of how close the two of you are. Sherice is a member of our family."

"I don't think Sherice feels that way." Cal's voice was tight.

Docia placed her hand on Cal's arm, pulling him around to look at her. "It's okay," she murmured. "Don't. Please."

Pete glanced down to find Janie Dupree staring at him with laser eyes. He knew that look. *Do something. She's your mother.*

Pete took a swallow of champagne, practicing his Bogart impression. *Sorry, sweetheart. I stick my neck out for nobody.* You couldn't stop Mom when she was in one of these moods.

When he looked back at Janie Dupree, she'd moved a lot closer to Otto Friedrich.

Docia bit her lip. "Mama, could you come over here, please?"

Reba floated across the floor from where she'd been dazzling some anonymous high roller, probably a Kent family relation. "What is it, sweetheart?"

"Could we add another bridesmaid, please? Cal's sister-in-law?" Docia's voice had a faint tremor.

Reba stared at her blankly, then looked back at Mom. Pete felt as if he'd stumbled into Duel of the Titans.

Mom gave Reba another counterfeit smile, backed by her Medusa look, the one that turned you to granite if you met it directly.

Reba blinked first. "Why, I suppose we could try. I'll call the shop and see if they have another dress. I'll need her size, of course."

"Size 4," Mom said promptly.

"Oh." Reba blew out a breath. "Well, then, I'll see what I can do."

"Sherice will be here tomorrow afternoon with Lars." Mom picked up her glass again and took another sip of champagne. "She can do the fitting then."

Reba's jaw firmed. "Lovely. I'll try to get it overnighted from Houston."

Mom smiled at Cal, resting a limp hand on his arm. "There now. I knew we could get everything worked out. Isn't it time for dinner?"

"Certainly." Reba's voice had a definite whip crack quality all of a sudden. "Let's eat. And let's have a lot more champagne while we're at it."

Chapter Four

The next afternoon, Pete stood in his kitchen, staring down at the greyhound huddled in the beige, molded-plastic crate at his feet. He was supposed to leave the dog's crate out in the apartment so she could hide inside it if she wanted to. Apparently, she wanted to. She hadn't ventured out since he'd opened the wire mesh crate door.

He slid his hand into his pocket automatically, running his fingers over his cell. He could check his voice mail—wouldn't take more than five minutes. Or he could grab his laptop out of his suitcase and check his e-mail. Just a few seconds.

No phones, Pete. No laptop. No business.

Pete sighed, extending his hand to the dog again so that she could sniff it. She trembled as he stroked her shoulders. "Look, Pookie, it's not that bad out here, okay?" he soothed. "No rabbits to chase. No cages. Nobody yelling at you. Cal's a great guy. You've landed in clover, Pookie old girl."

The greyhound didn't budge.

Pookie. Holy crap. "Okay, let's face it, pup, the name has to go. For your dignity and mine."

Pete stared down at her, trying to be creative. His last girlfriend had been named Misty, but he didn't want the dog to start out jinxed. Mrs. Hebert, who lived next door when he was a kid, had had a cocker spaniel named Lillian, not that Pete had particularly pleasant memories of either Lillian or Mrs. Hebert. His mind was suddenly awash with male dog names: Butch, Bowser, Max, Killer.

The greyhound raised her large, moist, black eyes to gaze at him.

"Olive," Pete blurted.

The dog cocked her head slightly, considering.

"C'mon, Olive. Works for me." Pete grinned at her. He might have imagined it, but she didn't seem to be trembling quite as much anymore.

Or she wasn't until Pete's cell jangled with the *Bad Boys* ringtone. "Sorry about that," he mumbled, scratching her ears again as she shuddered. He flipped the phone open.

"Hey, bro." Cal was grinning again. Pete could tell. "How's Pookie?"

"Her name is Olive and she's terrified but coping. What's up?"

"Olive." Cal paused, considering. "Sounds okay. I forgot to tell you, we've got a tux fitting in fifteen minutes. Down at Siemen's Men's Wear on Spicewood."

Pete frowned. "I thought you said I needed to spend the day getting Olive acclimated to civilian life."

"Well, somebody does. Docia said she'd dog-sit for you. She's downstairs in the bookstore right now."

Olive trembled slightly under his fingertips, turning large kalamata eyes in his direction. Pete sighed. "How about if I bring her along? She could stay in her crate."

Cal sounded dubious. "Okay, I guess. Siemen probably won't like it, but he's making out like a bandit on the tux rentals so he hasn't got much room to complain. See you there."

Pete folded his cell and dropped it back in his pocket, then reached down to stroke the dog again. "Easy there, Olive, time to meet the outside world."

Ten minutes later, Pete hoisted the crate and Olive through the door of Siemen's Men's Wear, ignoring the surprised look he got from a sales clerk. "Toleffson wedding," he grunted.

"Through there." The clerk winked at him. Pete had a feeling the Toleffson wedding was a topic of considerable interest in Konigsburg.

The dressing room was full of half-dressed men and one harassed-looking tailor. Wonder Dentist was pulling off his tuxedo pants in the corner, the tails of his pleated shirt hanging down stiffly below his rear. The other groomsman, Horace Rankin, Cal's partner, was pulling on his shirt. Horace was somewhere on the far side of sixty, but his upper body still looked surprisingly muscular. Pete wondered if that was the result of hauling around dogs in crates all day.

Horace nodded toward Olive's crate. "Who's in the box?"

"Olive." Pete put the crate down in the corner and opened

its wire mesh door again. Olive extended her nose into the room and then quickly withdrew.

Horace stared, then blew an impatient breath through his walrus mustache. "Toleffson, you goddamned bleeding heart, don't tell me you're adopting another one."

Cal grinned at him. "She's a nice dog, Horace. Pete, grab your pants. Over there."

Pete raised an eyebrow. Cal was wearing boxers and nothing else. He looked like an affable grizzly. "Are you telling me they actually have tuxes that fit us? I thought the Toleffson physique defied formal dress."

"Us and Lars, as soon as he gets here. Reba had to call every store in San Antonio and Austin, but she finally rustled up three matching tuxes in size elephantine." Cal started buttoning a tuxedo shirt across his chest.

Pete picked up a pair of pants and pulled them on. The waistband actually reached his waist and the pants broke nicely over the tops of his running shoes when he put them back on. Amazing.

"All three of you are this big?" Wonder cocked an eyebrow as he pulled his regular pants back on. "Holy crap, I thought Calthorpe here was some kind of mutant."

Pete shrugged. "Viking throwbacks."

Horace folded his tuxedo jacket and pants into a box, humphing. "Looks okay to me, Siemen. Or as near okay as one of these monkey suits can get. Can I just take it now or do I need to pick it up later?"

The tailor waved an impatient hand. "Sure, sure, take it now. All of you take 'em with you. Less to worry about."

Horace and Wonder left, carrying boxes under their arms, leaving Cal and Pete in different states of undress and Siemen trying to adjust seams and general fit.

The tux shirt was a little tight across Pete's chest, but then he'd never yet seen a rental tux that could comfortably accommodate somebody six-feet-four-inches tall who weighed upward of one-ninety.

Cal was trying to tie a bow tie under his beard with considerable difficulty. "Let me do it." Pete pulled the tie up and tried to remember how to tie it backward.

Cal raised his chin higher so that Pete could loop the tie under his collar. "Did you bring a coat for the rehearsal dinner?

47

Mom won't be happy with anything less than sport jackets."

Pete kept his eyes on the tie, stepping back to study the effect. "All I brought was a blazer. You told me I was on vacation. I left my working clothes back in Iowa."

Cal began inserting studs into his shirt front. "Fine by me. So what's up with Mom and Sherice?"

Pete pulled on his tuxedo jacket, squinting at himself in the mirror. "Your guess is as good as mine, Calthorpe." He shot his shirt cuffs below the edge of the sleeves, showing a nice quarter-inch of white.

"So what would your guess be, Peter?"

He sighed. "You know Mom. Keep the family together, no matter how obnoxious the individual members might be. That means Erik and Sherice and even Aunt Roslyn, far as I know."

"Erik and Sherice have Aunt Roslyn beat by a mile, if we're talking obnoxious." Cal fiddled with his cuff links. "How serious is she about getting them both into the wedding?"

Pete frowned as he tied his own tie. "About as serious as usual. She won't come out and order you to do it, but she'll make your life miserable until you do."

"Terrific. I think Reba managed to work Sherice into the line-up, but I'll be damned if I let Erik in."

Pete shrugged. "Up to you, Calthorpe. Just put your head down and ignore her, then."

Cal studied himself in the mirror, straightening his collar around the bow tie. "Do you ever see him?"

"Erik? Not for a couple of years." Pete half-turned away from him, pulling out his cuff links a little more decisively than he'd intended. One of them bounced onto the floor. "He moved to Marshalltown, then someplace in Illinois. I guess Mom and Dad have kept tabs on him. From what I hear, he's cleaned up his act. Mom said he got a degree from some community college someplace, but I don't know what he's doing now."

"I don't have a single good memory of him, bro. Not one." Cal's eyes were bleak.

Pete's stomach tightened. "Well, we got through it, growing up with King Kong. Think of it as a learning experience."

"You took the worst of it." Cal began to pull the shirt from his shoulders, reaching for a hanger. "Keeping him off Lars and me."

Pete pulled his T-shirt back over his head. "He wasn't some kind of psycho serial killer, Calthorpe. He was just a bully. And like most bullies, once we were big enough to fight back he lost interest."

"Maybe. I'm still not inclined to say welcome back, big brother." Cal sat on a creaking chair in the corner and pulled off his dress shoes.

Pete took a deep breath and blew it out. Stress reduction time. "Then don't. Dad'll be here in a couple of days. He'll get Mom to back off. Or I can talk to her. Maybe I'll do that." Right. A conversation he was really looking forward to.

Cal shook his head. "You don't have to look out for me, Pete. I'm not ten anymore."

Pete's jaw tightened. "I know that, but maybe I could—"

"Let it go." Cal's voice was flat. "If I need to talk to her, I will."

Siemen entered the room again. "Jacket will be ready tomorrow, Cal." He picked up Pete's shirt and jacket from the chair, then waited for his pants.

Cal knelt beside Olive's crate, reaching in to scratch her ears until Siemen left again. "You feeling okay, bro?"

"Hey, I'm fine. I'm here to relax, remember? Vacation time in Texas?"

Cal gave him a slightly rueful smile. "I don't know how much of a vacation this is—taking care of all this wedding stuff and riding herd on Mom." Olive whimpered as he took his fingers away. Dr. Doolittle on steroids. "Anyway, I'm glad you're here, Pete."

Pete nodded slowly. "Yeah, bro, so am I." He was amazed to realize he wasn't lying—much.

Janie arrived at Reba's headquarters at the Woodrose Inn right after lunch. Reba had taken over the whole place, sleeping in one of the big bedrooms upstairs and using the other rooms to store all the various bits of wedding paraphernalia she was accumulating.

The bridesmaids' dresses were draped over the chairs in the Woodrose's parlor. "Aren't they lovely?" Reba cooed. "Just perfect. I'm so glad I found them. Docia needs to come out here and look at them, but of course she'll love them too."

Janie wondered if there was an opposite of Bridezilla. Whatever it was, Docia was it. Janie wasn't sure Docia had any idea what her bridesmaids' dresses looked like. On the other hand, Reba might be moving into Momzilla territory, assuming such territory existed. This was Reba's wedding in every way except the actual marriage part.

The dresses shimmered in the early afternoon sunshine— soft champagne satin with toast-colored sashes below the strapless tops and bands of matching color around the hems. Janie thought they were the most gorgeous things she'd ever seen.

"Where's the other dress?" she asked as she spread one satin skirt across the chair back.

"You mean for the sister-in-law?" Reba's smile curdled slightly. "Fortunately, Claudine was able to find another dress in the right size. Unfortunately, the dress was in Chicago. It's being flown in. At least the sister-in-law can pair up with her husband the groomsman, so we're even. That's one less thing to worry about."

Janie took a breath. "What about my dress?"

"Not yet." Reba smiled at her. "I'll show you yours when the other bridesmaids get here."

Voices sounded in the hall outside the parlor as Allie walked in with Bethany Kronk. Both of them had on their working clothes, chef's pants for Allie, multi-colored scrubs for Bethany.

Reba smiled again. "Right on time. Let's get you all into these gowns."

Janie watched as Reba and her seamstress fluttered back and forth, nipping and tucking. The champagne color made Allie and Bethany glow. They were going to be beautiful. Janie frowned at herself in the mirror, wishing she had a dress just like theirs.

"And now, Miss Janie, let's get you dressed up too." Reba gave her a slightly sly smile, then reached into an open box resting on the sofa.

Janie caught her breath. The dress Reba shook out in front of her was like the other two, but not exactly. For one thing, her dress was a pale lavender. The sash below the bust was a darker shade of bluish purple, like the band at the bottom of the skirt.

Where the other dresses shone with a smooth light, like burnished metal, Janie's dress almost glistened, changing colors subtly as the skirt moved, like a twilight-colored pearl.

"Oh Janie," Bethany murmured. "How beautiful."

Janie stripped off her jeans and camp shirt. She raised her arms and let Reba drop the dress over her head, then turned so that she could zip it up.

The bodice hugged her breasts, pushing them up as if they were being offered for inspection. The skirt hung straight to the floor, pooling slightly over her bare feet.

"Shoes." Reba dug through a pile of boxes until she emerged with a pair of lavender kid sandals. Janie slipped them onto her bare feet, then pushed her hair back from her face.

From across the room, Allie and Bethany stared at her.

Allie swallowed. "My god, who is this woman and what have you done with Janie Dupree?"

Janie turned to look at herself in the mirror. The lavender made her skin almost golden, emphasizing the black sheen of her hair. Suddenly, her dark brown eyes had developed navy highlights. The woman in the mirror was mysterious, ethereal, sexy.

Beautiful.

Janie caught her breath. It was the most amazing dress she'd every put on. "Oh thank you," she whispered, turning to Reba. "Thank you so much."

Reba grabbed a tissue from a box on the coffee table, dabbing at her nose. "You're more than welcome, sweetheart. Now let's see if we can make any sense out of these hair ornaments."

Janie headed to the Dew Drop at five, although Reba had given her a couple of glasses of champagne while the seamstress had made her adjustments. Janie figured she'd had more champagne over the past week than she'd had in her entire previous life. And they hadn't even gotten to the major events yet.

Inside the bar, Docia sat at a table at the side, watching a bunch of men in back shoot darts.

"Where's Cal?" Janie slid into a chair.

Docia shook her head. "Who knows. Trying something on, picking something up, dropping something off." Her lips firmed to a thin line. "I knew this whole wedding thing would turn out to be a pain in the ass. That's why I didn't want to get into it."

"Your mama's got everything covered." Janie smiled encouragingly. Clearly, it was her turn to be on keep-Docia-with-the-program duty.

Docia gave her a slightly mutinous look. "She's got it all covered, all right. Every time I try to tell her what I'd like, she says her way is just the same only better. The whole thing is such a hassle."

Janie tried to think of something soothing to say. It would have helped if she hadn't been absolutely spot on about Reba's persuasive techniques. "Well anyway, Docia, the bridesmaids' dresses are absolutely fantastic. We look great!"

"Do you?" Docia's lips curved up again. "I love the one Mama found for you—she showed me a picture. Did she say anything about Sherice's dress?"

Janie nodded. "It's being air-lifted in as we speak."

"Good. By the way, Daddy's having a barbecue tomorrow night at Buckhorn. You and Otto are invited."

A chorus of groans arose from the dart game spectators. "No offense, Toleffson, but you might want to take up bridge," Wonder crowed from the back of the room.

Pete Toleffson lounged at the side of the room, leaning his shoulder against the wood paneling as one of the other men picked up the darts. He wore jeans and a gray T-shirt with DMPD across his chest.

His extremely broad chest. Janie took a deep breath. Well, so what? Otto's chest was broad too.

After the other player finished, Pete pushed himself up from the wall and pulled the darts loose from the target. He moved easily across the floor, cutting through the crowd to stand at the dart line. Something about him reminded Janie of a large tom cat, strolling effortlessly along a rooftop.

No. More like a cheetah strolling across the plains, looking for prey to chase.

"Watch and learn, Wonder, watch and learn," Pete crooned, raising his hand. He let fly with a dart.

It pierced the center of the target neatly. A chorus of raucous male voices hooted in the background, and Pete raised his arm again. Janie watched his hand move back and then forward in a perfect arc, sending the dart arching toward the target.

It pierced near the center again, just below the first dart.

This time the hoots were mixed with whistles. "Double bull!" somebody yelled.

Pete raised his hand once more, balancing the dart on his fingers before he sent it flying. The arc looked a little flatter this time. The dart *thunked* into the wall beside the target.

The whistles and hoots were deafening.

Pete shrugged. "Just give me a chance to get my rhythm back, boys."

"Bridge, Toleffson," Wonder yelled. "Maybe croquet."

Janie watched the ripple of muscle across Pete's back as he loosened his shoulders. Otto had muscles too. Otto was solid muscle.

Pete wasn't. He flexed his long arms above his head, then leaned back against the wall again, raising narrowed eyes to study the target. His eyes were the color of strong coffee in the dim light of the Dew Drop. Strands of his dark hair flipped over his ears and drifted across his forehead.

God, he was gorgeous.

Janie bit her lip. No. She was not going to be attracted to Pete Toleffson. He was a jerk. Besides, he'd be heading back to Des Moines after The Wedding. Otto lived here in Konigsburg, full time, and so did Janie.

Nonetheless, she had to admit it, at least to herself. Pete Toleffson was one gorgeous hunk. Janie dropped her gaze to her hands on the table in front of her. Staring at Pete Toleffson was not a good idea.

Said gorgeous hunk slid into a chair opposite Docia. "Vanquished."

Darts. He's talking about darts.

"Olive okay?" Pete took a swallow of beer.

Docia was smiling now, relaxed and easy. "She's under the table."

Janie looked under the table for the first time and saw a large plastic crate resting beside Docia's chair. "Olive?"

"The dog." Pete's hand disappeared into the crate. A long, slender snout edged slightly beyond the edge of the door.

"You're really good at darts," Docia remarked. "I don't think I've ever seen Cal get two bulls-eyes in a row. And he plays a *lot*. He's even got the rest of us doing it."

"Misspent youth." Pete shrugged as he sat up again. "Dad had a dart board in the rec room. We all played a lot. So how are your scores?"

Docia grimaced. "I can hit the target most of the time. I consider that a plus."

"Definitely." Pete grinned now. "In some bars that's enough to make you the champ, particularly late in the evening."

Docia shook her head. "Janie's better than I am."

Pete raised an eyebrow as he turned to her. "You throw darts, tiny? Never would have guessed."

Janie's gut tightened. She really hated being called tiny. She wasn't all *that* small. "I learned when I was a kid."

"In Janie's hands, darts are a lethal weapon." Docia rested her elbows on the table, cupping her chin in one hand. "You should never get in her way. Just ask Joe Roy Ellison."

Janie's face grew warm. She hoped the Dew Drop was dark enough to hide her blush. "That was just once when he wouldn't get away from the target. He thought he was being funny. He said the target was the safest place to stand since I'd never come close."

Pete frowned slightly. "So what did you do?"

"She darted him." Docia's lips spread in a slow grin. "He got off easy."

"You...darted him?" Pete's brow furrowed. "What does that mean exactly?"

"I hit him in the butt with a dart." Janie said it in a rush, hoping it didn't sound as bad as she knew it did.

Pete's eyebrows rose almost to his hairline. "You put a dart in him?"

"He was wearing his work pants so it didn't really penetrate much beyond his back pocket," she said through gritted teeth. "I was super careful not to aim for anything vital. I was surprised it didn't bounce off."

So was Joe Roy, of course, although his surprise had been more centered on the fact that she'd done it at all. That was the end of that relationship, not that Janie was all that sorry to see him go. Joe Roy had a big mouth and nasty ideas.

"He spent the rest of the evening rubbing his ass," Docia chortled.

Janie dropped her gaze to her hands again. "Better him than me."

Pete threw his head back and guffawed. "I hereby apologize, Ms. Dupree. You're clearly a very dangerous woman. I will never call you tiny again."

"Good. See that you don't."

The door swung open behind Docia. Two broad figures were silhouetted against the fading evening light.

"Cal!" Docia called, waving. "Over here."

Cal stepped into the muted dimness of the Dew Drop. The man who followed him looked a lot more polished but still clearly a Toleffson. His dark brown hair was close cropped, and he wore a burgundy knit shirt with impeccably creased khakis.

Pete jumped to his feet, grinning, one hand outstretched. "Lars!" He pushed away from the table and started toward his brothers.

As Lars moved away from the doorway, a woman stepped inside behind him. Her long, perfectly straightened blonde hair fell to her bare shoulders above a tight black halter top. Her denim skirt stopped somewhere around mid-thigh, revealing a significant amount of bare, tanned leg. As she glanced around the room, she raised a hand to push her bangs back from her forehead. Gold and jewels flashed at her fingers and wrist. The woman's gaze slid across Docia and Janie with minimal interest.

The entire male population of the Dew Drop seemed to go still, staring. Janie thought she heard a faint, awed whistle from one of the dart players.

The woman looked back at Pete Toleffson again, still not smiling.

"What a dump," she said in the silence of the bar.

Pete's grin faded. "Hey, Sherice. Welcome to Konigsburg."

Chapter Five

That night Pete dreamed he was sharing a bed with his brothers again, as they had when the three of them were small—well, smaller, anyway. Lars was crowding him, and Pete gave him a push. Lars whimpered and snuffled, and then licked Pete's nose.

Pete's eyes popped open.

A warm weight nestled at his hip. Someone was snoring, and it took him a moment to realize it wasn't anybody related to him. Olive lay sprawled across the other side of the bed, her head resting lightly on the pillow.

Right. The first female to share his bed in at least six months, and she was leaving hairs on the sheets. His luck was running true to form.

"Night, Olive," Pete muttered. He thought he saw Olive's eyelids flutter in response.

Several hours later, he was dimly aware of whimpering and scratching sounds somewhere near the back of the apartment. He jerked abruptly awake, his head cranking from side to side, then stumbled into the kitchen to see Olive scratching at the door to the stairs. "Okay, dog," Pete sighed, "gimme a minute."

He pulled on a pair of jeans, clipped a leash to Olive's collar, and headed down the stairs and out the door to the street just as Janie Dupree walked by. Olive jerked into her path, sending her crashing backward into Pete. He dropped the leash as Olive galloped into the backyard.

Pete placed a steadying hand on Janie's shoulder, suddenly aware of soft feminine curves pressing against his partly naked body. Instantly, he was totally awake.

"Morning," he mumbled. "Sorry about that. Apparently, this was more of an emergency than I realized."

Olive was already peeing on the nearest live oak. Janie stood, straightening nonexistent creases in her shirt. "That's okay. How are you two getting along?"

Pete shrugged. "So far, so good. I need to get her out for more exercise. I thought I might take her to that shindig tonight."

"The Kent family barbecue? Do you need a ride?"

"I hadn't really thought about it." Getting Olive outside had taken precedence over less pressing matters.

"Billy's lodge is about fifteen miles from here, up in the hills. The road's a little rough, but Otto's got a heavy-duty truck. You could ride with us."

Pete considered the joys of experiencing Otto Friedrich at close quarters for fifteen miles. "That's okay. I'll hitch a ride with Cal or Lars." Whoever wasn't taking his mother.

"Okay." Her brow furrowed. "I don't suppose you've ever run a bookshop, have you?"

Pete shook his head, leaning down to pick up Olive's leash again. "Nope. I ran a snack bar at the lake back home, but that's the extent of my retail experience. Why?"

"Docia's got the final fitting for her gown this morning, and I wanted to go with her. But we don't have anybody to look after the store."

"I'll do it. How hard can it be?"

Janie's lips curved up in a faint smile. "That sounds like a lead-in to one of those sitcom scenes where the store gets trashed."

"I promise to return the shop to you in the same shape I found it." He grinned back at her.

"Great. Come on down around ten and I'll show you how the cash register works."

Her eyes were almost as dark as Olive's, Pete realized suddenly. Not that anything else about her reminded him of a dog. "Right. See you later."

Olive tugged at the leash in his hand, and Pete turned back toward the door. After a moment, he gave in to his baser self and watched Janie disappear around the corner, gazing at the perfect apple shape of her behind.

He took a deep breath and ignored the slight tingle of arousal in his groin. He was a grown man, and he wasn't going to get a hard-on over every woman he saw walking down the street.

Of course, he had to admit—Janie Dupree didn't strike him as just any woman anymore. Unfortunately, she appeared to be attached to that human support pillar known as Otto Friedrich. For some reason, Pete found that thought particularly depressing.

Otto spent ten minutes driving around Main looking for a place to park his truck. He didn't know why the city wouldn't break down and build a parking garage—hell, the tourists would probably pay for it in a year.

He figured he had a couple of hours before he had to get back for the afternoon practice. He could entice Janie Dupree away from the cash register for a little lunch and then maybe some heavy petting in the grotto over by the city park.

That wasn't what he really wanted to do, of course, but Janie had turned out to be a lot slower about putting out than Joe Roy Ellison had led him to believe. In fact, if it hadn't been for Joe Roy's stories about Janie and her hot bod, he would have said the hell with it by now. He'd never waited three months for nookie before.

Still, having invested all this time and money in getting Janie Dupree in the sack, Otto wasn't backing off yet. At least he knew she wasn't frigid. When he thought it through, he decided she was just a little intimidated. After all, she'd probably never dated anybody like him. He was sort of a local hero around here, what with the team making it all the way to the state semis last year. Maybe she had to get used to the idea he really wanted her.

He'd already planted the seed, told her he wanted to take it to the next level. Now he'd just give her a little more time to get used to the idea. Not too much time, though. Summer was almost over, and he had other things to do.

Otto swung open the door to the bookstore and stepped inside, already sliding his best seductive smile into place. But instead of Janie Dupree or Docia Kent, a large male stood behind the counter talking to Helen Kretschmer.

Otto goggled. Nobody talked to Helen Kretschmer. Helen Kretschmer was a cop, and she was the single most terrifying woman he'd ever seen, the only woman he'd ever thought could take him in a fair fight. Now Helen was not only talking, she was...ye gods...smiling.

At Pete Toleffson.

It took him a couple of seconds to identify the man behind the counter, and then he was doubly annoyed. What was Toleffson doing running the bookstore? And where was Janie? His lunch hour was ticking away.

Helen turned gimlet eyes his way, her smile fading. Otto's gut clenched.

Toleffson glanced at him and raised his eyebrows. "Morning, Friedrich. Something I can help you with?"

"Where's Janie?" he blurted.

"Off helping Docia and Reba with something wedding-related." Toleffson leaned a hip against the counter. "I'm filling in."

"You're running the bookstore?" Otto stared. He'd heard Toleffson was a lawyer. What the hell did a lawyer know about running a cash register?

"Filling in, like I said." Toleffson grinned, but it didn't reach his eyes.

Otto felt a quick rush of adrenaline. He could take Pete Toleffson, even if he was the size of a red oak. No problem. He'd enjoy it. "When's she coming back? I'm taking her to a party tonight."

He figured Toleffson already knew about the party, since the party was because of the wedding and his brother was the one getting married, but it wouldn't hurt to remind the man who Janie Dupree belonged to.

"Oh, yeah." Toleffson went on grinning. "Janie said I should ride up there with you."

Otto's gut clenched again. Goddamn! He wasn't going to take anybody in his truck except Janie. He had some plans of his own for the evening.

He worked on keeping his teeth from gritting. "Is that right?"

"That's right." Toleffson waited a moment before he spoke again. "I turned her down, of course. I'll ride with my brother."

Behind him, Otto heard Helen Kretschmer snicker.

Okay, not only could he take Pete Toleffson, he was pretty sure he'd be doing it before the week was over.

Reba's command center at the Woodrose had become a mass of tulle and satin ribbon, which Janie gathered had something to do with table runners. Reba and her seamstress, Mamie, had dragged Docia away as soon as the two of them had arrived, Reba muttering about strapless bras and body shapers.

As far as Janie was concerned, Docia didn't need any more shaping than Mother Nature had already provided. She was about as shapely as anyone Janie had ever met, and most of the men in Konigsburg agreed with her, judging by the usual reaction when Docia walked into a room.

Now she stared at Docia as she stood reflected in the three-way mirror. The bottom of her gown looked like a cloud of ivory chiffon. Her satin-clad torso rose above it, a mermaid emerging from a wave, the fabric clinging to her generous curves and shimmering with sprays of subtle, rainbow-colored brilliants.

Just looking at Docia made Janie's eyes prick with tears. Brides were supposed to look just like that.

Reba ran her hands through the chiffon, lifting it slightly. "Oh my, baby." She smiled. "Look at you!"

Docia stood silently, staring at herself in the mirror.

"Isn't she lovely?" Reba turned toward Janie, fumbling in her pocket for a handkerchief. "Isn't she just so gorgeous?"

Janie nodded, sniffling.

"Oh where's my mind?" Reba clapped a hand to her cheek. "I forgot all about the veil. Come on, Mamie, I'll need help unpacking it." The two women scurried back toward the dining room where Reba had stacked the dress boxes.

Janie glanced at Docia. She stood frozen in the dressing room lights, her face a blank mask.

"Docia?"

Docia let out a breath, pressing a hand to her stomach. "I don't recognize myself."

"Oh, honey, I know. I didn't recognize myself either when I had on the maid of honor dress. It's just...it's like a fairy tale, isn't it?" Janie dabbed at her eyes again.

Docia shook her head defiantly, sending her bronze curls tumbling from the cluster Reba had gathered at her nape. "No, it's not. I don't recognize myself, Janie. It's not me. None of this is me! It's just pretend, make-believe. How can I go through with this?"

Janie's fingernails bit into her palms. Reba should be here. Reba would know what to say. She took a deep breath. "Docia, Cal is the most wonderful guy ever. You know that."

Docia waved an impatient hand. "Of course Cal is wonderful. I'm nuts about him. This isn't about Cal, or about getting married to him. This is about—" her lips pursed again as she waved her hand at the mirror, "—this. All this...stuff. I don't dress like this. I don't look like this. This isn't me! This is some prom queen or something."

"Docia, nobody dresses like this normally." Janie knelt down to fluff out the chiffon cloud again. "But don't you want to look like Cinderella just once?"

Docia looked down at her, still frowning slightly. "I'm not exactly the Cinderella type, Janie. Can you imagine me being intimidated by a couple of raggedy-ass stepsisters?"

The corners of Docia's mouth began to inch up again. Janie's shoulders relaxed slightly.

"I can't even imagine you in heels, let alone glass slippers." She stepped back again. "Oh, Docia, you really do look so beautiful. Cal will just be bowled over."

Docia stared into the mirror, smoothing a hand over her hip. "Maybe. I'm telling you, Janie, giving Cal the surprise of his life is the only reason I can see for going on with this production. That and making Mama happy."

"What's making me happy?" Reba bustled in again, carrying another chiffon cloud, rising from a simple band of crystals. "Here, sweetheart, try this on."

Docia straightened her spine, letting Reba settle the band of crystals in her hair so that the chiffon dropped in graceful folds over her shoulders.

"Oh, baby." Reba clasped her hands against her chest. "You look like Cinderella getting ready for the ball."

In the mirror, Janie saw Docia roll her eyes.

Pete rode to the barbecue with Cal and Mom after all. Docia was already there, having ridden up with Reba, and Pete decided he couldn't abandon Cal to a solitary drive with their mother.

He loaded Olive's crate into the back of Cal's SUV while his mother frowned.

"What's that?"

"Olive." He climbed into the front seat beside Cal, strapping on his seat belt.

"She's a dog, Mom," Cal explained. "Pete's taking care of her for me." He pulled out onto the highway, heading toward the edge of town.

The silence from the back was deafening. Pete took a deep breath and turned around to look at his mother.

She sat with her hands folded over the leather purse resting on her lap. The pattern on her blouse looked like tiny green tarantulas. Pete blinked. Okay, not tarantulas—ladybugs. Freud would probably have a field day with his family psyche.

His mother's brow was pleated in a frown. "Why are you taking care of the dog when you don't even live here?"

"Cal needed someone to look after her while he was getting ready for the wedding."

His mother's eyes stayed narrow. "How are you going to take care of it while they're on their honeymoon?"

"Cal has somebody else lined up." Pete turned back to gaze out the windshield.

"You could stay here then and look after things. Maybe you could take a vacation."

Pete was careful not to look into the back seat. "I'm on a vacation right now." He glanced in the rear view mirror to see his mother's scowl.

"I still think...Mercy!"

The SUV turned onto a dirt road that looked like it had last been graded in the Carter administration. "Hang on," Cal yelled cheerfully as he pulled the SUV to the side, managing to avoid a car-eating pothole. "Billy's lodge is back in the woods a ways."

Mom grabbed the panic handle above the door. "Why would anyone want to build all the way out here—without a good road?"

"It's real pretty, Mom." Cal flipped the four-wheel drive switch. "Billy's tried to get the county to fix the road, but it's not high on their list right now."

Cal was grinning again, but Pete couldn't argue with him this time. This was living, just like the good old days. They'd driven over every cow track in southern Iowa, looking for ways to relieve the general placidity of Lander. And finding enough of them to cause their father to confiscate their car keys on a regular basis. Or Pete's car keys, anyway, since he was usually the one who let his younger brothers drive.

The road dipped down between limestone cliffs, crossing meadows dotted with the deep olive of live oaks, striped with the lighter lime greens of mesquite. Pete saw flashes of water now and then through the trees.

"Placitas Creek," Cal explained, sliding right to avoid a particularly nasty washboard rut. "It covers the road once or twice a year, but not enough to keep Billy from getting in and out."

"Why aren't they having the wedding out here if it's so pretty?"

Pete glanced back at Mom again. She was leaning forward in her seat, still holding onto the panic handle for all she was worth.

"Too small," Cal called back to her. "Buckhorn's only got room for a hundred or so people."

"Some hunting lodge." Pete remembered a couple of pheasant hunting trips he'd taken with Lars. Cal, of course, wouldn't kill any animal unless it was already in mortal pain. "You don't hunt up here, I take it."

Cal shook his head. "Took Billy a while to accept it, but I don't think it bothers him now."

He pulled the SUV to a stop at a wrought-iron gate with B K splashed across the middle in brass.

"Tell me again—this is his little 'get-away place'?"

Cal blew out a breath. "Just open the gate, Pete, you're riding shotgun."

The road wound around more limestone hills until the house came into view—an immense wood-and-granite building spilling over the crest of a hill on the other side of the valley. Pete could see the corner of a turquoise swimming pool around the back. Cal parked in front of the triple garage at one side.

He raised his eyebrows, but Cal shook his head. "Don't say anything, okay? I'm marrying Docia, not Billy."

"A decision we all applaud." He helped his mother out of the backseat, then turned as the door of the house opened and Reba and Billy walked toward them.

Reba was wearing knit slacks in apricot with a silk blouse that had the colors of a fall sunset.

Pete heard his mother's slight sniff as she surveyed the ryegrass-covered yard. "Where are Lars and Sherice?"

"Somewhere around here. That's his rental car." Cal glanced back at the other cars parked at the edge of the driveway.

"Everybody's out by the pool," Reba trilled. "Did y'all remember to bring your suits?"

Mom looked momentarily as if she'd been asked to perform a human sacrifice. Cal took her arm and herded her toward the swimming pool in back. "C'mon, Mom, let's go find Lars."

"Lars and a margarita," his mother said in a hollow voice.

Janie sat beside the pool between Allie and Bethany. Allie was wearing a red maillot that did great things for her olive complexion. Bethany had draped a denim shirt over her black one-piece and wore a floppy straw hat to protect her from the sun. Janie wore the two-piece she'd picked up at a sale at the Lucky Lady—yellow flowers on a bright blue background. It looked...okay. Not as good as it had in the shop, unfortunately.

She sighed and went back to watching Otto swim. Droplets of water gleamed along the long muscles of his back and arms as they bunched and stretched with his strokes. His short brown hair made him look a little like a seal when he raised his head slightly to breathe.

He flipped onto his back and the muscles of his chest flexed as he sliced through the water again. She had the odd feeling that she was supposed to be looking at the stacked rings of his abdominal muscles where they formed a perfect six-pack. Instead, she found herself studying his expression as he grunted with the effort of swimming.

He really was a very good-looking man, she told herself again. She was a very lucky woman. She could have sex with that body. She could even do it tonight if she wanted to.

If she wanted to.

Janie sighed again and took another sip of her margarita. It had started out frozen, but now it was just cold.

"Holy crap," Allie murmured beside her, "what a body!"

Janie looked back at Otto again. "Yep."

On her other side, Bethany sucked in a breath. "Not real," she said. "Definitely plastic."

Janie blinked at her, then glanced at the other side of the pool.

Sherice Toleffson was wearing two small strips of cloth that passed for a black bikini, with a black scarf wound around her platinum hair. From where Janie was sitting, it looked like Des Moines had at least one salon that knew how to do a nice Brazilian wax.

"I don't know," Allie mused. "Wouldn't the scars from a boob job show in a swimsuit that size?"

Bethany made an impolite sound. "She's five-foot-five or so and weighs about as much as the average wren. Believe me, honey, nobody that size naturally has tits like cassava melons."

Janie bit her lip to hold back the laugh. Unfortunately, it came out as a snort. She picked up her margarita for a quick swig.

"Watch it," Allie warned, "the Girl from Ipanema is heading this way."

Sherice sauntered around the pool, a magenta canvas bag draped across her arm. Her black leather mules clicked against the pebbled concrete. She stopped a few feet away from them and angled herself above a black metal lounge.

Janie's conscience took a quick bite. "Sherice," she called.

Sherice turned slowly, staring in Janie's direction from behind a pair of huge black sunglasses that made her look vaguely like an insect. She didn't smile.

Janie took a quick breath and pushed the corners of her mouth into a semblance of friendliness. "That lounge has been out in the sun all day—it's probably pretty hot. Would you like to join us?"

Sherice stared at her for another moment, then shrugged. "Whatever."

She ambled to a fabric-covered chair on Allie's other side, then pulled a bottle of sunscreen from her bag and began to rub it onto her arms.

After a moment, Allie cleared her throat. "I'm Allie Maldonado, and that's Bethany Kronk at the end. I guess you met Janie yesterday."

Sherice raised her sunglassed eyes to stare in Janie's direction. "I guess."

She turned back to rub sunscreen onto her legs, then glanced across the pool. "Lars!" she called. "Bring me a drink, will you?"

Janie looked up. The three Toleffson brothers were clustered together on the far side like a small stand of redwoods. Three dark heads turned to stare across the pool. Only one of them smiled.

"Sure, Sherice," Lars Toleffson called, heading toward the bar Billy Kent had set up at one end of the pool.

Sherice pulled off her sunglasses and began applying sunscreen to her face. "So what do you people do around here for fun?"

Janie managed to keep her smile in place although it made her jaws ache. "Right now we're getting ready for The Wedding. That's about as much fun as most of us can handle at one time."

Sherice rubbed sunscreen down her throat with the kind of motion that probably raised a sweat on most male brows. "Lars said I'm supposed to be some kind of bridesmaid. Do you know anything about that?"

Janie nodded. "Right, Allie and Bethany are bridesmaids too. You can come over to the Woodrose tomorrow and try on your dress. I think Reba said it came in this afternoon."

Sherice shrugged. "Tell Lars. He remembers stuff like that."

"Stuff like what?" Lars Toleffson walked toward them with a margarita balanced carefully in one huge hand.

Janie wondered briefly what it would have been like to give birth to three sons the size of Paul Bunyan. Maybe that accounted for Mama Toleffson's general temperament.

"I'm supposed to go somewhere tomorrow and try on a dress." Sherice didn't sound as if the prospect filled her heart with anticipation.

"Okay." Lars smiled at the four of them. "We'll get you there, no problem. Hey, you want a tour of the house? Billy's going to take Mom through."

Sherice raised a languid brow, then slowly slid her feet back into her mules while she pulled a gauzy wrap from her bag and draped it over her shoulders. "Why not?"

She rose from her chair, plucking the margarita from Lars's hand, and headed toward the end of the pool without glancing back.

Lars's shoulders tensed for a moment, then he smiled again, without a lot of warmth. "Want to join us, ladies?"

Allie gave him a leisurely wave. "That's okay. We've already been around."

Janie watched Sherice's hips sway gently as she sashayed toward Billy Kent. Billy looked like he was trying very hard not to look at anything below Sherice's chin. At his side, Reba was smiling very brightly indeed.

Allie glanced back at Sherice's magenta bag, pushing her sunglasses down her nose. "You suppose she has any extra tits in there? I have a feeling I'm going to need something more impressive than mine if I want to keep Steve's attention at this bash."

Bethany shook her head. "Aw, hell, sugar, they'll look but all they have to do is listen to her for a couple of minutes to know she'd be pure hell to spend any time with. My sympathies are with Lars Toleffson."

One corner of Allie's mouth tipped up in a half smile. "Honey, the kind of time they'd want to spend with her has nothing to do with talking and everything to do with tits."

Judging from Otto's expression as he watched Sherice undulate by, Janie had a feeling Allie was absolutely on the money.

Chapter Six

Sherice Toleffson was bored. As she walked around the pool, she glanced at the mansion Lars kept calling a hunting lodge and saw nothing she was even remotely interested in pursuing—with the possible exception of Billy Kent.

Not that feeling bored was all that unusual. Sherice had been bored ever since she'd walked down the aisle to join Lars Toleffson at the altar. Getting Lars to that altar had been fun. Having Lars afterward was a lot less so.

Lars was wearing his old swimming suit along with a knit shirt. She'd bought him a classy black Speedo, but he persisted in wearing a suit that made him look like an aging surfer. Typical. Lars would never look like a billionaire, much less be one.

Sherice had started reading about billionaires and their wives around the time she'd realized her looks were her greatest asset, probably sometime in grade school. Urbandale, Iowa, hadn't provided much in the way of role models, but *People* magazine filled in the blanks. Women who married billionaires got to wear great clothes and even better jewelry. They lived in houses that were written up in magazines. Sometimes they became fashion designers or jewelry designers or handbag designers—all things she was fairly certain she could do, given half a chance and a lot of money. How hard could it be to design a purse, for god's sake?

Billy Kent led the way through the lodge's living room, yammering something about a couple of maps hanging over the fireplace. Sherice managed to pretend some low-level interest, given Billy's probable net worth.

Finding available—or even unavailable—billionaires in Iowa had always been tough.

Her first job out of community college had been as an office manager in a medical clinic in West Des Moines. She'd figured rich doctors would be good billionaire candidates. But most of the doctors in the clinic were busy paying off their student loans, and none of them gave Sherice the impression they'd be attending cocktail parties with venture capitalists in the near future. She'd almost decided to try another office when the accountant arrived to go over the books.

Lars was six-five or so, with curling brown hair and laughing brown eyes. Sherice went to bed with him on their second date.

She narrowed her eyes, studying Lars now as he bent down slightly to speak to Billy Kent. He was still gorgeous. But, as she should have known very well, gorgeous wasn't enough.

Lars had fallen hard. He'd asked her to marry him after six weeks. Sherice had carefully considered her options. Lars was a junior executive in a large accounting firm and made a decent salary, which would increase sizably if he made partner. He also had a nice stock portfolio that he'd described to her on their third date, never noticing when her eyes glazed over.

She'd realized she could do worse. The question was, could she do better? For once, Sherice had been cautious. Lars was the proverbial bird in the hand. Besides, she sort of liked him. He looked great and he was terrific in bed.

At least at first. Lately, Lars hadn't been much interested in the bed part of things. She figured his lousy performance was the result of exhaustion from work or from Daisy.

She'd gotten pregnant within a year of their wedding. A lot of billionaire wives had a baby quickly. A baby was great job insurance, plus it meant a guaranteed income no matter what happened, at least until the kid was eighteen or so.

And the baby, Daisy, wasn't half bad. Sherice enjoyed shopping for her and dressing her up like a gorgeous live doll. For the rest of it, she had Lars. Lars loved playing with the baby. He even got up to feed her in the night and changed more than a few diapers. Sherice hadn't changed as many herself since she'd convinced Lars to hire a nanny. That way she could get by with seeing Daisy a few times a day, preferably after someone else had cleaned her up.

She wrinkled her nose slightly, remembering the god-awful fuss Lars had made when she'd refused to bring Daisy to the wedding. What was he thinking, anyway? Society weddings were no place for a toddler. Besides, Sherice didn't particularly want to be seen as somebody's mother when she might be circulating among the rich and famous.

She sighed. Living in Des Moines was torture—no parties like the ones she saw in magazines, no jetting off to the Caribbean for a weekend, nobody who owned a yacht or a house in the Hamptons (the Wisconsin Dells just did not count). And Lars wasn't interested in moving anywhere more exciting.

Sherice took a quick glance at herself in one of the large mirrors that hung on the walls of the main hall. She knew she looked very good, despite the slightly mutinous gleam in her eyes—the bikini had been worth every penny of the outrageous price she'd paid.

Maybe she'd see what kind of opportunities presented themselves at this wedding. This was Texas, after all. Billionaire central.

Billy Kent's house tour took them through another massive entry hall leading to an equally massive dining room with a limestone fireplace that looked big enough to roast an ox.

Billy apparently liked things oversize. Sherice gave him a quick once over and decided his taste didn't necessarily reflect his other attributes. Then again, he was undoubtedly loaded in the financial sense.

Mom Toleffson was walking with Billy's wife, which made flirting a little tricky. While Lars might not always notice if she did a little trolling, Mom T. was a lot more observant. And she'd never been reluctant to call Sherice on any apparent transgressions.

Still, she might have been tempted to try a few come-hither looks if Billy's wife hadn't been welded to his side. His wife had hips the size of a bus, but Billy didn't seem to notice. He kept his arm around her waist and his eyes away from Sherice.

Sherice grimaced carefully, trying not to create a new wrinkle. A pity. Billy was probably in the general economic bracket she was interested in. And she'd look far more appropriate on his arm than his current wife did.

Billy waved them into a room with a pool table and an oversized flat-panel television on one wall. The game room. Two of the groomsmen were playing pool—the dentist whose name she'd forgotten and the old guy with the mustache that made him look like an extra in a Western movie. She'd already dismissed both of them as billionaire candidates.

Lars's brother Cal and his fiancée were cuddled together on the couch. They jumped up a little guiltily when Billy and Reba walked in. The woman, Docia Kent, clearly took after her mother and clearly needed to be a lot more careful about what she put on her plate if she didn't want to end up with hips to match. On the other hand, the way Cal looked at her made Sherice feel grumpy.

Lars had looked at her like that. Once upon a time.

Docia was dressed in jeans and a white cotton blouse, not what Sherice would have chosen if her father had been a billionaire. She glanced at Sherice's bikini as they walked back to the pool together, then managed a tight smile. "I think Mama got your bridesmaid dress this morning. Did you get a chance to look at it?"

Sherice shrugged. "Lars said he'd bring me over tomorrow. I'll try it on then."

"Good." Docia giggled. Sherice turned to see Cal pull her back into his arms.

A tight little ball of discontent bounced around in Sherice's stomach. She turned back to the pool. A man stood at the far end rubbing himself with a towel. He was talking to one of those women who'd been sitting at poolside, the one in the flowered bikini. Someone should have told her about the advantages of solid colors in concealing figure flaws.

The man stretched and she saw an expanse of hard muscle and gold-flecked brown hair across his chest.

Yummy. Maybe Konigsburg had something interesting after all.

Pete took Olive for a quick trot around the yard, although for a greyhound she wasn't all that enthusiastic about running. "Come on, Olive," he panted, "let's show your stuff here."

Olive paused to sniff at an oleander bush and Pete surveyed the pool. Janie Dupree stood at the far end, talking to Otto Friedrich. As she turned slightly, Pete suddenly got a more complete look at her figure.

Whoa.

For somebody as small as she was, she had major league curves. Along with that perfect bottom he'd already noted, she had perfect breasts, full and round, just the right size to go along with the rest of her. Clearly, his earlier judgment that they were *smallish* needed to be revised.

Janie suddenly turned her head in his direction, and he quickly shifted his attention to Olive. When he glanced back, Otto Friedrich was scowling at him.

Oh suck it up, coach. You think nobody else notices her? Pete grinned at Otto, nodded at Janie, and started herding Olive toward an umbrella table where Lars sat by himself.

Lars had a margarita in one hand, sunglasses propped halfway down his nose.

"Hey, bro." Pete dropped into the chair beside him. "How do you like Texas so far?"

Lars raised one eyebrow. "This isn't Texas, Pete, this is billionairesville. Has no relation to ordinary life." He took a long swallow of margarita, leaving a slight dusting of rock salt on his nose. "I've heard a lot about the place over the years—never actually saw it before myself."

Pete frowned. Lars gave every indication of being slightly plastered. Of all his brothers, Lars was the most upright. Lars was responsible, Cal was nice, Pete was pigheaded and Erik was a jerk. They'd gotten all of that worked out when they were kids. For a moment, he tried to remember if he'd ever seen Lars drunk before. Not since his bachelor party, anyway.

Lars squinted at Olive. "What's with the pooch?"

"She's Cal's. I'm dog-sitting."

Lars looked up at him, then nodded slowly. "Good. Good for you. Get the hell out of Dodge, right?"

"Right." He had no idea what Lars was talking about or what he was agreeing to, but Lars was satisfied. He leaned his head back against the chair cushions and closed his eyes.

"Where's your wife?"

Lars didn't move. "Somewhere," he mumbled. "Look around. You can't miss her."

"What the hell kind of dog is that?" a man's voice boomed from Pete's left.

He looked up at Otto Friedrich, dressed in tight-fitting swim trunks that outlined his package like the outfits of some of the male strippers Pete had prosecuted over the years. His chest was broad and tanned, and the white towel around his neck contrasted nicely. No doubt an outfit meant to make maidenly hearts flutter.

"Olive's a greyhound." Pete kept his voice affable—no point in starting a fight unless Otto really wanted one. Of course, if he really wanted one, he'd be honor-bound to oblige.

"Not much to her, is there?" Otto glanced down at Olive and then smirked at Pete.

"Racer," he snapped. "They don't build up a lot of fat."

Otto raised his eyebrows. "You're racing her?"

"No. She's retired." Pete reached down to scratch Olive's ears.

Otto made a sound that combined incredulity with scorn. He reached a hand toward Olive, holding his fingers in front of her nose.

Olive growled.

"Down girl," Pete crooned. "Gee, Friedrich, she doesn't seem to like you. Funny—she hasn't acted like that with anybody else."

Otto straightened, resting his hands on his hips. After a moment, he turned toward the other end of the pool. "Janie, sweetheart," he called, "could you bring me my shirt and sandals?"

He turned back to Pete with a vaguely challenging stare. Pete wondered if having Janie at his beck and call was supposed to make up for Olive disliking him?

No comparison, as far as Pete could see.

Janie Dupree picked up a blue T-shirt and leather sandals from the side of the pool. "Are these yours? I can't remember."

Otto's brow furrowed. Pete figured not being memorable was probably a new experience for him. As Janie walked up, Otto slid an arm around her shoulders, hugging her against his slightly damp chest.

"Those are mine. Thanks, sweet thing."

For a moment, Pete thought he saw a flicker of distaste cross Janie's face, but then it was gone. She bent down at Pete's feet, extending her hand. "Hey, Olive."

Olive sniffed at her fingers, then gave her palm a quick lick. *Good girl.*

Otto folded his arms across his chest, then glanced back and forth between Lars and Pete. His mouth curved into a smile that Pete found mildly threatening. "Okay, who's up for some touch football?"

Pete and Lars glanced at each other and sighed. "Football," Lars groaned, doing his best Harrison Ford voice. "Why did it have to be football?"

"Oh, c'mon, Indy, why not?" Pete managed a grin for Janie. "Look after Olive for me, okay?"

In Janie's opinion, the game between the Toleffsons and Otto, Allie, Docia and Wonder should have been quite a battle. After all, except for Wonder, all the men were built like oak trees and coordinated to boot.

All the men were shirtless. If you didn't count Wonder (and no one did except Allie), that expanse of gleaming, muscled flesh was quite a sight.

However, all in all the game wasn't really a fair fight. The Toleffsons were getting creamed.

Janie wasn't exactly sure why this was happening. The three of them together were a solid, dark-haired, six-foot-plus wall of power. They should have been able to beat anybody, including Otto, given that Wonder was one of his teammates.

Assuming, of course, that the Toleffsons took the game halfway seriously. Unfortunately, that wasn't the case.

The snickering gave it away. Every time one of them missed a catch—and that was pretty much every time one of them threw the ball—all three would collapse into snorting laughter, pointing at the offender and making insulting comments about a lack of coordination and grace that went back to the cradle.

They reminded Janie of three puppies tumbling around on the ground. Three very large, very well-built puppies.

When Pete had thrown his fourth interception of the game, allowing Otto to cruise across the goal line once again, all three of them howled with laughter.

"Jesus, you were on the baseball team," Cal crowed, pointing at Pete. "Lars and I were runners. You should at least be able to throw a ball. You've got no excuse, man. You're just bad."

"Basketball." Pete mopped his brow with his forearm. "I was only on the baseball team one year. And throwing a baseball is freakin' nothing like throwing a football."

"*I* was on a baseball team, and I can manage to throw a football. So far as I can tell, none of you guys can throw a football worth a damn," Docia said affably. "Cal's brain is probably mush, but the rest of you have no excuse."

All three Toleffsons collapsed in giggles again. Olive barked, dancing around them as they snorted.

Janie glanced at Otto. He didn't say anything. As he watched the Toleffsons, his face was frozen, his mouth twisted in scorn. Janie drew her brows together in a frown. Otto wasn't enjoying himself, even though his team was winning by a mile.

Pete picked up the ball again, moving back behind Lars to throw. Suddenly, Lars's feet slipped out from under him on the grass and he collapsed on the ground in another gale of snickers. Pete's throw bounced somewhere in front of Wonder.

Otto pushed Wonder aside quickly, scooping the ball up and running toward the makeshift goal they'd set up at the end of the yard.

"Get him!" Lars yelled from his position flat on his back.

Cal took two steps toward Otto, reaching to slap him on the back. Otto twisted suddenly, his shoulder catching Cal in the middle of his chest and sending him crashing down against the concrete strip that ran around the side of the pool.

Cal lay very still.

Janie clamored out of her chair and sprinted across the lawn, hearing the sound of thundering footsteps behind her.

"Cal," Docia cried. "Oh god, Cal!"

She dropped to her knees beside him, one hand pressed to her mouth. Janie bent down to put her hand on Docia's shoulder.

Both Toleffson brothers were huddled around Cal's inert form. Pete leaned forward, grasping Cal's arm. "Cal, can you hear me?" he bellowed.

Cal reached a shaky hand to his forehead, eyes closed. "Of course, I can hear you. Hell, they can probably hear you in San Antonio." He began to push himself up slowly, rubbing the back of his head.

Lars pulled Cal's arm across his shoulders as they stood together. "You okay, bro?"

Cal blinked a few times, then shook his head. "Yeah, sure. Now I remember why I always hated football."

Janie glanced back toward the rest of the players. Otto stood holding the ball negligently at his hip, his lips slightly pursed. He was doing a great job of concealing his concern.

Pete turned toward Otto, his face thunderous. "Cheap shot, Friedrich."

Otto shrugged. "He was over-balanced. I didn't realize. Sorry."

Janie took a breath. Otto didn't sound that sorry. She glanced at Pete Toleffson again.

His hands were flexing at his sides, and his eyes were dark. Suddenly, he seemed huge, his shadow spreading across the grass in the late afternoon sun.

Lars stepped beside Pete quickly, laying a hand on his shoulder. "Football, Pete. It happens. Remember?"

"Football sucks." Pete's voice sounded hoarse. His gaze stayed locked on Otto.

"The way you play it, sure." Otto's mouth curved up slightly.

"Time to cook dinner," Reba chirped, stepping in between the two men. "That fire looks just right! We've got three grills over there. Who all's gonna be our barbecue chefs? Peter, Otto, you start grilling now." She pushed Pete gently toward one of the huge gas grills set up at the far end of the pool.

After a moment, each man headed toward a grill, regarding the other through narrowed eyes. Janie took another deep breath and blew it out. She had a feeling she was about to see barbeque become a competitive sport.

Chapter Seven

Janie studied Otto as he walked toward the nearest grill. His chest was marked by thick ridges of muscle. The fine dusting of reddish brown hair glinted in the sunlight. He looked like his body had been sculpted from bronze.

And she suddenly realized she hadn't the slightest desire to know what it felt like to have him thrusting inside her.

Pete's bare chest was broader but less muscled and covered in a thick pelt of black hair arrowing down to the waistband of his jeans. He was still breathing hard from the game and reaction to Cal's accident, his chest rising and falling in the dying sunlight. Right then, he looked like the most dangerous man Janie had ever seen.

She took another deep breath. Her brain reeled with visions of Pete Toleffson, his shoulders gleaming in a darkened bedroom, his face taut with desire.

Clearly, she was losing her mind.

She wandered toward the grill where Otto regarded a small fleet of burgers and sausages with narrowed eyes. He held a long-handled spatula in one hand.

"Can I help?" Janie managed a smile.

Otto raised his eyebrows at her. "Women grilling? Don't think so, sweet thing."

Janie's jaw tightened, her smile fading. "I grill at home all the time, Otto. It's never been all that difficult."

"You have to have a feeling for it." He shrugged. "Men know meat."

She pressed her lips together hard. *So many things to say. So little time.* So little chance that Otto would understand more than a fraction of it. She walked toward Pete Toleffson's grill, trying not to grind her teeth.

Janie blinked. Pete was grilling zucchini.

Also eggplant, onion slices, and what looked like a few portobello mushrooms. A bowl of tomato slices sat on the shelf next to the grill.

Pete glanced at her. "Got any idea what eggplant looks like when it's done?"

"Is it marinated?" Janie stepped forward, peering at the vegetables.

"Haven't a clue." Pete grinned at her. "Reba handed all of this to me and I'm following orders."

Janie removed the tongs from his hand and rolled an eggplant wedge to its other side. "Marinated. And it's got grill marks."

"You think I should salt and pepper it?" Pete's brow furrowed. "You don't salt meat, but I'm not sure about mushrooms."

"Nope, it makes them sweat. Plus they've all been marinated." Janie flipped the eggplant wedges then handed Pete the tongs. "There. Now do the rest of the slices. Only don't turn the mushrooms—the juice will spill out if you do."

"Okay." Pete industriously flipped vegetables. "You want to put those tomato slices out? I figure they go last."

Janie nodded, picking up the bowl.

"You're letting her grill?" Otto's voice was tinged with outrage.

Janie glanced over at him, feeling Pete stiffen beside her. "Pete's doing the vegetables, Otto," she snapped. "I'm helping."

"Vegetables? At a barbeque?" The outrage was definite now.

Janie took a deep breath, turning toward Otto's grill. "Grilled vegetables are really good, Otto. Besides, Cal's a vegetarian."

Otto looked as if she'd just told him Cal was a devil worshipper. He would have been hilarious if he hadn't been her date. After a moment, he recollected himself and pushed his shoulders back slightly. His naked chest gleamed in the late afternoon sunshine.

Pete had put his shirt back on again, Janie noted with a feeling of vague disappointment. The buttons hung tantalizingly open, reminding her briefly of his thick mat of chest hair.

Janie took another in a series of deep breaths. Okay, she was being unfair. Comparing Otto to Pete wasn't right. Otto was

Konigsburg. Pete was…somewhere else.

She glanced back at Pete's grill. He was nudging the vegetables with his tongs, his forehead creased in concentration. Olive sat at his feet, watching him carefully. "Take a look at this, will you?" he muttered. "I can't tell if they're ready to come off or not."

Janie studied the vegetables. "A few more minutes." She turned slightly to look at his face. "So why don't you guys like football? You all look like a high school coach's dream team."

Pete's mouth twisted briefly. "Football was our big brother Erik's game. We all went out for other stuff. The football coach wanted us, but we didn't necessarily want him."

Right. The big brother nobody liked. "So you played basketball?"

Pete nodded. "And baseball. Even wrestled one year." One corner of his mouth rose in a half grin. "It was a small school."

"Hey, sweet thing," Otto called. "Come and get it! Burgers are done."

Janie picked up a plate and started toward Otto's grill, then stopped. Pete was flipping vegetable chunks onto a platter. They looked a little charred around the edges, but overall good.

"Got any extra eggplant there?" she asked.

Pete glanced at her, one eyebrow raised in question. Then he grinned. "Have at it, ma'am. My veggies are your veggies."

Pete sampled the portabella with a certain amount of trepidation. He was okay on grilling, but he hadn't ever grilled a mushroom before, particularly one that looked like it had a glandular disorder. Tasted good, though, in a mushroomy sort of way. He leaned back in the lounge chair he'd grabbed in the pool pavilion, reaching for his beer.

Cal looked like he'd recovered from being sucker-punched by Friedrich. At least he'd eaten a full plate of Pete's veggies and gone back for seconds. Beside him at his table, Docia munched on a hamburger, along with a healthy portion of bacon-studded baked beans and potato salad.

Obviously a mixed marriage. Good thing Cal was Mr. Nice.

Lars reclined in a lounge chair next to Pete, poking a little nervously at a piece of zucchini. Pete wasn't sure why they'd all decided to go for vegan barbeque. Some kind of nutsy Toleffson solidarity, he supposed.

"You can get a burger. I won't be offended." Pete grinned at Lars's scowl.

"Naw, it would give that SOB too much satisfaction."

Friedrich glanced up at them. Pete raised a piece of eggplant in salute, then popped it into his mouth.

Friedrich regarded him as if he'd suddenly grown an extra head. He took a bite out of a hamburger that might have fed three or four members of his team and quickly transferred his attention to the big-screen TV in the corner of the pavilion that was showing a preseason football game.

Beside him, Janie Dupree nibbled delicately on a piece of tomato. She hadn't taken a hamburger, Pete noticed, but she did have one of the rib-eyes Billy Kent had been fixing on the third grill. Nice compromise.

He watched as her small white teeth nipped a bit of beef off her fork. His groin tightened.

Right. Knock it off. Clearly this whole thing was getting way out of hand. Competing with Friedrich was one thing, but pursuing Janie Dupree was something else entirely. If he hurt Janie, even inadvertently, Docia would mutilate him, with good cause.

Music boomed over the sound system Billy had installed around the pool—Willie Nelson and "Yesterday's Wine". Pete wasn't up on country music, but he recognized the basics. Billy and Reba waltzed enthusiastically on a concrete slab at the other end of the pool. Reba threw back her platinum head and laughed.

"Dance with me."

Pete turned to see Sherice standing over Lars, hands on hips. She'd changed out of the minimal strips of cloth that had passed as a bikini into a halter top and pair of shorts that stopped just below her butt cheeks. She wasn't smiling.

Lars tipped his head back to look at her. "I'm eating," he said in a flat voice.

"You can finish later." Pete noted a significant firmness in Sherice's jaw.

Lars waited a moment longer. Long enough, Pete suspected, to piss her off even further. Then he pushed himself up from his lounge, extending a hand in her general direction.

The music shifted to a woman singing a song Pete didn't recognize as Lars pulled Sherice stiffly into his arms.

Pete glanced at Cal.

"Not good." Cal shook his head.

"Nope."

Pete concentrated on his mushroom, half-listening to the music until he heard Cal's sharp inhale. He looked up to see Billy Kent waltzing carefully with Mom. "Holy crap!"

He and Cal leaned forward in unison, bodies taut. The dance would either be terrific or disastrous, depending on how Mom felt about the whole thing. As the music ended, Billy gave Mom a quick twirl under his arm, which she handled with surprising ease. As she walked past, she flashed both of them a raised eyebrow.

Cal exhaled, collapsing back against his chair. "For a minute there I thought I was hallucinating."

Pete drained his bottle, then reached for another beer. "An evening of surprises, Calthorpe. At least some of them are pleasant."

A series of guitar chords, rhythmically hypnotic, came over the sound system. Docia jumped to her feet. "Come on, ladies, let's do it," she called, heading for the concrete slab. Allie trooped behind her, as Janie turned to beckon to Bethany.

"Oh, Christ," Cal murmured. "Here we go."

"Here goes what?"

Cal shook his head. "You'll see."

The song had something to do with a red dress. Pete managed to get his brain to register that much. The singer seemed to be upset because his girlfriend was wearing a red dress he didn't recognize and he figured she was playing around.

The slow, sensuous rhythm of the guitar and bass filled the air and the four women moved their bodies more or less in unison, like some cowgirl chorus line.

Pete glanced at Wonder and saw him swallow hard as he watched Allie.

Then he looked back at the women again.

Janie Dupree moved in a graceful swaying motion, her eyes closed, as if she were dancing for herself alone. She raised her arms above her head and moved her body back and forth, the most elegant bump and grind he'd ever seen.

Every muscle in his lower body went on high alert. "They do this a lot?" he managed to ask.

Cal's gaze was locked on Docia. "Only when they've had a couple of margaritas. And when the right song comes on. My guess is Docia made sure the right song would come on this time."

"I don't know what you've got goin' on..." the singer crooned. The four women gyrated harder.

Pete's blood roared in his ears.

"Did we ever remember to send James McMurtry a thank-you note for that song?" Wonder croaked.

"Thank you note, nothing. Let's bring him to town and buy him a beer. Or a case. Or maybe the whole Dew Drop."

Back on the concrete slab, the women had joined hands and were shimmying back and forth as the singer asked his girlfriend again where she'd gotten her red dress.

Pete couldn't take his eyes off Janie Dupree.

Docia was a seventies fashion model, all long hair and muscled thighs. Bethany Kronk was a good-natured country girl having the time of her life. Allie Maldonado was a Rubensesque vision of generous breasts and thighs. But Janie was like nothing he had a label for. Small and curvy, moving like a beam of light. Like something not exactly of this earth. Maybe that was what sylphs were supposed to look like.

Assuming that sylphs were the kind of creatures you wanted to jump, which he definitely did at this point.

She threw her head back and laughed from pure joy, stamping her feet and undulating her marvelous body to the final strains of the music.

Bethany and Allie applauded. "Go, Janie," Docia yelled.

Pete discovered he was holding his breath. He exhaled in a single whoosh as the song drew to a close. "Interesting," he croaked.

The women's laughter fluttered over him like Luna moths as they walked back to the tables. Somewhere in the distance a dog barked as the music segued into something bland and mainstream. Olive's cold nose pressed against the back of Pete's hand.

He couldn't take his gaze away from Janie Dupree.

She stood next to Otto Friedrich's chair. "Dance with me?" she asked.

Friedrich pumped his fist in the air as someone made a touchdown on the television set. He glanced up at Janie in surprise. "Say again?"

"Dance with me." Pete thought she narrowed her eyes.

Friedrich shrugged and got to his feet, towing Janie to the concrete slab.

Pete was suddenly absolutely certain that Otto hadn't seen Janie dance. Either that or he had no functioning body parts below the waist, which was always a possibility, given his steroid-fueled muscles.

Otto pulled Janie into his arms and moved somewhat jerkily around the concrete slab. Pete shook his head. Did he even know what kind of woman he was dealing with? Apparently not.

"Peter?" Pete glanced up to see Mom bearing down on him, a cardigan over her shoulders even though the temperature still hovered in the eighties. "I need a ride back to the bed and breakfast. Are you ready to go?"

Pete pushed himself up from his lounger. "Sure. I'll tell Cal."

His mother shook her head. "Don't bother. He can ride back with Lars and Sherice. They're enjoying themselves."

Pete glanced at Cal, who was embracing Docia in a slow waltz. He was, indeed, enjoying himself. On the other side of the slab, Lars and Sherice weren't having that much fun judging by their expressions.

Beside him, Olive whimpered. Pete reached down to scratch her ears. "Yeah, girl," he murmured. "I know exactly how you feel."

Otto was definitely trying to impress her, Janie reflected as she stared at the ceiling of the truck. Unfortunately, he was trying to impress her currently with his sexual prowess, which involved a lot of wet tongue and heavy breathing. She'd managed not to get wedged underneath him on the front seat, but she was still pinned against the door. Otto was stroking her breast, although "stroking" wasn't exactly the right word. "Kneading" was closer.

Janie really liked having her breasts touched, or she had before Otto had started going at it. Right now she wished he'd just move on. The breast thing wasn't working for either of them.

She moved her hands lightly across his chest, trying to give him a hint about what she wanted him to do.

Otto stuck his tongue in her ear and slurped. "Baby, you make me so hot!" he groaned.

Janie bit back a sigh. What was she supposed to say to that? *Yeah, I noticed you were sweating like a pig?* She moved her hands to cup Otto's face, turning him back toward her. She'd give him one more chance.

Janie pressed her lips to his, slowly, running her tongue lightly across his lower lip. Hoping he'd get the message. *Finesse. Subtlety. Build to a climax.*

Otto attempted to stick his tongue down her throat. Simultaneously his elbow jammed up against the horn button on his steering wheel, so that sound blared into the night.

Janie jumped back, then placed her hands on his chest and pushed. She'd meant it to be light, but it took her a moment to get Otto's attention, and by then push had come to shove. He raised his head abruptly to stare at her with dark, glittering eyes.

Janie's neck muscles felt unpleasantly tight. "I need to go in now. That horn probably woke up everybody on the block, including Mom."

"Now?" Otto dropped his hand to her breast again, kneading hard.

Janie managed to keep the annoyance out of her voice. "Yes, I've got to work tomorrow." She pulled further away from him, reaching for the door handle.

"Stick around, sweet thing." His voice dropped an octave. "We're just getting started. One little horn blast won't mean anything to anybody."

"Not tonight, Otto. I'm tired." This time she let the annoyance show. For once, she didn't care if he heard it.

He hauled himself upright. In the dimly reflected light from her front porch, she could see the firm line of his jaw. "You got somebody else, Janie? Is that why you're getting all pissy with me?"

She blinked at him. She'd expected him to be irritated, but

not loopy. "Somebody else?"

"Yeah." Otto's voice grated. "You got something going with that Toleffson asshole?"

For a moment, Janie thought about asking him which Toleffson, but she knew who he meant. "Otto, you're losing your mind. I don't have time to have anything going with anybody except you."

Otto's jaw stayed firm. "So how come he's always watching you?"

She picked her purse up from the floor. "He isn't. You're imagining it. I'm going inside now. Did you still want to go to the movies tomorrow night?" She ignored the brief hollow feeling in her stomach. After all, they always went to the movies.

He shook his head. "Got a meeting with the department. I won't be out of it until late."

"Okay, then, I'll see you later. Good night. Drive carefully."

Janie climbed out of the truck, telling herself what she was feeling wasn't really relief.

Otto stared at Janie's ass disappearing in the front door. Goddamn it! Three months and the pissy little bitch still wasn't putting out! He jammed the truck into gear and pulled away from the curb, letting the tires squeal slightly. Enough with Mr. Nice Guy.

As he drove down Main, he considered his options. The easiest one was just to dump her and move on, find somebody who appreciated him and what he could do in the sack. Clearly, Janie didn't.

But now it was sort of the principle of the thing, or anyway, what he thought of as principle. You didn't invest three months in a woman and walk away empty handed.

People were still walking down Main, heading toward the Silver Spur or the other night clubs. There were some picnics going in the city park—Otto could smell charcoal and beer, and he almost felt hungry again.

One of the couples ambling up the street caught his eye, mainly because the man towered over everybody else. Toleffson. That lousy son of a bitch.

Otto slowed his truck, narrowing his eyes. Maybe now was the time to have that little "discussion" the two of them had been building up to for the past couple of days.

Then the man turned toward the light, and he realized his mistake. Toleffson, all right, but not the right one. The other one, the one with the wife. And there she was, walking beside him.

Otto's already-aching groin grew tighter. She still wore the black halter top along with a white skirt that was a little longer than her shorts had been. He pulled into a parking space a couple of doors down.

Toleffson and his wife stopped outside the Silver Spur. He leaned down to talk to her while she bent her head back. Not a friendly conversation if Otto was any judge. After a few moments, Toleffson turned around and stalked back up the street.

The wife stood staring after him.

Well, hell, no sense letting something like that go begging. "Hey, there," Otto called. "Remember me? We met at the barbeque up at Billy's." Let her think he was on a first-name basis with Billy Kent.

The wife turned toward him, tilting her head slightly as she pushed her bangs away from her eyes. "I remember you." Her voice sounded like warm syrup, with maybe a little bit of jalapeño underneath. Oh yeah, definitely one hell of a woman.

"Can I give you a ride anywhere?" He managed to keep his voice neutral. No need to scare her off.

The wife watched him for a moment, then her lips spread in a slow, seductive smile. "No thanks. Not this time."

She turned and ambled up the street after her jerk of a husband. Otto watched her hips swing until she disappeared around the next block.

Not this time. His lips moved into a grin. Didn't that open up all kinds of interesting possibilities?

Chapter Eight

Janie opened the shop at nine without seeing Pete Toleffson. She told herself she wasn't disappointed. Just because she'd seen him on his fire escape for the last two mornings didn't mean she'd see him every day. He probably had best man errands to run. Assuming he'd ever bothered to find out what a best man did.

Docia clumped in around ten, her jaw set. "Okay, you're on Mama duty today. Sherice is going to be at the Woodrose at noon to try on her dress and I can't trust myself not to say anything nasty to her."

Janie raised an eyebrow. "I didn't know you knew her well enough to be nasty."

"I talked to her last night." Docia shrugged. "A little Sherice goes a long way."

"Lars seems nice," Janie said tentatively.

"Lars is a sweetie. Yet another reason I'd like to say a few nasty things to Sherice. She doesn't deserve him. Anyway, Mama asked me specifically to send you over to help. She doesn't trust me either." Docia's mouth spread in a sly grin. "I'm crushed, of course."

The Woodrose dining room was filled with an even greater clutter of table runners, candles, favor bags, and something that looked like a silver fountain. The Wedding in all its various pieces. Reba looked a little fragmented herself.

Janie didn't think she'd ever seen Reba scowl before. She definitely wasn't the scowling type. Even when she was unhappy, she managed to keep a broad smile pasted firmly in place.

However, right now, Reba was staring at Sherice Toleffson with a very definite scowl.

Sherice was wearing a bridesmaid dress identical to the ones for Allie and Bethany. She regarded herself critically in the three-way mirror. Mrs. Toleffson, her mouth a thin line, sat behind her in one of the few empty chairs.

With a quick turn, Sherice studied herself from all sides, then shook her head. "Sorry. It doesn't work for me."

"Doesn't work for you?" Reba drew in a deep breath. "How do you mean?"

Sherice shrugged. "The color's all wrong. It makes me look washed out. Blondes shouldn't wear beige, you know."

"It's champagne," Reba said between gritted teeth.

"Whatever. It's the wrong color for me. Sorry." Sherice didn't sound sorry at all.

Mrs. Toleffson nodded slowly. "She's right, Reba. The color's all wrong for her hair."

Janie thought about all the possible responses to that statement, including pointing out that beige might work very well with Sherice's real hair color, whatever that color was. "That's too bad." She stepped beside Reba's chair. "The color looks wonderful on both the other bridesmaids."

Sherice glanced back at Janie briefly, and then studied herself in the mirror again. She reached around to the back, unfastening the top hooks. "Sorry," she repeated, "I just can't wear this."

"What a shame," Reba said through clenched teeth. "I guess we'll just have one less bridesmaid."

"But then Lars won't have anyone to walk with." Mrs. Toleffson's chin rose to combat level. "That's not right. Sherice needs to be there too."

"The wedding is at the end of the week." Reba's voice was very quiet, but Janie felt like ducking suddenly. "There's no time to have another dress made in a different color. I had a hard enough time getting this one."

Mrs. Toleffson pushed herself to her feet and began to prowl around the room, pausing to inspect candles and fountains and the yards of tulle table runners. Suddenly, she stopped. "What about this one?"

Reba walked up behind her, peering over her shoulder. She shook her head. "No. That's Janie's. It's the maid of honor dress."

In Janie's heart, the last flickering ember of optimism promptly went out, to be replaced by a cold spike of dread.

Sherice walked purposefully across the room to stare over Mrs. Toleffson's shoulder. "That could work," she mused.

"No it can't." Reba's voice was tight. "As I said, that's Janie's. It's for the maid of honor."

Mrs. Toleffson turned to give Janie an assessing look. "They could switch. Sherice could be matron of honor. Then she could wear the dress. Janie could wear the other one."

Sherice picked up Janie's glorious lavender gown, holding it tight against her. "Needs to be taken in," she said, narrowing her eyes. "Particularly around the hips."

Janie had a sudden memory, so strong it made her catch her breath—twirling in front of the mirror in her lavender dress. Mysterious. Ethereal. Beautiful.

Shit.

"That dress was designed specifically for Janie!" Reba's voice was low and sharp. "It fits her perfectly."

Sherice nodded. "Yes, as I said, it'll have to be taken in for me. But the color's better."

"Now look here..." Reba's voice rose dangerously.

Janie closed her eyes. Docia's perfect wedding to her prince. Happily every after. *Somebody has to make it happen.*

"It's all right." She thought her own voice sounded rusty, as if she hadn't used it in a long while. "She can wear it. It's okay. I'll be a bridesmaid."

Reba's forehead furrowed. "Janie, no. Don't do this. You don't have to."

Janie found herself nodding. Her head felt as if it were suspended from strings. "Yes, I do. It's okay. Really."

"Fine, then!" Mrs. Toleffson smiled triumphantly. "Everything will work out. Sherice will be the matron of honor. Lars can be best man. Let's go find that seamstress." She walked purposefully toward the dining room.

Sherice draped the lavender dress over her arm and strolled after her mother-in-law.

Janie stood staring at the other bridesmaid's dresses, trying to control her breathing so that her eyes wouldn't overflow. A hollow pain blossomed somewhere in the general vicinity of her heart.

Reba stepped up behind her, wrapping her arms around her and pulling her close, so that Janie's head rested on Reba's ample bosom. She patted Janie gently on the back.

"Janie Dupree," she murmured, "you are too nice to live. But sooner or later, that woman is going to get her comeuppance."

Janie took a deep breath. *Just a dress. It's just a dress.* "Which woman?"

"Take your pick." Reba smiled wryly. "And now, missy, which one of us gets to tell Docia she's got a new matron of honor?"

"No," Docia snapped. "Absolutely not. You can forget this, Janie. I'll call this whole dog and pony show off before I let that woman be my matron of honor. That's final!"

Janie sighed. She felt like a small ice-pick was boring into the base of her skull. "It's not my idea, Docia, it's Mrs. Toleffson's."

Docia's mouth turned down as she pressed her lips together. "She's not running this wedding."

"No, but she's going to be your mother-in-law."

Brenner's restaurant glowed with golden light from the candles on the tables. The chairs were full of couples who were drinking wine and smiling. Happy people everywhere Janie looked.

She really wanted to lean back and close her eyes, so that she could pretend she was happy too. Instead, she had to explain the facts of life to Docia.

Lee Contreras leaned over the table smiling. "Docia, my treasure, how goes the wedding?"

"Like the Battle of Antietam," Docia said through gritted teeth, "only with fewer laughs."

Lee winced and placed a bowl of olive oil and a bread basket within reach. "Here, eat this. I'll send Ken over with some alcohol."

Janie put her hand on Docia's arm. "Listen, Docia, we've been friends for a long time and we'll go on being friends, knock wood." She rapped her knuckles on the tabletop. "But Mrs. Toleffson is Cal's mother and she'll be your mother-in-law. In the great scheme of things, she's more important in your life than I am."

Docia stared up at Ken Crowder as he poured wine at the next table, her lips still tight. "This sucks, Janie."

She sighed. "What do you want me to say, Docia? Sure it does. But I can't see any other way around this one. Unless you want to start some battle that will put you on one side and your mother-in-law and Sherice on the other. Then Cal and Pete and Lars would all have to decide how to line up and it could get very messy."

"What's messy?" Cal slid into a chair beside Docia, leaning over to kiss her cheek.

Pete dropped into a chair across from Janie. His orange T-shirt said "You can't handle the truth!" At least it looked clean.

Docia gave them a short and very profane summary of the day's activities.

Cal stared at Janie. "Holy crap!"

Pete sighed, tearing a slice of bread into pieces on his plate. "You mean just when I found out what a best man is supposed to do, I'm not best man anymore? Shoot!" He winked at Janie, his lips quirking into a grin.

She managed to push her lips into a flat smile.

"Cal, you've got to talk to your mother." Docia grabbed a piece of bread and jabbed it viciously into the bowl of olive oil. "I'm sorry, but I don't even know Sherice. How can she be my matron of honor? It's nutsy."

"I can talk to Mom—so can Pete. But chances are we won't be able to get the dress back." Cal rubbed the back of his neck, frowning. "We need to figure out what's going on here. I don't remember Mom ever being all that big on Sherice before. In fact, I've heard her say some fairly caustic things about her over the past couple of years." He turned to Pete. "Have I missed something?"

Pete shook his head. "Nope. Sherice has definitely not improved with time. And Mom has never been one of her fans. But I've got a theory about this, though."

"And that would be..." Cal raised his eyebrows.

Ken reached over his shoulder to plunk down a bottle of Super Texan. "Lee said y'all needed a rapid infusion of booze." He placed four glasses in the center of the table. "Let me know when it runs out. We'll start a tab."

When they'd each been supplied with a full glass of wine, Pete began again. "Okay, as you may have noticed yesterday,

Lars and Sherice are having some big problems, as in heading for a crack-up. I think Mom's decided that putting them together in this wedding will help out. And before you ask—" he shook his head, looking at Docia, "—no, I have no idea *how* it's supposed to help out. Maybe remind them of the wonders of marriage or something. Make them think it's worth another try. Anyway, if Sherice has to have that dress to be in The Wedding, Mom's going to get her that dress. And remember, it's Sherice who's decided she needs the dress, not Mom."

Docia exhaled an irritated breath. "I don't think Sherice is all that hot to even be part of the wedding, to tell the truth. She certainly doesn't act like it."

Pete shrugged. "Nope. I'd guess weddings aren't Sherice's thing."

Janie took a sip of wine, trying not to gulp it down. It had a certain numbing effect. "So the bridesmaid obsession is all your mom's idea? Sherice had nothing to do with it? I guess that goes along with the way she acted at the barbecue."

"Oh Lord, it sounds like Mom." Cal pinched the bridge of his nose, closing his eyes. "Once she gets her teeth into something like this, it's really hard to get her to change her mind."

"That assumes you could get her to admit that the changes in the wedding were her idea to begin with." Pete gave them a dry smile, sipping his wine. "By now, Mom has undoubtedly convinced herself that Sherice is really invested in being part of this wedding and removing her would not only be an insult to the Toleffson family honor but a heartbreaking assault on Sherice's psyche."

"An assault on Sherice has a lot of appeal right now, heartbreaking or otherwise." Cal grimaced.

Lee appeared beside their table again. "You people need some food." He motioned to a waitress with a tray. "I grabbed one of every tapa we've got in the kitchen right now. Eat them. Then you can plot."

The next ten minutes were taken up with passing small bowls of baked goat cheese and hummus and something made out of eggplant that tasted really good spread on crostini. Amazingly, Janie felt her headache begin to recede slightly. Maybe she'd been more hungry than heartbroken.

Docia bit the end off a barbecued shrimp, dipping it into

the lime butter sauce. "Okay, I'm less inclined to decapitate people now, but what are we going to do about this, Cal? I'm still not willing to have Sherice take over for Janie. I don't even *know* Sherice."

Pete shrugged. "Believe me, if you knew her, you still wouldn't want her to be your maid of honor."

"Matron," Janie corrected. "She's married. She can't be a maid."

Cal and Pete glanced at each other, smirking.

"I can't do it," Pete grumbled. "It's too easy."

"What?"

"The punch line." Cal reached for a marinated mushroom. "It could go in so many ways. We could make fun of Sherice's housekeeping skills, which are nonexistent, or we could talk about her sex life prior to her meeting Lars, which was the extreme opposite of nonexistent."

Pete grimaced. "Making fun of Sherice doesn't take any skill. I refuse to stoop."

"So why did Lars marry her?" Janie was briefly amazed at herself for asking. She must have had more wine than she realized.

"She was a trophy wife. Of course, trying to imagine a contest where Sherice could actually be the prize boggles the mind." Pete waggled his eyebrows at her.

Cal snickered and Pete shook his head. "See what I mean? Much too easy."

"Enough. Back to the problem at hand." Docia sighed. "How do we get out of this?"

Cal grimaced, settling back in his chair. "All right, how's this for a compromise? I don't think we can pry that dress out of Sherice's hot little hands, and Janie's already made the sacrifice." He lifted his wine glass in her direction. "For which I thank you. Anyway, that's a wash. But I'd say we're on solid ground in refusing to allow Sherice to become maid—matron—of honor since you just met her two days ago."

"Damn straight," Docia muttered.

"Right." Pete leaned forward. "Here's how we play it. Go for Mom's cheap gene. Tell her the programs have already been printed with Janie's name as maid of honor and mine as best man, and that it would cost too much money to change it."

"But…" Janie stopped, trying to pull her thoughts together. Definitely too much wine. "Sherice's name isn't in the program either. Won't your mother get upset about that?"

"An addendum." Pete nodded decisively. "Print up a little slip of paper. Insert it in the program. 'The part of third and least bridesmaid will be taken for this performance only by Sherice Toleffson.'"

"An addendum?" Docia raised an eyebrow. "In a wedding program?"

"Sure. Suits the occasion, don't you think?" Pete grinned widely.

"Oh, Lord, yes," Docia moaned. "The way this is going, it certainly does."

Pete wasn't sure exactly why he and Cal had wandered over to the Dew Drop after dinner. Cal should have been with Docia. As a matter of fact, he also wasn't sure what had become of Docia and Janie—they'd ambled off in the other direction, muttering something about calling Allie.

Now he stood in the dimness of the Dew Drop's back room, studying the dart board on the rear wall. He wasn't really drunk, just slightly happy. He raised his arm and sent a dart flying toward the target in a smooth arc.

It hit the floor in front of the board.

Cal shook his head. "Your problem has always been consistency. One minute tournament quality, the next a menace to life and limb. So tell me about Lars and Sherice."

Pete leaned over and picked up his dart. "Come on, Calthorpe, you don't need me to tell you anything. You already know what the problem is."

"Woke up, didn't he?" Cal stared at the bottle of beer in his hand. "I wondered how long it would take him to realize what he'd done when he married her. Has she been cheating on him?"

"I don't know. Maybe. It would be in character. On the other hand, if Lars knew she was cheating, I don't think he'd hesitate to get a divorce. Except for Daisy."

Cal groaned, closing his eyes. "Oh, yeah. Our one and only niece. So this is why Lars is suddenly drinking margaritas?"

"Yep." Pete let fly with another dart. This time it landed in the outer circle at least.

Cal shook his head. "This wedding is rapidly turning into a train wreck."

"All weddings are train wrecks, Calthorpe." Pete pulled the dart out of the target and took his stance again. "This one is just a more interesting train wreck than most." The dart made a beautiful arc, landing just shy of the target center.

"It took me a year to get Docia to set a wedding date, after the weeks it took me to get her to move in." Cal's voice was soft. "A year, bro. She was scared to death of the whole thing. I had to convince her that it wouldn't go bad, that we were going to be good together."

Pete turned to stare at him. Of his three brothers, Cal had always been the one women flocked to. "What did you do to scare her off?"

"Nothing. I fell for her five minutes after I saw her. But she'd had some lousy experiences with men. All in all, she was very anti-wedding."

Pete braced one shoulder against the wall. He'd always been able to tell when Cal's Mr. Nice Guy exterior concealed major anxiety. "She's not going to back out, Calthorpe. The lady's in love. Anybody can see that."

Cal shook his head. "I don't know, bro. Everything's going south right now. I'm afraid she's going to hit a point where it goes one screw-up over the line."

"No she won't." Pete slid into a chair across from Cal, spreading his darts on the table in front of him. "I'm your hired gun, remember? Say the word and I'll do a little breaking and entering at the motel. Once we get that dress back, Sherice is history."

"Hold the thought." At least Cal was smiling again, although the smile itself was pretty thin. "You won't have to dance with her, anyway, once Janie's back as maid of honor."

"Dance?" The hairs on the back of Pete's neck began to rise. "I'm not dancing with anybody, Calthorpe. You know I don't dance. None of us does." Except, now that he remembered, Lars and Sherice had done a few turns around the dance floor at Billy Kent's—so had Cal and Docia.

"Dancing's not so bad." Cal studied his beer bottle again. "It's definitely got its points. With the right person, of course."

"Fine." Pete's shoulders tensed. "You guys dance. I'll watch."

Cal grinned at him. "Nope. Best man dances at least once with the maid of honor. Another reason to make sure Sherice doesn't fill that particular role."

"So I'm supposed to dance with Janie?" Janie who could light up a dance floor with a quick flip of her hips? Lord have mercy!

Cal raised an eyebrow. "You have a problem with Janie?"

"No, not really." Pete gulped. "But...well...she's pretty small, you know?"

"Don't worry, bro, she's a lot tougher than she looks." Cal pushed himself up from the table. "Besides, I have a feeling this wedding is going to require lots of alcohol. At the point in the reception when you take to the floor we may all be so blitzed it won't matter. I'm heading home. See you tomorrow."

Chapter Nine

Olive had spent the evening on her own in the apartment, her first evening by herself. A chance for her to try out her solo skills since Pete wasn't going to be gone that long.

Or originally, he wasn't. As it turned out, he'd been gone a bit longer than he'd planned.

Olive gave him a slightly resentful look, as if to say she'd expected better of him, then shot out the street door to take advantage of her favorite oak tree. Pete wandered into the back yard and sank into a lawn chair.

Dancing. The family joke was that the three of them could send a dance partner to the emergency room with one careless misstep. The punch line was that Pete had actually done it.

It hadn't exactly been a misstep, of course. A couple of middle school idiots had been playing keep-away with some girl's scrunchie, and one of them had gone barreling into Pete's back. He'd already been off-balance, trying to count steps as he slow danced with Bernice Keener. The keep-away game had shoved him down on top of her, knocking her flat—to the great hilarity of all the boys within twenty feet. Until they'd discovered she was unconscious.

Waiting to find out whether he'd given Bernice a concussion was the most embarrassing, excruciating memory of Pete's early teenage years. He'd never been much interested in dancing after that, and the entire incident had established the Toleffson brothers as the Dance Partners from Hell.

But now Cal and Lars had both deserted him. Pete was left the sole remaining Toleffson lummox.

Crap.

Olive wandered over to his chair and dropped at his feet, pushing her nose against his hand. Reflexively, Pete reached down to rub her ears. His alternatives were clear—he could hide or he could try to get through a dance with Janie Dupree. Given his size and build, hiding wasn't a viable option.

But if he danced with Janie—sexy, sylphlike Janie—he had to do it right. He couldn't embarrass them both.

Of course, Pete figured he was going to be embarrassed regardless, given the lummox factor. But all of a sudden he didn't want to embarrass Janie Dupree.

"Okay, Olive, let's see what we can do."

He climbed back up to the kitchen and grabbed Docia's boom box off the counter. He wasn't sure what stations he could get in Konigsburg, but at least he'd get a chance to practice without anybody watching.

Back in the yard, he set the radio on the table next to his lawn chair and turned it on. Thank heaven for batteries. After a moment, he found a station playing oldies. Patsy Cline was singing softly about faded love. Pete stood straight and closed his eyes for a moment. Then he began to waltz through the darkened backyard.

Janie was trying to walk off the effects of the wine she'd had at dinner and the margarita she'd had at Allie's. She didn't drink much as a rule, and her head still felt a little loopy.

She turned up Spicewood, heading for home. Soft music was playing on someone's radio—a woman singing "Making Believe". It almost sounded as if the music was coming from the bookstore.

Janie stopped. It *was* coming from the bookstore. From the backyard behind it anyway.

She began to walk again, as quietly as she could. At the gate, she stopped and peered into the yard.

Pete Toleffson was dancing. Sort of.

Janie loved to dance. She even loved dancing in Docia's chorus line, although she could only do it now and then, when she felt particularly raucous. She'd been known to waltz around her backyard on a summer night to the sound of her own humming, reveling in the feeling of the grass beneath her toes and the warm night air on her face.

Pete Toleffson didn't look like he was reveling in much of anything. His upper body was impossibly rigid, as if he wore a solid steel jacket that kept him from bending at the waist. He held his arms stiffly in front of him in a parody of a waltz position. Apparently, his partner wasn't cooperating. As he passed beneath the reflected street light, his face looked pinched and tense, like he expected something very painful to happen at any moment.

Olive sat beneath a lawn chair watching him, her head canted to one side. After a minute, she got up and trotted to his side, then jumped away quickly as his feet brushed against her. Pete ground to an immediate halt.

"Shit," he muttered. "Sorry, girl." He bent down and rubbed her ears.

Janie cleared her throat.

Pete stood straight, his back rigid. After a quick glance at her, he fastened his gaze on the back fence. "I suppose it's too much to hope that you didn't see anything." His voice sounded oddly choked.

Janie opened the gate and stepped into the backyard. "You didn't look as if you were enjoying yourself."

"That, as they say, would be an understatement." Pete sighed and finally looked her way. "I'm a total non-dancer, but you and I are supposed to dance at the reception. I'm trying to remember enough about waltzing not to cripple you for life."

Janie grinned. "I'm pretty agile. I think I can deal with a dance."

She wasn't sure what was wrong with what she'd said, but judging from Pete's expression, she'd just made the whole thing worse. "I'm hoping agility won't be needed," he said stiffly.

The music on the radio changed to Lyle Lovett and "If I Needed You". Janie extended her hands. "Come on, it's not that bad."

"Yeah, it is." Pete sighed, but he moved toward her, taking her hands. "This isn't a waltz."

"No, it's not." Janie smiled. "It's just beautiful." She swayed back and forth lightly, letting the music move into her bones.

After a moment, Pete began to move with her in a sort of tentative way.

Janie shuffled lightly to the left and back again, taking the rhythm from the music and pulling Pete gently in her wake.

He stumbled, half-catching himself, but Janie kept hold of his hands, sliding back and forth easily, humming along with

Lyle. The tension began to fade in his arms.

On the radio, Emmylou Harris started singing "Cattle Call". Pete stopped in his tracks. "What the hell?"

Janie laughed. "C'mon, it's a waltz. Dance with me." She extended her arms.

Pete pulled her closer, one hand at her waist, the other holding her hand out rigidly. After a moment, he began leading. Emmylou's sweet soprano yodeling followed them around the yard. Janie found herself emphasizing each downbeat, enjoying herself immensely as Pete's arms began to loosen slightly.

The music slowed and shifted to another slow one. Without thinking, Janie moved closer, letting Pete slide his feet alongside hers. She could feel the hard muscles of his shoulders beneath her fingers, flexing slightly as he moved her in careful circles. She let him push her along, keeping her spine straight but moving steadily closer until their bodies finally touched.

She hadn't meant it to happen, really. Pete came to an abrupt halt, his shoulders stiff again. Janie started to move, but his hand at the small of her back held her in place. Then he began to dance again, more slowly this time. Another waltz began to play. Apparently, the DJ was psychic.

Janie could feel the smooth plane of his body pressing against her breasts. An ache had started low in her body that had nothing to do with exhaustion and everything to do with Pete Toleffson. She closed her eyes and let her cheek rest against his chest for a moment, feeling warm skin and smelling faint hints of sweat and aftershave, letting herself relax against the hard muscles of his chest and thighs.

One muscle was very hard indeed.

What the hell was she doing? Janie's head popped up abruptly. Pete Toleffson was staring down at her, his eyes obscured in the dim light. "Something wrong, Ms. Dupree?" he murmured.

Janie shook her head, feeling a weird bubble of panic rise in her chest. This was just a dance, after all. She danced all the time.

Pete's fingers spread against the small of her back, nudging her closer as their bodies moved slowly back and forth. Her hips brushed against him, and she was aware again of the hard shape of his erection.

Okay, she wasn't imagining it—something was definitely going on beyond a quick turn around the backyard.

The music faded and changed to a muted commercial. Pete stopped moving.

Janie felt as if she were standing on the edge of a precipice, looking down. She could step back. Or she could leap over the edge and fly.

Pete's hand moved from the small of her back to cup her cheek, and Janie stood very still, looking up at him. His eyes were dark in the dim light of the backyard, but she could see the fire behind them as he moved closer. Then his lips touched hers.

For a moment, she tasted traces of beer and salt before heat blossomed in her belly, burning away the ache of the dance. His tongue moved across the seam of her lips, touching, teasing. She opened for him, winding her arms around his neck so that she could feel the heat of his chest against hers.

His tongue touched her lightly, rubbing against her teeth, her mouth, her own tongue. Janie rose against him, her legs opening against the warm heat of his arousal, trying to find the right spot as her head swam.

Trying to find the right spot? She was losing it—she needed to pull away, right now. But she didn't.

She moved closer, slipping up onto her toes until the V of her crotch fit across his groin. Pete groaned, his arm fastening tight around her waist, pulling her flat against him.

And then he raised his head to stare down at her. "Janie Dupree," he said softly, "you are lightning in a bottle."

The world whirled around her for another moment, and then the genes of several generations of Texas ladies yanked her back to reality. "Oh my," she gasped. "Oh my goodness." She stepped back from him, staring wide-eyed.

One corner of Pete's mouth curved up in a dry smile. "I take that to mean the dance lesson is over for the night."

"I...yes, I guess I'd better get on home. I mean, I was on my way when..." Janie stuttered to a halt, swallowing hard.

"I'll walk with you," Pete said, swinging the gate open.

Janie shook her head. "It's just one block over. You don't need to."

"Yes." Pete's voice was firm. "I do."

They started up the darkened street, a warm night breeze shivering through the live oaks in the yard next door. Janie hadn't the faintest idea what to say to him. At least she managed to keep quiet rather than babbling.

Pete walked beside her with easy grace. Why couldn't he dance like that?

"Why don't you like dancing?" Janie blurted.

She saw his grin in the streetlight. "Because I'm a lummox. Lummoxes don't dance."

What to say to that? Janie saw the porch light her mother had left burning ahead to her right. She turned in front of Pete and extended her hands.

After a moment, he took them. Janie looked up into his warm brown eyes, feeling the soft night air envelop her. "You're not a lummox, Pete Toleffson. Your inner dancer is longing to get out, believe me. Just give him a chance."

Without pausing to think, Janie reached up and brushed her lips lightly across his. "Thank you for dancing with me. We'll do it again some time." She turned and started toward the front porch.

"Have I ever told you what a knock-out you are, Janie Dupree?" Janie glanced back at him. He was grinning. "Night, ma'am."

Janie smiled, then slipped through her front door.

Long after he should have been asleep, Pete still lay staring at the ceiling of his bedroom. Beside him, Olive snored happily, oblivious to all of his moral struggles.

Pete grimaced. He refused to be envious of a retired greyhound, no matter how uncomplicated her life might be.

His mind wandered to Sherice and Lars and how difficult it would be to get Mom to give up on the whole Sherice-in-the-wedding thing.

Thinking about the wedding reminded him he had to talk to the bartender at the Dew Drop about the bachelor party he and Lars were supposedly hosting tomorrow night. He hadn't discussed it with Lars since he'd left Iowa. Right now, Lars didn't seem to be in the mood to talk about anything relating to marriage, even somebody else's. Pete sighed. He was going to be designated driver since he doubted either Lars or Cal planned on staying sober, and a DUI arrest would definitely put a chill on the evening.

He tried not to think about Janie Dupree. And failed miserably.

He couldn't really explain what had happened in the backyard. One minute they'd been dancing and he'd been worrying, as usual, about stepping on his partner. The next minute, he'd been overwhelmingly aware of that partner's perfect breasts and sensuous hips pressed up against him.

His body had responded in a completely predictable way by immediately going rigid. His brain was still counting steps and suddenly his cock was urging him to pull Janie down into the lawn chair for an extended session of body-bumping boogie. It took all his self-restraint to push his brain back into control again.

He'd been about to pull back and thank her for the dance, suggesting maybe they could practice again sometime— preferably in broad daylight so that he could put a block on his unruly hormones.

But when he'd looked down at her beautiful face, her brows shadowed by the streetlight, her full lips slightly parted, his brain had simply gone missing.

She smelled of jasmine and honeysuckle—warm southern nights that sent his cold northern soul into a daze. Her taste was as exotic as the rest of her, like nothing he'd had before but needed to have again, soon.

Every cell in his body was screaming at him to keep going, but Janie had ended it. Not a moment too soon. She'd stood blinking in the dim light of the backyard as if she'd suddenly awakened from a weird dream to see a strange man looming in front of her.

Pete had been ready to categorize the whole thing as an anomaly. One terrific kiss that wouldn't be repeated because the lady had better things to do. And then she'd turned back at her doorstep, with a quick whispering kiss and a promise. He didn't know exactly what to make of it all, but he knew one thing for sure.

He and Janie Dupree had some definite unfinished business. Even if it did put him squarely in Otto Friedrich's sights.

Mom hadn't been waiting up for Janie when she came inside after her dance, about which she was profoundly glad. There were times with Otto when she'd been very grateful for the fact her mother was sitting on the other side of the front door and she couldn't possibly invite her date inside for anything other than a glass of tea.

She didn't exactly feel that way with Pete Toleffson, but she definitely wasn't ready to introduce him to her mom.

But of course Mom was sitting at the kitchen table the next morning when Janie went down for breakfast. She had a cup of coffee on the table in front of her and a concerned look on her face.

Oh boy. Interrogation time.

"You were late coming in last night, Janie," she announced.

Janie sighed. Mom didn't have to be sitting in the living room to see what went on in the front yard. Her bedroom window faced the street.

"We had some problems with the bridesmaids' dresses." Janie poured herself a cup of coffee, carefully keeping her gaze on the coffeepot. "Then I had dinner with Docia and Cal."

"Was that Cal who walked you home?" Her mother's voice was tense.

Janie could have laughed with relief. Mom had seen that kiss and drawn her own conclusions. She thought Cal was cheating on Docia with her? And pigs fluttered by regularly!

"No." Janie took her seat at the table opposite her mother. "That was Cal's brother Pete. He's the best man. All the brothers are sort of the same size. They look a lot alike."

Her mother's shoulders relaxed slightly, but her expression remained guarded. "He's just here for the wedding, though, right?"

Janie shrugged. "So far as I know. He lives in Des Moines. He's a lawyer there."

Mom stared out the kitchen window at the backyard where a cardinal circled the bird feeder. "It's a funny thing about weddings. Sometimes people act like what happens there doesn't really count."

Janie stared at her. She had no idea where her mother was

heading with this, but she doubted it would be someplace fun. "I suppose that's true. I hadn't noticed."

Her mother continued as if she hadn't spoken. "The problem is, once the wedding's over, things that happened don't go away. You have to live with them." She gave Janie a level look. "You don't want to do anything you'll end up regretting later."

Oh, man, I've really got to get my own apartment.

Janie took another sip of coffee and shrugged. "So far I haven't regretted much of anything." Except possibly wasting so many months on Otto Friedrich.

Her mother reached out to place her hand over Janie's, giving her a level look. "Otto's a terrific man, Janie. He'll be able to support you and give you a good home. And he's handsome too." She gave Janie a hopeful smile.

Janie managed to bite back her immediate response about Otto's lack of spousal potential. "Mom, I'm not marrying Otto. I'm not even considering it. Neither is he, so far as I know. Like I told you before—it's not that kind of relationship. We're not serious."

Her mother's mouth popped open, but then she reconsidered whatever she'd been ready to say. "Why not?"

Oh lord, how to begin? He doesn't even know how to touch my boobs right? "We have almost nothing in common, Mom."

Her mother made an exasperated sound, tongue against teeth. "Janie, for pity's sake, you'll find things in common when you get to know each other better. After you've spent a few years together you'll have all kinds of things in common. That's how marriage works."

Janie took a swallow of orange juice. "I'm not going to marry somebody I can't have a conversation with, Mom. In fact, I'm not thinking about marrying anybody at the moment."

Mom gave her a look, but at least she let it go. She started gathering up the dishes from the kitchen table. "Dinner at six tonight. I'm making lasagna. You be sure and call if you're going to be late."

Janie rinsed her cup in the sink. Maybe she'd ask Docia what her plans were for the apartment over the bookstore once Pete Toleffson went back home.

Funny how thinking about that event made her heart feel just a little heavier.

Chapter Ten

Early the next morning, Pete took Olive for a run in the hills above Cal's house. She loped along beside him as he trotted down the gravel road, trying not to wear himself out in the first five minutes. In front of them, a roadrunner paused to stare with bright peppercorn eyes, then zipped back into the underbrush. Buzzards circled lazily overhead, riding the thermals on broad black wings, as a hawk cried somewhere in the distance.

A redbone hound in a yard barked as they passed, then came galloping up to the cyclone fence to yip at Olive. Olive ignored him, turning instead to sniff at a clump of firewheels.

Pete felt closer to happy than he had for weeks. *Texas. It could grow on you.*

After twenty minutes he was slightly winded and more than slightly sweaty—ready to go back and take advantage of Cal's shower. His cell phone began vibrating as he and Olive approached the back yard. Pete slowed to a walk and pulled the phone off his belt.

He recognized the number as soon as he saw it. Evan. The Bureau Chief who'd taken over his cases while he was in Texas. He listened to another ring. It wasn't like he'd called the office— he was just answering. Technically, he wasn't breaking his promise to Cal. *Yeah, right.*

He flipped the phone to his ear, leaning down to sit on Cal's back steps. "Yeah?"

"Pete?" Evan Hughes's politician voice boomed from the receiver. Evan was clearly in big-buddy mode. "How's that wedding coming along? You got 'em churched up yet?"

"A few more days." Three actually, but who was counting? Besides Docia, Reba, Cal and the entire city of Konigsburg.

"Well, hang in there, buddy, just a few more days of that Texas heat, right?"

Pete tried to remember if Evan had ever sounded quite this obnoxious before. Normally, he kept it in check, but his general asshole qualities were definitely running amok at the moment. "Right, Evan. So what's up?"

"Oh, not much, just wanted to check in, keep you in the loop," Evan continued smoothly. "I filed the motions on Tancredi, and Samuels is taking over the Parsons continuance. I put Larkin on Amundson."

A quick spike of acid burned in Pete's stomach. "Larkin? You mean Claire? The new assistant?"

"Right. The one who started in May."

Pete swallowed hard—his stomach was clenching. "What the hell were you thinking, Evan? She doesn't have the experience for Amundson."

"Don't worry about it—she'll be fine." Evan's voice was still chipper, but it had begun to take on an edge. "Nothing's happening on that one anyway. She needs to get her feet wet."

"Get her feet wet? With an SOB who almost killed his wife?" Pete shifted the phone to his other hand and stretched his fingers. He'd been holding it in a death grip.

He heard Evan sigh. "Look, Pete, I know you feel like Amundson's some kind of big deal, but it's really a routine spousal abuse case. Larkin can handle it."

"Not without help." Pete spoke almost on top of him. "Put Libby Fineman on it. She knows the case. She was involved."

"Libby's got other things to do." Evan began to sound annoyed. "I'm telling you Larkin's fine. Besides, Mrs. Amundson has a restraining order, doesn't she?"

Pete moved into the shade of Cal's back wall, reaching out to lean one arm against the door frame. "Yeah, and those always work so well. If Amundson gets out, are you willing to take the risk that he'll kill his wife this time?"

"Nobody's letting Amundson out. He'll be tucked away until you get back." Evan's voice crackled through his phone, not even trying for folksy anymore. "You want me to have Larkin call you so you can second-guess her from a thousand miles away?"

Pete started to tell Evan where he could put his phone and how long he could leave it there, then stopped. He *was* a thousand miles away. He couldn't run the case if he wasn't around to see what was happening.

He sighed. "No, Evan, let her alone. I think you're making a mistake, but it's your call."

"That's right." Evan's voice was soft but lethal. "It's my call. You took off and left the case hanging. Now it's up to us to make sure it doesn't tank."

Ah, yes, leave it to Evan to play the guilt card. Of course, in this case he was full of crap. "Come off it, Evan. I haven't taken a vacation in two years. And before I left, I got everything lined up for you. If you screw this up, you're doing it on your own."

"Yeah, well, just because you're not around, that doesn't mean the office is going to hell. The rest of us can practice law too, Wonder Boy." Evan's voice rose. Pete could picture the clerks in the outer office leaning toward the door.

He stared out at the cedar-covered hills. The buzzards were circling again. Why did he feel that had some personal relevance? "Right now I've got a wedding to worry about, Evan. I'll be back sometime next week."

"Yeah—" Evan's voice was heavy with sarcasm, "—somehow we'll get along without you. You have yourself a real good time there."

"I'll talk to you later." Pete disconnected.

He clipped the phone back onto his belt. Olive was gamboling around Cal's backyard, chasing a butterfly. Docia's cat was sitting on a fencepost regarding Olive with burning eyes, while Cal's Chihuahua huddled at the back door.

Pete rubbed his chest. The burning sensation behind his breastbone was fierce. Acid reflux. Maybe he should take a pill. He stared down at the cell phone on his belt. The feeling of approaching doom was well-nigh overwhelming. After a moment, he picked his cell up again and punched in the office number.

"Hey, Pete!" At least Corinne, the administrative assistant, sounded glad to hear from him. "How's the wedding?"

"Exhausting," Pete lied. "Do you have Claire Larkin's cell phone number handy, Corinne?"

"Sure, but I can patch you through if you want. She's in the office right now."

"No." Pete gripped the cell tighter. "I'm in the middle of something. I'll call her later, but I need her number."

"Right." Corinne sounded dubious, but a few moments later Pete entered Claire Larkin's number into his address book. He probably wouldn't call her.

Probably.

Right now, what he really needed to do was call Janie Dupree about the bachelor party.

Janie called Allie from the bookstore after Docia had gone off with Reba for their daily wedding confrontation. "Are we set for tonight?"

"Are we ever! You made sure we've got Lee's back room, right? I don't think some of this stuff should be seen by the average Brenner's customer." Allie giggled.

Janie didn't think she'd ever heard Allie giggle before. Allie was usually more the belly-laugh type. "I thought we decided just to give her lingerie."

"Well, there's lingerie and there's lingerie," Allie temporized. "Some of this stuff is a little on the risqué side."

Janie closed her eyes. Normally, Docia would have loved risqué lingerie. Currently, Janie had a hard time telling what Docia liked and didn't like, besides The Wedding. That she definitely didn't like. "Maybe I should look it over before we give it to her."

"Oh, don't be a nudge." Allie giggled again. "This is Docia, remember?"

"Docia isn't herself these days, Allie. Her sense of humor is a little shaky." Not to mention the fact that just about everything that happened seemed to upset her.

Allie paused for a few moments. "Okay, you've got a point. I'll check it all over myself and make sure there's nothing that might set her off."

"Thanks." Janie plopped onto a stool behind the cash register. Already, she was exhausted and the day had hardly begun.

"Say, we don't have to ask her mom and her mother-in-law to come to this, do we?" Allie's voice sounded slightly panicked all of a sudden.

Thinking of the lingerie they were probably going to be giving Docia, Janie could see her point. Showing that stuff to Cal's mother might cause palpitations at the least. And Reba would undoubtedly get a snickering attack.

"No, this is a bachelorette party—strictly single bridesmaids only."

"So no Sherice?"

Crap. Crap. Crap.

Janie sighed. "I guess we need to invite her since she's a bridesmaid. I'll call her. Maybe she'll be busy."

Allie chuckled at the other end of the line. "The sound you hear is me knocking wood. Talk to you later."

Janie considered who might have Sherice Toleffson's phone number. Docia, but she didn't want to ask since it involved the sort-of-surprise bachelorette party. Cal would be able to get in touch with Lars, but he'd probably say something to Docia.

Pete.

Pete would definitely have Lars's number, maybe even the number of their motel room. And if nothing else, Lars could give Sherice a message. Or not, depending on how he felt about it. Up to him, anyway.

Janie checked the numbers on her cell and then pressed the one for Pete.

His voice when he answered was clipped. "Yeah."

"Pete?"

A moment's pause, then he was back again. "Janie? Sorry, I didn't recognize your number right off."

"That's okay. I need Sherice's phone number. I thought maybe you might have it—or Lars's."

"I've got Lars's number for sure, and the number in their motel room."

Janie wrote the numbers down carefully, trying to think of something else to say to Pete that didn't sound really dumb.

Say, that was some kiss last night, wasn't it? And how 'bout them Longhorns?

"So why do you need Sherice?" Pete's voice sounded slightly wary.

"I need to invite her to Docia's bachelorette party. I forgot to do it yesterday." Yesterday, of course, Sherice had been too busy absconding with Janie's dream dress to pay attention to minor details like a party in the bride's honor. And yesterday Janie wouldn't have been capable of inviting her to a dogfight.

"Oh. That's tonight?"

"Yes. At Brenner's. Why?"

Pete chuckled. "Because we're also doing the bachelor party tonight. At the Dew Drop. Can we visit back and forth or is this gender-specific? I could see a quick run to Brenner's. Food at the Dew Drop doesn't strike me as a transcendent experience."

"Just avoid the pizza. If I were you I'd have Al Brosius send over some burgers from the Coffee Corral. And, no, you cannot visit us at Brenner's. This party is strictly female."

"Ah, something to dream about. Have fun." Pete disconnected.

Janie looked down at the number she'd copied on her scratch pad. Oh well, no time like the present. She dialed the motel.

The phone rang several times before someone picked up. "What?" a sleepy female voice muttered.

Janie checked the clock. Ten-thirty. "Sherice?"

"This is Sherice Toleffson." The voice sounded more awake now but fairly pissed. "Who's this?"

"This is Janie Dupree, you know, Docia's maid of honor?" Janie wasn't sure why she'd slipped that in, but it suddenly felt good to say it.

"Yeah. So?"

"So we're having a bachelorette party for Docia tonight. Seven o'clock at Brenner's restaurant. I wanted to invite you." *No, I didn't. Not really.* And Janie was pretty sure they both knew it.

"Which place is that? The dump on the corner?" Sherice yawned loudly.

"No." Janie managed not to grit her teeth. "Brenner's is a couple of blocks down from Docia's bookstore. There's a sign outside. You can't miss it."

Unfortunately. Although one could always hope.

"All right." Sherice yawned again. "I'll see if I can make it. Depends on what Lars has planned."

"Lars has the bachelor's party tonight," Janie blurted. Why on earth was she making it easier for Sherice to come to her party?

There was a slight pause on the other end. Then Sherice came back again. "No shit. Well, like I said, I'll see if I can make it."

Janie heard the click of her hang-up and fought the urge to

snarl. Just one of life's trials.

Now all she had to do was find time to go to Allie's bakery to make sure the lingerie for the party wasn't going to send Docia over the edge.

Gosh, who knew weddings were so much fun?

Janie didn't decorate the room they'd reserved at Brenner's. As she glanced at the massive fireplace in front of her, she wondered if she should have. Were bachelorette parties like showers? They'd wanted to give Docia a shower, but she'd told them she'd throw them all out of the wedding if they did. Apparently, she'd seen some Web site that had shower suggestions, and the games they'd described had made her hyperventilate.

The bachelorette party was as close to a shower as they'd been able to come, and the only way they'd gotten Docia to agree to letting them do it was to promise her lots of alcohol and no doilies.

Once upon a time, Docia had taken things like shower games in stride—or at least with a healthy snicker. These days, she'd forgotten how.

Now Janie gazed around the room again and decided she'd made her first mistake. It was the same room where Reba had hosted the Toleffson-Kent get-together a few nights before. The five of them were going to be dwarfed by the fireplace alone. A few silver bows and a little white netting wouldn't have helped.

"Lee?" She turned toward Lee Contreras as he brought in a tray of appetizers. "Could we maybe switch to a table out in the restaurant? There are only five of us."

Lee grinned. "Honey, I figure y'all are going to be carrying on in a manner guaranteed to shock the blue hairs from the tour buses. We need to preserve their innocence. This way you get to be as bawdy as you want to be. And Ken and I can join in the fun when we have a spare minute."

"Oh. Okay." Janie bit her lip as she surveyed the room again.

Happy. This was supposed to be a happy occasion.

Lee's grin dimmed slightly. "What's the matter, sweetheart? Wedding of the century not proceeding as planned? Don't tell me I need to have a talk with the bridegroom? Or the bride?"

Janie managed to push the corners of her mouth up into something that might pass as a smile. "Nobody needs to tell Cal anything. He's a rock. And if you try to talk to Docia, she's liable to take your head off. On the other hand, if you could tell the fates to lay off for a couple of days, I'd appreciate it."

Lee stretched an arm around her shoulders, giving her a brotherly hug. "Listen, sweetheart, let Ken and me pamper all of you for the evening, okay? Don't worry about anything. If I know you, everybody has you doing their dirty work and listening to their problems. Forget all of that for now. You just drink your wine and relax."

Drink your wine. *Right.* "Sorry." She sighed. "Club soda only for me. I'm the designated driver."

Lee pursed his lips at her. "Oh, Lord, why am I not surprised?" He left, shaking his head.

Janie surveyed the room once more, wishing she'd at least found a naughty centerpiece of some kind. But these days who knew? A salacious centerpiece might have had Docia in tears.

Oh well. Janie sighed again. She hadn't had a chance to check Allie's gifts before she headed for the restaurant, but she could always hope that Docia's sense of humor had returned or that Allie's innate taste had prevailed.

Or she could take the cautious route and batten down the hatches.

Docia, Allie and Bethany arrived in a group, Docia sandwiched between the other two as if they were guards to make sure she couldn't escape.

"Y'all sit down and start on the appetizers." Allie grinned. "I've got stuff to bring in from the van."

Docia squinted at the tapas Lee had set out on the table. "I'm not in the mood for mussels. Does he have any shrimp?"

"Let me get you a glass of wine." Janie started toward the bottles Ken had left on the side table.

"It's not champagne, is it? If anybody gives me another freakin' glass of champagne, I swear I'll throw up."

Okay, Docia's sense of humor was apparently still missing.

Allie bustled back with several gift bags. "Still snarling, are we? I've seen hysterical brides, Docia, and a couple of true Brideszillas, but you're the first morose one I've ever run into. Give me a glass of whatever you're pouring there."

Janie poured three glasses of viognier and handed them around. "You're not drinking?" Allie asked.

"Designated driver." Janie grinned at her a little sourly. "Somebody has to make sure you party hearty types get home."

Docia took a sip. "Not bad. And I'm not morose. If I were morose, I'd have killed several people by now."

"The great Konigsburg wedding massacre," Bethany mused. "The Merchants Association could probably create another festival centering around the occasion or at least a couple of wine dinners. Konigsburg loves gore."

"Don't you dare make lemonade out of my lemons," Docia grumbled, the corners of her mouth edging up into an unwilling smile.

"Come on, toots, live a little." Allie handed her a small plate. "Try this one. Looks like Lee's baked goat cheese."

Docia nibbled on a tapa, closing her eyes. "God, I love Lee Contreras. Too bad he's not available! Ken would probably kill me if I tried to lure him away."

Janie helped herself to a mussel with a little pale green cilantro mayonnaise. Her shoulders relaxed marginally—maybe things would work out after all.

Beside her, she heard Docia's quick intake of breath. "What's she doing here?"

Janie glanced toward the doorway. Sherice Toleffson stood surveying the room with the same air of boredom she'd shown when she'd first set foot in the Dew Drop. She wore a purple jersey dress that looked like she'd had to be sewn into it.

Janie started to wave, then stopped herself. The four of them weren't exactly a crowd, for Pete's sake. "Hi, Sherice. Come join us."

Sherice moved briskly into the room. Apparently, she didn't bother to undulate when no men were present.

"Why is she here?" Docia muttered.

"Because she's a bridesmaid who's going to be your sister-in-law," Janie muttered back.

"Would you like some wine?" Bethany asked politely. "We've got viognier and syrah right now."

Sherice extended her lower lip slightly. "No margaritas?"

"They don't have that kind of liquor license," Janie explained. "But the wine is terrific. The syrah comes from one of the local wineries."

Sherice shrugged. "I don't like wine. Give me some of that white, I guess."

"Oh yes," Docia murmured, "this is going to be loads of fun."

Chapter Eleven

Pete stood outside the Dew Drop, staring down at the cell phone in his hand. The bachelor party was already in full swing. He needed to get in there. Really.

He sighed and pressed Claire Larkin's number.

It took her a few rings to pick up, probably because she didn't recognize the number he was calling from. "Hi, Claire," he said after her tentative "Hello", "it's Pete Toleffson."

"Oh. Mr. Toleffson. Hi." Claire's voice sounded slightly strangled. Pete had a sudden mental image of her seated at her desk in the office—tall, thin, likely to disappear in a crowd. Not his first choice for a future prosecutor.

"I just wanted to check in with you on the Amundson case, see if you had any questions." Pete managed to keep his voice genial. *No big deal here, Claire. Just checking in.*

"The Amundson case." Claire paused long enough to make Pete believe she didn't exactly remember which Amundson case he was talking about. "Oh. The spousal abuse. No—no questions really."

Pete rubbed his chest absently, willing the pain behind his breastbone to go away. "Well, if anything comes up—any problems—you can always reach me at this number. Any time."

This time Claire's voice sounded slightly wary. "Okay. I'll keep that in mind."

Pete closed his eyes. Great. Now she thought he was coming on to her. "Okay, well, good luck with it."

"Thank you," Claire said in a still-wary voice and hung up.

Pete clipped the cell back to his belt and popped an antacid. Not that it would do much good—his acid reflux ate antacids for lunch.

The guys were already halfway through the first pitcher of beer when Pete got back to the table, along with a couple of bowls of pretzels. He hadn't really thought about food since he'd talked to Janie. What did they usually eat at bachelor parties? In the past, he'd been too drunk to notice. He tried to remember what they'd had at Lars's party, but he'd been so numb with shock over Lars's bride that he couldn't recall too many details.

Now he studied the frozen pizza Ingstrom had plopped on the bar for his inspection. Somehow, it didn't look like it would feed the multitudes. "Can I bring hamburgers in?"

Ingstrom shrugged. "Sure. There's a McDonald's down on the highway."

Right. Well, serving fast food at the bachelor party would certainly go along with the train wreck aspect of The Wedding so far. Pete tried to remember the name of the place Janie had recommended, then grabbed his cell again.

Janie picked up after a couple of rings, her voice slightly incredulous. "Pete?"

"Right. Where did you say to get the burgers?"

"Coffee Corral. Just tell Al that you want burgers for Cal's bachelor's party. He'll know what to do."

"Thanks. Everything okay with the females?"

He thought Janie paused for a fraction of a second. "Sure, everything's going great."

"Okay, check back with you later." Pete snapped his cell closed and then wondered what the hell he'd meant by that. He hadn't planned to check on Janie and the bachelorettes tonight. Hell, "Janie and the Bachelorettes" should be recording for Motown.

Pete got the number for the Coffee Corral from Ingstrom. The man who answered, probably the Al Janie had mentioned, promised to send over multiple orders of burgers and fries. "This is Cal's bachelor party, right? I'll send over a couple of toasted cheese sandwiches for him, too. Is Wonder there? Better make sure you get enough food for a small army, then."

Back at the table, Wonder was into his third or fourth beer. He gave Cal a dark look. "Marrying Docia sets a bad precedent, Calthorpe. First thing you know we'll all be in chains. Right, Horace?"

Horace shrugged. "Speak for yourself, Wonder. Doesn't strike me as such a bad idea."

"For Docia and Calthorpe, you mean."

"For all of us." Horace took a healthy swallow of beer.

"Dorothy and I were married for twenty-two years before she died. Lately, I've been thinking it's not such a bad idea to try it again."

"You see what I mean, Idaho?" Wonder snapped. "You've already started the rest of us on the downward slide."

Cal grinned. "Are you all that averse to marrying the best baker in Konigsburg, Wonder? If you are, you're a bigger idiot than you seemed to be up to now."

"See, this is what happens." Wonder stared morosely at his beer. "Soon as one goes, they start dragging others along with them to share the misery. First you, then Horace, then the next thing you know I'll be off the market. Who's going to be left for the women of Konigsburg?"

To their credit, no one snickered. Pete sipped his soda and reflected that being a designated driver would not be his occupation of choice in the future.

"Once they've got you, they've got you," Lars muttered from the corner of the booth. The others turned to stare at him. "Nothing you can do. Women. They're always ready for you. That's what they do. Get you tied down so they can stick it to you."

The silence at the table was deafening. Pete realized he probably should have checked to see how much alcohol Lars had already consumed before he arrived.

"Hey, bro," Cal said softly, "tell us about Daisy."

Lars looked up, his face creasing in a smile. "She's a real Toleffson. Ten pounds four ounces at birth. Black hair and eyes like Dad's. Gonna be a holy terror on the soccer field."

"How old?" Horace took another swallow from his beer stein.

"Eleven months." Lars grinned again. "Already a holy terror to tell you the truth."

Wonder looked aghast. "Your wife is, what, five-foot-three? She gave birth to a ten pound baby?"

"Yep." Lars finished his beer and smiled.

A wiry, dark-haired man appeared in the doorway carrying a very large box. "Bachelor party?"

"Just in time." Pete pulled a burger and fries from the box and handed it to Lars. "Here, bro, I think you need some food."

For a woman who said she didn't like wine, Janie noted that Sherice had managed to consume a considerable amount of it. The viognier disappeared within fifteen minutes, to be followed by a goodly portion of the syrah.

After her second glass, Docia began eyeing the presents. "Are those serious or funny?"

Allie leaned back in her chair, her face solemn. "Serious, of course. This is a kitchen shower. We all think it's time you took your domestic duties in hand, Docia. I myself provided some oven cleaner."

Docia stared at her wide-eyed.

"Oh for god's sake, lighten up, toots." Allie shook her head. "It's a freakin' bachelorette party. What did you think we'd give you—an engraved pocket watch?"

Docia blew out a breath, pulling her hair back from her face. "I've been opening wedding presents for at least the last month, usually with Mama looking over my shoulder. You wouldn't believe the stuff people think you need when you get married."

"Like what?" Bethany sorted through the remaining tapas with her index finger, selecting some flatbread with sirloin and blue cheese. "All I got when I married Lloyd was a set of Corelle. I should have known that marriage was doomed."

"Place card holders." Docia grimaced. "Silver. Swear to god. Like I'd ever give a party where I needed to show people where to sit."

"Maybe we could use them in the shop," Janie mused. "I'm always looking for something to hold up the display cards."

Allie guffawed. "That should start a new Konigsburg legend—the bookstore with sterling silver display card holders." She reached for a gift bag. "Here, babe, take a look at this."

Docia opened the bag and pulled out what looked like a pair of panties.

Or not. A strip of lace with a large bow and a thin string hanging down below. Janie hadn't ever seen anything quite like it before.

"What the hell is this, and how does it work?" Docia frowned, holding it up for inspection.

"The bow goes in back," Allie explained.

"That string looks uncomfortable." Bethany shook her head. "Geez, I hate thongs."

"Crotchless," Sherice said.

All four women turned to stare at her.

Sherice reached for the panties. "Crotchless. Works like this." She spread the string apart so that it formed a thin border around a very large hole.

Janie swallowed. "I never really understood the logic behind crotchless panties. I mean, if you're going to do the dirty, why wear panties in the first place?"

"Men." Sherice shrugged. "They like mystery."

Janie studied the panties. They were undoubtedly the least mysterious item of clothing she'd ever seen.

Bethany swallowed. "Still looks really uncomfortable."

Sherice shrugged. "It's not that bad." The corners of her mouth edged up in a slightly smug smile. "You usually don't wear them long, anyway."

Janie fought the impulse to say "Eeeew".

"Good to know," Docia muttered, staring at the other bags. "What else you got there?"

Lee appeared with another tray of food. "Oh good, you're opening the gifts. Anything interesting?"

Docia hurriedly dropped the panties back into the bag. "Not for general inspection, no."

Janie picked up a plate, checking the contents. "Bruschetta?"

"Close to it." Lee grinned at her. "Just eat, sweetheart, you look like you need sustenance." He patted her on the shoulder, then walked back out the door into the dining room.

As soon as Lee was gone, Allie handed Docia another bag. "Try this one."

Docia reached in and pulled out something that resembled a white satin placemat. "Gee, this looks...intriguing."

"Oh, hold it up," Bethany cried. "We can each take a shot at guessing what it is."

"I *know* what it is. It's a nightgown," Allie explained.

Docia's eyes widened. "Like hell."

She gave the placemat a shake. It unfolded to reveal two satin panels, attached by three small straps on each side, with two more at the top.

Docia shook her head. "There is no way this will cover me, Allie, not even slightly."

"Nonsense." Allie got to her feet, a bit shakily. Apparently, they'd gone through more bottles of wine than Janie had counted. "C'mon, toots, stand up here. I'll show you."

Docia stood and Allie held the satin panels in front of her. They extended from the top of her breasts to a couple of inches at the top of her thighs. "See? I told you."

Docia stared down at her front, the corners of her mouth quirking up slightly. "That's not an accurate measure."

"Sure it is." Allie grinned. "Everything essential is covered."

"Look, Al, let me put it this way—my cups runneth over." Docia moved forward slightly so that her breasts pushed against the fabric. It moved up an inch.

"Still," Allie mused, "you've got essential coverage, I tell you."

"But why bother?" Docia's eyebrows inched up. "Why wear anything at all?" She sank into her chair again, peering at the satin panels in Allie's hands.

"Mystery." Sherice shrugged. "Like I said before."

"She's right." Allie plopped into her chair, staring off at the fireplace. "Sometimes I make yeast rolls at the restaurant."

"Your yeast rolls are terrific," Bethany mused. "A life-changing experience."

"Thanks. Anyway, I make yeast rolls. And then when we serve them we put them in these wicker baskets with a white linen napkin over the top. You can't see the rolls, just the outlines under the napkins, but you know they're there."

"Yeast rolls." Docia stared at her.

Allie closed her eyes, her voice low and crooning. "All warm and round and smelling like bread. Just under that linen napkin."

"Yeast rolls." Docia's lips began to tremble.

"Yep." Allie smiled beatifically. "All in the presentation."

Docia threw her head back and whooped. "Oh, god, yeast rolls." She put her arm around Bethany's shoulders.

"Lord yes," Bethany cried, guffawing, "yeast rolls."

They both embraced Allie, and the three of them leaned together, laughing so hard that tears rolled down their cheeks.

Janie glanced at Sherice, who was staring at the three

women, her face blank.

Sherice raised an eyebrow at her, as she tipped back the last of her wine. "What's so funny?"

Janie shrugged. "Maybe you had to be there."

Lars was in marginally better shape after he'd had a couple of burgers. At least his eyes were focused. Pete wondered if he could manage to avoid giving Lars any more beer without being too obvious about it.

The Dew Drop was full of the normal patrons, mostly Konigsburg males, leaning at the bar. Otto Friedrich held up one end, Pete noted, a beer stein clenched in his beefy fist. A few more years spent at the Dew Drop and Otto might find his six-pack transformed into a case.

From the back room, he heard the distant *thonk* of darts hitting the board.

"How's your game, bro?" Lars stared at a neon Corona sign over the bar.

"Which bro?" Cal was grinning again, but Pete didn't find it too dismaying at the moment.

"Either. What's the plural of 'bro', anyway? 'Bros' sounds like it belongs on a sign or something—Toleffson Bros., Inc."

"Spoken like an accountant." Pete took a sip of his Dr. Pepper.

"Are we talking about darts, here?" Wonder put down his stein. "Because I'm not sure anybody at this table is in shape to handle sharp objects."

"Pete is." Cal nodded in Pete's direction. "He's the designated sober guy."

Lars began to push himself to his feet. "Darts. Let's do darts."

Lars was the one most likely to hit something other than the target, Pete reflected, given the way he was weaving.

Cal put his arm over Lars's shoulders, steering him toward the back. "Come on, Lars, let's watch Pete show us all how it's done."

In the back room, Ingstrom placed another pitcher on a nearby table. "Okay," he called to the other men, "everybody stand back. Bachelor party coming through."

The dart players glanced at the five men wavering in the doorway, then placed the darts on the nearest table and fled to the main room. That struck Pete as a very wise idea.

Wonder picked up three darts and stepped to the throw line.

Horace leaned toward Cal. "Care to place a side bet? I'm saying no darts in the target."

Cal smiled beatifically. "At least one. He might be better than usual after a couple of pitchers."

Wonder squinted, then leaned forward, flinging a dart in the general direction of the wall. It lodged around three feet from the target.

"Good thing I cleared everything and everybody off that whole wall," Ingstrom mused. "You do realize you're liable for any damages, Toleffson?"

"Right." Pete leaned back against a pillar, watching Wonder.

His second shot arced high and ended up in the floor a couple feet in front of the throw line.

"Not looking good," Horace muttered.

"Have faith." Cal leaned back in his chair, folding his arms behind his head.

Wonder peered at the target, as if he was trying to locate it exactly. Pete thought about suggesting he clean his glasses. Wonder raised his last dart, eyes narrowing. The dart arced through the air and bounced off the target's outer rim.

"You gonna count that?" Horace cocked an eyebrow.

"Sure." Cal clapped his hands. "Nice going, Wonder."

"Your turn, Horace." Wonder shrugged. "Only fair."

Otto Friedrich wandered into the room, stein in hand, as Horace gathered up the darts. "Bachelor party, huh? Y'all think you can hit the wall?"

Lars glanced at him. "Pete can."

Otto turned to study Pete. Behind them, Horace's first dart *thunked* into the wall next to the target while Wonder jeered.

"You play darts, Toleffson?" Otto took a swallow of beer.

"Occasionally." Pete leaned against his pillar, watching Horace raise his arm. The dart landed closer to the target this time.

"Up for a game?" Otto watched Horace raise his arm once

more.

"Sure."

Horace's third shot landed in the outer ring of the target.

"Lucky shot," Wonder mumbled.

"Okay, new shooters," Cal called. "Everybody back."

Otto picked up three darts from the table and took his stance. His first dart arced through the air, landing in the double ring at fourteen.

"I'll keep score," Horace called. "Twenty-eight."

"You'll keep score?" Otto narrowed his eyes at Horace. "You sure you can see the numbers?"

Horace pulled off his glasses, polishing them on his shirt tail. "You just throw the darts, boy. I'll keep track if you hit something."

Pete stepped to the line, weighing the dart in his hand then lifting it carefully. It landed in the triple ring at seven.

"Twenty-one." Horace stretched his legs in front of him.

"Tough luck." The corners of Otto's mouth edged up. "Could have been thirty-two if you'd gone up a little."

"Could have been seven, if I'd been down." Pete folded his arms. "Your shot, Friedrich."

Otto picked up a dart. "You running this party, Toleffson?"

"More or less." Pete kept his gaze on the target.

"I guess Janie's running the bachelorettes."

"Nobody's running the bachelorettes, Friedrich," Wonder mused. "They are a law unto themselves."

Otto raised his hand, sighting down his arm, then let fly. The dart landed in the outer ring at ten.

"That's thirty-eight total." Horace sipped his beer.

"Nice girl, Janie." Otto gave Pete a long look. "Known her a long time."

"No, actually." Pete smiled at him. "I've only known her a week or so."

"No." Otto scowled. "I mean *I've* known her a long time. Years. We've known each other for years."

"Oh, well, you know what they say about familiarity." Pete stepped to the throw line.

"What's that?" Otto was still scowling.

"Breeds contempt." Pete's dart landed at eighteen. "Or something."

"Thirty-nine," Horace called.

Otto stepped to the line with his third dart. The back of his neck was slightly pink, Pete noted. Otto's dart flew to the target, landing in the triple ring at five.

"Fifty-three," Horace called. "Your turn, Pete."

Pete stepped up to the throw line, squinting at the target. He raised his arm.

"She's my girl," Otto snarled. "Remember that, Toleffson."

Pete's dart *thonked* at ten.

"Forty-nine," Horace called.

Pete turned to Otto, managing not to grind his teeth. "Two out of three?"

"Sure." Otto's mouth curved in a tight grin. He took his stand at the throw line.

"I didn't get the impression Janie belonged to anybody," Pete mused. "She sure doesn't act like it."

Otto stepped back from the line. "What do you mean by that?"

Pete shrugged. "Nothing in particular. Your shot."

Otto's dart arced in the air and bounced off a metal rim.

"Goose egg." Horace sighed, leaning back in his chair.

Pete stepped forward, picking up a dart.

"She acts like it with me," Otto snapped.

Pete looked over his shoulder. Otto stood straight, his arms folded across his chest. His eyes were faintly bloodshot. Pete wondered about the effects of combining alcohol and 'roid rage. Great. As if he didn't have enough drunks to contend with already.

He turned back to the target. *Party. It's Cal's party.* He raised his dart and let it fly before Otto could say anything else.

The dart landed in the outer bulls-eye.

"Bull," Horace called. "Nice one. Twenty-five."

Otto stepped up almost before Pete had stepped back, raising his dart and throwing it.

"Eleven," Horace called.

Pete waited for Otto to step aside. It seemed to take him a long time to pull his dart free. He raised his dart and threw as soon as Otto had moved.

"Twenty-two," Horace called. "That's forty-seven total."

Pete reached to pull his dart loose and something flew by

his hand. Otto's dart *thunked* into the triple circle.

"Jesus," Cal cried. "Watch what you're doing. Pete was still next to the target."

Pete looked back at Otto.

He shrugged. "Sorry. Thought you were finished."

Horace turned slowly, fixing Otto with a look. "That's twenty-one. Thirty-two total, unless we disqualify you for being an asshole."

Otto's expression turned mulish. "I said I was sorry, Doc."

Horace's gaze flicked to Pete. "Right. Your shot."

Pete stepped back to the line, sighting down his arm, then sent the dart arcing toward the target.

"Thirty-six," Horace yelled. "Way to go. Eighty-three total. Pete takes it."

"Two out of three, you said," Otto snapped.

"So I did." Pete dropped his dart onto the table beside him.

Next to Cal, Wonder momentarily returned to consciousness. "If you're going with Janie Dupree, you're one lucky man, Friedrich. She's one of the sweetest ladies in Konigsburg. Even if she can't make scones."

Otto's dart *thunked* into the target. "Double bull," he crowed.

Cal ambled toward the target, squinting. "Not quite. Still in the outer circle."

"Like hell," Otto pushed Cal to the side.

"Hey, don't push my little brother." Lars was on his feet suddenly, lurching toward Otto until Horace stepped in his path.

"Best have a seat, Lars, game's still on. Wouldn't want you to get darted." Horace guided Lars into a chair and dropped next to him. "It's a single bulls-eye, Friedrich, live with it. Twenty-five."

Pete stood at the line, aiming for the double twenty. Of course, aiming never worked too well for him.

"Twenty-four," Horace called.

Otto shot Pete a look. "Stay away from her. I've been working on her for three months. Just keep your distance." He tossed his dart with considerable force. It bounced off the metal ring with a clatter.

"Oooh!" Horace grinned. "Another goose-egg. Tough luck,

Friedrich."

"Working on her." Pete stared at the target. "You make her sound like a construction project." He sighted down his hand again. Maybe if he didn't aim... He let fly.

"Thirty-six," Horace called. "Total of sixty."

Otto stepped up to the line again. "She may not be a construction project, but she's built like a brick shithouse. *My* brick shithouse. Back off, asshole."

His dart hit the exact center of the target.

"Okay," Horace sighed. "That one was a double bull. Seventy-five."

Pete stared at the target as Otto ambled slowly forward. If he got a bulls-eye of his own, single or double, he'd beat him. That would be the mature way to take his revenge.

Otto reached languidly toward the target, deliberately drawing his time out. His voice still echoed in Pete's brain. Janie Dupree. Sexy, sylphlike Janie Dupree. *She's built like a brick shithouse.*

Ah hell, screw maturity.

Pete raised his hand and let fly. The dart pierced Otto's ass neatly through his left rear pocket.

Chapter Twelve

"Okay..." Docia wiped the tears from her eyes, "...what else have you got in those magic bags? I think I'm in the mood for it now."

"Right." Allie's lips twitched. "Well, these are the interesting presents. I got them off the Web, and before you ask, I have no idea how well they work."

"Maybe you can tell us when you get back from San Francisco," Bethany chirped. She took a long look at the box Allie had lifted from the gift bag, then blew out a quick breath. "Or not."

The picture on the box looked a little like ponytail holders, but Janie had a feeling that wasn't what they did. "What are those?"

"Cock rings." Allie's voice was breezy. "My understanding is they're supposed to make things, well, bigger and better."

Docia cleared her throat. "Yes, well, thanks for the thought but bigger is not exactly a problem here."

"Not with the Toleffsons," Sherice muttered darkly.

Docia glanced at her then looked back at the sack. "I shudder to ask, but what else have we got here?"

She reached in and pulled out a box with a picture of another ponytail holder, this one made out of six rows of small pearls. "What on earth?"

Allie shrugged. "Sort of more of the same, except these are supposed to work on both partners simultaneously as it were."

Docia studied the beads for a moment, then fanned herself with her hand. "Oh my, my, my. This has some possibilities."

"Indeed it does." Bethany picked up the ponytail-holder-that-wasn't and held it up for study. "Indeed it does."

"Is there more?" Janie felt slightly giddy.

"A couple of things." Allie pulled two more boxes out of the sack, handing the first to Docia.

"Glow in the dark condoms?" Docia raised an eyebrow. "Won't this make him look like a monster out of some fifties horror movie?"

"The Attack of the Monster Penis?" Janie blurted and then slapped a hand across her mouth.

Bethany and Allie both shrieked, as Docia stared at her wide-eyed, then dissolved into another series of whooping guffaws.

"Oh god," Allie gasped, "I can see it now. Bouncing across the room. Sort of like this giant green pogostick."

All four of them were gasping for breath. Janie fumbled for a tissue in her purse.

"Okay, what's so funny this time?" Ken stood in the doorway, his all-American boy face perplexed.

Janie's cheeks were flaming again. "Oh, gosh, Ken, I'm sorry. Were we too loud? Did we upset the blue hairs?"

Ken shook his head. "The blue hairs are safe, but you're intriguing the hell out of me. What have you got there?"

Docia handed him the box—her cheeks were flaming too, Janie noted.

Ken read the label, snorted, then collapsed into snickers. "Oh, no, Docia. Don't do this to your sweet doctor. No, no, no."

"Don't do what?" Lee set another tray of tapas on the table, peering over Ken's shoulder. "Oh sweet lord, Docia."

"All right, all right." Docia grinned at them. "I get the message. I'll refrain. At least on the wedding night. Who knows what we might do if we get bored later on, though."

"In San Francisco?" Ken shook his head as he collected empty wine bottles. "Not likely, sweetie. I brought you all some more syrah and a new gewürztraminer from Sonoma."

"Enjoy, ladies." Lee smiled at them indulgently. "We'll check back on you in a little while."

"What's the other box?" Bethany nodded toward the box beside the glow-in-the-dark condoms.

Docia picked it up, her brow furrowing. "More condoms?"

"Specialized." Allie shrugged. "Or so they tell me."

"'Uniquely Textured'?" Docia frowned at the box. "What does that mean?"

"Got me." Allie shrugged again. "You won't know until you

try it, I guess."

"But texture? I never thought a textured dick was a necessity."

Bethany choked on her wine, then let Allie pound her on the back.

"You could ask those two queers who run this place if they work," Sherice said flatly. "I'll bet they use stuff like that all the time."

The silence in the room was suddenly deafening. Janie's fingernails bit into her palms. "What did you say?"

"Those two. They're queers, right? Geez, they do everything but swish."

"They don't have gay people in Iowa?" Docia's voice was dark. She was no longer smiling.

Sherice shrugged. "Probably. I don't interact with them. Except at the hairdresser's, but there you expect it. I guess it's different here."

"Yes," Janie snapped, "it's definitely different here." She swallowed hard, trying to loosen her shoulders. "Lee and Ken are my friends. *Our* friends."

Sherice shrugged. "Whatever. I figure they wash their hands before they do any cooking."

Janie stared at her, her breath catching in her throat.

She's Docia's sister-in-law. She's a bridesmaid.

She's a hairy-assed bitch.

Janie stood abruptly. "Get out."

Sherice raised an eyebrow. "Sorry. Didn't mean to tread on toes. Since they're your friends and all."

"Yes, like I said, they're my friends. But you aren't. Now go away. Or I'll probably do something both of us will regret." Although Janie didn't figure she'd regret it much. Her pulse pounded in her ears.

"Oh for heaven's sake." Sherice stood, straightening the creases from her skirt. "All right. It's not like I said anything other people don't say all the time. You're sure touchy about this."

"Yes—" Janie nodded, "—I definitely am. My friends are important to me. Can you find your way out or do I need to show you where the door is?"

Sherice gave her a quick, pointed look. "I'm going—don't get your knickers in a twist." She undulated toward the door, giving them the full treatment. In the doorway, she paused. "By the way, that lavender dress wouldn't have looked nearly as good on you as it will on me."

Janie stood watching the empty doorway for a moment after Sherice had gone. Docia's voice came from beside her. "Did I ever tell you Lee Contreras was the first person to say 'Hi' to me in Konigsburg? The second day I was here."

Janie practiced taking deep breaths, willing her pulse to slow down. "Really?"

"Really." Docia's voice was flat. "That woman will not be part of my wedding. I don't care who gets upset. I wonder if I could rescind her invitation, assuming I could do it without excluding Lars."

Allie stepped to Janie's other side, giving her a quick hug. "Way to go, tiger. You did what the rest of us wanted to do, and you did it with style. Want some gewürztraminer?"

Janie shook her head. "I'm designated driver. Why don't you all just have several glasses in my place?"

Not for the first time, she wished she could be just a little irresponsible, at least for tonight.

The party broke up a half hour or so later. Sherice's exit had put a bit of a damper on things, Janie reflected.

"So are you going to tell me what happened to send the Cotton Bowl Princess stomping out into the night?" Lee packed the remaining tapas into Styrofoam boxes, throwing in a little extra cilantro mayonnaise for good measure.

"Nope." Janie had already decided she'd rather have her fingernails torn out than admit that she'd thrown Sherice out to protect Lee and Ken's honor. Among other things, she figured they'd both find that hilarious.

"Ah well, at least Docia is smiling again. Or is that the result of the six bottles of wine you all consumed?"

Janie sighed. "They consumed. I had club soda, remember?"

She surveyed her three remaining guests. Docia was indeed smiling, although Janie wasn't sure whether her smile was the result of Allie's gifts or Sherice's exit. Whichever—the smile was worth it.

"You think that bachelor party's over yet?" Bethany raised an eyebrow. "I've never seen Horace drunk. I'd hate to miss it."

"Well, if it's not over yet, let's crash it. They can't keep us out of the Dew Drop, can they? It's a public place." Allie was grinning, not entirely as a result of the wine.

"You're on." Bethany hopped to her feet. "Come on Docia, don't you want to see what they're up to?"

Docia sighed. "*Down to* is probably more like it. By now they could all be under a table at the Dew Drop. I may need help getting Cal upright, although I'm not sure the four of us would be able to do it by ourselves."

Lee handed Janie a bag of Styrofoam containers. "Here, sweetheart, lunch for tomorrow. Or you can share it with the drunks at the Dew Drop. Give 'em some of the wasabi dip if you want to sober them up!"

Outside the night air was like velvet, perfect late summer, with a slight breeze blowing down Main. Janie could hear the faint sounds of music from the patio stage at the Silver Spur, the hum of cicadas from the hidden front lawns, and the sharp bark of angry voices.

Several angry voices.

"What the hell?" Allie murmured.

A knot of men stood in front of the Dew Drop, yelling at each other. Actually, Janie realized, only one of them was yelling. The other voices were too low to hear.

The crowd shifted as the yelling man took a swing at someone else. Janie strained to see who it was, but the men kept moving around the two figures at the center.

And then she recognized the yelling voice—Otto.

"Oh, man," Docia groaned as they approached the crowd, "what now?"

"...assault, goddamn it! He threw that goddamn thing at me on purpose! I want him in jail!"

Janie moved into the outer circle of the crowd, staring at Otto. The only time she'd ever seen him that upset was when Johnson City beat one of his teams in the state semifinals. He kept swinging his fists at somebody she couldn't see until Cal grabbed hold of his arm and spun him around.

"Oh for god's sake, Friedrich," Cal snapped, "nobody's arresting anybody. You really want to take Pete to court over jabbing you with a dart? You really think anybody's going to take that seriously?"

"He did it on purpose, I tell you," Otto snarled. "I don't care if he's your freakin' brother. That's assault."

Cal blew out an exasperated breath. "Friedrich, just get over it. You go to court over this, and you'll have everybody in town laughing at you. Is that what you want?"

Janie was close enough now to see the other man at the center of the circle. Pete Toleffson stood opposite Otto, long arms loose at his sides, his mouth curving into a faint grin. Janie suddenly knew exactly which Toleffson had thrown that dart.

"I'm going to whip your ass, Toleffson," Otto yelled at Pete, moving toward him. "You smug son of a bitch."

Cal shoved Otto back again. "Knock it off, Friedrich. If you don't stop throwing punches, I'm going to call a cop to take you in so you can sleep it off."

Horace, Wonder, and Lars lounged on a bench in front of the Dew Drop, watching Cal, Pete, Otto, and the crowd of interested Dew Drop customers who surrounded them.

Docia walked to the other side of the crowd and slid her arm around Cal's waist. "My, this looks like a fun party. Didn't they give you anything in the way of bachelor gifts?"

Cal glanced at her and smiled. "Just entertainment. Looks like the party's over, though. Time for everybody to go home now." He narrowed his eyes at Otto.

Otto grunted but stayed where he was.

"Good." Docia nodded decisively. "Let's get out of here, Doc. I need to show you my booty."

Cal raised an eyebrow, grinning.

"I mean gifts," Docia stammered. "I need to show you my gifts."

Lars pushed himself up from his seat beside Horace. "Where's Sherice?"

"She left early," Docia said quickly.

Lars shrugged. "Probably walked back to the hotel. It's not too far from here, right?"

"You want a ride back, bro? Maybe we can find her if she's still walking." Cal glanced back at Lars.

"Nah." Lars shook his head. "Let her find her own way. I'm going to stumble back there myself. Too drunk to drive anyway." He gave them a slightly vacant grin, then shambled up the street toward the Silver Spur.

Cal turned back to where Otto and Pete still faced each other in the middle of the street. "Come on, gents, get over it. Like I said, it's time for everybody to go home."

Allie helped Wonder to his feet. "Okay, Steve, you need to sleep it off. Tell me you don't have a root canal scheduled tomorrow morning."

"Nope." Wonder leaned heavily on her shoulder. He looked a little the worse for wear. "Nothing until noon. See, I planned ahead. Of course—" he glanced back toward Pete and Otto, "—I never planned on it being this exciting. Maybe somebody will knock some teeth loose."

"You can tell me all about it while you have your cocoa," Allie crooned, nudging him up the street.

"Cocoa," Wonder mumbled as they moved away, "you are kidding, right?"

Janie and Bethany sat on the bench with Horace. Bethany leaned her head against the wall. "You think this is gonna take much longer?"

"Depends on Friedrich's stamina," Horace rumbled. "Personally, I'm ready to go home."

Bethany dropped her head on his shoulder. "Me too," she murmured.

Janie watched them. Horace was in his late sixties and looked sort of like Wilford Brimley in *The Firm*. Bethany was probably pushing fifty, although Janie wasn't sure which side she was pushing. Now they snuggled together like a couple of teenagers.

It gave a person hope.

Cal still had one hand on Otto's beefy chest, holding him back from Pete. "Are we done here, Friedrich? You ready to go home now?"

Otto's mouth was pursed in a thin line, his gaze fixed on Pete. "You son of a bitch. You did that for no reason. Just because you were losing."

"I had a reason, Friedrich," Pete snapped. "You shouldn't go tossing Janie Dupree's name around in a crowded bar."

"Janie Dupree's my girl, Toleffson. I'll toss her name around if I feel like it."

Janie leaned her head back against the wall, feeling utterly exhausted all of a sudden. "Oh for pity's sake."

She pushed herself up from the bench and stepped in front of Pete. "Go home, Pete," she snapped. "You're just making it worse."

Behind her, she heard Otto snicker. She turned, pushing him back up the street in front of her. "Go home, Otto. Just go home. It's over now. We can talk about it later."

Otto squinted at her, as if he wasn't sure exactly who she was. His close-cropped hair was slightly mussed, his eyes bloodshot. He flexed his large hands at his sides. "Janie?"

Janie thought of all the nights in Otto's monster truck. His damp hands, his thrusting tongue. "Just go home now," she repeated, giving him a slight push on his chest.

Otto caught her wrists, gazing down at her, his eyes suddenly dark. "Don't want to."

For a moment they stood staring at each other. Otto's grip on her wrists was almost painful. Janie's mouth slid into a grim line.

"Do it anyway." She pulled her hands away from him, then stepped back. After a moment, Otto turned on his heel and stomped off down Main.

Janie stood for a moment longer, catching her breath. She hadn't been afraid of him. Not really. She turned and looked back. The crowd in front of the Dew Drop had faded away. Horace and Bethany trudged off toward the clinic. Cal and Docia were already gone. Sighing, Janie started to head up Spicewood toward home. The sack of leftovers she'd grabbed from the bench banged against her leg as she walked. Oddly enough, she was suddenly hungry.

"Ladies shouldn't walk alone at night, even in Konigsburg." Pete Toleffson fell into step beside her.

Janie sighed again. "Is that a fact? Even if they've lived here all their lives? Even if they're heading home?" She'd never felt less like being a gracious lady.

"So they tell me." Pete nodded toward her sack. "Did you get presents too?"

"No." Janie held it up. "It's leftovers from the party." The sack looked slightly crumpled. She must have been holding the top too tightly. Oh, well, the contents still probably tasted okay. "What about you. Did you get the burgers?"

Pete shrugged. "Everybody else did. I had an order of fries

Wonder missed."

Janie stared down at the sack in her hand. She really should be getting home. Where Mom would probably ask about Otto, if she was still up. Janie glanced up at Pete. "Want some tapas?"

"Yep." Pete smiled at her. "I can even offer you a beer, now that I'm off duty. Nobody needed me to drive them anyway. They all had women to guide them home."

"Yeah, well, those women weren't in any better shape than they were." Janie sighed one more time. "A beer would be great about now."

Chapter Thirteen

Sherice realized her mistake before she'd gone fifty feet from Brenner's—three-inch heels were not made for walking. But god it had been so great to wear them in front of those losers, to show them what a real woman looked like.

She had very little use for other women, for the most part. Most of them didn't come close to her in looks, and they all resented her for it. She served on committees with lots of women like that. They kept her off the boards of the charities where she needed to be if she and Lars were going to move up in Des Moines society. Sometimes they managed to blackball her altogether when she tried to join.

The minority of women who did come close to her in looks were her competitors. Hanging around with them had never occurred to her. She'd never understood why women thought they needed to be friends with people who might cause them trouble in the end.

She managed to walk a block down Main before she turned onto a side street and pulled off her shoes. It wouldn't do for anyone important to see her walking barefoot, but she figured nobody important would be living in these dinky little houses.

They reminded her a lot of Urbandale. Which didn't mean they made her homesick. She'd already been thoroughly sick of home when she'd left.

Sherice tucked her shoes under her arm and began walking in the general direction of her motel. In reality, she wasn't all that eager to get there. Lars would probably still be at the party for Cal, and then he'd probably be too drunk to do anything when he got back.

He'd been too drunk to do anything for most of the week. Not that Sherice particularly wanted him to do anything, but she did like to remind him of her importance every once in a while.

The more she thought about it, the more convinced she became that this whole marriage thing wasn't working out, but she hadn't yet decided what to do about it. She'd wait until the wedding was over and then start making plans when she got back to Iowa—where there were some lawyers who weren't related to Lars, and where she had a perfect bargaining chip in her eleven-month-old daughter. Caution also told her to hold off until she had a few prospects lined up before she jumped.

She turned down another dark street lined with houses. She was pretty sure it ran in the same direction as Main. If she followed it, she could cut up to the motel when the time came.

Sherice pushed the hair back from her forehead, feeling the dampness of sweat at the roots. Now she'd need to wash her hair again, and she hadn't yet found a stylist in town that she'd trust to do a decent blow-out. She wasn't sure how she was going to manage looking great at the wedding. No matter what she'd said to that Dupree woman, that dress wasn't going to work for her. Too long, for one thing. Her legs were one of her best assets.

She was sweaty, her make-up was running, her hair was beginning to frizz, and her feet hurt. Goddamn Texas anyway! Sherice was one very unhappy woman.

And then she was a nervous one. A man stood under the street light just ahead of her. A very big man.

He was leaning against his truck, drinking a beer. He wasn't aware of her yet, but he would be soon. Sherice studied his shoulders for a moment. They looked vaguely familiar.

Ah, yes, the barbeque. And then in the street afterward. She knew who the man was now. The guy with the abs. "Evening," she called. "Got another one of those?"

Olive lay curled on the living room rug when Pete and Janie entered the apartment, but she got up and followed them as soon as Pete closed the door. He walked into the kitchen, trying to keep that light tone he'd managed to come up with in the street.

He didn't know who he blamed more for the generally stupid situation he'd found himself in—Otto or himself. Before Janie had stepped up, Pete had been ready to punch Otto's lights out just for the hell of it. And then she'd settled things, simply, politely, firmly.

Pete watched her lift Styrofoam containers out of her paper sack and place them on the kitchen table, giving a great imitation of someone who wasn't thoroughly pissed.

Yeah, right.

He studied her stiff shoulders, the way her arms moved. Alcohol was definitely called for. He went to the refrigerator and pulled out two bottles of beer, setting them on the table next to the food.

He lifted one of the Styrofoam boxes and looked inside. "What's this?"

Janie glanced at the box. "Pita chips with goat cheese and chives."

Pete pulled a chair back from the table for Janie and then settled himself across from her, munching on a chip. He took a deep breath. "You know they were all drunk, right?"

She closed her eyes for a moment, then nodded. "I thought that was the idea of the party. I didn't know Otto had been invited, though."

"He wasn't." He pulled over another box—flatbread with something that looked and tasted like steak and blue cheese. "He joined us later."

"And you played darts."

Pete nodded, chewing. He wondered if he could come up with a way to detour around this part of the conversation. Probably not.

"Who won?"

He shrugged. "We each won one. We were working on the final match when things sort of deteriorated."

She reached into a box and pulled out some cheese. "What did you do to him?"

"Well, I sort of took my inspiration from you—I mean you and that guy who was giving you trouble that one night when you were in the darts match."

"Oh my god, you darted him in the butt!" Janie stared at him, the corners of her mouth trembling.

He shrugged. "What can I say? It seemed like a good idea at the time."

She shook her head. "You could have hurt him, you know. Those darts are sharp."

"Nah." Pete crunched into another pita chip. "I aimed for his ass. I figured he had enough muscle there to protect anything vital."

Janie's trembling lips finally resolved themselves into a grin. And then she threw her head back and guffawed. "I wish I'd been there."

He shrugged. "If you had been, it probably wouldn't have happened."

Her grin disappeared, and she reached into another box, then pulled out something green.

"What's that?" Pete started to reach into the box himself, but Janie snapped the lid down.

"Mussels with cilantro mayonnaise, and they're all mine."

He settled back in his chair, peering at the other boxes. "So how did your soiree go?"

She sighed. "I ended up ordering Sherice out of Brenner's, but otherwise it went fine." She opened the box again, reaching inside.

The corners of his mouth edged up. "And you did this because... Not that you really need a reason for ordering Sherice out of your life."

"She insulted Lee and Ken. They weren't in the room at the time, but they're my friends. She called them 'queers'. I couldn't let that go."

Pete blew out a breath. "Interesting. I didn't realize Sherice was also homophobic, among all her other sterling character traits."

Janie raised her eyes to his, dark brown, the color of bittersweet chocolate. "Like I said, they're my friends. It just...I got fed up with everything, I guess. Docia's ready to kick her out of the wedding again."

"Yeah. Sherice has been known to do that to people. I'll talk to Docia tomorrow. Maybe we can work something out." He pulled something else out of one of the boxes and bit down. And felt as if his mouth had exploded. "Holy shit, what was that?"

"Wasabi sauce." Her grin returned. She handed him his bottle of Modelo Negro. "Here. Drink."

Pete let the cold liquid slide down his throat, counteracting the small brush fire occurring in his sinuses. "Okay," he gasped, "that constitutes revenge, right?"

"No, that constitutes carelessness." Janie snapped two of the now-empty boxes shut and tossed them into the sack again. "You should look before you put something into your mouth. Besides, why would I want revenge on you?"

He leaned back in his chair. "For having a Y chromosome? For darting your boyfriend?"

Three boxes were left on the table. She reached into one and pulled out a spring roll. "That assumes I consider him my boyfriend. After the past few days, I'm not sure I do. Do you want to tell me what he said about me at the Dew Drop that made you so mad?"

"Nope." He got up and headed for the refrigerator, pulling out a couple more bottles. He twisted the top off one as he sank back into his chair. Time to bite the bullet. "Otto probably wouldn't have said anything about you if he hadn't been drunk, and if I hadn't been needling him. Don't take it seriously." Olive pushed her nose against his hand and he scratched her ears.

"I've known Otto for a long time," Janie mused, sipping her own beer. "We went to high school together. By now, I know what to take seriously and what to ignore."

She ran her fingers up the neck of her beer bottle, absently rubbing around the ridges at the top. Pete worked on convincing the unruly parts of his body that no particular subtext was involved.

Olive whimpered slightly, pushing her nose against his hand again.

"Ah hell." He sighed. "I forgot. I need to take her for a walk."

"It's time for me to go home anyway." Janie smiled at him. "Thanks for the conversation."

"We'll walk with you." He reached for Olive's leash.

As usual, Olive had her own ideas about walking. She tugged Pete in the opposite direction he'd intended on going, but Janie didn't object. She walked along beside him, moving through the pools of light along the street. After a couple of blocks, he unfastened the leash and let Olive amble along at her own pace.

Janie looked up at him as Olive trotted across the street in front of them. "How do you like living in the apartment?"

"Docia's apartment?" He shrugged. "It's good. A little bare, but good."

"I was thinking..." she began, then stopped.

141

Olive sniffed at an oleander bush. She'd already marked a succession of live oaks and a couple of pecan trees.

"Thinking about what?"

"I'd like to find a place of my own. Maybe something like that. After you head back, I mean."

Pete felt an odd pang in his gut. *After you head back.* "It's comfortable. You'd like it."

Janie nodded. "I think I would. And I'd be right upstairs over the store, so I could open up in the morning, the way Docia used to." She looked up at him, eyes dancing.

Without thinking, he reached out and took her hand, lacing his fingers through hers and feeling the warmth of her palm pressed against his as they walked up Spicewood.

Just an illusion, this feeling of rightness. He didn't really belong here.

"I've got this case I'm worried about," Pete blurted. Where the hell had that come from? He hadn't been going to talk about the Amundson case. "I mean, not worried, exactly, just...concerned, sort of."

She stared up at him. "What is it?"

He shrugged. "This guy who hurt his wife, hurt her bad. I thought I had it locked up tight when I left, but now they've given the case to a new prosecutor. I'm not sure she's up to it."

"Why wouldn't she be?" She raised a questioning eyebrow. "Is there something unusual about it?"

"No," He said slowly. "It's just...I don't want anything to go bad. That woman's suffered enough."

"Maybe the new prosecutor will do a good job. If it's her first big case, she'll probably put a lot into it."

"Maybe. She didn't sound like it when I talked to her, though." Ahead of them, Olive was suddenly fascinated by a sunflower. She paused to sniff. Somewhere nearby he could hear a car alarm bleeping.

Janie turned toward the sound. "Gosh, that's really loud."

"Isn't that Cal's clinic building over there?"

She nodded. "That's the parking lot."

Pete paused to snap the leash on Olive's collar again, then headed up the street, Janie at his heels.

The sound got louder the closer they came, but he was no longer sure they were hearing a car alarm. He squinted at the parking lot.

A large pickup was parked at the far side under a live oak. The horn blared at irregular intervals, while the light bar on the top flashed occasionally.

"What the hell?" Pete muttered.

Janie's hand flexed on his arm. "That's Otto's truck. How can it do that on its own?"

"It can't, unless it's haunted." Now that he looked at it, he noticed the truck was also rocking back and forth gently.

"Should we go up and see what's going on?" she asked. She didn't seem particularly eager to do that.

Neither was he. He handed her Olive's leash. "Here, hang onto Olive for a minute, okay?"

He thought the rocking had diminished slightly. The horn still blared every few seconds, but not as often as it had before. In between the horn blats, Pete thought he heard voices.

The headlights of a car turning into the parking lot swept across him, and a Konigsburg police cruiser pulled up beside Janie. Pete stepped back from the truck with a feeling of intense gratitude.

"Hey, Nando." Janie nodded. "Pete Toleffson, this is Nando Avrogado. He's one of our town cops."

A large man in a tan uniform had stepped out of the cruiser, pushing his Stetson back on his head. "Evening. So what's happening here?"

"We don't know exactly." She frowned. "We heard the truck horn over on Navarro. I guess it's been going for a while."

"Yeah, neighbors called the station to complain." Avrogado squinted at the truck, then turned to Pete. "You check inside?"

Pete put his hand on Janie's elbow. "Nope. I guess we can leave you to it."

"Wait." She dug in her heels. "Don't you want to know what's going on?"

He had a fair idea of what was going on, which was why he wanted to be back walking Olive in the opposite direction when Avrogado opened the truck door. "We'll probably find out later."

"I want to find out now." She gave him a level look.

"Okay." Protecting her suddenly didn't strike him as necessary.

Avrogado pulled his baton from his belt and rapped on the

driver's window. "Anybody in there?"

The rocking stopped abruptly, as did the horn and the lights. The night became very quiet all of a sudden.

"What?" The voice from inside the truck was muffled but masculine.

"Konigsburg police," Avrogado snapped. "Open up." He stepped back so that he was behind the door, holding the baton in front of him.

After a moment, the truck door swung open and a man's head emerged. "Nando?"

Avrogado grimaced, sliding his baton back in his belt. "Otto, you moron. You woke up the whole neighborhood."

"Oh. Sorry."

Otto turned toward the front and caught sight of Janie. Pete found himself staring at a lot more of Otto Friedrich than he wanted to see.

"Shit," Otto gasped. He pulled back inside the truck abruptly.

Avrogado cocked his head around the side of the door. "You okay in there, ma'am?"

"Of course," a woman's voice snapped.

Pete stood very still. *Shit. Goddamn.* "Sherice?"

The silence was deafening. "Yeah?" Sherice replied finally.

Beside him, Pete heard Janie suck in a hissing breath.

Otto cleared his throat. "It's not what you think."

"Oh for Christ's sake, Otto," Janie snapped. "Of course it is!"

The door on the passenger's side of the truck opened and Sherice stepped down onto the asphalt. Her hair was a mass of tangles and her eye make-up gave her the look of a marauding raccoon. But she was dressed. She braced one hand against the truck as she pulled on her shoes.

Her gaze fixed on Pete. "I assume you'll be talking to Lars."

He shrugged. "I wouldn't know what to say to him."

"I'm sure you'll think of something." Sherice straightened, glancing behind them. "Or you may not have to."

Pete turned to see a small crowd gathering beside the clinic. Apparently, he and Janie weren't the only ones who'd heard the horn. Some people he figured were neighbors stood at the side of the building, along with Cal and Docia.

Behind them, Lars stood frozen, staring at Sherice. For a moment their eyes met, and then he turned on his heel, stalking back up the street.

Pete stared after him, balancing on his toes. Ready to follow.

"He won't want to talk to you." Janie rested her hand on his arm. "Not right now."

Sherice stared after her husband for a long moment, then ran her hands over her hair, pulling it back into a semblance of order. Her gaze moved across the small crowd with exaggerated disinterest.

Otto jumped out of the driver's seat and started toward Janie, buttoning his shirt. "Look, Janie..."

She closed her eyes. "Don't even try, Otto. Just let it go."

Otto turned toward Pete, his bloodshot eyes blazing. "You son of a bitch! You're always poking in where you've got no business."

Pete stared at him. He had a feeling Otto was on the verge of being sick as a dog, but not quite there yet.

"I'll teach you to mess with my girl." Otto took a step toward him, swinging a roundhouse punch in his general direction. Pete had an impression of Avrogado turning toward them. Before his good sense could kick in, he buried his fist in Otto's gut.

Otto was indeed sick as a dog then. All over Pete's shoes.

Chapter Fourteen

Pete rinsed off his shoes with the garden hose in the backyard. Fortunately, they didn't appear to have suffered any major damage. He wished he could say the same for Janie Dupree.

She sat on the lowest step of the fire escape, absently scratching Olive's ears. He tried to decide if the blank look in her eyes came from exhaustion or pain. Whichever it was, he decided, he needed to do something about it. He didn't stop to wonder when Janie Dupree had become his responsibility. She just had.

"So are you hungry? Thirsty? Need to throw something? I have some bricks you can toss." His voice was unnaturally hearty. Pete suspected he sounded like an asshole, but he wasn't quite sure how to stop.

Janie raised her blank gaze to his, the corners of her mouth inching up faintly. "You don't have to take care of me, Pete. I'm okay. Really."

Just what he'd said to Cal earlier in the week. He suddenly had a lot more sympathy for his brother's point of view. Pete squinted at her. She didn't look okay, but maybe that depended on your definition of *okay*. He walked over and sat beside her on the step, his wet shoes squishing. Olive stayed where she was, curled between them. "Quite a night."

"Quite a week. Quite a month, now that I think about it." Janie scratched Olive's ears again, staring off into the night sky.

He blew out a breath. The whole thing was like pretending the mud-covered elephant in the room wasn't there. "He's an asshole, Janie. Probably always has been. You must know that."

Janie nodded. "Oh, yeah."

"It had nothing to do with you."

She nodded again, then shrugged. "It had something to do

with me, but not much. And whatever happened to me was nothing compared to what happened to Lars."

Pete groaned, leaning back against the step. "Would you believe I forgot about that part of it—just for a minute?"

Olive stretched out, resting her muzzle on Janie's foot.

"We never were all that...serious, Otto and me." She narrowed her eyes, staring up at a streetlight. "We've dated for a couple of months, but I always knew he wasn't going to be The One."

"Yeah?" Pete leaned back on his elbows. He wasn't the kind of man people shared confidences with as a rule, but at least he knew how to keep his mouth shut.

"People in town really look up to him, though. When this gets out, it's going to be a blow to the town's pride. They'll probably find a way to blame Sherice. Or the Toleffson family. Or me. Probably me."

Janie stroked Olive's ears. Olive was the one who was really making out in this situation, Pete reflected. "How can they blame you?"

"They'll figure Otto wasn't getting enough action at home so he had to find something on the side." Her voice sounded remarkably matter-of-fact.

"Gee," Pete mused, "so Konigsburgers are assholes just like the rest of us."

"The thing is, though, they're all going to assume I'm heartbroken about losing him, so they'll feel like they need to tiptoe around me or find some way to make me feel better." She grimaced. "I'm going to hate that."

"Yeah, I can see how you would. Maybe you could find the bull goose gossip in town and tell her Otto was always a jerk. With any luck she'd spread it around."

Janie stared out into the darkness again, considering. "Rhonda Ruckelshaus. But it wouldn't work. She'd just figure I was being brave, putting the best face on it. Damn it!"

Pete glanced up at her. She was staring at him now, her eyes burning.

"I'm so sick of being nice, you know?" Her voice shook slightly. "I'm so sick of being the one everybody goes to when something goes wrong. I'm so tired of being the one who takes care of stuff. I want to be a real bitch for once, but I don't even know how to start."

He squinted at her in the shadows of the backyard. "You might need to start slower. Start with being testy, then work up to obnoxious. Then you can make the leap to bitch. I mean Sherice had years to hone her craft. You're just starting out."

Janie shook her head, her mouth spreading in a faint grin. "You know what I mean."

"Yeah." He took her hand. "You want to just tell everybody to screw off. Sounds good to me."

He pressed his palm against hers, sliding his fingers in between her fingers, feeling the warmth of her skin, the slight dampness. A night breeze moved through the live oaks, shaking the leaves into a whispering mass.

"Why did you become such a nice girl in the first place, Janie Dupree?" He watched her now, dark eyes to dark eyes. "Nature or nurture?"

"I'm from Konigsburg." Her smile turned wry. "Females here are bred to be nice. My daddy was from East Louisiana and Mama's from Lampasas—they both knew how girls were supposed to behave. I've spent most of my life living up to that standard, even after Daddy died."

"What happened to him?"

"He was killed in an accident on the highway—his truck collided with a semi. I was nineteen." Janie shook her head. "I had three semesters at UT, and then I had to come home and help my mom."

"Nice girl," Pete said softly.

She nodded. "Nice girl. I always wanted to go back and finish, but I've never had time."

"So now?"

"So now I'm assistant manager of the bookstore, thanks to Docia." She shrugged. "I never thought I'd get this far. I figured I'd be a waitress for the rest of my life."

"Gratitude's a bitch," He murmured.

"No. I don't resent her. Not Docia. And not Cal. He's the best thing that ever happened to her. I'm so happy for her. I want her to have the best wedding ever."

Pete nodded. "Yeah. Same for him and me. Although my little brother has never had a problem finding women. Girls always flocked after him like swallows headed back to Capistrano, not that he ever seemed to notice."

"They didn't do that with you and Lars?"

He paused to consider. "Lars, yeah. Lars is Mr. Responsible—or he used to be, before Sherice. Women always thought he was a great husband candidate."

"And you?" Janie cocked her head.

Pete stared up at the streetlight on Spicewood. "Nope. Nobody has ever considered me much of a candidate for Mr. Right. I'm a great candidate for Mr. Right Now, however." He glanced back at her, feeling his groin tighten. This was definitely not the direction he'd originally planned on going. But then lately his plans had had a tendency to go south.

Part of his brain screamed at him to say good night and go upstairs, but it couldn't make the connection to the rest of his body, particularly not when she smiled at him like she was doing now.

"I guess that's one way to get rid of sympathizers. Jump into bed with somebody else."

She was going to keep talking, and he was going to say something supremely stupid. That was almost a given. Pete leaned over abruptly and covered her mouth with his own.

Heat flashed through his body, sucking the breath from his lungs. She was soft and warm against him, her breasts pressed lightly on his chest. He cupped her face in his hands, angling his head to deepen the kiss.

Janie's hands moved up his chest to his shoulders. And then she pushed, gently. She tipped her head back, staring up at his face, her eyes narrowed. "Tell me the truth, Pete Toleffson—are you doing this because you feel sorry for me?"

"Sorry?" He was having trouble focusing. What exactly was she talking about? And why had she stopped kissing him?

Her jaw firmed. "Are you sorry for me because Otto dumped me so publicly?"

Good Lord, she was serious!

It took him a moment to remember just who Otto was. "If I'm sorry for anybody, it's Otto," he muttered. "The freakin' idiot blew it big time."

Janie gave his shoulders a small shake, like a miniature Rottweiler. "I'm serious, Pete. I don't want pity."

Pete took a deep breath, closing his eyes. If only he could get enough blood back to his brain to form a sentence. "I don't believe in pity sex, Ms. Dupree. Among other things, pity doesn't really do much to get me in the right mood."

She grinned up at him. "Are you in the right mood?"

Too much talking. Entirely too much talking was going on right now. "Lady, I've been in the right mood since I saw you walk into the Dew Drop my first night in town."

He dropped his head, opening his mouth against hers again. One arm locked around her shoulders as he pulled her against him. Then Janie's arms wrapped around his neck, and she pressed her body to his, shoulder to hip.

Pete felt as if a small rocket had ignited in his groin. He leaned back against the stair, moving his tongue into the warmth of her mouth, his fingers spearing through her soft hair. All of his senses were suddenly in play—pinwheels of light went off before his eyes, he tasted something sweet, spicy, felt the warm, wet rasp of her tongue, smelled a faint echo of lavender, heard the distant humming of the street lights—or was that him?

Janie's fingers slid beneath his shirt, smoothing across his chest. Her palm touched the jut of his nipple and every inch of his body was suddenly like rock.

Somehow he had to get her upstairs. Now.

In some corner of her mind, Janie was amazed at herself. She was on the verge of tearing Pete Toleffson's T-shirt in two and rubbing herself against his naked chest so that she could feel the rasp of his hair against her nipples.

She knew ladies didn't do this. Even if the ladies came from Texas.

She had all kinds of reasons to call a halt. Her mother might still be waiting up for her at home. Olive was draped across her feet. She'd just had a nasty shock, and she might be doing this for all the wrong reasons.

It didn't matter a damn. She was going to have sex with Pete Toleffson right here in his backyard and worry about the consequences later.

Then Pete pulled back from her, gently, raising his head. Oh, hell, he was going to be noble.

Except he didn't look noble. His face was set in hard lines, his jaw impossibly square. His chest rose and fell as he stared down at her. Janie was suddenly afraid he was going to snarl.

"We need to go upstairs," he rasped.

She tried to kick-start her brain. "We do?"

"Yes, we do. We're not going to get caught doing this in the backyard. There's been enough of that already tonight." Pete stood, pulling her to her feet. "Come on."

He started up the fire escape, his hand clamped around hers. Janie hurried after him, trying not to trip on the stairs. At the top, he pushed the window up, stepping through. "Watch your head."

She ducked and followed him over the sill. Then they were standing in his bedroom.

"Oh." Somehow being downstairs on the fire escape had made the whole thing a lot easier. She could always claim she'd been swept away by the moment. She heard a scrabbling sound behind her and a whimper.

"Oh crap," Pete muttered. "Olive."

He stepped to the window and lifted the greyhound through. Then he carried her to the door.

"Sorry, Olive, tonight you get to sleep in the kitchen."

The door closed on Olive's yip. Janie had an unreasonable urge to giggle.

Pete pulled his shirt off as he walked back toward her, and all urges to giggle vanished. "Holy crap," she whispered.

He was beautiful. He was also huge. His shoulders were impossibly broad. She could just see the outlines of the muscles of his chest in the darkened room, and the thick pelt of hair that formed a triangle pointing downward to the button at the top of his fly.

Oh, gosh.

Pete stood in front of her, reaching for the top button on her blouse. Janie swallowed hard.

"Okay?" His brow furrowed slightly.

She took a deep breath. "Oh yes." *Yesyesyesyesyesyesyes.*

The buttons seemed to slide open all at once. His hands skated across her collar bones, pushing the blouse down her arms. Janie tried to remember which bra she had on, hoping it was one of her good ones.

Oh, please, tell me it isn't cotton.

His fingers returned to the front clasp of her bra. Okay, good, one of the lace ones. And then the bra was gone.

My breasts are too small. They're a weird shape. They're not right. Who cares?

Pete leaned down and took one nipple into his mouth. His tongue rasped across it quickly, pebbling the areola. Heat prickled across her skin.

Her fingers itched to touch him and she spread her hands across his chest, rubbing against the crinkling hair. *Oh my. Oh my, my, my.*

She heard him gasp as she palmed his nipple. He raised his head then, and she wrapped one arm around his neck.

Pete stumbled forward, pushing her in front of him, and the edge of the mattress pressed against the back of her knees. Her body jackknifed as Pete angled to the side at the last minute so that he didn't land on top of her.

She stared up at him. His face was taut again, deep grooves running beside his mouth, his chest heaving. For a moment, Janie wondered if they were moving too fast here. Then the moment was gone and she wrapped her arms around his neck again, pulling him down.

His mouth covered hers, his hands moving up to cup her breasts. His thumb dragged across her nipple, and then he pinched hard. A line of fire stretched between her breast and her core, flaming.

Janie caught hold of his waistband, pulling at the button and yanking his fly open. She could feel the weight of him, the hard shape barely contained by the ribbed cotton of his underwear. She stroked him with one hand, feeling the outline of his shaft, the swelling head.

"Oh Christ," he gasped.

Cool air brushed against her body as he rolled away from her. He struggled to push his jeans down over his feet. And then he was back, fumbling with the zipper on her capris.

Janie was pretty sure he broke the zipper when he jerked it down. Oh well, she could always buy another pair.

Naked now, she rolled her body back against him, feeling the hard jut of his cock against her stomach.

His very large cock.

She suddenly tried to remember just how long it had been

since she'd last had sex. Doug Ferguson. Eight months? A year?

Oh god.

Pete's mouth moved in a line down her body—light kisses whispered across her skin from breast to abdomen. Then he touched his mouth to the tender skin at the top of her thighs, and Janie thought she'd probably die.

Except that he wasn't finished yet.

His thumbs moved into the soft folds of her sex, opening her, and then his tongue was sliding across her clitoris, sending pinpricks of sensation tickling up her abdomen.

"Oh Pete, oh yes," she groaned.

His tongue moved to her opening, stabbing inside her as she dug her fingers into his shoulders.

Words failed her, literally. Janie found she couldn't say anything at all. The sounds that came from her mouth were like no sounds she'd ever made before—moans more than speech. And gasping. A lot of gasping.

She felt as if she were in the back seat of a car speeding down a mountain road. Everything was happening way, way, way too fast, and she had no control whatsoever. Waves of sensation washed over her, pushing her upward.

"Pete," she groaned. "Please. Wait...just... Oh lord!"

Pete rose above her, his shoulders tight. "Wait?"

"Just..." Janie gasped, trying to get her brain to work again. "It's all so... I'm sorry."

He sank beside her on the bed, his face a few inches from her. "Do you mean 'wait' as in 'stop'?" His face was tight again, with those tense grooves along the sides of his mouth.

Janie ran her fingers across the line of his jaw, feeling the taut muscles along his throat. "Not stop. Definitely not stop."

Pete sighed, the breath whooshing out of his chest. "Then what?"

"It's been...a long time for me." She traced the lines of his face with her fingers, her thumb rubbing across his lips. "I'm having trouble keeping up with you."

His lips moved almost automatically, kissing her thumb lightly. "Okay, then, your turn." Janie watched as he rolled onto his back, hands behind his head.

Beautiful. He was so beautiful. His body was ribbed with muscle, covered with dark hair. If she'd ever pictured a warrior

153

god, he was close. She ran her hands over his chest again, reveling in the contrast of soft and hard, then slid her hands down to his hips, resting them for a moment on the sharp point of his hip bones.

His cock jutted up, hard and straining, smooth skin and bulging veins. Janie took hold of him, running her hand down the shaft, feeling rock beneath satin.

She heard Pete catch his breath and glanced back at his face. His eyes were closed, his jaw straining. "Janie," he gasped, "please tell me you've caught up now."

"Not just yet," she whispered, dipping to take the head of his cock into her mouth.

He gave a strangled cry, balling his fists in the spread on either side. "Good Christ, woman, my control's about gone here."

She ran her tongue around the head, licking lightly just behind it.

Then Pete's fingers were biting into her shoulders and she was rolling onto her back. She heard the sound of a drawer sliding open and saw him tearing at the corner of a foil packet with his teeth.

"Let me," she said, reaching for the condom.

"Not on your life. No more touching. Trust me on this." Pete rolled the condom over himself, then dropped to his elbows above her.

Janie's breath caught in her chest. This was it. And she hadn't the foggiest idea whether or not she was ready for it, for him.

His fingers skimmed across her folds again, testing her, teasing her. Her hips jerked, canting up toward him as if they were no longer under her control.

Nothing was under her control anymore.

Pete looked down at her and then dropped his head again, his mouth opening against hers as his tongue slid in softly, gently. The gentlest kiss she'd ever had.

Her knees fell open as she felt him move against her. And then he was sliding inside, opening her, stretching her. The length of him was more than she could bear and all that she wanted. He was much too big and not big at all. Janie knew she wasn't making any sense, but she couldn't manage to pull her mind together.

She wrapped her legs around his waist, tucking her heels against the small of his back. He moved inside her with a kind of desperate rhythm, resting on his elbows above her, holding her face tight between his hands as if he wanted to make sure she wouldn't run away.

She reached up to stroke his cheek. "It's okay, it's okay."

He looked down. "Just okay?"

But she was lost by then, feeling the wave of sensation, driving her up, up, up. "Oh, Pete, yes," she moaned. And then she rode the wave up, up and over.

She felt as if her body had shattered against him. She flexed her fingers into his shoulders, trembling as she cried out—a high peak she'd never climbed before.

Above her Pete lost his rhythm, moving wildly, his body jerking as he drove into her again and again. Then he groaned and plunged deep, touching her darkest place, setting off another round of shocks that made her scream.

He lay still for a long moment, panting, his body damp with perspiration. And then he rolled to his side, carrying her with him, still deep inside her body, and dropped his head to her shoulder.

Janie closed her eyes. Somewhere at the back of her mind something told her she should go home. Her mother was waiting.

Her mother could wait.

She moved her hands to the sides of Pete's face, bending over him, then rubbed her nose against his. "More than okay," she whispered. "Believe me. Way more than okay."

Chapter Fifteen

When he woke the next morning, Pete felt as if his brain had melted during the night. He lay still, holding Janie Dupree against his chest, and tried to solidify the pieces again.

Cool light filtered through the curtains. He didn't look at his clock, but he figured seven, or maybe six thirty. For a moment, he tried to remember how long it had been since he'd last slept with a woman in his arms. But it didn't matter. Whenever it had been, it hadn't been anything like last night.

Nothing had ever been anything like last night.

Janie's body was curled against him now, small and lithe, almost like he'd cajoled some forest sprite into his room and then taken her to bed. Which made it sound like he'd seduced an elf.

Except he hadn't really seduced her because seduction implied some reluctance on her part, and as far as he could remember, Janie hadn't been reluctant at all. Just the contrary, in fact—she'd been warm and willing and exciting as hell, the partner of his dreams.

Whoa. He was moving into a dangerous area here. He'd only met her a week ago. Less than that really. Pete took a deep breath. He was getting way ahead of himself, moving far too fast. What was it about Janie Dupree that did that to him?

Janie moved against him, murmuring in her sleep, then settled back with a snort. She snored. Pete loved that she snored. It made her a little less perfect.

He closed his eyes, settling back against the pillow, folding Janie closer against his body. He wasn't going back to sleep, but he wanted to spend a little more time holding her before the morning got started. He had a feeling the day wasn't going to be pleasant for a whole lot of reasons. Janie rubbed her nose against his collarbone, and he looked down. Her eyes were open, barely.

"What time is it?" She yawned.

"Seven o'clock or so. Go back to sleep." He kissed the top of her head, tucking her back under his chin.

"Do I have to?"

The tip of Janie's tongue traced a line down the side of his throat. Suddenly, he didn't feel nearly as relaxed as he had a couple of moments before.

"Do you want to?" His voice sounded a little choked. Possibly because his blood supply was rushing to other parts of his body.

Janie tipped her head back, so that she could look at him again. Her eyes were wide open now, dark and lustrous. "What do you think?"

Pete thought his first kiss of the morning was probably not going to be a transcendent experience, but taking time out to brush his teeth wasn't exactly practical. Or desirable since it would mean stopping. He touched his lips to her forehead, then slid down her nose to her mouth.

She was ready for him, wrapping her arms around his neck as her tongue swept across his teeth. Her leg swung up over his hips.

He pulled back to look at her again. "Fantastic way to start the day, Ms. Dupree!"

"I thought so myself." The corners of her mouth edged up.

Pete touched his lips to the soft skin behind her earlobe just as he heard the front door creak open. *What the hell?* He jerked upright, putting himself in front of Janie.

"Pete?" Cal called from somewhere in the living room.

Pete closed his eyes, exhaling hard as Janie rolled across the bed, scrambling to pull the sheet up over her breasts. "Well, crap," he growled, reaching for his jeans.

The first thing Pete saw when he walked into the kitchen was Docia pouring coffee out of his coffee pot. Well, actually, it was her coffee pot since it had been in the apartment when he arrived, but still...

"Gee, to what do I owe the pleasure of your company at this ungodly hour of the morning?" Pete fumbled through the cupboard until he found a mug. "And where's Olive?" With any luck he could take care of whatever Cal wanted and get them out of the apartment before Janie had climbed back onto the fire escape.

"I let Olive out into the backyard," Cal said, his voice grim. "We need to do some planning."

Pete turned to stare at him. "What happened? Is Lars okay?"

"Lars is fine." Cal grimaced. "Well, not 'fine', exactly. But he's okay. We took him back to the house with us last night. Figured it would not be a good idea to let him go back to the motel alone. He's taking it a lot better than I would have expected. Maybe it's less of a surprise to him than it is to us."

Pete felt a quick jolt of guilt. He should have taken Lars back to the apartment. He hadn't thought of it—he'd been concentrating on Janie. He dropped into a chair opposite Cal. "So what's up? What do you need?"

Behind him, the kitchen door swung open. Pete willed himself not to look. He saw Docia's eyes widen, and then Janie walked into his line of vision. She was wearing one of his T-shirts that reached down almost to her knees. He wasn't sure if she had anything on underneath, and he didn't really want to check under the present circumstances.

Cal cleared his throat. He was biting his lip, and Pete was pretty sure he was doing it to keep from grinning.

"What are we planning, Calthorpe?" Pete moved into Cal's line of vision, blocking his view of Janie.

"How to make this godawful train wreck of a wedding work," Docia grumbled.

Pete glanced at her. Dark shadows circled her eyes, and thin lines outlined her mouth. She looked as if she'd aged a couple of years since he'd last seen her.

Janie slid into the seat beside her, slipping an arm around Docia's shoulders. "What can we do to help?"

Docia bit her lip, thinking. "Attendants," she said finally. "We need to get the attendants lined up again. Sherice is out— no question at this point. I want you to wear that freakin' dress." She raised a mutinous gaze to Janie. "Think you can take care of that?"

"Done." Janie set her mug on the counter.

Janie sounded like getting the dress back was one duty she'd enjoy. Pete wasn't so sure, but at this point he was willing to take on anything that involved her and getting The Wedding back on track. "All right, we'll take care of getting the dress from Sherice. Assuming that's okay with Lars."

Cal sighed. "I don't think Lars is processing much right now. He'd probably go along with anything you come up with, but try not to make it too nasty, okay? Things are screwed up enough already."

Pete nodded. "Strictly business. Or something."

Janie's brow furrowed. "We'll need some time to work on this. I doubt Sherice will be up before ten at least. What about the store?"

"I'll run it." Docia sighed. "It'll keep my mind off everything. Besides, you need some time to cool off a little before you have to meet the public again. Right now, you're radioactive."

"Radioactive?" Janie's mouth became a thin line. "Right. The shattered woman. Tell everybody I'm off on a three-day drunk, pining for my lost love. That's what they'll expect anyway."

Cal's mouth edged up into a slightly guarded smile. "Funny, you don't look too shattered to me."

Janie turned toward Pete, her face suddenly radiant. An ache throbbed in his chest. Lordy, he was responsible for that!

"If there's an opposite of shattered, that's what I am." Janie grinned at them both. "Go. Relax. Pete and I will take care of everything."

Pete took a deep breath. *Sure they would.*

Janie had to admit that part of her really wanted to just pull on her clothes from yesterday and head off to Sherice's motel. But her blouse was thoroughly wrinkled and her capris did indeed have a broken zipper.

And she couldn't put off seeing her mother forever—Mom was probably getting ready to call out the bloodhounds as it was.

"Do you want me to come inside?" Pete asked as they walked up in front of her house.

"No." Janie shook her head. If her mother saw her in rumpled clothes with a spare Toleffson brother, she'd probably have a heart attack.

"Okay, then. I'll go back and take a shower. I'll meet you back here in thirty minutes or so."

Janie almost suggested fifteen minutes instead, but it sounded cowardly.

Mom was sitting at the kitchen table in a pair of butterscotch knit slacks and a bright green shirt with embroidered daisies on the collar. She had on a lot of makeup, which was supposed to cover up the lines of fatigue around her eyes.

"Good morning," Janie trilled, feeling like a jerk.

Her mother studied her, taking in her generally rumpled appearance. "You could have called."

"Yes ma'am." Janie swallowed hard. "I'm very sorry."

"There's some coffee, and I warmed up some Sara Lee sticky buns." Her mother took a sip of her coffee. "I've already heard all about it, so you don't need to spare me."

Janie froze, one hand reaching for the coffee pot. "'Heard all about' what?"

"Otto. Carolyn Burnside called me thirty minutes ago. Rhonda called her last night."

Her mother took another sip, and Janie's heart began to beat again. "That was fast. The gossip express gets around."

"Oh, news like that is too juicy to wait." Her mother's mouth twisted slightly. "Carolyn wanted to make sure she was the first to tell me."

Janie sighed. "I'm sorry, Mom. I should have told you last night. But at least you found out before you went in to the shop."

Her mother squared her shoulders, lifting her chin. "Listen to me, Janie, men are like that. They do stupid things. From what I've heard, that Toleffson woman is no better than she should be. Maybe she was out to get Otto. Maybe she took advantage of him. Carolyn said he'd been drinking at the Dew Drop Inn."

Janie grasped her cup, staring down at the table while she counted to ten. "Otto is a total slimeball, Mom, he always has been. He and Sherice deserve each other, but Sherice's husband didn't deserve what they did to him. And believe me, both of them were definitely involved."

Her mother stared at her blankly, her mouth hanging slightly open.

Janie took a deep breath and blew it out, then gulped the

rest of her coffee. "I need to get dressed. I've got things to do today." She stood, heading for her room.

"Did you get any sleep last night?" her mother called after her.

"Yes ma'am." Janie increased her pace. "Some."

She took the world's fastest shower and shampoo. When she came out of her bedroom, Pete was sitting at the kitchen table, staring at a sticky bun. Mom appeared to have developed a new set of lines on her forehead. Pete looked like he was trying unsuccessfully to be invisible.

"We've got some wedding stuff to take care of," Janie said briskly as she propelled Pete toward the front door. "I probably won't be home for dinner. Don't wait up."

Pete slowed as they reached the front walk. "Should I ask what that was all about?"

She shook her head. "Trust me, don't. What about your mother? Did anybody tell her about last night?"

He grimaced. "I didn't. Maybe Cal did. It would be just like him to take it on since Lars isn't exactly in shape to do it himself."

"Have you seen Lars this morning?"

"Not yet." Pete's mouth compressed in a thin line. "Let's go see if Sherice is receiving visitors."

The Gasthaus was one of the better motels in Konigsburg, but probably not as plush as the hotels Sherice usually stayed in. Pete pulled up outside the entrance to the courtyard. He and Janie sat for a moment in silence, steeling themselves.

"Would you like me to do this?" Pete asked. "You don't really need to be there. I'm used to Sherice by now."

Janie shook her head. "Nope. I'm going to face her, for better or worse. I told Docia we'd take care of things, and I'm part of that 'we'."

"Okay." Pete squared his shoulders. "Let's go see how bad this is going to be."

Lars and Sherice had a room facing into the courtyard with its oak-tree-edged pool. Pete moved up the covered walkway and then stopped.

Lars was sitting in a lawn chair in front of the door to his room. His eyes were closed—Pete wasn't sure whether he was asleep or meditating. After a moment, he cleared his throat. "Morning, Lars."

Lars opened his eyes a little blearily. Pete wondered if he'd had anything to eat since the hamburger at the Dew Drop last night.

"Morning," he mumbled.

Pete hunkered down beside him. "You had any coffee yet?"

Lars shrugged. "Something in the room that was advertised as coffee. Between you and me, I think you could make the case that it was potentially lethal."

Pete chewed on his lip for a moment, trying to figure out how to phrase his next question.

"She's not in there," Lars grunted, closing his eyes again.

Pete frowned. "What?"

"Sherice. She took off sometime last night. All her clothes are gone." Lars opened his eyes again, his forehead furrowing. "Well, not all of them, I guess."

Behind him, Pete heard Janie inhale sharply. "Did she take the matron of honor dress with her?"

There was a long pause, then Lars shook his head. "It's in the closet."

Janie blew out a relieved breath. "We need to get it. Is it okay if we go in?"

Lars didn't open his eyes. He nodded slowly. "Go ahead."

Pete waited a moment longer, frowning. He'd expected Lars to be upset, but *upset* wasn't exactly the right word for this. He pushed himself to his feet and opened the door for Janie.

Inside, the room smelled slightly stale. Sunlight leaked through the window blinds, reflecting off the dancing dust motes. Janie headed toward the closet door. "She's got both dresses, you know, the matron's dress and the bridesmaid dress that Reba had flown in for her. But I don't think she ever got the alterations done on the matron's dress. I hope not anyway." She opened the door and started to reach inside as Lars appeared in the doorway behind them.

The sound she made tipped Pete off—that faint gasp of distress.

"Janie?" He stepped toward her.

Janie reached slowly into the closet. He couldn't see her

face, but her shoulders were trembling.

He stepped closer. "What's happening?"

"Why?" Janie whispered. "Why would she do this?"

Pete looked over her shoulder into the small closet. The two dresses hung side by side. A rip extended from the middle of the bodice to the hem of each dress, threads dangling from the jagged edges. It looked as if Sherice had simply sliced each dress in half before hanging what was left of them neatly on their hangers.

"That isn't all she did." Lars pushed the sliding doors down to the other end of the closet. "She was very thorough."

His tuxedo hung in tatters, the vest, coat and pants all ripped apart.

Pete sat on the end of the bed, staring into the closet. "I gather she was pissed."

Lars shrugged. "Maybe. Or maybe this was just a parting shot. I need to go home, bro." He raised his red-rimmed gaze to Pete.

Pete shook his head. "Why? What's waiting for you there? Aren't you better off here?"

"Daisy's there." Lars closed his eyes again. "I don't want Sherice to get her. I don't trust her not to grab Daisy and take off somewhere without letting me know where they are. The perfect revenge."

Pete stared down at his hands. No way he could argue with that. "Cal will miss you." To say nothing of Mom. Pete sighed, thinking of the battles on the horizon.

"Cal understands. We've already talked about it—I called him just before you got here. And it's not like I can be in the wedding now, anyway, right?" Lars looked back at his shredded tuxedo.

Pete glanced up at Janie. She still stared into the closet, her hands balled in fists at her sides. As he watched, her shoulders began to tremble again.

Uh oh.

Pete got up quickly, moving to put his arms around her. Janie leaned against him for a moment, then drew a shuddering breath. "Looks like Plan A just went all to hell."

Pete nodded, rubbing his cheek against her hair. "I'd say so, yeah."

"Any ideas?" Janie raised her wide eyes to his.

Pete started to shake his head when he heard the sounds of footsteps headed their way. "Close the closet door," he said quickly.

The front door swung open without any knock, and Pete stared into the bright sun suddenly filling the room. A man stood silhouetted in the light, a familiar shape. His broad shoulders blocked the sunlight momentarily—one hand was tucked behind him.

"Lars?" the man said.

"Dad?" Lars pushed himself slowly to his feet.

Pete stared up at his father's face, darkened by the dazzling sunlight at his back. He felt a sudden wave of relief, almost as if he were still twelve years old and his father had arrived to save him from the results of his most recent stupidity. "I thought you weren't due for another day."

His father shrugged. "I finished up early. And I brought another guest for the wedding. Hope that's okay."

A small figure was suddenly silhouetted alongside him, blinking in the sunlight. Pete heard Lars catch his breath.

"Daisy," he murmured. "Oh, baby, it's so good to see you."

He knelt in front of his daughter, pulling her into his embrace.

"Da!" Daisy crowed, grabbing his nose. She giggled as he swept her up into the air.

Pete's eyes prickled while his chest constricted. He looked down to see Janie watching father and daughter. Her eyes were suspiciously bright. "Maybe we should go get a cup of coffee."

"That sounds good." His father put an arm around Janie's shoulders. "C'mon, sweetheart, you can tell me exactly who you are and what the hell happened to this nice little wedding I was supposed to be part of."

Chapter Sixteen

Looking at Asa Toleffson, Janie had a very clear idea about where the Toleffson boys got their size. He loomed over one side of the table at the Coffee Corral in the same way Pete loomed over the other. She suddenly felt a little like a munchkin.

Asa's thick sable hair was sprinkled with gray, but his eyes were the same dark, velvety color as Pete's. He was still a remarkably good-looking man. Janie wondered if Pete would look like that when he was in his sixties.

Asa took a swallow of coffee and sighed. "Good stuff. Not up to Norwegian standards, maybe, but still good."

"Konigsburg's German," Janie explained. "I don't know how they feel about coffee."

Asa shrugged. "Lots of sugar and cream, I imagine."

"Okay, Pop, how'd you get Daisy down here?" Pete leaned forward on his elbows. "I thought Sherice had parked her with her relatives."

"Sherice's mother called me a couple of days ago. She had a chance to go to Las Vegas with some friends for a week. Asked if I'd look after Daisy." Asa shrugged. "I never understood why Sherice didn't want her here. Little girls like weddings, don't they?"

He paused to inhale part of a kolache. "I guess bringing Daisy along was a better idea than I realized. I haven't seen Lars looking that bad since he was in college. And that was only during Homecoming."

Pete narrowed his eyes. "How much do you know?"

Asa shrugged. "Basically nothing. But I'm guessing the situation's not good. Maybe you can start by telling me why Sherice wasn't in their room."

Pete had a gift for summary, Janie realized. Maybe it went along with being a lawyer. Asa said nothing as Pete ran through the events of the previous week, but his expression became progressively darker as Pete described last night, or rather the part of last night that didn't involve their activities in Pete's bedroom.

When Pete had finished, Asa sat shaking his head. "Well, damn, son. You tell your mother any of this?"

"No. Cal may have, but I haven't checked in with her yet."

"Best get me over there, then." Asa started to rise from his chair. "Somebody needs to fill her in, fast."

"You didn't see Mom when you got here?" Pete raised an eyebrow.

"Just for a few minutes." Asa's expression changed slightly, but Janie didn't know him well enough to interpret what was going on.

Pete's brow furrowed as he stared at his father. "What's up, Pop?"

"We'll get into that later. For now, I need to go talk to Millie. You want to come along in case she has any questions?"

Janie reached over to touch Pete's arm. "Go ahead. I'll go relieve Docia at the bookstore for a while."

"Don't tell her about the dresses yet, okay?"

"Don't worry. I'm not going to take that on by myself."

She watched the two Toleffsons walk out of the Coffee Corral, then looked around the room. Every woman was turned toward the door. A couple of them wore slightly dazed expressions, as if they'd just seen something so amazing they weren't sure it was real.

If nothing else, the Toleffson family had definitely spiced up the fantasy life of Konigsburg's female population.

Pete told himself to relax as they approached the bed and breakfast where his mother was staying. Maybe he wouldn't have to say anything. Maybe Cal had already talked to her. And maybe he could get a side of fries with that large order of denial.

His mother was sitting in the dining room, a folded newspaper beside her breakfast plate. Pete had the feeling she hadn't gotten much reading done, though.

His father took a chair across from her, reaching a large hand to cover hers. "Well, Millie, looks like we've got ourselves a real mess here."

His mother raised her gaze to his, blinking. "Yes, we do. Poor Lars. And poor Sherice."

Pete felt as if he'd taken a cannonball in his stomach. He collapsed into the chair opposite her. "Poor Sherice?"

"Every story has two sides, Peter." His mother's lips thinned. "She stopped here this morning on her way out of town."

"Why would she stop to see you?"

"I imagine because she wanted me to hear her side of it before I started hearing all the other versions." His mother picked up her cup of coffee from the table in front of her, her brow furrowing.

Pete's chest constricted further, if that were possible. "Sherice's version? Oh, this ought to be good!"

"Now that's just why she came here." His mother's chin came up mutinously. "That kind of attitude. At least I was willing to listen when nobody else was."

"Well, Otto sure as hell did," Pete muttered.

"Peter." His father's voice was sharp. "Shut up for a minute. Okay, Millie, what was Sherice's story this time?"

"She said she went to that bachelorette party with Docia, but some woman insulted her, so she had to leave."

Some woman. Pete pressed his lips together, fighting the red surge of anger. It wouldn't help to yell at his mother. He knew that from long experience.

His father gave him a quick warning glance. "What happened next?"

"Well—" his mother looked down at her coffee cup again, "—I guess they'd been drinking a lot at that bachelorette party."

His father nodded. "And?"

"And Sherice and Lars haven't been getting along..." His mother still wasn't looking up. Pete had a feeling even she wasn't buying this part of Sherice's story.

"So anyway this Otto person came along as she was walking back to her motel and offered her a ride. Then he lured her into...well...petting, I guess."

"Lured?" His father's eyebrows lifted almost to his hairline.

"Petting?" Pete croaked.

His mother shrugged. "Sherice said she didn't know what came over her. She'd never done anything like that before." She finally looked up at his father, her mouth a tight line again. "She said she's very sorry."

"Mom..." Pete found it difficult to talk through clenched teeth.

His father gave him another level glance. "Pete, don't you have wedding stuff you need to do with Ms. Dupree? Don't worry. We'll work this out."

Pete blew out an acrid breath and headed out the door to find Cal. *Better you than me, Pop, better you than me.*

Janie hadn't had too much trouble keeping the news about the dresses from Docia. The shop had been busy, and she had the feeling Docia didn't really want to think about anything else just then anyway.

Janie didn't want to think about it either, but of course she had no choice. She spent the morning fending off the mingled sympathy and curiosity of all the Konigsburg customers. By mid-afternoon her face ached from maintaining her blandest smile.

Around four, Lars walked in, looking happier than she'd seen him look since he'd arrived in Konigsburg. His daughter rode on his shoulders, her chubby fingers knotted in his dark hair.

Lars swung her in front of him, one arm around her middle, while she giggled.

"Da!" she squealed. Her mop of dark curls reminded Janie of Pete. Particularly when he first woke up. Janie chewed on her lip and hoped she wasn't blushing too visibly.

"Daisy, this is your Aunt Docia, your almost-Aunt Docia, that is." Lars grinned up at them blissfully.

Daisy stared at them with the same laughing black eyes Janie had seen with Lars, Cal, Pete, and, of course, Asa. "Da!" she said.

Docia dropped to her knees in front of her. "In the ballpark, sweetie. Can you say 'Docia'?"

Daisy gave her a wide-eyed look, then extended a dimpled hand toward Docia's red curls. "Da!"

"Close enough." Docia leaned forward and gave her a hug, while Daisy giggled, running her fingers through Docia's hair.

"Do you mind if I bring her to the wedding? I know she wasn't invited. I didn't know if you were allowing children."

"Are you kidding?" Docia swung Daisy up in her arms. "I'll invent a new role for her. We can all waltz down the aisle together."

Lars shrugged. "Oh, that's okay. I mean, since I can't be in the wedding anymore, I'll just hold her."

Docia stared at him blankly. "You can't be in the wedding? Since when can't you be in the wedding?"

Lars glanced at Janie. The creases in his forehead became more pronounced. "Well, I mean, since the tuxedo got...ruined, I just figured..."

Docia turned to stare at Janie, her expression stony.

Janie sighed. "You'll need to have a margarita in front of you before I explain this one."

They left Lars to finish checking out the few customers who were still in the shop. Daisy had discovered Docia's cat, Nico, and was rapturously in love. Nico, in residence on top of one of the bookcases, was playing hard to get.

Janie positioned Docia in a booth at the Dew Drop and brought her a margarita, then gave her a summary of what she'd found in Sherice's motel room. It probably wasn't as good as Pete's, but she figured nobody's summary would make Docia feel happy about the whole thing. "It's not that bad, Docia," she lied. "We'll work something out."

"Absolutely." Pete slid into the booth beside her. "As far as I'm concerned we're already ahead here. We traded Sherice for Daisy. You can't tell me that isn't a great exchange."

"Daisy's here?" Cal slid into the other side of the booth with a wary glance at Docia's stony expression. "How did that happen?"

"Dad brought her." Pete waved two fingers at Ingstrom, who slid a couple of beers across the bar for him and Cal.

"Dad?" Cal stared at him blankly.

"Oh, man, let me guess—you've been hiding in the clinic all day."

"I've been *working* in the clinic." Cal humphed. "I'm trying to make up for the amount of time I'm going to be gone for the honeymoon. Dad's here?"

Pete nodded. "He's with Mom. The general message is, butt out for now."

Cal took a long pull on his Dos Equis. "Gladly. So the crisis is over, right?"

"Wrong." Docia drained her margarita. "Tell him."

Pete did. Cal's eyes widened as the story unfolded. He set his bottle down sharply on the table.

"What the hell was that all about? Why take it out on Lars? He didn't put her into that truck!"

Pete grimaced. "Oh, it gets even better. Sherice made a stop on her way out of town."

When he'd finished speaking, Pete and Cal sat staring at each other.

"So why did she stop to talk to Mom? Does she want to get back with Lars?" Cal shook his head. "But if she does, why shred his tuxedo?"

Pete shrugged. "I don't think she wants to get back with anybody. I think she just wanted to stir things up a little more before she left. And she knew Mom was her best bet for doing that."

"Okay," Docia snapped. "Good riddance." She turned to look at Cal. "Did you tell them what we decided last night, Calthorpe, in case there were any further disasters?"

Janie leaned forward so that she could look Docia in the eye. "This isn't a disaster. It's minor."

"Minor?" Docia narrowed her eyes.

Janie shrugged. "So you're down one attendant, so what? You've still got Allie and Bethany."

Cal closed his eyes. "Okay, go ahead. Tell her."

Docia waved at Ingstrom for another margarita. "The wedding's off. We figured we should tell you before we told anybody else."

Beside him, Pete heard Janie catch her breath. "No, Docia, don't. Please. You're perfect for each other. All this other...stuff. It just doesn't matter."

Docia shook her head impatiently. "That's not what I mean, Janie. The marriage is on, it's the wedding that's off."

"You mean the ceremony?" Pete asked carefully. He was slightly dizzy all of a sudden.

"This whole misbegotten...mess. Yes. The friggin' ceremony. *That* is off." Docia took a swallow of her drink. "I am not doing this dog and pony show anymore. It's over."

"We're going to Vegas." Cal's voice had a hollow quality.

Pete stared at him. "You hate Vegas."

Cal shrugged. "Better than the Ozarks."

"We're going someplace where this whole wedding business can be taken care of in an hour or so," Docia explained. "No dresses. No cakes. No family. Just us." Her mouth compressed to a thin line.

"You could come with us," Cal mumbled. "We could go to some shows or something. Maybe even gamble."

Pete tried to picture Cal gambling. It didn't compute.

"Docia, please." Janie's voice was soft. "Your mama's worked so hard on all of this. You'll break her heart."

"Mom will be very...disappointed," Pete added, carefully. In fact, of course, their mother would make their lives a living hell for the foreseeable future.

Cal didn't look at him. Bad sign. "She'll get over it."

Pete exhaled in a sigh. Cal obviously was dealing with his own large order of denial. "I'm not sure I will."

"Docia, why do you think you have to cancel?" Janie took a long sip of her own margarita. "What exactly is the problem?"

"The problem? What's the problem?" Docia's voice crackled, and then suddenly her face crumpled, her eyes swimming. Cal reached for her, pulling her against his chest.

Pete's hands fisted on the table, helplessly. *Damn Sherice. Damn Otto. Damn everybody.*

"The problem," Docia continued, her voice thick, "is that this whole thing has spun out of control. It's a train wreck. Everything we plan goes wrong. Every time we try to fix something it gets worse. I'm tired of it. I'm just..." she waved a hand, helplessly, "...tired of it."

"What if we could fix it?" Pete heard himself say. He had no memory of planning to say anything like that. Maybe he was possessed.

Janie turned toward him, nodding. "Yeah. We can fix it. You just relax and trust us."

Cal stared at her for a moment, then turned to Pete. "Fix it how?"

Oh, good question. Too bad he had no answer whatsoever. "We'll take care of it. Tell us what the problems are and we'll make them go away." Whatever spirit had possessed him clearly wasn't finished yet.

Docia's brow was still furrowed. "Take care of it how?"

"Give us a problem." Janie leaned back against the booth. "Any problem."

Docia blew out a breath. "The last I heard, Mama had the guest list up to around four hundred, and that's just for the ceremony. She may be up to eight hundred or so for the reception. I'm not going through with this whole Hollywood wedding idea. Make this less of a grand opera and more of a country wedding that fits in Konigsburg. Get that guest list down to under a hundred and make it our friends and relations."

Janie nodded again. "We can do that."

Pete had a feeling she was going to nod at everything Docia said. He forced himself to open his fists. "Okay, simplify the wedding. We can work on that. That strikes me as enough for one day, but, of course, you can always call us if you think of something else."

"I'm not done." Docia turned back to Janie. "You're my maid of honor. Period. End of discussion. I need you back in the wedding."

Janie closed her eyes. "Docia, there's no way we could get another bridesmaid dress here in time, let alone the maid of honor dress. I can run the guest book or something. It really doesn't matter."

"It *does* matter." Docia's voice cracked. "I'm not doing this without you."

"Couldn't you just wear a different dress?" Cal asked innocently.

Docia and Janie both stared at him.

"No, no, of course you couldn't, what was I thinking!" Cal took a hurried swallow of Dos Equis.

"Wait a minute." Pete's brow furrowed. "Why couldn't you wear something else? What's stopping you?"

"Because it's a wedding." Janie looked at him as if he'd

taken leave of his senses. "Everybody has to match."

"Why?"

"Because...they just do, that's all."

"Look—" Pete leaned forward, "—Docia says she wants to get out from under this train wreck. Well, why not change its direction? Who says this has to be the second coming of Di and Charles—hell, just look how well that one turned out, anyway!"

"So, I get to stand up there in my prom dress, while everybody else wears those luscious bridesmaid dresses?" Janie grimaced. "Excuse me, but I don't see how that's going to help."

Pete shook his head. "Not just you. Me too. And Lars."

"You're going to wear a prom dress?" Cal raised an eyebrow. "Good entertainment value, but mixed messages."

"No, wait, I see what you mean." Docia leaned forward. "As long as we're not going with tradition here, let's take it to the limit. No bridesmaid dresses. No tuxes."

"Right." Pete nodded. "You and Cal can wear your finery, and the rest of us will wear stuff that will make us fade into the background."

"Speak for yourself," Janie cut in. "Even if I'm not going to get to wear that dream dress, I'm still wearing something nice. It's Docia's wedding."

"No." Docia stared down at her margarita, her forehead furrowed.

Janie blinked at her. "No, you don't like it or no, you prefer me to fade like Pete?"

The corners of Docia's mouth quirked up slightly. "No, I'm not wearing any finery. Why should you guys be the only ones who get to wear what you want?"

"Oh, but Docia, it's such a beautiful dress!" Janie sighed.

"It's a beautiful dress for someone who isn't me," Docia said gently. "For me, it's like playing dress-up. I've never wanted to be Cinderella, even when I was a kid."

"Okay, hold up a minute." Cal frowned. "What do we have here? No wedding clothes I get. But what about the rest of it? We'll look pretty weird wandering into this extravaganza dressed in jeans and boots."

"Oh, god, Mama," Docia moaned. "I forgot all about the wedding of the century part of it."

Janie narrowed her eyes, thinking. "You wanted to cut the

guest list, right?"

"Right." Docia grimaced. "Four hundred isn't a wedding, it's a convention."

Janie shrugged. "So your mama's production becomes the reception. And we have the wedding someplace else. Maybe even sometime else."

"Such as?" Cal was leaning forward now.

"I don't know." Janie's eyes danced. "Maybe in the morning. Or even the night before. But we'll have to clear that with Reba."

"You know where I want it to be?" Docia leaned back, her eyes meeting Cal's. "Morgan Barrett's winery. The patio outside the tasting room. I've always loved that place."

Cal looked slightly confused. "Then why didn't you suggest it for the wedding when your mama was doing the planning?"

"I did. She vetoed it because it won't hold four hundred guests." Docia was grinning now. "Which means it's currently perfect for our purposes."

"*If* your mama agrees," Janie cautioned. "I'm not going to get into this if it's going to upset Reba too much."

"Oh you can explain it," Docia said airily. "Mama listens to you."

Janie looked as if her stomach had suddenly dropped to her toes. "Me?"

"You." Docia nodded in Pete's direction. "And him. Your impossible mission, should you choose to accept it."

"Is the alternative Vegas?" Janie croaked.

"It is." Docia gave her a faintly feline grin. "The two of you are still invited if we go."

"In that case we accept."

"Huh?" Pete's head whipped toward her.

Janie sighed. "I mean we accept the mission. We'll talk your mama into it, Docia."

Chapter Seventeen

"So explain to me again why we're doing this," Pete murmured as he wandered up the street behind Janie.

"Well, Docia wanted a smaller wedding, and we're down by a dress and a tux, and..."

"No." He shook his head. "Explain to me why we're not just letting them head for Vegas."

Janie paused, leaning one hand against a live oak tree. *Why weren't they?* "Well, Reba would be upset."

"She'd get over it eventually." He placed a hand on the tree trunk above her head, angling over her.

"Your mother would be upset."

Pete didn't say she'd get over it. Janie was willing to bet Millie Toleffson didn't get over very many things. She probably had a memory like an elephant on ginko.

"We'd survive."

"Docia would be upset. Once she realized what she'd done, she'd be unhappy."

"She's already unhappy. You think she'd feel worse than she already does?"

"Right now all she can think about is the fuss and the disasters." Janie leaned her head against the tree trunk. "But the thing is, every time she and Cal have talked about getting married for the past few months, Docia has said her one nonnegotiable demand is that the wedding happens here with all her friends. If she bolts off to Las Vegas, she'll lose that. And she won't be happy when she understands what she's done."

Pete's mouth edged up in a grin. "So you're saving her from herself? You're being a nice girl again? I'd say this isn't going to help you in your ambition to become a bitch."

"Oh well, I'll have other chances." Janie grinned back, then her grin turned into gritted teeth. "And if we do this, we keep that true bitch Sherice from screwing everything up like she planned to. We *will* make this wedding happen."

Pete's smile turned fierce. "I'll drink to that."

"Look, I'll talk to Reba." Janie pushed herself up again. "It's probably better if I do this alone. She's more likely to listen to me after all the work we've done together."

Pete nodded as he fell in step beside her again. "Okay, but we need to check in with each other. Keep in touch. Maybe have dinner."

He was looking carefully at the other side of the street, his face neutral. Janie thought he was adorable. Also super hot.

"Right. We can get together later."

Pete sighed. "Yeah, I guess I need to check back with my dad to see what's happening on the other front. Call me when you're done, okay?"

Janie sailed home, almost literally. She was pretty sure her feet were several inches above the ground. The wedding was on, Sherice was gone, Lars was smiling, and she had Pete.

Her feet hit the ground with a thud. *She had Pete?* What did that mean? She didn't *have* Pete—nobody did. As far as she could tell, Pete preferred it that way.

And, of course, so did she. Independence. Her own apartment. The new, vaguely bitchy Janie Dupree. She started up her front walk, then stopped, her chest constricting. Suddenly, she was having trouble breathing.

Otto's truck was parked in the driveway.

A muted pain began somewhere around Janie's sinuses. She had a feeling Mom had something to do with this. For a moment she considered heading back toward Main, but she waited too long. Mom stepped out onto the front porch.

"Janie, honey, come inside." She glanced a little fearfully at the houses on either side, her voice dropping. "You need to talk to him."

No, I don't. On the other hand, maybe talking to Otto now would lead to a clean break. Preferably of one of Otto's major bones.

Otto himself was sitting at the kitchen table with a coffee mug in front of him. He looked like he needed it. His complexion reminded her of bread dough—moist and pale. His brown hair was plastered against his skull as if he'd been wearing a close-fitting hat. Janie didn't think she'd ever seen him looking quite so bad. She tried not to be delighted. Delight was beneath her. "What do you want, Otto?" she snapped.

"Janie," her mother said from behind her, "don't be rude. Otto is our guest. Sit down. I'll make some sandwiches."

Janie sat. She decided she'd save her battles for more vital things. On the other hand, she needed to dispense with extended conversations. "I don't have time to eat right now, Mom. I've got errands to run. I'll get dinner while I'm out. What was it you wanted, Otto?" She figured that sounded marginally more polite at least.

Otto turned red-rimmed eyes in her general direction. "Came to apologize," he mumbled.

"All right." She folded her arms across her chest. "Go ahead."

"Janie!" Mom stood behind Otto's chair, her eyes narrowed.

Janie gritted her teeth. "Mom, maybe you could go check the mail."

"The mail? It's almost five. The mail came at two." Her mother glared at her with mutinous eyes.

"Then find something else to do in the living room, Mom." Janie managed to keep her voice level. "Otto and I need to talk. In private."

She watched her mother's jaw become square, as her chin moved up. She walked stiffly toward the kitchen door, her eyes sending messages all the way. *Don't blow it! Last chance! Good catch!* Janie looked away.

Otto took a long swallow of coffee, shuddering slightly at the taste. Janie thought about standing again to try to hurry him on his way. "So what do you have to say, Otto?"

"Well, you know." He rubbed his eyes. "Like, I'm sorry."

Janie swallowed down the words that leaped to her tongue. "Sorry for what exactly?"

"Well, last night." He waved one hand in the air, vaguely. "What happened and all. I was drunk. I'm sorry."

As an apology, she figured it ranked right up there with Helen of Troy apologizing for causing that misunderstanding with the Greeks. "Okay. You've said you're sorry. Now you can go."

"Oh come on, Janie." Otto winced, rubbing his eyes again.

"So I'm not good with apologies. I came over here to make it right. Give me some credit at least."

She blew out a quick breath. Clearly, he wasn't going to get the hell out of her kitchen yet. "I accept your apology, Otto, but I don't really have much more to say about it. In fact, I don't see that the two of us have much more to say to each other at all."

Otto gave her an incredulous look. "You're not gonna break up with me over this, are you? It's not like I really cheated on you or anything."

She stared at him, fascinated. She'd never seen self-delusion on this scale before. "What exactly would you call it?"

"I just..." He gave a one-shoulder shrug. "Like I said, I was drunk. And she was willing. And the Toleffsons have been like a burr in my ass all week long."

"So this was a chance to get back at the Toleffsons?" That didn't exactly speak well for Sherice's charms, not that she found that idea all that upsetting, of course.

"Bunch of smartasses." His face darkened. "He threw a dart at me."

Janie sighed again. Had dealing with Otto always been this annoying? Probably. She just hadn't focused on it before. "Look, Otto, let's just forget the whole thing, all right? It's not like we were going steady or anything. You've said you're sorry, I've accepted your apology, we can be friends. That's that."

"Friends?" He glared at her. "We weren't friends!"

"Okay," she said through gritted teeth, "we can be distant acquaintances. Is that better?"

Otto ignored her. "We've been going out for weeks. You're my girlfriend, damn it!" He pushed back his chair and stood, then leaned over her, resting his fists on the table. "What do you mean we weren't going steady?"

Janie sat very still, staring up at him. He seemed to loom over her, like some backstreet thug. She'd never been afraid of him. She wasn't now. *Not exactly.* "I can't talk about this now. I've got things I have to do. And we both need time to cool off."

Otto straightened, his face thunderous. "Cool off? Yeah, right. Believe me, honey, you don't need any more cooling. You're already so frigid you're like a fucking icicle." He turned and walked out of the kitchen without looking back.

Janie sat very still, concentrating on breathing. She wasn't going to take anything he said seriously. She wasn't frigid. Pete hadn't thought so.

Had he?

She heard her mother's step in the doorway and closed her eyes. She really wasn't up to this right now.

"Janie?" her mother said, tentatively.

Janie pushed herself back from the table. "Mom, I've got to go talk to some people. I don't know when I'll be back. Don't wait up."

Mom watched her go with worried eyes, but Janie willed herself not to slow down or look back.

Pete parked outside the B&B where his parents were staying, trying to remember which rental car was his dad's. If they'd gone out to dinner with Lars or Cal, he'd catch up with them later.

He tried the front door, knocking quickly when he found it was unlocked. "Hey, anybody home?"

"Just me."

Pete froze. Sherice sat on the couch wearing a tank top made out of shiny black fabric and a skirt that ended the usual six inches above her knees.

The corners of her mouth edged up in a thin smile. "You should see your face."

"Why?" Pete blew out a quick breath, trying to regroup.

"You look like you've had the shock of your life. At least I'm ahead of you for once." Sherice looked out the window, squinting slightly.

"Is Mom here?" he asked.

Sherice shrugged. "Haven't seen her. Is Lars coming over now?"

Pete sank into the easy chair opposite her couch. "Why? Do you want him to?"

"Not especially. I assume you've already closed ranks."

"Well, we saw your little goodbye present. I figured if you wanted to make it up to him, you wouldn't have burned your bridges."

"There's no point in my talking to him now, is there?" Sherice inspected her sunshine-yellow fingernails.

Pete shrugged. "Depends on what you've got to say, I

guess."

She glanced up at him, her mouth narrowing to a thin line. "You're all so smart. You've got it all decided, haven't you? You know who the good guys and bad guys are. What chance do I have?"

"Let me get this straight. You're asking me to feel sorry for you, to think you got some kind of raw deal." Pete blew out a disgusted breath. "C'mon Sherice. You were screwing a near stranger in the front seat of his truck. How is that Lars's fault? How is that anybody's fault but yours and Otto's?"

She gave him a faintly feline smile. "Your mother doesn't think it's all my fault. She thinks you've all been mean to me."

He rubbed his eyes. He had an overwhelming desire to kick Sherice in the butt. "Mom has her point of view. I have mine."

"You should keep something in mind—all of you Toleffson boys." Sherice leaned forward in her seat, her voice dropping to a rasp. "I've got Daisy. She's with my mama. If you push me too hard, I can send them away to some place where you'll never find her."

Pete felt a quick surge of rage, followed by an equally quick surge of guilty delight. He managed to keep his face blank. "You'd do that to Lars? And to Daisy? They're nuts about each other."

"Then Lars had better think twice about throwing me out with nothing." Sherice stood, smoothing the wrinkles in her skirt. "I'm looking for a decent settlement, and I've got all the cards here, Mr. Attorney of Record. Just keep that in mind."

"I will." He sighed. "Oh, believe me, I will. Are you staying here with Mom?"

Sherice narrowed her eyes as she opened the front door. "You never mind where I'm staying. I'll be in touch." She closed the door behind her with a snap.

Janie called Morgan Barrett from the car as she headed toward the Woodrose.

"The tasting room patio?" Morgan sounded mystified. "Yeah, sure, it's available on Saturday morning. We don't open until noon. Why do you need it?"

Janie took a deep breath. "For Docia's wedding."

Silence spread at the other end of the line, then a sigh. "I thought Docia was getting married at the Woodrose. I mean that's what my invitation said."

"She was. There's been a slight change in plans."

"Well, okay, I guess. What all do you need from us?"

"I'm not sure yet." Janie turned into the Woodrose's drive. "I'll get back to you after I talk to Reba."

Janie found Reba on the Woodrose's spacious side porch, a very large glass of wine on the table beside her. Billy Kent was sitting next to her on the wicker settee, his arm draped across her shoulders.

Janie had decided that she'd tell Reba about the dresses without any preliminaries, sort of like jerking out a splinter without discussing it. Reba sat perfectly still when she'd finished, then slowly lowered her head to her folded arms.

Janie wondered if she should have indulged in some preliminaries after all.

Billy leaned forward, stroking his wife's shoulders. "Hey there, sweet thing, we'll take care of it. We'll just fly in another one, and another tux too. Hell, how hard can it be?"

Reba raised her head fractionally to stare at him, then sighed, dropping her head back on her arms. "There's no time, Billy. The wedding's day after tomorrow. Besides, I think that bridesmaid dress I got for the sister-in-law was the last one in the country. And finding a tux for someone Lars's size is no simple thing."

"So we'll figure out something else. It's not right that Janie here can't be in the wedding—or Lars either." Billy's mouth twisted. "Besides, I'll be damned if I'll let that goddamned little gold-digger ruin my daughter's wedding."

Reba sat up again, eyes narrowed. "There is that. Maybe I can get something from Dallas."

"We had a thought."

"We?" Reba raised an eyebrow.

"Pete and I, but Docia and Cal too." Janie swallowed. "We were sort of discussing it." If she could only get through this part of it, the rest would be minor. She took a deep breath. "Maybe we could make the wedding a little less formal."

"Meaning?" Reba's other eyebrow lifted as well.

"Well, we could have the wedding in the morning at

Morgan's winery. We'd all wear something we could get in town—my Mom can help us at the Lucky Lady. Then we could have the reception out here in the afternoon. Just sort of explain to everybody that this was a party for the wedding rather than the wedding itself, which would already have taken place."

Janie's voice trailed off. Reba and Billy both stared at her as if she'd sprouted a third eye.

"So who would come to this wedding at the winery?" Reba asked faintly.

"Well, maybe just family and close friends. I mean the patio is really beautiful, but it's pretty small. Not like the grounds here." Janie studied her toes. She couldn't bring herself to look at Reba. If she was going to have a meltdown, Janie would rather not know in advance.

"Family and close friends. Well, that should whittle it down some, although when you consider all those Toleffsons, it wouldn't narrow it down a whole lot." Reba's voice sounded slightly choked.

Janie glanced at Billy. He looked like he was preparing himself for a nuclear attack. "Um…sweetheart…" he began.

"Fine." Reba took a healthy swallow of wine.

Billy stared at her. So did Janie.

"Fine with me." Reba nodded. "This whole thing spun out of control a long time ago anyway. If we went ahead with the wedding we planned, I'm afraid we'd get hit with the plagues of Moses or something. Not that that Sherice doesn't resemble a special kind of plague all on her own."

Billy's face split into a cautious grin.

Reba cradled her glass in her hands. "I assume that woman will no longer be participating."

Janie frowned. "Sherice? I think she's gone. She cleaned out her closet anyway."

"Perfect." Reba drained her glass. "I don't suppose you could get Millie Toleffson to join her."

Janie and Billy both blinked at her. Reba waved a hand. "Forget I said that. You think you can get your mama to open up her dress shop tonight?"

Janie nodded. "Maybe not tonight, but tomorrow morning for sure."

"Tomorrow at the latest." Reba stood. "I want this whole thing settled. Give her a call and then give me a call. Billy, when this is done, you and I are going off someplace where they don't have phones."

"Bora Bora?" Billy smiled hopefully.

"I was thinking more like Mars." Reba stomped back into the Woodrose dining room.

Pete asked Janie to meet him at the Coffee Corral for dinner and an update. His mom and dad were having dinner at Brenner's. Lars and Daisy were at McDonald's. Cal and Docia were God knows where, probably making good use of their time. And Pete really wanted to see Janie Dupree.

Even in the midst of the day's insanity, he hadn't forgotten last night.

She breezed into the Corral, looking thoroughly delighted with herself. That was fine with Pete. He was delighted with her too.

Janie slid into the seat across from him at the table. "She bought it!"

"Who?" He yanked his wandering thoughts back to the situation at hand. Apparently, her delectable smile wasn't a reaction to him after all.

"Reba. She's okay with the new, improved wedding. And Morgan says the patio isn't booked for the morning, so we can have it there. We can look it over tomorrow—the rehearsal's tomorrow night. I'll try to get Mom to open up the Lucky Lady early in the morning so we can pick out some bridesmaid dresses. And the bride's gown, I guess, if Docia really wants something different. Have you eaten? I'm starving all of a sudden."

After Pete ordered burgers and fries, Janie leaned back in her chair, still glowing. "I know today was one disaster after another, but I really think we've got it back on track. Docia should be happy now."

"Why should I be happy?" Docia pulled up a chair and dropped down at their table.

"Because the new, improved Wedding of the Century is finally on track. Your mama's okay with it. The patio's booked. Everybody's going to rally round." Janie beamed.

Pete thought of Sherice and her parting promise to be in touch. "Most everybody anyway."

Cal slid into a chair beside Docia, toasted cheese sandwich in hand. "Has anyone thought to inform Judge Farber that he needs to be at the winery instead of the Woodrose and in the morning instead of the afternoon?"

Janie's face fell. "No. Rats, I didn't think of it. I'll call him first thing."

"I'll call him." Docia pulled her cell phone out of her purse. "It's my wedding, I can take some heat for a change. Besides, I found him that first edition Tony Hillerman he was looking for. Y'all just hang on for a few minutes." She walked back to a spot in the hall where it was marginally quieter.

Cal watched her, smiling. "God, I love that woman."

"Good. It's too late to find you a sub at this point." Pete took another bite of his burger, chewing happily until he heard Cal's gasp.

Pete looked up. Cal sat rigid, staring at the doorway, his jaw tight.

Pete turned and looked back. A tall man was standing in the entrance to the dining room. At first glance, he thought it was his dad, but then he looked more closely.

That face had haunted his nightmares for most of his early childhood and even beyond. It still showed up now and then in his dreams when he was under stress. Like now.

The man caught sight of them and headed slowly toward their table, one corner of his mouth turning up slightly in a tentative grin. He stopped beside Cal, raising his hand in a cautious greeting. "Hey, bro." His voice sounded rusty from disuse.

Cal sat silent, staring up with furious eyes.

Pete pinched the bridge of his nose, closing his eyes for a moment. Of course. The general disaster had lacked only this. "Hey, Erik." He sighed. "Long time, no see."

Chapter Eighteen

Janie stared curiously at Erik Toleffson. He looked taller than either of his brothers but less formidable in other ways, softer, less muscular. His face was worn, deep grooves running across his forehead and from his nose to the corners of his mouth. His thick dark hair was beginning to gray at the sides. He looked like he needed to sit down.

"What are you doing here, Erik?" Cal, usually the warmest, friendliest man she knew, sounded like an Albanian border guard.

Erik shrugged. "I came with Dad. He was supposed to tell you I was here, but then he got busy with other stuff. I guess he didn't let you know."

Cal flexed his hands on the table, gripping them into fists again. "No, he didn't." He still hadn't looked at Erik after that first startled stare.

"I think what Cal really wants to know is *why* you've come, Erik." Pete stared up at him.

Erik shrugged again. "I wanted to be here for my brother's wedding."

"Even if that brother didn't want you to come?" Cal finally raised his gaze to Erik's face. Janie felt like wincing. She'd never seen that much hostility in Cal's eyes before.

"Yeah, even then." Erik's shoulders slumped. "I'm in this twelve-step thing, have been for a while. One of the steps is to atone for things you've done in the past, people you've hurt. And that's you guys and Lars. More than anybody else in my life, I guess."

Cal closed his eyes, his shoulders stiff. "I don't know if I'm ready for that, Erik."

"I figured you might not be." Erik smiled slightly, looking more like a Toleffson than he had before. "I'll hang around anyway, in case you think you might be able to listen to me sometime." He nodded to Pete. "You too."

"Where are you staying?" Pete's voice sounded grudging, as if he really hated to ask.

"There's an extra room in the B&B Mom and Dad rented. I'm bunking there."

Pete blew out a breath. "Okay, Erik. We'll think about it."

"Good enough." Erik ambled toward the door without looking back.

As soon as he was gone, Cal slumped back against his chair. "Well, shit."

"I thought Dad was being a little cagey about something this morning. Didn't realize he was planning anything this big, though." Pete drew a french fry through his ketchup, then sat staring as it dripped onto his plate.

Docia returned to the table, beaming. "We got the judge—he can come to the winery and to the Woodrose." She slid into her chair. "So who was that standing at the table just now? I thought it was your dad, but it wasn't, was it?"

"Nope." Cal wrapped his sandwich in a napkin and handed Docia her burger basket. "C'mon. Let's see if Al will wrap this up for us. I'll explain everything on the way home."

Docia widened her eyes at Janie, then hurried after him. Janie glanced over at Pete.

He sat with his hands folded on the table, staring down at his half-eaten hamburger. "I need to take Olive out for a walk. You want to come?"

"Sure, we can talk about the wedding." Janie glanced at his set face. "Or not."

Pete's mouth twisted in a parody of a smile. "I vote for not."

At the apartment, Pete opened the door to a frantic Olive. "Hey, come on, I just took you out before dinner. You can't be desperate again."

Olive scrabbled her paws against his thighs, blinking her large black eyes as Pete rubbed her ears.

"She just missed you." Janie watched Olive lick his hand.

"Novel idea." He gave her another half smile. "I'm not used to anybody missing me."

I will. She clamped down on that particular thought very quickly. She absolutely wasn't going to go there. *Not yet, anyway.* She watched Pete clip the leash to Olive's collar.

"I guess you'd like to know what that was all about back there at the Coffee Corral." He herded Olive out into the darkening night.

She shrugged. "Only if you'd like to tell me."

"C'mon, Janie." His grin was somewhat lopsided, but still more of a grin than he'd shown before. "No more Ms. Nice, remember? You just saw a family meltdown. It's okay to be curious."

They walked back toward the residential streets, away from the lights of Main.

"So I guess Erik is your big brother, right?" She figured that was a neutral enough thing to ask.

He nodded. "He's two years older than I am."

"Two?" Janie thought of Erik's tired eyes and worn face. "He looks older than that."

Pete grimaced. "He's had a hard life. Most of it by his own choice."

"Y'all didn't get along."

"At least you didn't make that a question." He glanced at her again, his eyes bleak.

"He looks..." she searched for a word that wouldn't throw everything off, "...tired."

Pete stopped, turning to look at her. "Erik made our early lives a living hell. I spent a large part of my childhood either trying to get away from him or trying to keep him from beating up on Lars and Cal. Dad stepped in frequently. Mom did occasionally. Didn't help. Once we all got big enough to defend ourselves we managed to fight him off, but it took us a lot of years to do that."

He tugged on the leash to pull Olive away from the oleander she was examining.

"You don't think his twelve-step program will help?"

"I have no idea whether it'll help him or not. The question is, do I care?" He looked up the street, then crossed to the side with a sidewalk. "My mom has decided we all need to forgive and forget. She's all about family sticking together."

"You don't think that's a good idea?"

He shook his head, staring down at Olive as she trotted ahead. "I'm now going to tell you something that would cause my mother heart palpitations if she ever heard about it, but here goes. My parents had to get married. Mom was pregnant with Erik."

Janie blinked at him. "She told you this?"

"Christ no! Lars and I figured it out when we looked through her wedding book one day."

She frowned. "Why does that make her big on family?"

"My mom made a choice." He ran his fingers along a picket fence beside them. From the far end of the street, Janie could hear children whooping. "She left college to have Erik, and she never went back. She's an administrator at the nursing home in town, but she could have gone a lot farther than that if she hadn't dropped out."

"Maybe she's happy."

Pete shrugged. "I think she is. Pretty much. The point is, Mom made that sacrifice because she believed in having a family. And I don't think she'll be happy if that family doesn't hang together, including Erik and, God help us, Sherice."

Janie sighed. It sounded logical. Also highly unlikely.

"See, I think it also explains why Mom is so set on keeping Lars and Sherice together." He nudged Olive forward again when she showed a little too much interest in a rose bush. "From Mom's perspective, people are supposed to stay together no matter what. Marriages take work."

"They do actually. My mom and dad weren't the world's happiest, but they bumped along together pretty well. Probably because they both worked at it."

"Amazingly enough, so do mine." Pete started walking again. "I guess Dad is trying to get all of us brothers to reconcile too, but I don't think it's going to happen."

She trailed along behind him, staring at the first stars that peeked through the trees at the intersection. "I always wanted a sister or a brother. I thought that would be neat."

He gave her a dry grin. "I have one I can pass on to you, but I don't make any claims for his being much of an asset to your life."

"You protected them, didn't you? Lars and Cal," she said slowly.

"I tried." His mouth twisted. "I don't know how much good I was in the long run."

"You do that, Pete. You look after people."

Pete sighed. "You make me sound a little like Olive."

Janie walked along beside him in silence for a while until he put his arm around her shoulders, pulling her closer.

She looked up into the molasses depths of his eyes, then stopped. Pete frowned slightly. "Everything okay?"

"Everything's fine." She stood on tiptoes, running the tips of her fingers along the sides of his face, then sliding them into his hair. He stood still, watching her. Janie closed her eyes and brought her lips against his.

She tasted salt and French fries. And Pete. Her tongue moved carefully against his, rasping lightly. Somewhere in the back of her mind she could hear Otto. *Frigid. Icicle.* She wondered if she was doing this right.

Suddenly, Pete's arms locked around her waist pulling her tight against his body. The hard swell of his arousal fit at the V of her legs and she found herself lifting up to cover him more completely.

Pete groaned into her mouth.

Janie felt a sudden jolt of power. She'd done that. She had. She'd definitely done it right. *In your face, Otto.*

He pulled back to look down at her. "I don't mean to alarm you, but right now, more than anything, I want to take you back to the apartment and make love to you until you scream."

"Oh gosh," she whispered.

He watched her, his face creased with strain. She'd done that too.

"Yes," she said carefully, trying to get her heart rate back into the normal range. "I think that would be a very good idea."

Pete threw back his head and guffawed. "Oh, man, Janie Dupree, you are the sexiest Ms. Nice I have ever encountered."

Janie Dupree, Janie Dupree, Janie Dupree. Her name pulsed along his brain like a heartbeat. It alternated with another pulse that said "Hurry, hurry, hurry, *now!*"

Pete leaned over her, running his hands under her T-shirt, feeling satin skin, the jut of her shoulder blades beneath his fingers. He probably should have undressed her before he pushed her onto the bed, but there was that whole *hurry, hurry, hurry* thing.

Janie grinned up at him, then grasped the bottom of his T-shirt, pulling it up over his head. "I want you naked, Toleffson."

"Yes ma'am." Pete unsnapped his jeans and kicked off the rubber sandals he'd been wearing all day.

She started to unfasten her shorts, but he put a hand on her arm. "Nope, I like to do that."

Janie leaned back, watching him. One hand stroked lazily across his stomach. Pete took a deep breath.

Her bra today was bright red lace. He could see the dim outline of her areola through the interstices, and felt himself grow harder. He'd always been a sucker for lace and satin. And areolas.

He pinched her nipple, feeling it pebble between his fingers, then rubbed it against the soft, textured surface of the lace. Janie moaned faintly and Pete leaned down to take the nipple into his mouth.

His tongue rasped over the fabric as he sucked. Her body moved against him, arching slightly off the bed. He pulled back and blew gently.

Janie moaned again.

Pete's hands dropped to the waistband of her shorts, unfastening, unzipping as he pushed them down impatiently. Her panties matched her bra—red lace and silk.

Hurry, hurry, hurry started pulsing through his brain again.

He pressed his palm against her mons, covering her, rubbing his fingers across the silk that enveloped her folds. Janie pushed her hands up against his chest, hard, and Pete glanced down at her face.

"You're not naked." She licked her lips.

He looked down. He was wearing his jockeys and nothing else. "Sorry." He moved to pull them off.

Suddenly, he was falling over onto his back and Janie was straddling him, one knee on either side of his hips.

She looked like a pocket Amazon, maybe an Amazon mascot. No way would Janie Dupree ever look fierce, but she looked...formidable nonetheless.

Pete lay still, staring up at her—a conqueror elf. She leaned forward, bracing her hands against his chest, and then she leaned down very slowly and ran the tip of her tongue along his collarbone.

He exhaled fast, feeling his breath whoosh out from his lungs. *Not going to survive this. Going to love dying, though.* He had enough wit left to reach up and unfasten her bra in front, so that her lovely, luscious breasts swung free.

Janie slapped his hands lightly. "You're supposed to lie still for now."

"Got it," he croaked. "No hands."

She reached up and tossed the bra to the side, and Pete realized he could reach another degree of hard just by looking at her.

Janie leaned over him again, running her lips and tongue along the side of his throat, while her hands rubbed across his chest, grazing his nipples lightly with her palms.

Pete closed his eyes and tried to breathe. Clearly, he needed to pump some oxygen into his brain.

She lifted her hips and slid down his torso, her silk-covered crotch skimming lightly over his erection. "Holy Christ!" he gasped.

Janie looked back at him, eyes wide. "Is there a problem?"

"Panties," he panted. "Still wearing panties."

"Yes?" Janie said politely. Her eyes were sparkling.

He'd kill her. After he finished having hot, wild, sweaty sex with her. "Take them off," he managed to wheeze.

"Not yet." Her hands glided down his body from his chest to his abdomen to his...

"Holy shit," he gasped.

Janie wrapped one hand around the shaft of his cock, moving down lightly. Her other hand cupped his scrotum, her fingers sliding underneath.

Hurryhurryhurryhurry!

"Janie," he wheezed, "sweetheart..."

"Just a minute." She let go of him and he almost moaned in protest. Then she was leaning up, pulling her panties off.

She reached into the bedside table and pulled out a foil packet. Pete held out his hand.

Janie shook her head. "I'll put it on for you."

Pete covered her hand with his own. "Nope. At this point, speed is of the essence, believe me."

He sheathed himself as Janie watched him, smiling that faintly wicked smile that made his heart rate speed up again.

"Is there any hope you'll be gentle with me?"

"None." Janie grinned at him. "But you can always beg if you feel like it. Actually, that might be fun."

Pete stared up at her—her short black hair like feathers, her full curving lips, her wonderful breasts above the slight swell of her belly. God almighty, she was the most perfect thing he'd ever seen! How had he ever gotten so lucky? He was the least romantic member of the family, wasn't he?

Janie leaned forward again to brace her hands against his chest, then pushed herself up on her knees. She moved her hips carefully and then began to lower herself over his cock.

Pete exhaled quickly, trying not to choke. Her warmth and wetness sheathed the head, then slid slowly down, her muscles gripping him like a glove.

Gloves. Tuxedoes. Boutonnières. Think about the wedding. Think about the White Sox. Think about anything other than the wild swirl of sensations that had just hit his brain. "Oh, god."

Janie rose again, very slowly, then lowered herself again, equally slowly. If she didn't speed up soon, he'd be dead before she finished.

Not from old age, however.

"Janie," he gasped, "sweetheart, if you could just..."

She ignored him. Her expression was thoughtful, as if she were comparing the feeling of riding him slowly to his grave with some other feeling—eating artichokes, say. Her hips moved up and down unhurriedly and Pete decided she had more control than anyone he'd ever met.

Damn it!

He reached up and abruptly grabbed her hips, pulling her down, impaling her neatly on his cock. He jerked his hips back and then rose again, moving into her.

Into heat, into moisture, into what was beginning to feel like insanity.

Janie closed her eyes above him and began moving more quickly, her hands braced against his shoulders. Pete kept hold of her hips, his fingers digging into the soft roundness of her behind. He couldn't have let go if his life had depended on it, and he had a feeling it did.

Janie's hips thudded against his, her luminous brown eyes staring down. A delectable sexual athlete, good enough to eat.

Which he would, he figured, a little later in the evening.

"C'mon Janie," he crooned, "c'mon. Now!"

And she shattered, her head thrown back, eyes closed, hands braced against him. The wild spasm of her muscles around him sent him spiraling after her, shouting her name.

She collapsed against his chest, then slipped to his side, burrowing her face into his shoulder. Pete lay still trying to catch his breath. All of his previous experiences suddenly seemed irrelevant. This...*this*...was what sex was supposed to be like.

He wasn't sure how long they lay wrapped around each other like vines. He might even have fallen asleep for a few minutes, given how totally relaxed his body was.

"Pete?" Janie's voice sounded oddly tentative. He glanced at her. Her eyes were dark, glowing. "Was it okay?"

It took him a minute to process what she was saying, given that his brain really didn't want to function at all. "Okay?"

"What I did. Was it okay for you?"

Pete gave himself a quick mental shake. *What the hell was going on?* "Okay?"

"Did I make you happy?" She chewed on her lower lip, her expression serious.

He pulled her closer, surrounded by her warmth, her vibrancy. "Janie, you are a goddess. Yes, you made me happy. How can you doubt it?"

"I just...I don't have much experience with this, and I've been told..." She nibbled on her lip again. Her very full, very pink lower lip.

"Told what?" He managed to say before his body took over again. *Down, boy.* Geez, he felt like he was back in high school again.

"Implied I was sort of...well...cold." Janie looked like she was holding her breath.

Pete stared at her, as his brain finally worked its way through what she'd said. Cold? This warm bundle of passion and mischief cold? What idiot would think that?

Oh. "Otto." Pete made a vow to whip Otto Friedrich's ass with relish if he ever wandered within striking distance.

"He was mad at me," Janie ventured. "I might not have understood him exactly."

Jesus, she was apologizing for the benighted lummox. Pete blew out a breath. "Otto is a moron. You are a marvel. Allow me to demonstrate." Mr. Happy was definitely showing signs of life. Maybe if they did it two or three more times she'd be convinced. Or four or five. Pete gathered her into his arms and began to slide his tongue behind her ear.

He heard Janie giggle.

Janie lay beside Pete and watched him sleep. He was so beautiful—looking at him made her ache. His dark, curling hair tangled around his head on the pillow. His eyelashes and brows were dark slashes against his face.

She reached out to touch his cheek, the slight shadow of beard, then stopped herself. Hands off.

In more ways than one, of course. Whatever they had here was temporary. Looking for more would only get her hurt.

Sex. Concentrate on the sex. Not that doing that was much of a hardship.

But her mind kept drifting back to earlier. Walking with Olive through the warm summer night, Pete's voice in the darkness. It was all so—comfortable.

She bit her lip. Comfortable or not, everything was going to end in three days. She didn't know how much longer he was staying after that, but she knew his plans wouldn't involve her. Why should they? He barely knew her. She barely knew him. And she wasn't going to embarrass herself—or him—by expecting anything else out of this relationship.

So it only made sense for Janie to keep her distance, to make sure she didn't get too involved with someone who was going to take off.

Right. Which is why you're in bed with him right now.

Janie took a slow, shaky breath. She really hadn't meant for this to happen. In fact, a week ago she wouldn't have considered it possible. She was normally such a cautious person. So level-headed. So careful. She'd never intended things to go this far. Never intended to get her heart involved. Still, there was no denying the truth.

Pete Toleffson made her pulse speed up whenever she looked at him. He made her palms sweat. He made her want to dance naked in places where that would be a very bad idea, like

Main Street. He made her forget all about the things good girls did and didn't do.

He made her want to keep him.

She was in love with Pete Toleffson.

Well, damn!

Chapter Nineteen

Janie called her mother from Pete's kitchen early the next morning to ask her to open the Lucky Lady. She could have gone home to do it, but she was a coward. Besides, Pete had better cereal.

"You and Docia want to go to the Lucky Lady?" Mom sounded faintly confused. "But why? I thought you already had all your wedding clothes."

"We did, but now we don't," Janie said hurriedly. "Anyway, it could mean a big order. LuAnn would be pleased." LuAnn Gottfried owned the Lucky Lady, and given the amount of money she stood to make on the New, Improved Wedding, LuAnn was about to become pretty lucky herself.

Janie could almost hear Mom's mental gears grinding. She really wanted to know what was going on, but she wanted the commission on the sale almost as much. "All right." She sighed. "Can y'all be there by nine?"

"Yes ma'am, I'll let everyone know." Janie started to hang up as her mother spoke again.

"Janie?"

"Yes, Mom."

"Are you all right?" her mother asked softly.

Interesting question, Mom. "I'm fine. I'll see you in a little while."

Pete raised an eyebrow over his granola. "What was that all about?"

"Replacement wedding clothes. What are you guys going to do?"

He gave a disgusted snort. "Crap. We have to get more clothes, don't we?"

"Unless you want to have Lars drop out or appear in his birthday suit, yes, you do."

His brow furrowed. "What should we buy?"

"Something that goes with whatever we're wearing."

"Which would be?"

Janie gave him a guileless smile. "Currently, I'm thinking tutus and cowboy boots."

Pete's expression passed through confusion to apprehension and landed squarely on horror.

She grimaced. "Oh just deal, Pete, you're the best man. The hired gun, remember? I'll give you an update when we've figured something out, but you'll need to herd the groom and groomsmen back to Siemen's."

Docia, Allie and Bethany were all waiting outside the Lucky Lady when Janie arrived. Considering that she'd had to wake Docia up and pull Allie away from her breakfast customers, only Bethany looked particularly delighted to be there. Janie figured that was because she'd otherwise have been dealing with sick deer hounds.

"I'm putting you all on notice," Docia snarled. "If I can't find anything here, I'm wearing jeans."

Allie sighed. "Fine by me. I recommend chef pants myself. They cover a lot of sins and they don't show tear stains." She brushed a bit of flour off the crimson chili peppers running down the side of one pant leg as Janie's mother unlocked the door from the inside.

Mom was concentrating harder on the potential sale than on the details of the story, Janie was relieved to note. "We don't really have any formal wear right now," she burbled, "but we have some lovely suits that might work."

Docia wandered along the side of the room, running her fingers over the hanging dresses, frowning slightly. Janie felt like holding her breath.

Allie and Bethany fanned out to either side, holding up hangers. "I need a new denim skirt," Bethany mused, holding one up against her waist. She turned to Janie. "What do you think?"

"That's it!" Docia murmured. "Oh yes, definitely."

Bethany frowned. "Well, it's nice but I don't know for sure. And it's not for the wedding."

Janie turned to look at Docia. She was holding up a hanger. The dress flowed to Docia's ankles—flowered voile, golden brown sprinkled with petals in green, yellow, and orangey red. A deep flounce edged the bottom.

"Oh, well, it's lovely, but I don't...for a wedding? A bride's dress?" Mom was struggling between her sales instincts and her sense of propriety.

"For a wedding," Docia said. "*My* wedding." She stepped purposefully into a dressing room and shut the door.

Allie raised her eyebrows. "You think?"

Janie nodded. "Oh, yeah. Let's see what matches."

Mom was pulling hangers off the racks. "Well, what are you looking for. More flowers?"

Janie shuddered. "Nope. No flowers. Solids."

"This," Allie declared. She held up a loose column of linen. "A shift. Straight sides. V-neck. Loose waist. And we can each grab a different color in our respective sizes, right Mrs. Dupree?"

Mom nodded, taking a deep breath. "Absolutely."

"Great." Allie began rummaging along the rack, looking for her size. "Let's try these suckers on. I've got bread to bake."

Ten minutes later the three of them stood staring into the three-way mirror. Pastel linen wasn't nearly as breathtaking as satin, but they actually didn't look too bad.

Mom smiled. "Y'all look lovely."

"As do I." Docia stepped out of the dressing room. The voile wrapped lightly around her bosom then dropped to a deep flounce at her ankles. Flowers rioted across her body.

She looked terrific.

Janie grinned. "Oh Docia, it's actually going to work, isn't it?"

"You bet, toots." Docia studied herself in the mirror. "Let's go for it."

Siemen wasn't particularly upset about Lars's shredded tux, but then again he was getting paid for it. Cal, Pete and Lars stared glumly at the clothing racks. Daisy was busy charming Siemen's sales staff.

"Why do we need new clothes?" Lars raised an eyebrow. "Why can't we just wear something we've already got?"

"I think we have to match." Cal sighed.

"Match?" Lars raised an eyebrow. "We're going to look like a boy band."

"We already did. Just a very formal boy band."

Pete took a breath. "What about Erik?"

Cal's grin faded. "Erik's not part of the wedding."

"Is he invited?" Lars moved to catch Daisy as she started to climb into the window with the manikins.

Cal shrugged. "I haven't decided yet."

Pete wandered around the shop, poking at hangers. He hated shopping. Nothing ever fit, and he always looked like the Hulk in mid-transition. Once he found something that actually worked on his body, he tended to buy in multiples.

He paused. Multiples.

"Blue blazers," he muttered.

"Excuse me?" Cal folded his arms across his chest.

"Blue blazers. Navy. You've got one, right?"

Cal frowned, thinking. "Yeah. Actually, I've got a couple, I think."

"I've got at least that many. And I brought one with me. Lars?"

Lars shrugged. "I don't know. I've never counted. Every man in the country has a blue blazer, and I might have brought mine along, too. So what?"

"So Wonder and Horace probably each have one of their own."

"Right." Cal stood. "Blue blazers and khakis. The national male uniform. Gentlemen, we have our boy band."

"Yep." Pete grinned for the first time since they'd entered Siemen's.

"Shirts." Lars was frowning.

"Blue Oxford cloth." Siemen began pulling shirts off the rack. "You want something everybody's got, that's it. And if you don't, I do. In every size."

Lars removed Daisy from a bin of plastic hangers before she could become too entangled. "So what else do we need? Socks? Shoes?"

"Ties." Cal began flipping through the rack. "We each need a new tie. One that matches."

"Right." Pete stood at his elbow. "I suppose Bugs Bunny is out."

Cal made a disgusted sound. "This is my wedding, damn it!"

"Dignity. Right. Definitely Elmer Fudd. Oh, man, look—Siemen's got one with the Tasmanian Devil!"

Cal put a hand on Pete's chest and pushed him away. "Hell, Daisy would be more helpful."

"Okay, you asked for it." Lars slung Daisy under one arm and carried her to the tie rack. "Okay, Dais, which one do you like?"

Daisy stared down at the rack and smiled beatifically. "Da!" she cried, reaching for a bright red tie with gold stripes.

Cal nodded, moving the tie out of her reach. "Looks like the Iowa State colors. Da it is."

Lars grinned. "Speak for yourself, bro. As a U. of Iowa man, I'll find my own."

By the time the rehearsal started, Janie had decided that maybe the whole wedding train wreck had turned around. They'd had almost ten disaster-free hours—a record. Maybe the fates didn't suck after all.

Morgan had dragooned some of the vineyard workers into rearranging the patio chairs to create a small wedding space at the far end, shaded by some ancient live oaks and a trellis with some grape vines. Reba had rallied enough to start decorating again, stringing swags of chiffon along the aisles between the folding chairs she'd brought over from the Woodrose. "I'll get some flowers over here tomorrow," she told Janie. "I don't want them to sit out in this heat until morning."

She and the judge worked out the details of the ceremony while Lars kept Daisy from trying to ride Olive, who hid under the chairs.

Asa and Millie Toleffson sat at the back watching the chaos beneficently—at least in Asa's case. Millie looked glum, as usual, but she also looked a little nervous. Janie wondered if she was worried about the wedding coming off. More likely she was worried about Erik Toleffson, who sat on her other side. His brothers hadn't exactly ignored him, but they hadn't said much to him either.

Erik wore sunglasses in the late afternoon glare, the dark lenses hiding his eyes. The sunlight made his face look weathered, deepening the lines around his mouth. He sat silently beside his mother and stared at the vineyards. Janie thought he was trying not to draw attention to himself.

Docia glowed. She wore jeans and a denim shirt knotted under her breasts, with an expanse of alabaster skin showing above her waist band. Cal kept one hand planted at the small of her back, as if he couldn't bear to stop touching her.

Whenever Janie looked at them, a tightness began in her throat and a prickling in her eyes that threatened to turn into tears. She told herself repeatedly that being envious of her best friend was not an attractive trait. It didn't help. Docia had found her prince. Janie just hoped it wasn't one to a customer, at least in her case.

Pete laughed with Horace over something the judge had said. Janie took a moment to study him. His dark, curling hair was like his brothers—all three of them, now that she'd seen Erik. But his jaw was different, more square. And his eyes. Cal had the kindest eyes. Lars's eyes were always laughing, now that he'd found Daisy. Erik's eyes were watchful. Pete's eyes were... She tried to think. Pete's eyes were strong. Steady. Whatever was wrong, Pete would do something about it. Whoever was hurting, Pete would be there to help.

A protector. A guardian. Janie watched him reach over to free Olive from a grape vine. Was that how he saw her? Another stray pup who needed to be looked after? To be rescued?

Well, he *had* rescued her, in a way. Two nights in Pete's bed had cured her of settling for anything less. No more Otto Friedrichs for her, no matter what Mom thought.

Unfortunately, no more Pete Toleffsons either. Not after tomorrow. Janie had no illusions about the likelihood of his staying. He hadn't made any promises, after all. And she wasn't going to demand any.

And really, that was perfectly okay. She didn't hold it against him—it wasn't his fault she'd fallen for him. She'd just have to get over it. Move on. She had a life to build on her own now.

Pete looked up, his dark eyes meeting hers across the stone-covered patio. One corner of his mouth inched up in a crooked smile. A quick tremble of goose flesh moved along Janie's arms. Get over it. *Yeah, right.*

"Okay, let's get this shindig started," the judge called.

Reba gestured from the end of the aisle. "Wedding party back here, please."

Janie trooped along after Allie and Bethany, keeping her head down. Maybe if she didn't look directly at Pete, she wouldn't be distracted.

"Line up, now," Reba called, "boys and girls. And Lars." Her mouth flattened slightly as she contemplated the uneven numbers.

"I've got my partner." Lars swept Daisy up into his arms again, as much to keep her from stampeding after the winery cat as to walk down the aisle with her.

Reba gave him a long-suffering look. "Fine. We're going to use recorded music for now, but we'll have the string quartet tomorrow. Just walk down the aisle together in time to the music."

A recording of Handel began to play over the loudspeaker, and Pete put his hand on her arm. "Shall we?"

She took a deep breath and looked up at him. *You can do this.* "Let's."

The judge was a comedian. Pete had been through that enough times in his life—laughing at judges' jokes even when they weren't funny. Fortunately, these jokes weren't all that bad.

The judge also made a couple of oblique references to the local county attorney and his need for good staff. Pete had given him a version of his Idiot Smile and pretended he didn't know what he was talking about. He already had a job, didn't he? A job he'd be going back to when all of this was over. So what if he had a hollow feeling in his gut whenever he thought about Des Moines.

Beside him, Janie seemed to vibrate with life and passion. Pete tried to concentrate on his best man duties, such as they were. Just being next to her was giving him a contact high.

The judge made a joke about losing the ring, and Pete was jerked back into the wedding again. Was he supposed to be carrying a ring right now? Something from Crackerjacks maybe? He patted his pockets surreptitiously.

Cal put his hand on Pete's arm. "Don't sweat it. I haven't given it to you yet."

"Oh." Pete nodded. "Well, good."

Janie looked up at him with a faint smile. She probably thought he was a halfwit.

He wondered if he could lure her back to the apartment again tonight. Of course, her mother might come looking for him with a shotgun and a quick jaunt to the justice of the peace if he did.

Would that be so bad?

A quick jolt of adrenaline sped through his system. *Later.* He'd think about all that later. Right now he had a wedding to get through. Cal's wedding.

"Okay, after I pronounce you husband and wife, you all recess back up the aisle." The judge grinned at them.

Docia stuck out her lower lip in a pout. "What, no kiss?"

"Sure, yeah, of course. I just figured we'd skip it for now."

"Skip my favorite part?" Cal wrapped his arms around Docia and bent her over backward in an enthusiastic kiss that made her lift one foot off the ground.

"Looks good to me." Horace pulled Bethany into his arms.

Wonder stood blinking at Allie for a moment, then bent his head and pressed a somewhat decorous kiss on her lips.

Janie looked up at Pete expectantly. *Holy crap!* He stared down at her full pink lips, remembering what they'd felt like on other parts of his body. He probably shouldn't kiss her. If he did, he had a feeling he wouldn't stop there. He reached for her hand, pulling her gently toward him. She raised laughing eyes to his.

"Ma!" screeched Daisy.

"Shit!" Lars muttered.

Pete stopped inches from Janie's lips. It took all the control he had to raise his head. Even then, he couldn't bring himself to let her go.

Sherice stood at the end of the aisle watching them.

Daisy wriggled desperately in Lars's arms. "Ma!" she yelled again.

After a moment, Sherice began undulating toward them, smiling a faintly bored smile. "Hi, baby," she cooed, "come over here to me." She extended her arms.

Lars slowly lowered his daughter to the ground and then watched her toddle into her mother's embrace.

Sherice lifted the child, pushing her black curls back from her eyes. "Ooh, you've gained weight, baby. Daddy must have been feeding you junk. We don't want you to get fat now, do we?"

She fixed Lars with a quick, dead-eyed stare, then turned and began walking back up the aisle again, much more quickly. "You better have dinner with me tonight, baby. Mama will make sure you get the right food. And a nice place to sleep."

"Goddamn it, Sherice," Lars growled.

"Watch your language in front of the baby," Sherice said automatically. "She's coming home with me, Lars. I'm her mother. You don't really want to make a scene with me, do you? You'll frighten the baby."

Pete was suddenly aware of Mom standing at the end of the aisle. "But Sherice, you're staying for the wedding. You promised." She reached tentatively toward Daisy, who stared at her wide-eyed.

"Don't be ridiculous," Sherice snapped. "Babies don't belong at weddings. And I'm going home."

"But you said..." Mom's eyes darted between Sherice and Lars.

"Whatever I said, Daisy's not staying and neither am I." Sherice turned toward the parking lot.

Pete was beside her in three strides. He took hold of her arm, his fingers clamping like a vice. "Put my niece down."

Sherice stared at him. "You can't stop me. She's my daughter. You're just her uncle."

"Put her down, damn it." Pete worked on keeping his voice level.

Daisy began to whimper. "Daisy," Lars murmured from behind him, "sweetheart."

The whimpers rapidly became sobs and then wails. Sherice glanced down at Pete's hand and then back up again. She tightened her hold on her daughter.

"Daisy, honey." Lars was standing beside her now. He reached out to stroke his daughter's hair. "Don't cry. It's all right."

Daisy dropped her head to Sherice's shoulder, staring at her father as she caught her breath in ragged sobs.

"Let her go, Pete," Lars said.

"Lars..." Rage closed his throat.

"No, Pete, just let her go."

Slowly, regretfully, Pete dropped his hand. Sherice gave him one last look of searing contempt, then turned back toward the parking lot.

"Lars." Mom stared at them, her lips trembling. "I thought...she said... She just wanted to see Daisy, that's all."

"It's okay, Mom." Lars sighed.

"I didn't...I never meant..."

"I know." Lars patted her shoulder awkwardly. "It's okay."

Beside her, Dad took a deep breath. "Come on, Millie, this is our fault. We've got to fix this."

"Let it go, Dad." Lars straightened. "It's my problem. I'll take care of it. All of you go on to the rehearsal dinner."

The wedding party milled around them uneasily. Cal held Docia against him as if he was afraid she might bolt.

"Go on," Lars said again. "I'll come later." He walked toward the parking lot where Sherice was loading Daisy into a car seat.

Pete sat on one of the chairs, pushing aside a swag of chiffon. All the others began to move toward their cars, Cal pushing Docia a little doggedly. Pete stared down at the weathered Saltillo tile beneath his running shoes. A pair of paws clicked into view.

Pete blinked, then looked up. Janie stood holding Olive's leash. "Do you want to drive," she asked, "or should I?"

"That's okay." He reached for Olive's leash. "Go on ahead. I'll catch up later."

Janie stood watching him for a moment, then sat on another chair beside him. "You couldn't have done anything."

Pete stiffened. "That's not the point."

"What is?" She reached down to scratch Olive's ears.

He sat silent for a few moments, then shrugged. "I don't know exactly. I just feel like shit."

"Lars is the only one who can deal with this. My guess is he will."

He stared out at the rows of grapevines climbing the hillsides. "You know my mother told her we'd be here. That's the only way she could have found out."

"Yeah. And now your mother feels awful about it. So maybe she'll stop trying to bring them back together again."

"There is that." Pete squinted in the late afternoon sun. "The whole thing's heading south again, isn't it?"

Janie shrugged. "Not a problem. We'll just work another miracle, now that we know how it's done. Olive and I are ready to go."

"Bag of tricks is about empty, ma'am. And no more walks with Olive. I'm supposed to take her over to Armando at the clinic early tomorrow."

Janie stood, handing him Olive's leash. "Come on, Mr. Toleffson. You've got a rehearsal dinner to host."

As he pushed himself up beside her, he felt his cell phone vibrate. He flipped it open, frowning. Claire Larkin. He nodded to Janie. "Go on ahead. I'll catch up."

She grimaced, then took Olive's leash again and headed for the parking lot.

Pete pressed the accept button. "Yeah, Claire."

"Mr. Toleffson?" Claire's voice sounded slightly breathy. "There's a sort of...problem. Bo Amundson's been released."

Chapter Twenty

The rehearsal dinner was in the same room at Brenner's where Reba and Billy had hosted the first wedding get-together a week ago. Pete paused, counting backward. Yeah, impossible as it seemed, it had only been a week.

Cal and Docia sat on the raised stone hearth in front of the massive fireplace, their heads together, whispering. Reba sat next to Billy at the side, looking slightly pole-axed. The other guests—Wonder, Allie, Horace, Bethany, the judge and some people Pete figured were behind the scenes types—milled around the room.

He was thirty minutes late. The only reason he wasn't forty-five minutes late was that he'd run out of people to call. Evan wasn't answering, which probably meant he was at Lake Panorama for a weekend of booze and bimbos. The detective who'd arrested Amundson was on vacation, as was the judge from the arraignment, as was Pete.

Which explained why Amundson's lawyer had been able to slide the request for bail through so easily—nobody had been around to stop him, or to notify Claire Larkin until after the fact.

Pete rubbed his chest absently, trying to ease the dull ache behind his breastbone. Stopping Amundson before he walked was a lost cause. Now they had to find his wife, Maureen, before he did, which was what Claire Larkin was currently trying to do, using a list of possibilities Pete had given her from memory.

He paused in the doorway, staring.

Erik was talking to Lee Contreras, motioning toward the table in the center of the room.

Pete stepped up quickly. "What's going on?"

Erik shrugged. "Mom and Dad went off after Lars. Mom told me to get things started. They'll be back."

Pete's jaw tightened. "I'll do this."

"Okay. Whatever." Erik stepped back, his face blank.

Lee gave Pete a professional smile. "It's all been arranged. I was just telling your brother—we'll bring the food in whenever you want it."

"Bring it in now." Pete sighed. "Did Dad remember to order any alcohol?"

"Wine with dinner." Lee gestured toward the bar at the back. "We can start it now."

"Do that. Sooner the better."

"Soda for me," Erik said.

Pete glanced at him curiously. Erik gave him a bleak smile. "Three hundred days and counting."

Pete nodded, then glanced at his phone. Nothing. No calls. No messages.

Janie had joined Docia on the hearth as Pete started back across the room. Cal stopped him with a hand on his shoulder. "Are we going ahead with this?"

"With dinner? Sure. Dad and Mom have it all set up and they're supposed to be back soon." He gave Cal a reassuring smile that almost hurt his lips.

Cal shook his head. "You suck at deception."

"What do you want me to say? They're chasing Lars and Sherice and Daisy. They'll be back when they get back. My guess is Mom's suffering from a belated attack of guilt."

"Belated is right." Cal glanced at Erik, his jaw hardening. "Is he staying?"

"Yeah, Mom asked him to hold down the fort until they get here."

Cal sighed. "Train wreck."

"Is Docia talking Vegas again?" Pete looked back at Janie, hovering on the hearthstone beside Docia. Her smile was a little too bright all of a sudden.

"Nah. Not with the wedding of her dreams set for tomorrow." Cal looked back at his bride-to-be and grinned. "Better go rescue Janie, though. She's tap-dancing so fast she's going to hurt herself."

As Pete started back across the room, Ken Crowder handed him two glasses of wine. "Viognier. From Morgan Barrett's vineyard. I've got more coming."

"Right." Pete nodded. "I have a feeling this had better be a very alcoholic evening." He glanced back a little guiltily.

Erik leaned against the table, a glass of soda and ice at hand. He shook his head. "Don't worry about it. If the booze starts to bother me, I'll leave."

Pete nodded a little stiffly, then walked to the fireplace and handed a glass to Janie. "If you keep smiling like that your face will freeze in that position."

Janie turned her glittering grin in his direction. "It already has."

"I've been trying to convince her she doesn't need to cheer me up." Docia took another glass of wine from Cal. "I'm okay, Janie, I'm not going to run for the border, honest."

Cal grimaced. "Lars is the one who should be running. With Daisy under one arm."

"Can she really do that, take Daisy away without Lars's consent?" All three of them turned to stare at Pete.

He raised his hands. "I don't do family law and I'm not licensed in Texas."

Janie put a hand on his arm, staring toward the door. "Oh my god. It's your folks. And they've got Daisy."

Pete turned back and caught his breath. His dad had stopped in the doorway to say something to Lee. His mom was walking across the room, carrying Daisy in her arms. She didn't look exactly happy about it, but she didn't look unhappy either. Just sort of...Mom.

He hurried toward her, and she glanced up at him as he approached. "Peter, good, I need your help." She shifted Daisy to her other arm. "See if you can find Daisy some mashed potatoes or some peas. Maybe a banana. Something I can puree for her."

"A banana?" Pete envisioned himself wandering around Brenner's kitchen, looking for overcooked vegetables. "Now?"

"I'll do it." Erik stood, placing his soda on the table next to the door. "I'll go talk to the manager. They'll probably have something."

He was gone before Pete could say anything. His mother gave him an annoyed look. "Erik had never even met Daisy, you know. Her own uncle."

"Well, she's got a lot of uncles to go around." Pete smiled at Daisy, who pulled back from him, thrusting out her lower lip.

Pete sighed. "Where's Lars?"

"Still talking to Sherice, I imagine." Mom's lips firmed. "Running away with a child like that. I don't know what got into her. Disgraceful."

Dad appeared behind them, holding two glasses of wine. "Here, Millie, drink up. There's more where that came from." He gave Pete one of his calmly beatific smiles. What was one more crisis after thirty-plus years of them?

Pete kept his expression carefully bland. "So Sherice let you bring Daisy back to the rehearsal dinner?"

"Let me? She put the child down." All of a sudden his mother's voice was trembling. "Daisy was crying, and Sherice just put her down on a picnic table. Like she was some kind of package that had got too heavy to hold. I picked her up."

Dad reached out to pat her shoulder, giving Pete a narrow-eyed look, but Mom had just gotten started. Her chin rose to a dangerous angle. "Daisy's staying right here with us. Just let her try and stop me. Daisy wants to go to the wedding, don't you, sweetheart."

"Ma!" Daisy crowed at her.

Pete's mouth dropped open, but he shut it quickly. "Right. Would you like some food, Mom?"

"If you please. You can hold Daisy."

Daisy's lower lip began to tremble as she looked at him. Clearly, Pete was not her uncle of choice at the moment.

"I'll take her." Cal swept her up into his arms. "Come on, sweetie, you can come drool on Aunt Docia."

"Da!" Daisy agreed.

Pete watched them go. "Is she always going to think I'm a monster after that scene with Sherice?"

"Don't be ridiculous." His mother sighed. "I need more wine too."

Pete took a bottle of viognier and poured her a healthy amount. "So you picked Daisy up. Then what happened?"

Mom sipped her wine and then pursed her lips. "I like the wine I get at home in a box better than this, but I suppose it's okay. Yes, I picked her up, and your father and I left."

"Sherice didn't object?"

Dad grimaced. "Sherice was too busy telling Lars how much money she expected him to give her for the privilege of divorcing her. I don't think she noticed we'd taken Daisy with us."

"She wasn't paying any attention to Daisy at all." Mom took another sip, this time without the pursing. Her voice trembled again. "I think she'd forgotten all about that child, except as a bargaining chip."

Pete took a sip of his own wine. Unlike Mom, he felt no urge to pour himself something out of a box. "So does this mean you're not trying to get Lars and Sherice to stay together?"

Mom stared down her glass, her gray eyes bleak. "It's better if parents stay together, Peter. Usually, that is. But Sherice isn't a good mother for Daisy, and I don't think she's good enough for Lars either. I never did, you know. I just pretended. For Lars's sake."

Pete couldn't resist. "So what do you think about Docia?"

Dad looked like he was holding his breath. Mom sipped and shrugged. "She seems nice enough. At least she's not after his money."

"Definitely," Pete agreed, watching Billy Kent bring Reba a glass of wine, "since she has tons and he doesn't have any."

"He does quite well." His mother straightened her shoulders. "He has a very successful practice. Your father and I are both proud of him. As we are of all of you. Except..." She turned to look at him again. "You need to get married and settle down, Peter. And find a new job. That Polk County Attorney's Office has wrung you dry. It's time you found a job that didn't make you sick."

Pete's mouth opened and closed soundlessly. He felt a little like a guppy. "I'll think about it," he croaked finally, then took a deep breath. "What do you think of Janie Dupree?"

Dad squinted across the room, studying Janie. "She's lovely. And a very sweet girl."

Mom nodded. "You could do a lot worse. And you have, as I recall."

Pete blew out a quick breath. "Yes, ma'am."

Mom patted his hand, absently. "You're a good boy. Now go find us some food."

Lee and his waiter were laying out a buffet on a table by the wall—cheeses and breads, fish, ham, turkey and grilled vegetables for Cal.

"How about that?" Cal grinned. "For once, Mom isn't trying to turn me into a carnivore."

"Mom is...a revelation." Pete began filling a plate. "Where's Daisy?"

"Playing peek-a-boo with Docia." Cal gestured at the fireplace where Docia and Janie were taking turns making Daisy laugh. "So where's Lars?"

"With any luck, putting Sherice on a fast plane to Des Moines. But I wouldn't count on it."

Wonder appeared at Cal's elbow, plate in hand. "Thank god! I was afraid all this drama was going to put me off my feed. Clearly, it hasn't."

"Clearly." Cal grinned at him too. "We all know the perils of putting you off your feed."

"Indeed." Allie slipped her arm into Wonder's. "Come on, gents, let's eat!"

The bridesmaids took charge of Daisy, although Pete wasn't entirely sure how it happened. One moment Daisy had been his mother's problem, the next moment she'd moved onto Bethany's lap and Allie was playing pat-a-cake, for which, as a baker, she had a natural flair.

Mom sat at a table with Reba and Billy. She was actually smiling for a change, but Pete wasn't sure how long that would last. Probably until she bit into Lee's take on potato salad—with anchovies.

He pulled his cell off his belt and checked the voice mail again. Nothing. Not even a text. What the hell was Claire Larkin doing?

A bowl of mashed potatoes and something that looked like squash had magically appeared on the table near Daisy. Erik dropped it and moved back quickly, as if he thought she might bite. However, the only uncle she was apparently interested in gnawing on was Pete, who provoked incipient tears every time he walked into her line of sight.

Pete felt close to tears himself. "Come on, Dais," he pleaded with her after he'd brought her a brownie. "I'm the one who taught you how to wade in the creek, remember?"

Daisy gave him an uncertain look, then stuck out her lower lip in protest.

"Come on, Daisy. You used to like me."

"Daisy!" Lars stood in the doorway, smiling at her. "Stop torturing your Uncle Pete."

"Da!" Daisy shrieked, wriggling off Docia's lap.

Allie sighed, watching her totter across the room to her father. "I want one of those."

A moment of profound silence spread while everyone avoided looking at Wonder.

"Better watch yourself, Doc." Horace grinned in Wonder's direction.

"Nonsense," Docia said crisply. "We all want one of those. I just want a guarantee that they'll be as cute as she is."

"I'll see what I can do," Cal murmured, nuzzling her ear.

Lars slid into a chair next to Pete. "Food." He sighed. "And drink. Mostly drink."

Pete passed him a bottle of syrah. They'd moved on to the reds, and it looked like there was a lot more where they came from. "Glad you could make it."

"Me too." Lars loaded up his plate with protein. "And no, I did not bring my wife back with me. I hope nobody's disappointed."

"I'm pretty sure we'll all bear up." Pete took the bottle from Lars and poured himself a glass. "So where is she?"

Lars took a large swallow of wine, then leaned back in his chair. "Headed back to Iowa, I trust. I figure she wants to get there before I do so that she can liquidate every asset she can get her hot little hands on. Fortunately, she can't empty out the bank accounts." He sighed. "I think I can guarantee I've got a really hellish year ahead of me."

"I know some divorce lawyers who could probably declaw her. I can give you a list." Pete handed him a plate of cheese and olives.

Lars shook his head. "I'll give her anything she wants, as long as she gives me Daisy. That's the only non-negotiable part of this debacle."

Pete sighed. "Lars, you don't have to cave."

"No, bro." Lars took another deep swallow of syrah. "I don't care about any of the rest of it, so help me. If she'll sign off on Daisy she can have the house and the cars."

"And you'll live where? With the folks?" Pete glanced at Daisy, currently giggling on Allie's lap.

Lars blew out a breath, staring at the metal star hanging over the fireplace. "To tell you the truth, I was sort of thinking about here."

"Here?" Pete blinked at him. "You mean Texas?"

"Right." Lars gave him a slightly lopsided grin. "I assume they need accountants in Texas. Even in Konigsburg. Is that so shocking?"

Pete frowned, watching the bridesmaids fuss over Daisy. The shocking thing was—the thought wasn't shocking at all. In fact, living in Konigsburg sounded almost, well, nice.

Sighing, he picked up his cell to check his messages again.

Janie told herself she wasn't tipsy. She did feel remarkably relaxed and good natured, but that was perfectly normal. She hadn't counted the glasses of wine she'd drunk, but she was sure they weren't that many.

She looked around the room. Cal, Lars and Pete stood in front of the fireplace, talking earnestly. Their parents were sitting with Reba and Billy in a slightly stiff version of friendliness. Other guests moved around the room talking. The whole thing was very pleasant, in a sort of waiting-for-the-other-shoe-to-drop kind of way.

Docia pushed a large, very gooey brownie in her direction. "Here, toots, have something to eat. You didn't even have the grilled veggies."

"I did eat something." Janie paused, considering. "Didn't I? I must have."

"Brownies," Docia repeated. "The staff of life."

Janie took a bite of brownie and suddenly felt very good natured indeed. "God, Docia, we're almost through with this."

Docia rapped her knuckles on the table. "Don't even mention getting through it, Janie, I swear. Did you check the weather forecast? Are we due for a tsunami?"

"All the weather web sites say it's clear sailing." She patted Docia's hand a little clumsily. "It'll be all right, I promise."

Docia sighed. "Janie, you are not responsible for the success of this wedding. Or its failure. You've been a good soldier, but now it's time to let up a little. Have some fun."

"I've already had fun," Janie mumbled, glancing unwillingly

at Pete where he leaned against the fireplace with his brothers, looking at his cell again.

Docia followed her glance, her eyes softening. "He's a nice guy, Pete Toleffson. He tried his best to be a jerk at the beginning, but it just didn't work for him."

"No," Janie agreed. "It wouldn't."

"Too bad he's not from around here. Not that he won't be back to visit." Docia gave Janie a faintly guilty look. "I mean he and Cal are close. But, well, you know. He's got his county attorney job back in Iowa. And he's really conscientious about it, according to Cal. Maybe a little too conscientious."

"It's okay, Docia, I know he's not going to stick around here." Janie managed to give her something that resembled a calm smile. "I'm okay with it."

"Yeah, right." Docia narrowed her eyes. "You suck at deception."

"What do you want me to say? Whether I'm okay with it or not, he's still going to leave. I might as well try to make the best of it."

Docia shook her head. "When I get back from the honeymoon, I'm going to work on this, finding a way to get you hooked up with somebody who deserves a girl like you. This is, of course, assuming we don't run into some new disaster tomorrow that screws up the honeymoon."

"Docia, for heaven's sake!" Janie rapped her knuckles on the table. "Don't even think about any more disasters, okay?"

"More disasters?" Cal pulled Docia to her feet. "Come on, I'm taking you home. Clearly, you've had enough wine for the evening."

"Oh, no, not yet," Docia protested. "I haven't had a chance to talk to Lee and Ken to make sure they're all straight about tomorrow."

Cal sighed. "Okay, let's do it now and then wander on. We've got a wedding tomorrow morning."

"That's right." Docia frowned. "I'll have to stay with Mama tonight, I guess."

Cal stared at her. "Your mother? Why would you stay with your mother?"

"You're not supposed to see me before the wedding, Calthorpe," Docia explained patiently.

"But that's not until tomorrow. Why can't I see you tonight?" Cal looked stricken.

"Oh, guts up!" Docia grinned at him. "It's only one night." She headed toward the doorway and Lee.

Cal stared after her. "Disaster," he groaned. "I should have known."

Janie gathered her purse and slid her shoes back on. Pete stood in a corner, talking into his cell. She considered going up to him for a moment, then rejected it. After all, she'd just told Docia she was making the best of things. Maybe that meant putting some distance between the two of them now, before she had to say goodbye to him tomorrow. Or the next day. Or the next.

The one thing that was certain was that she'd say goodbye to him eventually. So maybe it was time to be a grown-up. After all, putting pain off didn't make it any better.

Or something like that.

She walked slowly toward the entrance, hoping against hope that Pete would notice her leaving and come after her. At the door she turned one last time. His back was toward her as he leaned into a corner, talking on his phone. Janie bit her lip.

God, Janie, you are pathetic. She squared her shoulders and walked out the door to the parking lot.

Outside, she stood by her car trying to decide whether to drive or not. She really hadn't had all that much to drink, but it would be truly embarrassing to be picked up for DUI the day before the wedding. Lee wouldn't care if she left her car here for now.

She turned and started walking toward Main.

"Janie?" a man called from the darkness.

She knew who the man was before she saw him, and for a moment she thought about walking on without saying anything to him. But he'd probably just follow her.

"What is it, Otto?"

"Eating dinner with the swells?" Otto sneered.

Janie turned to look at him, keeping her expression neutral. "This was the rehearsal dinner. The wedding's tomorrow."

Otto looked even worse than he had the last time she'd seen him. His hair needed brushing, and he hadn't shaved for a while. He was wearing jeans and a T-shirt instead of his usual polo shirt and khakis. He stepped closer, and Janie smelled stale beer.

She was suddenly absolutely sober. "I need to get home. I have to get up early in the morning. Good night, Otto."

"Good girl." Otto reached toward her, sliding his finger along the inside edge of her collar. "You're always such a good girl."

Janie pulled back from him slightly. She wasn't afraid of him. He was just Otto, for god's sake.

He stepped closer again, his hand closing around her upper arm. "What'll you do when this is all over, Janie? When they all take off again. When he goes back home to wherever it is he comes from."

She stood very still, keeping her breathing even. "I need to go home now, Otto. Let go of my arm."

He leaned over her. His breath, hot and faintly moist, fanned against her cheek. She smelled the cigarette smoke on his clothes. "You wouldn't do it with me, but you'll do it with him. What does that make you, Janie? How about a kiss for old time's sake? Or are you too good for that now? How about more than that? Maybe I could show you a few things he can't."

"I think you should let the lady go," a man said from the doorway. He stepped forward into the lot. "Since that's what she wants."

Janie stared up at his silhouette against the parking lot lights. At first, she thought the man was Pete, but the body wasn't quite right.

"Who the hell are you?" Otto growled.

"I'm Erik Toleffson," Erik said quietly, "and I believe the lady asked you to let her go."

Otto blinked at him. "*Erik* Toleffson? Never heard of you."

Erik's mouth moved into the ghost of a smile. "I'm the one they don't talk about."

"Well, stay the hell out of my way, Erik Toleffson," Otto snarled. "You've got no business here. This is my girl and I'll hold onto her if I want to. We got stuff to talk about that doesn't concern you."

Erik turned to Janie. "Ms. Dupree, would you like to go back inside?"

Janie swallowed. "I think I would, yes."

"Let her go." Erik's silhouette seemed much bigger all of a sudden.

Otto dropped her arm, then took two steps toward Erik. "Look, asshole, I told you to butt out! Goddamn Yankees coming down here from goddamn Yankeeland. Texas for Texans!"

Janie snorted. "Oh for heaven's sake, Otto, your folks moved down here from Indiana when you were in middle school. I remember."

But Otto had apparently reached his limit. He swung a fist toward Erik's face.

A couple of things happened at once. The door swung open behind them and Janie was suddenly aware of people standing in the entrance. Erik moved back easily, and Otto's fist swung by his face, missing him by several inches.

"Oh for Christ's sake, Friedrich, not again. Knock it off!" The voice sounded like Horace. The people at the door started to move toward them.

Otto swung again, and Erik ducked again. "I'm going to give you one last chance here," he said. "Walk away now, and you won't get hurt."

"Fuck you. I'm not the one who'll be getting hurt." Otto swung one last time.

Erik ducked under the punch and brought his knee up squarely and very hard between Otto's legs.

Otto collapsed to the asphalt in a gasping, retching heap.

Erik leaned over him almost casually. "Now here's where you're in luck because I'm a reformed man. If I weren't, I'd be wailing away on you right now. I might break your nose." He touched the bridge of Otto's nose lightly. "Maybe knock out a few teeth. Definitely make it so you couldn't walk away from here without a lot of help. But because I don't do that stuff anymore, you're just getting off with sore nuts."

Otto rolled over on his back, his knees bent to his stomach.

"But keep this in mind." Erik loomed over him for a moment. "The next guy you push around may not have reformed. And Toleffsons look after their own." Erik turned to Janie. "Nice meeting you again, Ms. Dupree."

Janie swallowed. "Likewise."

Erik nodded at her and began to walk back toward the street.

"Erik!" Cal called, stepping to the front of the group still clustered at the door.

Erik paused and looked back, his expression blank.

"Wedding's at eleven tomorrow. See you there."

Erik stood still for a moment longer, then nodded. "Right."

Janie thought she saw that ghost of a smile again as he walked away.

Chapter Twenty-One

Pete walked Janie up Main Street, even though it meant leaving both their cars in the Brenner's parking lot. He didn't trust himself not to run over Otto.

He should have been out there, of course. He should have been looking after her instead of bothering Claire Larkin about finding Maureen Amundson. Claire had a lead, but it hadn't panned out yet. Pete was giving her names of cops who could help. He hadn't expected Janie to leave without telling him.

And none of that was any excuse for the fact that big bad Erik had been the one to rescue her from Otto.

He should have been out there.

"It's okay, you know," Janie said softly.

"What is?" Pete kicked a pebble out of his way.

"That Erik took care of Otto and not you. It's okay."

Pete felt an entirely unreasonable surge of annoyance. "He wasn't much on rescuing people in the past, you know. More like putting people in a position where they needed to be rescued."

Janie nodded. "I get the feeling he has a lot to make up for."

"Why did you leave?" Pete glanced down at her.

She looked away. "Oh, you were on the phone, and I didn't want to bother you. I mean there was no reason you had to take me home."

Except for the fact that Otto Friedrich had tried to attack her in the parking lot. No reason at all.

"I wanted to take you home," Pete grumbled. Which was sort of accurate—he wanted to take her to *his* home.

"Well, now you can." She looked up at the moon hanging high in the dark Texas sky.

For a night that had started out with such promise, this

one was rapidly turning into a bummer. He rubbed his chest where the usual burning cinder had lodged itself behind his breastbone.

As they approached the door to the apartment, he tried to figure how he could get her upstairs. Maybe she needed to be comforted after Otto. Maybe *he* did. "Want to come up?" he asked.

She looked up the stairs and then back at him. It was too dark to see her face clearly, and Pete had a feeling he needed to. "Janie?"

"I don't think I'd better." She sighed. "Big day tomorrow and all." Her voice trailed off.

"Oh. Well...okay." He felt like a kindergartner all of a sudden. He wanted to yell "Why not?" but he was afraid of her answer.

"I guess I'll go on home then," she said softly. "See you tomorrow."

She started to walk up the street. Out of his apartment. Out of his life. "Janie?"

She turned back, blinking in the street light.

"Please?" Pete called softly.

He watched her lips quirk up as she looked at him, then she turned and walked toward him again.

This is a really dumb idea. The voice of reason muttered in Janie's ear. Janie decided the voice of reason was a real pain.

Olive was very glad to see them, but even gladder to gallop out into the backyard. Pete stood watching her.

"What are you going to do about Olive?" she asked.

"Do?" Pete frowned. "What do you mean?"

"Well, I mean, when you leave. Are you really going to take her to the clinic again? Couldn't you take her back to Des Moines with you? I thought the two of you had sort of bonded."

For a moment, he looked stricken, but then he shook his head. "Cal's going to adopt her when he gets back from his honeymoon. She's Cal's dog. I was just supposed to get her used to people."

"Oh." Janie sighed. "She'll miss you." And, of course, she wasn't the only one. *Come on, Janie, buck up.* This was no way to start her new, independent, bitchy life.

Pete's cell phone buzzed to life on his hip, while Olive wandered back from her visit to the live oaks. He glanced at the number, then snapped the phone open. "Yeah?"

Olive butted her head against Pete's hand, but he turned away from her. Janie knelt down, hand extended. "Here, Olive," she murmured.

"What?" Pete snapped. "Who? Who was hurt? Goddamn it!"

Olive whimpered as Janie scratched her ears. "It's okay," she crooned, hoping she was telling the truth.

"Look—" his voice was harsh, "—have Larkin call me. Or if she can't do it, have the detective in charge call me. I need to know what the hell is going on, and I need to know it yesterday!"

He snapped the phone closed savagely. Staring at it as if he'd like to toss it across the yard.

"Problems?" Janie asked.

Pete nodded, blowing out a breath. "A wife abuser got out of jail on a technicality. I've been trying to get his wife into protective custody long distance. Now a cop I know says somebody's been hurt at her sister's house but he doesn't know who, and I can't raise the DA in charge." He rubbed his chest absently.

"The new DA you were worried about?"

He nodded. "That's the one. I just..." He closed his eyes, rubbing harder.

"Pete?" Janie stood quickly. He was bent over slightly at the waist, breathing through his mouth.

"It's okay," he muttered. "Just...acid reflux..."

"Do you need a doctor?" She put her hand on his shoulder. Did his skin feel clammy? Was he perspiring? She tried to remember the other signs of a heart attack.

He shook his head. "Don't worry. It's not...shit, that hurts!"

Janie bit her lip. "We should go to the emergency room. Only we don't have a car. I'll call 911."

"No!" He grabbed her hand. "Don't! Tomorrow's the wedding. I'm not going to the emergency room over this. Just get me upstairs, okay?" He draped one arm across her shoulders.

She narrowed her eyes. Having the best man in the hospital

would put a damper on things. Of course, so would having the best man dead. "Pete..."

"Janie, trust me." He raised his head slightly. "I know what it looks like, but it's not a heart attack. It's just bad acid reflux. I've had it for a couple of months. Stress makes it worse."

Janie sighed. "Okay. But if you die, I may never forgive you."

In the shadows, she saw Pete's lips edge up. "I'll keep that in mind, Ms. Dupree."

The burning in his chest had diminished slightly by the time they got upstairs. The general mortification of having to be helped upstairs by Janie Dupree, however, wasn't likely to diminish in the foreseeable future.

She was still peering up at him with concerned eyes whenever she thought he wasn't looking. Pete sighed and dug out the bottle of pills his doctor had given him. "These will take care of it," he mumbled.

"Good." Janie nodded a little doubtfully.

Olive pushed her cold nose against the back of his hand, and he scratched her ears as he poured himself a glass of water. "Sorry."

"For what?" She sank into a kitchen chair.

"For being such a fun date." He popped a pill in his mouth and swallowed.

Janie shook her head. "You couldn't do anything about this. Well..." She paused. "I guess you could do something."

"Like what?" He raised an eyebrow.

"Like slow down a little and let other people do what they're supposed to at your office."

He stiffened. "I'm a Bureau Director. It's my job to keep track of this kind of stuff."

The corners of her mouth edged up slightly. "Then your job sucks, Pete. It's making you sick."

He wanted to argue, but right now wasn't the best time. Anyway, the pain in his chest had diminished to its usual ache. "I'm okay," he repeated.

Hell, how many times had he said that over the past year? Too many. Had it ever been true?

Janie rose gracefully from her chair, moving around the table. "Are you really, Pete?"

He started to nod, rubbing his hand across his chest, then stopped. Would somebody who was okay be rubbing his chest all the time?

She stopped behind him, resting her hands on his shoulders. "Come on. You need to be de-stressed. You've got a wedding to get through tomorrow, which should provide enough stress for anybody."

He gazed back at her. What she made him think of wasn't exactly stress-free. On the other hand, it would improve his attitude a hundred percent.

Janie made a face. "It's not what you think. I'm giving you a massage, Toleffson. Your stomach probably isn't ready for much more."

"A massage." He shrugged. Massages could always lead to other things, right? "Ms. Dupree, your talents never cease to amaze me."

Janie managed to get Pete to lie down on his stomach, although clearly he had other ideas. So did she, but she wasn't about to rush him.

He'd scared her half to death in the backyard, but he didn't look like he was suffering from a heart attack at the moment. Janie ran her hands lightly over his back, feeling the ridges of muscle flex beneath her fingertips.

Oh, yes, definitely other ideas!

She placed her thumbs alongside his spine, pressing lightly as she moved up his back. "Does that feel okay?"

Pete mumbled something that sounded positive. She slid her palms down from his shoulders to his hips, wishing she had some oil. She worked back up his body to the shoulders again, digging her thumbs into the base of his neck. His muscles were bunched in knots. She slid her hands down again to the small of his back, then the top of his hips. "God, you're tight."

"You have no idea," he muttered.

"Am I hurting you?" She stopped, resting her hands on his buttocks.

He exhaled in a whoosh. "Just keep doing that, please."

Janie returned to the small of his back again, digging her fingers into the knots of muscle there, then worked her way up again to his shoulders. "I don't exactly know what I'm doing, you know. Just sort of."

"'Sort of' is fine." He sighed. "God that feels good."

She circled her fingers along his shoulder blades. "But are you relaxing?"

"If I were any more relaxed, I'd be dribbling off the bed." He moaned slightly as her fingers moved across his shoulders again.

"Good, this is all about de-stressing you."

"Oh, Ms. Dupree, you do that." Pete rolled over slowly, his gaze rising to hers. His hands slid up her arms to her biceps, then he slowly pulled her down on top of him.

She touched her lips to his, gently, gently, feeling the warmth of his breath against her mouth. His hands were at her waist, pulling her up his body so that she lay upon him full length.

"Ah, Janie," he whispered. "Sweetheart."

His mouth angled against hers and she opened for him, rubbing her tongue against his, then sucking him lightly. His hands tightened against her back.

She could feel the swell of his arousal against her mons, pressure mounting low in her abdomen. She brought her hands to his shoulders, kneading lightly across them, feeling the pull and bunch of the muscles. Somewhere at the back of her mind she heard music.

"Shit!" Pete slid out from underneath her and reaching for his phone.

Janie rolled onto her back, trying not to snarl in frustration.

"What?" he barked into his phone, and then he leaned back against the headboard. "Okay, Claire, tell me what's happening."

She watched his face. His eyebrows moved together in a scowl. "What?" he snapped. "Say that again. Good god, Claire!" Slowly the corners of his mouth began to inch up as he listened. "No shit? Then what?" After another moment, he began to chuckle, shaking his head. "No. No, you did fine. You're sure you're all right, though? And Maureen?"

There was another longish pause as he listened, then he nodded. "Right. His lawyer will ask for bail, but there's no way in hell. Just make sure you're there for the hearing. Okay, Claire. Good work. Very good. I'll see you in a few days."

He clicked the phone closed and sat staring at it for a moment, shaking his head.

"What happened?" Janie asked.

"Claire happened, bless her." He leaned his head back against the headboard. "She found Maureen Amundson about twenty minutes before her husband showed up. Ol' Bo had stopped to toss down a few, so he was good and soused. Claire locked the door, called 911 and yelled at Bo that the cops were on the way. Which, of course, really pissed him off."

He turned to her, grinning. "So he put his fist through a window, cutting up his hand and also setting himself up since his fist was caught and he couldn't move without cutting himself up worse. Claire said he went on yelling insulting things so she hit him with some pepper spray. The cops got there a few minutes later and took him into custody. Turns out Claire's a hell of a fighter."

"So it all worked out," she said carefully.

"Yeah."

"Without your being there," she added.

His grin began to fade. "Yeah, but I should have been. The whole thing was just luck..."

Janie shook her head. "From what you just told me, I'd say it was more than luck."

Pete's smile narrowed, then he shrugged. "Maybe."

"It sounds like you have some competent people in your office, Pete."

"We have a lot of competent people. I'm one of them. I help keep everything on track. If you'll notice, Ms. Dupree, I was the one who put all of this together. Claire was the one on the ground, but I was the one who ran it."

His jaw was remarkably square all of a sudden. She took a breath. "Do you like your job, Pete?"

He gave her a guarded look. "Like it? I worked hard to get it."

She managed to keep her expression bland. "So you enjoy what you do?"

This time he was quiet for a moment before he answered. "I believe in what I do. That's more important than enjoying it. If I didn't do it right, the bad guys would win. I'm trying to keep human pond scum off the streets."

She nodded slowly, thinking. "I understand that. Is that what keeps you going then?"

"Keeps me going?" His forehead furrowed. "Sure. Like I say, it's an important job."

"Do you get vacations?"

He looked momentarily uncomfortable. "Yeah."

"Where did you go last year?"

"I didn't take one last year. Too much was going on."

"The year before that then."

After a moment, he shook his head.

"When *did* you take a vacation?" Janie raised an eyebrow.

"Vacations are overrated."

"Not by those who take them."

"Well, I'm on vacation now," Pete snapped. "Look how well that's turning out, stress-wise."

She sighed, pushing herself to the side of the bed. "Maybe I should go home." Sort of the last thing she wanted to do, but this conversation definitely wasn't headed anywhere good.

He caught hold of her hand. "I'm sorry."

"Pete..."

"No, I'm sorry." His gaze held hers, dark coffee eyes in the shadowed bedroom. He took a deep breath and blew it out. "I guess it's a sore point with me right now. I used to like my job a lot, back when I was an assistant county attorney. Prosecuting felons was better than corporate law. Now..." He shook his head. "I still believe in it. I still know it's important. But I don't like it as much, I guess."

"You don't like being in charge?"

He gave her a bleak smile. "Nope. But, hey, somebody's got to do it. And I'm good at it, unfortunately. And there's no going back, once you start moving up the ladder."

There were a lot of things she could say about that, a lot of topics they could discuss. Except talking wasn't at all what she wanted to do right now. Janie wondered if there was any way they could get back to what they'd been doing before his phone call.

Pete took hold of her other hand. "Is this what you want to do right now? Have me explain how the Polk County Attorney's office works?"

She shook her head slowly.

He exhaled a sigh. "Me neither. Please stay with me tonight, Ms. Dupree. I promise not to mention my office for the rest of the evening."

Janie's lips trembled. Tonight. And tomorrow. And then he'd be gone. Back to his important job that he felt he had to do, that was the major thing in his life. While she stayed here in Konigsburg. Because that was the way these things worked. Everybody said so.

In which case, she'd better get as much of him as she could tonight.

"I'd be honored to stay with you, Mr. Toleffson."

Chapter Twenty-Two

Pete thought he'd wake up early the next morning, but Janie woke up earlier. He heard her in the kitchen at six and groaned. Already up and probably fully clothed, dammit. If he didn't get up, she'd leave before he could kiss her again.

Not acceptable. He pulled on his jeans and stumbled into the kitchen.

Janie was making coffee. She glanced up as he came through the door. "Oh. Sorry, I didn't mean to wake you."

She was wearing his T-shirt again. Pete wanted nothing more than to throw her over his shoulder and take her back to bed for the rest of the day.

"I need to get home and get my clothes. All the bridesmaids are meeting Docia and getting dressed at the winery."

Okay, so there *was* a reason they couldn't spend the day in bed. The Wedding. His reason for being in Konigsburg in the first place. Pete sighed, running a hand over his face as he headed for the coffee pot. "Run me through the schedule again."

"We all get to the winery by ten in case there are last-minute disasters. Wedding's at eleven. Then the reception starts at two at the Woodrose."

He poured himself a large cup of coffee. "And between the wedding and the reception?"

"We grab some lunch. Or we go somewhere and collapse in a heap. Our duties will be more or less officially at an end except for the toasts at the reception."

Pete raised an eyebrow. "Can I collapse in the same heap you do?"

Janie's lips quirked. "We'll never make it to the reception if we do."

"And that's important?"

"Yes," she said decisively, "that's important. We each have

to give a toast to Cal and Docia, and I want to dance with you."
She put her cup into the sink. "I've got to go. I need to talk to
Mom before I head out to the winery. I have a feeling she'll have
heard about what happened with Otto at Brenner's by now."

His grin curdled. He'd managed to forget about Otto since
last night. He hoped the SOB was off nursing his nuts
somewhere remote, preferably in a nice dank jail cell. "Okay,
how about I give you a ride to the winery?" That should ensure
that she had to at least spend some time alone with him today.

Janie shook her head. "I'm riding with Allie this morning.
Maybe you can take me to the reception."

Pete sighed. "I think that can be arranged, Ms. Dupree."

Janie walked through her front door with what she hoped
was a clearly purposeful stride. Maybe if she looked like she
had things to do, Mom would leave her alone.

Vain hope. "Janie, where have you been? People have been
calling ever since last evening."

Mom was dressed in sweats with her hair in curlers and
cotton balls between her toes. Janie sighed—of course she was
going to The Wedding. Half of the town would be going to The
Wedding.

"What were people calling about?" Janie tried for an
innocent look.

"Otto, of course," her mother snapped. "How that man beat
him up."

Janie stopped cold. "You've been talking to Rhonda
Ruckelshaus, haven't you? She always gets everything wrong."

Mom narrowed her eyes. "He didn't beat Otto up?"

"He had a fight with Otto, but Otto richly deserved
everything he got."

Her mother opened her mouth and then shut it again. She
slapped her hand against the chair next to her. "Sit down."

Janie shook her head. "I don't have time for this now. I
need to take a shower before Allie gets here."

"Sit down right now, Janie Ann Dupree!" Her mother's lips
were pursed and her eyes flashed fire.

Janie sighed. There was no way around this, and it was
probably better to get it over with than to have it hanging over

her head. She flopped into the chair.

"It's time—past time—you got a grip on things here." Her mother raised her chin. "He's leaving, Janie. In a couple of days he'll be gone and he won't ever be back. Otto Friedrich has lived here most of his life and he'll be here tomorrow and next week and next month. Just like you. You're making the mistake of your life here."

Janie took a deep breath, holding onto her temper with her fingernails. "Okay, Mom, this is what happened—for real. Last night Otto was drunk and obnoxious. He grabbed me and wouldn't let go. I don't know exactly what he had in mind, but it was nothing good and it involved dragging me off against my will. Erik Toleffson made him leave me alone."

Her mother at least looked slightly doubtful. "He was probably drunk because he was upset. Because you were two-timing him with that other Toleffson."

"The only way I could be two-timing him would be if we actually had something between us. We didn't. The only thing driving Otto is hurt pride, believe me." Janie stood again. "Now I have to go."

"Janie, listen to me now..."

"No, Mom!" Janie's voice was considerably louder than she'd meant it to be. Mom blinked at her. "You listen to me this time. Otto Friedrich doesn't want to marry me. He never did. He wants to have sex with me, but I've never been interested. Yes, Pete Toleffson is leaving, but so what? He's a nice guy and I've enjoyed all the time I've spent with him. That's it, Mom, end of story. I don't want to hear anything more about this, ever again. Otto Friedrich is out of my life as of right now."

Mom was blinking rapidly. Janie had the awful feeling she had tears in her eyes. "I just don't want to see you break your heart, sweetheart."

"Well trust me, my heart's not broken." *Dented maybe, but definitely in one piece.* "Now I have to get ready to go."

"But...what should I say if Otto comes by?" Mom's brow furrowed.

"Tell him if he comes by again, I'm getting a restraining order," Janie snapped and headed for her bedroom.

Allie was a few minutes early—unfortunately, since Janie was still drying her hair. "Docia just called from the Woodrose. Her battery's dead. We need to go get her."

"Great," Janie moaned. "The first disaster of the day."

"The *only* disaster of the day," Allie said firmly. "You should see my cake. It's going to be the talk of Konigsburg for the next two months."

Docia looked calm enough when they got to the Woodrose, but in close-up her eyes were sort of glassy. "Docia," Janie murmured, "are you okay?"

Docia swallowed. "Sure. I mean I'm absolutely doing the right thing, so why wouldn't I be okay, right?"

"You are absolutely doing the right thing, and this is going to be the most beautiful wedding ever." Janie restrained herself from finding some wood she could rap her knuckles against. If she kept rapping, she was going to hurt herself.

She pried the garment bag out of Docia's fingers and hung it in the back of Allie's van along with their bridesmaid dresses, then pushed Docia gently toward the back seat. "Do you have everything you need? Underwear? Stockings? Shoes? Garter?"

"Garter?" Docia gave her a panicked look.

"You toss your garter to the male guests. Don't worry, I brought one for you." Janie opened the door for her.

"Oh god, oh god." Docia sank into the seat. "I'm never going to get through this without screwing up."

"Sure you will." Allie started the engine. "You're already halfway there, and we'll push you down the aisle if we need to. Trust us."

Janie had the feeling it would be a good idea to keep Docia talking. "What's your old?"

"Old?" Docia blinked at her. "Oh. Okay, my earrings. They were Granny Brandenburg's." She touched the small gold hoops.

"The new is your dress, right?"

Docia nodded. "And my shoes, stockings, and underwear. None of which I wear as a rule." Docia grimaced. "I mean shoes and stockings. Of course, I wear underwear. I *like* underwear. Oh Lord, I sound like some coked-up starlet."

"What kind of shoes?" Allie turned into the drive that led to the winery.

"Sandals. Gold." Docia shook her head. "So I probably shouldn't wear stockings right? But then what do I put the garter on? God, I'm already messing up."

"Docia, chill." Janie put a hand on her arm. "You're fine. What's blue?"

Docia grinned at her. "My panties."

"Okay, have you borrowed anything?" Janie raised an eyebrow.

Docia clapped a hand to her lips. "No!"

"Then, here." Janie reached into her tote bag and pulled out a handkerchief. "It belonged to my Great Aunt Lucille, so I want it back."

Docia's lips trembled for a moment, then she gave her a watery smile. "Thanks, kid. I'm going to take you in hand when I get back from the honeymoon, you know."

"Don't think about that now," Janie said crisply. "Here we are."

Morgan Barrett stood at the door to her winery's tasting room. "We've closed for the morning, so you can use the tasting room to get dressed without worrying about some tourists from Lubbock wandering through."

Janie gave her a grateful grin. "Thanks, Morgan. Could you send Bethany in when she gets here?"

"Sure. No problem."

Docia seemed to wake up as they walked through the door. A full-length mirror was propped against one wall and the bar had been cleared for a make-up space. Docia unzipped the garment bag and shook out the shimmer of flowered brown voile, smiling. "It really is gorgeous, don't you think?"

"It's lovely." Janie sighed, trying not to think about how spectacular Docia had looked in Reba's wedding dress.

"Best of all," Docia continued, "I recognize myself when I look in the mirror. It's not like I'm trying to be Princess Buttercup or something."

"Don't you need a slip with that?" Allie narrowed her eyes. "It looks pretty sheer."

"Nope." Docia pulled the dress around her so that the soft ruffle framed her collarbone. "It's lined. Besides, no slip means Cal gets glimpses. Glimpses are good. They'll get him a little stirred up." She grinned.

Bethany slipped in the door, carrying her dress on a hanger. "Glimpses are great. Who are you stirring up?"

"Cal, of course, and he's already stirred up." Allie dropped her dress over her head and then turned her back to Janie to be zipped. "You made him stay by himself last night."

"So I did." Docia grinned even more widely.

"You're just evil, Docia." Bethany grinned back, fastening her own dress.

"What are you going to do for a veil?" Allie frowned.

Docia snorted. "You know what veils symbolize? Depending on who you read, it's either the woman's submission to her husband, which I'm not buying, or the woman's modesty, which is a nonstarter in my case, or her chastity, about which the less said the better. No veils for me, thank you very much."

"You need something in your hair." Allie pursed her lips. "Maybe we can borrow some grapes."

"Don't you dare!" Docia snapped. "They're about two weeks from harvest. I'd look like Bacchus."

Janie smiled, smoothing the linen of her skirt. "It's all taken care of. I had these delivered to the winery this morning." She opened the tasting room refrigerator and took out a cellophane package.

"Oh god," Docia groaned, closing her eyes. "That sounds like famous last words."

"It's fine," Janie soothed. "Just look."

Docia touched a fingertip to the circlet of yellow roses. "Oh my, Janie. They're just lovely." She threw her arms around Janie's shoulders, hugging her enthusiastically.

"Watch it," Janie wheezed. "This is linen. I'll get all wrinkly."

"Are those for us?" Allie picked up a matching circlet of pink.

Janie nodded. "Pick the one that matches your dress. Or contrasts. Or something. These were the colors the florist thought would work best."

"Dibs on the lavender," Bethany said quickly. "It'll look best with my yellow."

"I'm in blue, so I probably need the cream." Allie picked up a circlet a little dubiously.

"Which leaves me all in pink." Janie sighed. "I'm going to look cute, aren't I?"

Docia grinned. "Adorable. But I don't think that will slow Pete down."

A bubble of silence filled the spaces between them as they all concentrated on placing circlets on their heads and trying not to look at Janie's face.

"It's okay," she said softly. "I'm okay. Don't worry about me."

Allie grinned. "But you're such fun to mother. Did you hear what happened to Otto after y'all left?"

Janie grimaced. "Nothing good, I trust."

"Depends on your definition of 'good'." Allie grinned more widely. "Nando took Otto in to the police station and had a long talk with him. Nando did the talking. Otto did a lot of moaning, according to Nando. Anyway, I don't think Otto will bother you again. He probably won't be bothering any women for a while, period. Wonder thinks Erik's had a lot of experience in dirty fighting."

Docia shuddered lightly. "He's kind of scary, but I'm getting used to him. Cal thinks he might be sincere about cleaning up his act this time."

Janie narrowed her eyes at her reflection, trying to position the pink roses so that she looked like a maid of honor rather than a flower girl. "I didn't know him before, of course. He just seems kind of tired now. I think he'd really like them to forgive him."

"Well, he's here today as Cal's invited guest. That's a start, at least." Docia bit her lip. "Has anybody peeked outside yet?"

"Nope, it's early. Janie had her contribution. Now here's mine." Bethany opened her tote bag and took out a bottle. "Champagne. First of the day."

Docia grimaced. "I think I'm going to get really sick of drinking this stuff before the day is over."

"Maybe so, but drink up for now." Bethany poured them each a glass, then raised hers in Docia's direction. "Here's to you, kid, you got one of the good ones."

Allie and Janie raised their own glasses in unison, then sipped.

Docia sniffed loudly. "Oh for god's sake, I should have used the waterproof mascara, shouldn't I?"

Pete made a brief trip to Cal's clinic to drop off Olive at her new temporary home. She stared up at him silently, almost as frozen as she had been when he'd first met her.

"It's okay, Olive," he whispered, rubbing her behind her ears. "Cal's a great guy. You'll be happy with him. You have a nice life, now."

The last he saw of her were those large, moist kalamata eyes staring up as he stepped back through the door.

Not my dog. He had enough problems to deal with already without that one. Except, of course, that he couldn't stop thinking about those eyes whenever he let his guard down. Those eyes and Janie Dupree.

Back at the apartment, he studied the clutter in his bedroom and tried to decide what to do about it. He ought to be packing. He was catching a plane early tomorrow with his parents and Lars and Daisy. Back to Des Moines. Back to real life. Back to his empty apartment and his equally empty job.

He shook his head. Self-pity was obnoxious, and not something he was going to indulge in. Occasions like weddings made you lose your perspective, made you think about stuff that you didn't normally think about. He did an important job as a county attorney and he did it damned well.

But you don't like it much anymore.

So what? Most people didn't like their jobs. At least his job was important—at least he made a difference. He absolutely wasn't going to go moping around after Janie Dupree.

Janie Dupree. With her dark hair and laughing eyes and lithe body. The most beautiful woman he'd ever had the good luck to entice into his bed. The sweetest woman he'd ever bared his soul to.

Pete took a breath, pushing down the ache in his chest. Packing could wait.

He wasn't sure why all the groomsmen showed up together at his apartment. He hadn't asked them to. They just sort of arrived on his doorstep a half hour later.

The first to come was Lars, managing to look crisp even though the temperature was already in the eighties. Pete figured he was practicing some kind of accountant's juju that he himself didn't have access to.

"Where's Daisy?" Somehow he'd expected Lars to have her tucked permanently under his arm.

"With Dad and Mom. Janie sent her a wreath."

Pete blinked at him, picturing holly and red ribbon. "A wreath? You mean like Christmas."

"No, you dope, a wreath of flowers. Daisies, actually. Daisy thought it was great. Of course, she tried to eat it, but I'm assuming Mom can keep it out of her mouth and on her head until the wedding's over."

Cal showed up a few minutes later, looking disconsolate. "Docia actually went ahead and stayed with Reba last night. I thought she was kidding."

"It was just one night. You've got a lot of them ahead." Pete poured him a cup of coffee.

Cal gave him a long look. "It was a night together. I'm not giving those up without a fight."

Pete felt a twinge somewhere around his heart. Before he could say anything, the downstairs doorbell rang and Wonder arrived, carrying a bag of scones. "From Allie. She figured we all needed to lay down a foundation of carbs before we started in on the champagne."

"Oh man!" Cal smiled blissfully. "Allie's scones. There is a God and He's happy."

Pete leaned back against the counter, sipping. "You do all have your clothes with you, right? I mean you're not going to be sitting here eating scones and drinking coffee and running down the clock."

Cal reached to the chair next to him and held up his garment bag. "Complete ensemble."

"I've got mine on." Lars shrugged. "It might get a little wrinkled, but with blazers and khakis, who can tell?"

"Mine's in the car." Wonder finished wolfing down a blackberry scone. "I'll get it when I've finished breakfast. Allie would kill me if I got blackberry stains on my shirt."

Horace strolled in from the living room. "You're concerned about what a woman thinks of you? How are the mighty fallen, Wonder."

Wonder sighed. "Allie's not just a woman. She's *the* woman. And no, I do not want to piss her off."

All four men stared at him blankly. Wonder raised his eyebrows. "What?"

"Quite a day." Pete gulped down some coffee, turning to Horace. "How did you get in, by the way?"

"You left your street door unlocked, also the apartment." Horace grinned. "Good thing I'm honest. I'm surprised you haven't been robbed blind."

Pete sighed. "Got your wedding outfit?"

"Such as it is." Horace shrugged his garment bag onto a chair. "I have to say, this is the most comfortable wedding I've ever been in. So when do we get the tuxes back to Siemen?"

"Well, that's the thing." Cal gave them all a slightly nervous smile. "Reba says the wedding may be Docia's, but the reception's hers."

Pete had a sudden sinking feeling. "Meaning?"

"Meaning we're supposed to wear the tuxes to the reception."

Pete frowned. "What about Lars?"

"Lars gets a bye. The rest of us have to dress up. Reba's orders."

"Aw hell," Horace grumbled. "Just when I was enjoying this wedding too."

"What about the women?" Wonder asked guardedly.

Cal frowned. "I'm not sure. Reba loves Janie, so she could probably show up in a gunny sack without any problem. But I've got a feeling Docia's going to be wearing that fantasy wedding dress whether she likes it or not."

Pete checked his watch, then stood. "Okay, gentlemen, it's time. Get those blazers on."

"All right. But first..." Wonder stood, his hand on his heart. "All together now, join me in a chorus of 'Another Man Done Gone'."

"Come off it, Wonder," Horace grumbled. "Toleffson's got a real winner and you know it. Plus he's made Bethany take a second look at marriage, even after her lousy divorce from Lloyd five years ago, which I've been trying to do for a year now. And if I'm any judge, Allie Maldonado will have you in a church sooner than later."

Wonder sighed. "True. The women of Konigsburg will hang their heads in sorrow, but true."

Lars raised his coffee cup. "To Docia and Cal. Go for it!"

Pete drank his last swallow of coffee, feeling oddly bereft.

Chapter Twenty-Three

Janie stood at the back of the winery patio surveying the layout. Banks of summer flowers lined the front in bright pink and yellow and white. Swags of chiffon were strung along the sides, linking stone urns filled with more flowers. Reba might not have had much time, but she'd done herself proud.

Almost every seat was filled with friends and family. Konigsburgers were scattered throughout the crowd—Armando from Cal's animal clinic, Al and Carol Brosius from the Coffee Corral, Arthur Craven from the Konigsburg Merchants Association, even Hank Ingstrom from the Dew Drop with his wife.

Janie's mother sat at the side, wearing one of her Lucky Lady outfits in bright blue Polyester. Janie kept out of her line of sight. She really didn't want to deal with any other problems for the next couple of hours.

A lot of slightly stunned people in very expensive clothes were scattered here and there in the audience, probably all related to Docia. Reba herself still fussed around the edges of the patio in a spectacular daytime wedding outfit—pale yellow lace with a wide-brimmed garden party hat. She was currently bullying Lee and Ken, who were serving as ushers and enjoying themselves hugely. Janie figured if four-star generals wore yellow lace, they'd look and sound just like Reba.

The Toleffsons sat together toward the front. Mrs. Toleffson was wearing her mother-of-the-groom dress—a forest green satin coat with brown accents. She was undoubtedly dying from the heat, but she refused to look wilted. Asa had on a dark suit and a splendid crimson tie with a small picture of the Tasmanian Devil. Janie wasn't sure where he'd gotten it, but it looked great.

Erik sat beside his father, wearing a navy jacket. He blinked in the sunshine as if he wasn't entirely used to seeing it. Daisy perched on his lap, playing with his keys. She wore a pink dress that was almost the same shade as Janie's. Her daisy wreath had slid down slightly over her left eye. As Janie watched, Erik carefully pushed it back onto her black curls then patted her on the shoulder a little awkwardly. Daisy paid him no attention at all.

At the end of the patio near the live oaks, the string quartet was working its way through some Vivaldi. Reba appeared at Janie's elbow. "Y'all ready to go now?"

Janie didn't think Docia could wait much longer without hysterics, ready or not. "Yes, ma'am. We're ready."

Reba pressed her fingers to her lips. "Oh my, have I forgotten anything?" Amazingly, her cornflower blue eyes began to glisten with tears. "Oh well, let's get this show on the road."

Janie heard a rustling behind her and turned. The groom and groomsmen stood in line, all of them in navy blazers and khakis. They looked like a college golf team on their best behavior, although three of them also looked a little like Paul Bunyan.

Reba eyed them critically, then sighed. "Where's Cal?"

"Right here." Cal stepped forward, smiling. Janie had a feeling he'd be smiling all day.

"All right." Reba nodded decisively. "Soon as I'm in my seat, you and the judge go on up there."

Cal looked behind him a little nervously. The judge pulled his collar away from his neck with a finger. "If I'd known y'all were going casual I'd have ditched this damn suit. You should have told me."

"You're an appeals court judge," Reba snapped. "You should look like one."

Allie took Wonder's arm and Bethany moved next to Horace. Janie wasn't sure she'd ever seen Horace in a suit before, even when he presided at city council meetings.

Pete stepped beside her and stood looking down, a faint smile playing around his lips. "Morning."

"Morning yourself." Janie let herself grin up at him, then faced front again.

"Time for me to sit down, I suppose." Reba extended her hand to Lee Contreras.

He placed her hand on his arm with a flourish, a private

escorting a general, then began a slow march down the aisle to the front row.

When she'd reached her seat, Reba raised her hand. The string quartet segued into Handel, and the judge gave Cal a slight shove, heading him down the aisle. Once they'd reached the front, Reba stood.

Allie grasped her bouquet of daisies and roses and looped her hand through Wonder's arm. "Let's do it, stud."

"I assume that's metaphoric," Wonder muttered, stepping forward down the aisle.

Bethany put her hand on Horace's arm, and he drew it close to his side, giving her a brief look that made Janie's throat hurt suddenly as they began to walk.

"Okay, my turn," Lars sighed.

"No!" Janie reached up to grab his arm, then placed her other hand on Pete's elbow, balancing her bouquet between them. "Together. Okay?"

Pete grinned at her. "We'll never fit in that aisle."

"Sure we will." Janie grinned back. "I'm short, remember."

She took a step and the other two followed. "Why do I feel like I should be saying, 'Lions and tigers and bears, oh my'," Lars whispered.

Cal grinned at them. Janie didn't have the courage to look at Reba, but she heard Horace's chuckle. At the front, she dropped the men's arms and moved to the left.

Allie patted her shoulder. "Nicely done, kid."

The string quartet segued again, and Janie looked at the end of the aisle. Docia stood with her hand on Billy's arm. Golden brown voile swirled around her ankles, the deep ruffle circling her throat and then angling across her body to the hem. Yellow roses were twined in her riotous crown of red curls. She carried a bouquet of white daisies, yellow roses, and trailing jasmine.

She looked glorious. Beside her, Billy Kent looked as if he couldn't quite believe they'd gotten there in one piece.

Docia took a step and the two of them came gliding down the aisle.

Janie heard sighs from the audience. She glanced at Cal. He looked like he needed to be reminded to breathe.

The judge cleared his throat. Pete patted his pocket to

check on the ring. Docia arrived at the front, handed Janie her bouquet, and winked.

Showtime.

"The votes are in," Wonder grumbled. "Being photographed is definitely the most boring activity on the planet."

Pete agreed with him. The past thirty minutes were the longest half hour he'd ever spent, made even longer by the fact that Janie hadn't stopped doing useless tasks long enough to talk to him.

Allie grinned at Wonder indulgently. "Come on and give them another smile, sweetie. Think of it as advertising your professional expertise."

The photographer was arranging Cal and Docia, along with Reba and Billy. Mom and Dad waited patiently for their turn.

Pete wasn't sure exactly what he wanted to say to Janie. "Whew!" maybe. Or maybe he wanted to take her up on her promise of collapsing in a heap. What he mainly wanted to do was sit with her for a while and let events roll by. He had a whole list of things he needed to tell her, but he wasn't sure where or how to begin.

Lars had retrieved Daisy from Erik, who looked simultaneously relieved and disappointed. Daisy had given him a dazzling smile over Lars's shoulder, then appeared to have promptly forgotten all about him. Women.

Now Lars sat with Daisy on his lap, playing "she loves me, she loves me not" with the flowers remaining in her wreath. Daisy had removed it and refused to put it back on again once she'd seen Docia's yellow roses. Pete figured she was planning to trade up.

Reba, freed temporarily from the photographer, gestured at Janie, then murmured something. Janie nodded and was gone again.

Pete sighed. What exactly did he want to say to her anyway? "Nice job. Cool wedding." Yeah, but that wasn't it exactly.

"Don't hook up with anybody else like Otto Friedrich." That was closer, but he didn't really think she'd do that anyway.

"Wait for me." He closed his eyes. Yeah, that was it. And he could just picture Janie staring at him with bewildered eyes.

Wait for you to do what?

To get the Amundson case straightened out? To figure out exactly what he wanted to do next?

Wait for you how long?

As long as it takes. Please put your life on hold until I get everything taken care of. Pete grimaced. If he were Janie, he'd tell himself where to go and what to do when he got there.

He couldn't ask her to do that. It wouldn't be fair to her. He couldn't ask her to do anything. He didn't have the right.

"Okay, now the wedding party." The photographer motioned them up under the live oak where he'd been positioning everyone. "Bridesmaids on the left, groomsmen on the right."

Pete glanced over at Janie again. Her rosebud wreath had shifted slightly down onto her forehead. He reached out to slide it back just as Reba took her by the arm and moved her beside Docia. He sighed and moved beside Cal.

"Problems?" Cal raised an eyebrow.

Pete shook his head. "Nothing I can't handle, Calthorpe. Enjoy your wedding day. Let me know what you need."

Cal gave him a slight smile. "You know, bro, you don't really have to take care of me anymore. Lars either. We're both full grown, and Erik looks to be out of the bullying business, at least as far as his brothers go."

Pete glanced back at the people milling around in front of the winery, waiting for their rides to the Woodrose. Erik sat on the winery steps, blinking.

"I'm still having trouble believing it, Calthorpe. But I hope it's true."

"Yeah." Cal nodded. "After what he did at the rehearsal dinner, I'm ready to give him the benefit of the doubt."

Pete blew out a breath. The rehearsal dinner. Where he hadn't protected Janie the way he should have. "Right."

Cal shook his head. "Look, Pete, take a day off, okay? The responsibility for the world's happiness does not rest on your shoulders. The future can wait until tomorrow."

"Everybody smile," the photographer called.

Pete did his best.

Janie's mouth hurt from smiling. She was also pretty sure her makeup had sweated off, and she was ready to shred the damn rose wreath that kept sliding over her eyes. She desperately wanted the photographer to stop, but Reba wouldn't let him go until every last person had been photographed multiple times.

Janie wiped her forehead with the back of her hand, pushing the wreath back in place one more time.

"So when do I start throwing things?" Docia muttered.

Janie blinked at her. "What did you have in mind?"

"Oh, you know, the bouquet, my garter, my mother, the usual." Docia grinned at her. "Relax, kid, it's almost over."

Janie sighed. "I'm just tired, I guess. And we all need to get over to the Woodrose."

"Did I remember to admit you were right, by the way?" Docia took a deep breath. "This was a terrific wedding. Thanks for talking me into it. I would have hated Las Vegas."

She reached down and gave Janie another enthusiastic hug. Janie didn't think she'd been hugged by so many people in a single day since she'd been an infant. Her lungs were permanently compressed. "My pleasure," she croaked.

"All right." Reba clapped her hands. "Time to finish up and head to the Woodrose."

"What about throwing my bouquet and my garter?" Docia frowned.

"You can do it at the Woodrose after you've changed." Reba began making shooing motions toward the parking lot.

Docia put her hands on her hips. "I want to do it here, Mama."

Reba put her own hands on her hips and frowned.

After a long moment, Billy put his arm around Reba's shoulders. "How about if she throws the garter here and the bouquet there? That way you each get your way. Sort of."

Docia grinned. "Fine with me. Where's my husband?"

Cal emerged from the crowd of groomsmen. He'd loosened his tie and his hair was mussed. He looked more like Cal than he had all morning. "Present, ma'am. What do you need me to do?"

"Take off my garter so I can throw it to y'all." Docia gave him a slightly feline smile.

Cal shrugged. "Okay. Put your foot on this chair, so I can get some leverage."

Docia rested one foot on a chair, bending her knee gracefully. Cal started to slide her skirt up her leg, then stopped and swallowed hard. "Docia, you're not wearing any stockings."

Docia smiled again. "Yes, I know."

"Then how do I remove your garter?"

"Oh, hubby dear—" Docia's smile became positively incendiary, "—you don't need stockings to wear a garter."

Cal closed his eyes briefly and then slid Docia's skirt to her thigh. The blue satin garter with its crystal accents glittered in the sun. He expanded it deftly and pulled it down over her foot.

Behind him, Wonder blew out a breath. "Well done, Calthorpe. Better throw it quick."

"He doesn't throw it, you dolt, I do." Docia plucked the garter from Cal's nerveless fingers and tossed it in the general direction of the groomsmen. They all stepped back as if something radioactive had landed in their midst.

Except for Pete, who caught the garter through reflex action. And then stood staring at it in a slightly confused way.

"Very good." Docia grinned at him. "Now we can all go dance."

Pete nodded slightly, still studying the garter as if it held the secrets of the universe. Maybe it did.

Janie wasn't sure whose car she was supposed to ride in. Allie had taken her bakery van back to Sweet Thing, followed by Wonder. She had no intention of riding with Cal and Docia, particularly since they looked like they'd be stopping at Cal's house before they got to the reception. Horace was driving Bethany and the Toleffsons in his SUV.

That left Pete. Janie took a deep breath. Time to start that conversation.

Or not. Reba took hold of her arm. "Come along, Janie, we need to get there before everybody else. We've got things to check on." She pulled Janie along behind her toward her black Mercedes.

Janie looked back to see Pete staring after her, looking faintly annoyed. She tried to wave, but by then Reba was stuffing her into the back seat.

The Woodrose hummed with activity. Tables were scattered

around the wide lawn behind the event center and an orchestra was setting up under a gauzy tent at the side. Waiters from Brenner's unloaded trays of food under Lee's watchful eye and cases of wine under Ken's.

Reba kept her hand on Janie's elbow, pushing her forward. "In here, sweetheart," she chirped, shoving her through the door into the room that had been her command center.

Janie stopped, staring. Her dress was hanging against the far wall.

Only, of course, it couldn't be her dress. Her dress had been shredded by Sherice. She walked forward slowly to run her fingers down the front. She couldn't find any evidence of repairs.

"It's a new one," Reba said from behind her.

Janie turned. Reba was smiling so widely it looked like her face might split.

"I had my friend Coralee check the Market Center in Dallas. She found a place that had one in the right color. It may not fit quite as well." Reba's brow furrowed lightly. "The seamstress is supposed to be here, but she might be running late."

She might also be lost in the gauntlet of catering trucks, musicians' vans, and rented limousines bearing Reba's guests. Janie didn't care. The dress shimmered in front of her, pale lavender moonlight on a hanger. It would fit, she knew it would.

"I never did give that woman the sandals," Reba burbled on, "so they're still here. I don't know what you want to do about something for your hair..."

Janie wasn't listening anymore. Her fingers itched to unzip the dress and pull it on. Outside the door she could hear voices—Allie and Bethany heading for the dressing room. She turned and gave Reba a fierce hug. "Thank you so much!"

Reba smiled at her tearfully, brushing her bangs back slightly from her forehead. "You're welcome, sweetheart. Now go be Cinderella."

Wonder grumbled all the way down the stairs to the Woodrose back lawn. By then Pete had tuned him out. Yes, they were wearing tuxes. Yes, tuxes had been invented by some thorough-going sadist, probably female. Yes, they could have prevailed and insisted on wearing their blazers, looking and behaving like a bunch of frat boys, but Pete preferred to keep peace with Cal's in-laws—or Cal's mother-in-law, at any rate. Billy Kent didn't appear to give a rat's ass whether they wore tuxedoes or bib overalls as long as they showed up and behaved themselves.

He'd managed to swing by home and take a quick shower before he'd gotten dressed up. The tux was wool, of course, but lightweight.

On the other hand, it had a vest. He hadn't worn a vest since his senior prom. He'd hated it then, and he hated it now. And he had a feeling he'd be sweating like a pig within an hour.

As they rounded the corner, heading toward the event center, Pete could hear an orchestra somewhere tuning up. Orchestras meant dancing.

He was going to have to dance with Janie.

He closed his eyes and stood still for a moment, remembering just what Janie felt like in his arms. Lordy, the vest wasn't the only reason he'd be sweating.

"There's Allie." Wonder sighed. "Why is it the more clothes we have to pile on, the fewer women have to wear?"

Horace grinned. "Think of it as a tradeoff, boy. You may be miserable, but at least you can enjoy the view."

Allie and Bethany both wore strapless satin dresses in a color Pete would call beige but that probably wasn't. They both looked cool, sophisticated and gorgeous. Clearly they could both do better than the two steamy males at his side.

"Come on!" Bethany waved at them. "Docia wants to throw the bouquet." She slid her hand beneath Horace's arm, smiling. "Looking good, Doc."

"You're not looking too shabby yourself, ma'am." Horace gave her a grin that was pure seduction, walrus mustache and all.

Pete wondered if there were any empty bedrooms available at the Woodrose, just for future reference, of course. "Where's Janie?"

Bethany glanced at Allie, then shrugged, smiling faintly. "She'll be along. Better get moving now." She walked quickly toward a set of glass folding doors at the side of the event center. "Docia's in here."

As he stepped through the door, Pete caught sight of Docia. She was in a white satin wedding dress that looked skintight.

Her feet and lower legs were encased in a cloud of translucent fabric, sort of like a mermaid ascending from the sea foam. She looked thoroughly pissed. Cal was keeping out of her way, probably for good reason.

"That's quite a dress." Pete tried to make it sound like a compliment.

"If you say I look like Cinderella, I'll find something small and hard to throw at you," Docia grumbled. "I thought everybody got dressed up in uncomfortable clothes for the wedding and then got to dress down for the reception. How did I get roped into this?"

"To please your mother. That's how all of us get roped into stuff like this."

"Thank you, O wise one. That makes me feel a whole lot better."

"Docia, honey, where's your veil?" Reba bustled into the room followed by an entourage of Woodrose staff and the photographer. "You need to get it on before you throw the bouquet."

"Mama, I don't do veils." Docia smoothed down the wrinkles that had already developed in her dress. "Let's get this show on the road. Where's my husband? He hasn't deserted this shindig already, has he?"

Cal slipped away from Wonder and Allie. "I'm right here. It's okay." He was grinning again. Oh, well, he probably had reason to at this point.

"Okay, where's Janie?" Docia craned her neck, looking toward the French doors.

"I'm here, Docia, go ahead."

Pete turned. Janie stood in the doorway. She was wearing a dress the color of summer twilight. Her skin glowed. Her hair had a dense blue-black sheen. She looked like she was wearing stardust. She turned toward him and smiled slowly.

Pete swallowed. He was in deep, deep trouble.

Chapter Twenty-Four

Sherice stood beside her rental car, smoothing her skirt. She really wished she'd had time to go to San Antonio and pick up a real Versace dress rather than this knock-off, particularly since Lars would be cutting off her credit cards soon—if he hadn't already. Still, this outfit would do nicely for her purposes. A red the color of Marilyn Monroe's lipstick, matte jersey that fit her like a second skin, cut low on top and high at the bottom. Perfect for her entrance into the reception.

She started up the path from the parking lot. Good thing she'd taken the wedding invitation with her when she'd left the motel. The security guards at the entrance to the event center hadn't even blinked when she drove up, just motioned her through like any other guest.

She headed toward the French windows at the back. Best to avoid the receiving line, although she figured they wouldn't want to make a fuss about her there in front of all the other guests. On the other hand, she didn't want to give Billy Kent the chance to have her discreetly thrown out. Not until she'd done what she'd set out to do.

Not that she knew exactly what she'd set out to do. Too many possibilities!

She could walk in when the bride was tossing the bouquet. That would sure as hell ruin Docia's aim. Maybe she'd hit one of the Toleffsons by mistake, preferably one of the males. Better yet, she could step forward as the best man started his toast. She'd love to see Pete Toleffson choke on his champagne. Or maybe she'd show up in the middle of the dancing. She could picture the floor clearing to let her through, everybody whispering, wondering who this gorgeous woman was. This gorgeous woman the Toleffsons had driven away.

Sherice tightened her lips to a thin line. The final scene in all these scenarios always featured Lars realizing what an asshole he'd been, what a loser he was to let her go.

Not that she wanted him back. Not even slightly. But she really wanted him to suffer.

At one point she'd considered trying to grab Daisy again. If she wanted Lars to suffer, that was definitely the way to go. But she figured she'd never make it this time. Mama Toleffson would probably snatch her bald-headed before she'd let that baby go again.

Sherice rounded the corner of the building, heading toward the back entrance, when she noticed someone sitting on the steps that led up to the glass doors. A very large someone. A very Toleffson someone.

She caught her breath. For a moment, she thought it was Lars, but the body wasn't quite right. Taller, but softer somehow. She came to a stop a few feet in front of him as the man turned her way. Erik Toleffson. The prodigal son.

She shook her head. "What the hell are you doing here? I thought they'd drummed you out of the family. Or did they send you out to sit on the steps this time?"

Erik regarded her through narrowed eyes, his mouth spreading in a slow grin. "Afternoon, Sherice. I thought you might show up. I've been waiting for you."

Sherice took a deep breath, assessing the situation. A frontal assault would work best, she decided. "I've got a right to be here. I'm still a Toleffson. My daughter's in there." She took a step forward. Erik didn't move.

He nodded. "A concerned mother. Interesting approach. Of course, the dress doesn't really work for that."

Sherice folded her arms across her chest, careful not to loosen the double-sided tape that was holding her breasts in place. "What's wrong with my dress?"

Erik shrugged. "Nothing, if you're looking to replace Lars with a sugar daddy. It's just not what most people think of as motherly, unless you're planning on breast-feeding her during the afternoon."

Sherice felt like stamping her foot. All those Toleffsons were such smart-asses. "Get out of my way, Erik. I've got an invitation and I'm going in."

Erik pushed himself slowly to his feet, running his gaze over her without much interest. "You might want to think about that for a minute."

"I have thought about it," she snapped. "Get out of my way."

"I know you believe this is the best kind of revenge," Erik continued, not moving, "but you need to do a little analyzing here."

Sherice pressed her lips together, tapping her toe. One thing she didn't want to do was think. On the other hand, she hadn't been thinking clearly when she'd dumped Daisy on that picnic table so she could argue better. A crying baby just got in the way when she was trying to make her point. Then Mama Toleffson had walked off with Sherice's best bargaining chip.

She blew out an irritated breath. "Look, I'm going in there. You can't stop me."

He shrugged. "You're right. I can't. None of us Toleffsons can do much to you right now, although if I were you I'd try not to piss Pete off any more than you already have, seeing as how he knows most of the lawyers and judges in Des Moines."

Sherice shook her head. "So? I'll get a lawyer from Ames or something. I'm not afraid of any of you Toleffsons, not even Pete."

"No, probably not. So how do you feel about the Kents?" His gaze flicked back toward the ballroom. "And the Brandenburgs?"

Sherice had a faint sting of uneasiness. "Who are they? Friends of yours?"

His grin became slightly lopsided. "Not really. I don't have many friends here. They're Docia's parents. And from what I hear, they're worth more than all the Toleffsons for several generations put together, in terms of money anyway."

"So?" She smoothed her skirt over her hips. "You're all poor, so what? I've got no problem with Docia Kent's family. It's you Toleffsons who've been giving me grief."

"But Docia's a Toleffson now."

Erik leaned forward slightly, and she found herself thinking of all the stories Lars had told her about him. All the things he'd done, things that made his straight-arrow brothers treat him like he was radioactive. For a moment, she almost wished she'd brought that big lummox Otto Friedrich with her.

She straightened her spine. "What's your point?"

"It doesn't matter whether you piss off the Toleffsons. Like I said, we can't do much to you even if we wanted to. On the other hand, I figure you're ready to trade up from Lars. Right?"

Sherice blew out a quick breath, then raised her head defiantly. "You think I can't?"

He shrugged. "I have no idea. But does it make sense to go in there and make trouble, when you'd be screwing around with two of the richest families in Texas?"

She dug her nails into her palms, trying not to listen.

"You think the Kents don't have long memories?" His voice was lazy. "You think Billy Kent won't go out of his way to keep the woman who ruined his daughter's wedding reception from cozying up to anybody in his tax bracket?"

Sherice's pulse pounded in her ears. *Shit, shit, shit.*

"C'mon, Sherice." Erik's voice softened. "Think it through. Go on back to Des Moines and get your lawyer. Just let them have their reception."

For a moment—a very brief moment—Sherice was ready to do it anyway. The thrill of bringing everything down, causing the kind of scene where everybody ended up furious and in tears while she walked out in triumph. But then her practical self kicked in.

He was right. Damn him.

She turned on her heel, stalking back up the path, then glanced back over her shoulder when she reached the corner of the house.

Erik still sat on the stairs where she'd left him, his large hands clasped in front of his knees.

Sherice narrowed her eyes at him. "Why are you helping them? They treated you like crap. Just like they treated me."

"Ah, but I deserved it," he said. "And once in a while you get a chance to make up for shit you've done. This is one of those times."

Sherice sucked in a breath, feeling a hot flush of irritation. "And you figure that'll happen to me?"

Erik grinned at her again, leaning back against the steps. "If you're lucky."

Janie managed to miss the bouquet Docia threw at her. It bounced once off the tips of her fingers, rather like a volleyball, and landed in Allie's hands.

Wonder turned slightly pale. So did Allie.

Janie knew they were all trying to help, but she wasn't sure why they thought giving her a bouquet to match the garter Pete had caught would change things. Pete had to go back to Des Moines. He had a job there, even if he didn't like it much. He had family. He had responsibilities, and she knew only too well how seriously he regarded them all.

It had been a lovely fantasy, but fantasy time was over now. She had to be a grown-up again. And she didn't mind too much. Really.

Janie bit her lip. Maybe if she repeated that mantra enough times it would take care of the hollow feeling in her chest.

The reception line passed in a daze. Janie fielded compliments on her dress from most of the Konigsburgers, along with a few piercing looks from those who still thought she was cheating on Otto. She also got some interested looks from the out-of-town guests, mostly the men but also a few wives. She ignored them all. She'd already decided the afternoon was going to be her one turn in the limelight, or rather in the light that reflected from Docia and Cal.

Docia glowed, partly from joy and partly from irritation that she'd gotten stuck in the Cinderella dress in spite of her best efforts. Janie was so happy for her that her heart contracted every time Docia laughed.

Happiness, she assured herself. That pain in her heart was happiness.

The reception dinner was lavish—beef in some kind of elaborate sauce with an array of vegetables so tiny they might have been grown by gerbils. Janie ate almost none of it. She sat next to Cal, who had his own plate of seared sea bass, with Lars on her other side. Whatever they said was lost on her. She couldn't think. She couldn't even hear most of the time, given the orchestra sawing away in the background. Her stomach had rolled itself into a tight little ball.

She drank water and avoided the champagne that everyone else was pouring down lustily. She had a feeling champagne would make her maudlin, and this was a joyous occasion. The only people who got to cry were Reba and Mrs. Toleffson, although Mrs. Toleffson looked thoroughly dry-eyed from where Janie sat.

Allie's cake was a marvel of engineering and imagination,

cantilevered layers dripping with flowers and curlicues and filled with a butter cream that was guaranteed to raise a person's cholesterol by twenty points. Even the groom's cake was a spectacular concoction of carrots and pineapple and raisins and cream cheese. Janie was sure it would have tasted terrific if she'd been able to choke down a bite.

After the last dish had been removed, Pete got to his feet, holding his champagne glass in front of him as the orchestra ground to a halt. "I'm supposed to make a toast, but I'm not much good at this." He sighed. Everyone in the tent stared up at him expectantly.

"To Docia and Cal." He raised his glass. "May you have the kind of wonderful life together you both deserve."

All around her people raised their glasses, nodding and smiling. Janie gulped down a swallow of champagne, then pressed her fingers to her lips, trying to hold back the panic rising in her throat.

What had she been going to say? She couldn't remember her toast. She tottered to her feet, bracing one fist on the table in front of her, her champagne glass extended in the other.

"Docia," she said, her voice trembling, "you're my best friend."

Docia looked up at her intently, her eyes suspiciously bright.

"Cal—" Janie turned to him, "—you're the nicest man I've ever met."

Cal stared at her, his forehead furrowing.

"Here's to you both." Janie took a deep breath. "You make us all believe in the power of possibilities." She took another gulp of champagne, managed a thin smile for the crowd, and sat abruptly.

Lars put his hand on her shoulder. "That was beautiful, Janie. Are you okay?"

Janie nodded, biting her lip. She really was okay. Really. Okay.

"Janie." Docia stepped behind her chair and hugged her again. "Oh, Janie."

Janie wanted to tell her to stop it, that she was tired of being hugged. But somehow her voice seemed to have deserted her. Somewhere in the background the orchestra was beginning to tune up again.

"Oh god," Docia moaned, "time for the dances." She turned to Cal. "Did you tell your mother you'd be dancing with her?"

"She'll figure it out. Come on, babe, we get to lead off." He grabbed Docia's hand and turned toward the dance floor that had been set up in the adjoining tent.

"Slow down," Docia snapped. "I can hardly move in this getup as it is." She gathered up a handful of chiffon and took a couple of teetering steps. Cal grinned and swept her up into his arms, carrying her toward the orchestra tent as she squealed.

All around Janie, people moved toward the sounds of music. She sat staring at her now-empty champagne glass. She wasn't sure just when she'd chugged the contents, but the champagne was undoubtedly all gone now.

"Janie?"

She looked up. Pete stood watching her. "You promised to dance with me, remember? That was a beautiful toast, by the way."

She blew out the breath she'd been holding. "Thanks. Yours was nice too." She stared back at her glass again. Her brain was a little woozy all of sudden.

"Dance?" He said again. His forehead was slightly creased.

"Dance." She nodded. "Sure, I can do that." The afternoon sunlight reflected off the edge of her champagne glass as she stared, dazzling her.

"Or we could go back inside the inn and see if we can find an empty bedroom," Pete added casually.

Janie stared up at him. His mouth was solemn, but his eyes sparkled with mischief.

"Okay," she murmured. "Let's do that instead."

It only took three tries to locate an empty room that was also unlocked. Since Reba and Billy had reserved the entire Woodrose Inn, Pete figured they wouldn't invade anyone's privacy as long as he didn't see anything in the room that reminded him of Reba. Late afternoon sunlight poured through the lace curtains, flickering shadows across the floor. The bed was king-size, fortunately. Pete locked the door behind them and threw on the deadbolt for good measure.

Janie stood framed against the windows, her moonlight

dress shimmering. She was wearing the most beautiful piece of clothing he'd ever seen, and he was going take it all off her anyway. He was a lust-crazed beast, and it didn't bother him a bit.

After a moment, Janie glided toward him. He was pretty certain her feet never touched the ground, but since she was made of moonlight he wasn't surprised. She ran the tips of her fingers along the line of his jaw.

"You look hot," she said.

Ah, if she only knew. "It's the vest," he croaked.

The corners of her mouth quirked up slightly. "Take it off, then."

His fingers fumbled with the buttons until her hands slid beneath his, opening his coat and vest, then pushing them off his shoulders.

Cool air caressed his shirt front for the first time in a couple of hours at least. But his skin still felt like it was on fire, particularly since Janie kept stroking her fingers across his chest.

He closed his eyes and let himself feel the whisper of her touch. "God, Janie."

When she took her hand away, he almost groaned. He opened his eyes to see her reaching for the zipper at the back of her dress. He pushed her hands away gently. "Let me."

He pulled the zipper down, then let his hands glide across her silken skin, moving his thumbs up the bumps of her spine. He blinked. "You're not wearing underwear."

"It's sort of built into the dress," Janie murmured.

Pete began to roll the dress down, careful to treat it like the piece of magic it was. Janie stepped out and stood in front of him, her arms crossed protectively over her breasts.

He reached for her hands and unfolded her arms slowly. He'd never get tired of looking at her breasts, he decided. Not even when they were both in their eighties. He'd still want to see them.

His heartbeat sped up suddenly—he couldn't quite catch his breath.

He wouldn't see her when they were eighty. He might not even see her tomorrow. He'd be packed and ready to go, heading for the San Antonio airport, back to Des Moines. Back home.

This could be the last time he saw her beautiful body. The last time he held her in his arms. The last time he kissed her. The last time they made love.

Or not.

Somewhere in his brain his practical voice was screaming. *What are you thinking of? You're the Deputy Assistant County Attorney. You have responsibilities. You have a job. An important job that everyone depends on. You have a freakin' condo in West Des Moines.*

My responsibilities could be taken over in a microsecond by any number of hungry assistants. The only reason people depend on me is that I'm there. My job is sucking my life away. My condo looks like Hotel Anonymous.

If you make love to her now, the voice screamed, *it will mean you love her. No backing out. No going away. It will mean Janie Dupree is The One.*

Pete felt something in the back of his mind, like an object dropping into place—a puzzle piece, a missing coin, the keystone in an arch. Suddenly, he knew exactly what he wanted.

I do love her. And she is The One. Now and always.

Chapter Twenty-Five

Janie lay on her side, watching Pete's sleeping face. He had a small scar over his left eyebrow and a slight indentation at the base of his chin. His beard was already growing in, a dark shadow on his cheeks.

She kicked a couple of pillows out of the way. The bed had an elaborate lace bedspread and more pillows than a seraglio. She kept finding them tucked into inconvenient places.

She dropped her gaze to Pete's chest, running her hands across it lightly. Thick dark hair crinkled beneath her palms, the pinkish brown disks of his nipples showing through like pebbles. She leaned forward and touched her tongue to one tip, then laved around it.

Pete inhaled with a quick hiss, his eyes popping open. "Not fair."

"Why not?" Janie slid her hands to his stomach, then down the arrow of hair that led to his groin.

"I'm over thirty. My body doesn't bounce back so quickly anymore."

Janie gave a quick glance downward. "Parts of you are bouncing back just fine. Are you saying the rest of you is too old to keep up?"

"You're going to kill me, aren't you?" Pete sighed. He rolled quickly, pinning her beneath him. "This is self-defense, Ms. Dupree."

He kissed her behind her ear, then traced a line down her throat with the tip of his tongue.

Janie caught her breath. She reached for him, but he trapped her hands above her head, holding her with one hand. "Self-defense," he murmured, running his mouth across her collarbone and down into the space between her breasts.

Janie's body moved without her consciously willing it. Before she knew it, she was rubbing herself against him.

Pete caught one nipple with his lips, pressing it hard against the roof of his mouth with his tongue. Janie made a sound she'd never heard before, one she didn't know she could make.

Chuckling, he moved on to feathery kisses across her stomach and abdomen. Janie moved her hips again, helplessly. She was on the edge of the biggest orgasm of her life, and Pete was taking his time.

"Pete," she gasped, "please. God…"

"Patience, sweetheart," he crooned. "We'll get there."

"Before I die please."

Pete chuckled again, the vibration rumbling through her body. And then his mouth was moving down. He dropped her hands and opened her folds with his thumbs. The heat of his breath blew across her clit, as one finger moved inside her.

"Pete," she panted, "I don't think I can hold out anymore."

"Then don't," he murmured and drew her clit into his mouth.

Janie arched off the bed. He slid another finger inside her, working them against the straining of her muscles as he sucked. The storm of heat and desire swirled around her, breaking her into shards of light as her body arched and swayed in his hands.

After a few moments, she lay panting, aware that she'd probably screamed. With any luck everybody was still dancing somewhere in the distance.

She brought her hands down, wrapping them around his shaft, caressing him, running her hands up and down his length.

"Christ, Janie," Pete groaned. "Oh Christ."

"Pete," she whispered. "Now, please."

He fumbled quickly at the side of the bed, then froze. "Shit. goddamn."

Janie looked up at his face, creased with strain. "What's the matter?"

"No more condoms," he groaned. "I thought I grabbed more than one."

He turned away from her, closing his eyes as he took a breath. "Sorry, sweetheart."

"It's okay." Janie nodded toward her clothes. "In my purse."

Pete blinked at her. "Your purse."

Janie closed her eyes, tying to form a coherent sentence. "Look in my purse. It's over there on the floor somewhere."

"But..." He stared at her, his eyes like obsidian.

Janie blew out a breath. "I bought some, okay? And I tucked them into my purse."

Pete's mouth edged up. "You were thinking..."

"What you were thinking," Janie snapped. She'd actually put them there a couple of days ago, although she'd told herself she was being silly at the time.

"Good girl," Pete murmured, digging her purse out from under her dress.

If she weren't so turned on, Janie figured she'd probably be blushing from her toes to the top of her head. As it was, her face was flaming.

Pete climbed back on the bed again, dropping the other condoms onto the bedside stand before he sheathed himself. Then his body moved against her, pressing her back against the pillows again.

And then he was inside her, thrusting deep, deeper than she could have thought possible. She tipped her hips, wrapping her legs around him, catching his head in her hands so that she could bring her mouth to his. Their tongues tangled, salty with her taste, mimicking their bodies, and another wave of feeling spread from her center to her fingertips, her toes, the top of her head, everything blending, exploding, finishing in a trembling blast.

Pete pounded into her body a few more times and then cried out. Janie held him as he shuddered against her, as he panted her name against her throat.

After a long moment, he lifted himself and touched his forehead to hers lightly, holding her in a loose embrace. "Oh, Janie, holy crap."

Janie snuggled in next to him. "So that was okay for you?"

"Sweetheart." He sighed. "Trust me, we've already moved way beyond okay."

Janie closed her eyes again, relaxing. She needed to be ready. Any minute now he was going to start telling her goodbye. He'd tell her he was sorry to leave. Maybe he'd suggest they get together sometime. Maybe he'd want to e-mail her.

Maybe...

But whatever he had planned, she wouldn't let him do it. She wasn't another responsibility for him to take on. And besides, it would be better to end it now than to let it drag on for months, breaking her heart a little more every day whenever she thought about how much she wanted him. How much she loved him.

Clean breaks were much better. Weren't they?

Pete lay in the gathering darkness, feeling Janie's breath against his cheek. Somewhere at the back of his mind a voice whispered, *What are you going to do?* Unfortunately, he didn't have any answer yet. But he knew what he wasn't going to do. He wasn't going to let her slip away from him.

"Janie." He took a deep breath, "I've been thinking."

Her head lifted fractionally from his shoulder as she squinted at him. "About what?"

"Well, the future, sort of." He blew out a breath. "You know, what we're going to do and all."

"Oh." She shook her head. "You mean that you have to go back home tomorrow. That's all right. Don't worry about it."

A sliver of ice invaded his stomach. "Don't worry about it?"

"No." She half pushed herself up so that the sheet fell back from her breasts again. "It's okay. Really. I know this was only temporary. I know you need to go back to Iowa and your job. I know it's important to you, that they need you. I'm okay with it. Really. Don't worry."

He couldn't see her face clearly in the dim light, so he couldn't be entirely sure how serious she was. Her voice sounded funny, slightly choked. "What if I'm not okay with it?"

Janie reached out to run her fingers along his cheek. "No, Pete, it's all right. Believe me. You don't need to take care of me—I'm a big girl. I'll get along okay. Don't worry about me."

"But..." Pete took a breath. He loved this woman. Why exactly was this going so wrong so quickly?

"I've thought about it—a lot." She might have swallowed. In the darkness it was hard to tell. "You always protect people, look after people. But you don't need to do that with me. I'll always remember this week, but you don't need to take care of me now. I know your job in Des Moines is really important, and that you're really good at it. And I know you need to go back to do it, although you do need to slow down a little bit, too, so it doesn't make you sick. But, well, I understand you have to go. I don't...you know...just don't worry."

Pete felt as if his breath was caught in his throat. She didn't want him. Of all the outcomes he'd thought of, this was one that hadn't occurred to him.

He'd have to let her go if that's what she chose.

But she didn't look happy about it. In fact, he'd be willing to bet those were tears she was blinking back right now.

Something here wasn't computing. And his brain was too fuzzed with sex and wedding aftermath to work right. If this was *Casablanca*, somehow he'd ended up playing the Ingrid Bergman part rather than Bogart. And that was clearly unacceptable. Time to get things straightened out.

"We need something to eat before we go any further with this conversation," he sighed, sliding out of bed.

Janie sat staring at the door that Pete had just closed, trying very hard not to cry. If he came back and found her in tears, he'd decide she needed to be looked after. And she didn't. Honestly. She was a big girl. An apprentice bitch, even. She didn't need a man to protect her.

She'd done the right thing. She'd beaten him to the punch, sending him off before he could try to find a way to let her down easily. After all, they'd only known each other for a week or so. Once he got over the whole wedding euphoria, he'd realize his job meant more to him than she did.

If he tried to keep something going long distance, it would just draw it out, make it worse. Basically, they'd both end up feeling like crap.

Which didn't mean that she didn't feel like crap at this very moment.

Janie bit her lip. *Guts up, Janie.* She'd always known it would come to this. This was just a fling. Her first fling. Now she had to be a grown-up and get over it. Get her own apartment. Move on with her life. Find someone else, someone who lived in the same place she did. Someone who'd be here tomorrow and the next day and the next.

She had an obligation. She was still the good girl. She was the one who was going to make the sacrifice here, make the break. People fell in and out of love all the time, and so could she. She just needed a little time to forget him. And then she'd move on to something else, find somebody else. That was the responsible thing to do, the considerate thing to do, the best thing to do. The thing that would allow her to hold onto her dignity and her self-respect.

Was she supposed to feel so wretched when she did it, though?

As he slipped downstairs, Pete could still hear the orchestra playing out on the broad lawn, but it sounded very far away. Food. There had to be some food left somewhere. He knew Janie hadn't eaten much—he'd watched her all through dinner. Maybe she was suffering from low blood sugar. Feed her a little bit, and maybe she'd snap out of it.

Besides, they needed some champagne to lubricate this conversation. And if things didn't get better fast, he intended to get very drunk indeed.

He slipped out onto the patio without encountering anyone other than a curious waiter or two. He found a buffet table where he managed to fill a platter with bread and cheese and something that looked like dry salami, along with some chips and dip. He added a handful of olives for good measure.

As he turned to head back up the patio stairs, he caught sight of his father sitting next to the door, watching him.

"I'm glad you're feeding her," he said mildly. "She looked like she was ready to keel over when she gave that toast."

Pete stood poised next to the door, trying to think of something relevant to say that was fit for his father's ears.

"So how's your evening going?" His father leaned his head back to look up at him.

Pete sighed, setting the platter down on the nearest table. "Not exactly like I expected."

"So she turned you down?" His father shook his head. "Naturally. I guess that figures."

Pete felt a quick rush of annoyance. "Why does that figure? You think I'm not good enough for her?" He sighed. "Of course, you could be right. Maybe I'm not."

"You're not only good enough for her, you're just what she needs." His father grinned at him. "But it seems to me the two of you are too much alike. You're both fixers. You both want to take care of everybody around you before you get around to taking care of yourselves."

"So you think we won't be good together?" Pete frowned. "Really?"

"I think you'll be great together. You just both have to learn to be more selfish. Convince her she's not doing you any favors—that you don't want her to save you. And stop trying to save her from anything yourself. That's my advice, for what it's worth." His father took a swallow from his bottle of beer. "Of course, what do I know? I'm here hiding out from Docia's mama—she keeps wanting me to dance with her. It's a known fact Toleffsons don't dance."

Pete stood staring at him. Several points suddenly became crystal clear. "Thanks, Pop."

"You need anything else?"

Pete paused a moment, thinking. "I didn't find any champagne. Is it gone?"

"Pretty much." His father shrugged. "On the other hand..." He leaned behind the table, pulling out a damp bottle. "I just noticed some left in this cooler." He handed the bottle to Pete. "That do it?"

Pete nodded. "Yes, sir. Thanks again."

"Any time. Any time at all." His father peered back down the stairs toward the spreading lawn. "You think Reba's hooked back up with Billy by now?"

"Probably." Pete gathered up his platter and his bottle and headed back up the stairs, tucking a couple of glasses into his pockets.

At least Janie hadn't moved from the bed when he stepped back into the room, which he considered an encouraging sign. He sighed. "Hey."

"Hey yourself." She pulled up to a sitting position, letting the sheet drop to her waist again, which started an ache somewhere south of his heart. "Is that for me?"

"Yep." He placed the platter on the bed next to her. "You didn't have dinner."

"No, I wasn't hungry then. Now I am." She piled several pieces of cheese on a slice of bread and dug in.

Pete opened the champagne and poured. "I figured we needed something. Here, have one."

Janie took the glass, staring at him over the rim. "More champagne—I'm not sure I can drink any more. You're not expecting another toast, are you? What's the occasion?"

"The occasion is we need to dump the bullshit." He cleared his throat. "This time around we talk about what we really want, not what we think we should want or what we think is good for each other. We've both got a bad habit of trying to take care of everybody else's problems. It's making us stupid."

She blinked at him, her mouth narrowing. "What do you mean?"

"Look, Janie, I can't take care of the world or even the people in the immediate vicinity—and you can't either. So no nobility, okay? No selflessness. No putting my needs ahead of yours because that's what you're supposed to do. None of that. Am I clear?"

Janie nodded, her eyes suddenly very wide.

"Okay." He swallowed hard. "I guess I'm ready then."

She blinked at him. "For what?"

"My marriage proposal. Because the thing is, Janie, we've got no judgment at all when it comes to each other. We want each other so bad our brains go missing, and then we get all noble when it comes to admitting it. Well, screw that!"

He picked up his glass and took a quick swallow, then raised it in her direction. "I'm making a pre-emptive strike here. I need you. We need each other. And we need to make it official, given the kind of people we are. I know we haven't known each other long, and I know I was a real asshole at first, but…"

"Yes," Janie said.

Pete raised an eyebrow. "Pardon me?"

"Yes. I'll marry you. The time doesn't need to be long, just deep. And we've had deep. And you said I should tell you what I want—so this is it. You're what I want. Yes."

A bubble of heat rose in his chest, filling his body with warmth. "We've had deep all right."

"But—" she raised her hand quickly, "—that doesn't mean you don't have to go back and settle things in Des Moines. You need to do that, Pete, for your own sake."

He nodded. "But I'm coming back here to live. Hell, if Cal

can be a Texas vet and Lars can be a Texas accountant, I figure I can be a Texas attorney."

She gave him a luminous smile. "That's wonderful. You'll like it here."

"Why don't you come with me now to Iowa while I get everything worked out? You can see Lander. Not that there's much to see, but fall is one of the better times to see what there is." He poured himself more champagne, then took her glass.

Janie frowned. "I have to run the bookstore while Docia's on her honeymoon. Three weeks, starting tomorrow."

"Okay." Pete shrugged. "I'll help."

"But they need you at your office, you need..."

He touched his fingers to her lips, quickly. "I need you. Now. And I've got a lot of vacation time built up, believe me." His mouth moved into a slow grin. "And I can get Olive back. Since she's my dog and since I'll be living here. You don't mind if I keep her, do you?"

Janie let her grin break through, shaking her head. "No. I already asked Cal if I could take care of her while he was gone, to tell you the truth."

"Good enough." He sighed and lay back on the bed again, folding his arms behind his head.

She took a deep breath and blew it out, then took another bite of bread and cheese. "So now what happens?"

He shrugged. "We take our time. Get Olive back from the clinic—tomorrow, if I have anything to say about it. Go back to Iowa when we can. Get everything set up here. Get married whenever you feel like it. Quietly. With very few people in attendance."

"Right. I guess we'll invite our friends." She grimaced. "And families."

"No tuxes," Pete mused. "No big deal wedding dresses."

"Well, maybe a little deal wedding dress." Janie grinned. "And Daisy gets to be the flower girl."

"Agreed." They clinked their glasses together and sipped.

Pete sat very still, watching her. It hurt to look at her suddenly. But he had a feeling it would hurt a lot more not to.

"I love you, Ms. Dupree."

Janie grinned up at him. "Good. I love you too, and I do prefer happy endings."

Epilogue

Lars sat in a fairly comfortable lawn chair on the patio of the Woodrose Inn watching people dance. The wedding was finally beginning to wind down two hours after Cal and Docia had taken off to catch a plane. The orchestra had been playing most of the evening, but they gave no signs of stopping. Lars figured, like everyone else involved in Reba's party, they must have been paid an exorbitant amount of money.

He took a sip from his glass of iced tea. He'd stopped slugging back champagne when he realized it made him want to either burst into tears or take a swing at someone. Time to pull himself together and start working things out. He had Daisy and the rest of his life to think about.

Wonder was sprawled at the next table, chewing on what looked like a roast beef sandwich he'd liberated from the kitchen. Allie was dancing with Lee Contreras.

Wonder raised an eyebrow. "Where's your daughter?"

"Sleeping, I imagine. Mom and Dad took off with her a couple of hours ago."

"So are the rumors true?" Wonder raised both eyebrows this time. "Are you settling here?"

"Thinking about it seriously." Lars reached for a butter mint. Not bad at all, especially the little tang of chilies at the end.

Wonder sighed dramatically. "Two Toleffsons in one town. I don't know if Konigsburg can take it."

"Lander, Iowa, put up with six Toleffsons for around twenty years, counting my folks. The last time I looked, the town hadn't suffered a whole lot."

Wonder pushed himself to his feet. "Yeah, well, we're more sensitive down here. Time to go dance again."

"You going to open up an office here?" Horace sat in Wonder's vacated seat, carrying a slice of wedding cake.

"That's what I'm thinking about doing." Lars took another swallow of iced tea. "I'm working for a national firm right now, but I figure I could go on my own here."

"Yeah, people always need accountants. Even me. My guy's thinking of retiring." Horace glanced up at the patio door, squinting slightly. "There's your brother."

"Pete? I haven't seen him since dinner." Lars started to turn and froze in mid-motion.

Horace cleared his throat. "Not Pete. Your older brother."

Erik was carrying a glass of something that looked like more iced tea. He slid into the chair beside Lars. "Evening."

"Nando Avrogado said you were looking for part time work with the town police. That right?" Horace shoveled in a bite of cake.

Erik shrugged. "Yeah. I've been working for the force in Davenport—I took some Criminal Justice courses at the college there. I was thinking about maybe moving down here. Heard they might be hiring." He leaned back in his chair, keeping his gaze on Horace.

"Usually are. Just part time, though. Put in an application." Horace pushed himself to his feet. "Time to collect Bethany and head off."

Lars stared at his brother as Horace moved away. "You're in the police department?"

Erik shrugged. "Yeah. Before that I worked for a private security company. Got my Associate's degree a few years ago at Eastern Iowa CC after the army. I like police work." He gave Lars a slightly crooked smile. "Ironic, right?"

Lars blinked at him. "Not necessarily. Go for it, bro."

Erik's smile became less guarded. "You don't mind my being here? I mean, Dad said you were moving down too."

Lars leaned back against his chair again. "I don't think you being here would cause any problems. Not for me, anyway."

Erik turned slightly, watching Allie glide by with Wonder. "I figure I could start over in Konigsburg without all the baggage I've got back home. I'll stay out of your way, though."

"Don't worry about it. But Wonder's going to have a heart attack. Three Toleffsons in Konigsburg."

Erik closed his eyes, resting his glass of tea against his chest. "First time we've all been in the same place in fifteen years."

Lars took another survey of the dance floor. Billy Kent and Reba were moving with professional ease near the bandstand. Various Kent relatives and business associates flowed around them, like something out of a forties society movie. He glanced toward the far end of the dance floor and stopped.

Pete glided through the shadows of a live oak, dancing with Janie Dupree—or anyway, standing with her on the dance floor. They didn't seem to be moving much. He wore his tuxedo pants and shirt. Janie was still in her lavender dress. Both were barefoot and neither of them was even slightly aware of Lars or anyone else. They stood together, Janie's head tucked beneath Pete's chin, holding hands as they moved slowly back and forth.

Lars considered pretending he hadn't seen them, but curiosity got the better of him. He ambled over to their corner. "Evening."

Pete glanced up a little blankly. "Lars. You're still here?"

"Yeah, just thinking about going back to the motel." Lars grinned at him. "I don't suppose you'd be interested in giving me a ride."

"Oh." Pete looked down at Janie, his lips inching up. "Are you ready to go, sweetheart?"

"That's okay. Don't leave because of me." Lars watched them gaze at each other. He'd never felt more superfluous in his life. "Um, Pete, are you still flying home with us tomorrow?"

Pete kept his gaze on Janie. "Nope. I'll come back and take care of some stuff later. Maybe in a couple of weeks." He glanced back at Lars. "I'm going to move down here, bro. As soon as I get everything wrapped up back in Des Moines."

Lars blew out a breath. "As far as you know, are Mom and Dad staying in Lander?"

Pete frowned. "Far as I know. Why?"

"Just checking." Lars turned back toward his table.

"Lars?" Pete grinned at him. "We're going to have another wedding in a few months. Will you be my best man?"

Lars closed his eyes, remembering Sherice, touch football, tuxes and dart games. He pinched the bridge of his nose. "Have you considered Vegas?"

Pete and Janie smiled at each other again. "Not a chance. Konigsburg, bro, get used to it."

"Right." Lars wandered back toward his chair. As far as he could tell neither of them even noticed he was gone.

About the Author

Meg Benjamin writes about South Texas. Her comic romances, *Venus in Blue Jeans* and *Wedding Bell Blues,* both published by Samhain, are set in the Texas Hill Country. When she isn't writing, Meg spends her time listening to Americana music, drinking Texas wine, and keeping track of her far-flung family. After living in Texas for over twenty years, Meg recently moved to Colorado. To learn more about Meg Benjamin, please visit www.MegBenjamin.com. Meg loves to hear from her readers. Send her an email at meg@megbenjamin.com.

GREAT
CHEAP
FUN

Discover eBooks!

THE FASTEST WAY TO GET THE HOTTEST NAMES

Get your favorite authors on your favorite reader, long before they're
out in print! Ebooks from Samhain go wherever you go, and work with
whatever you carry—Palm, PDF, Mobi, and more.

Samhain
Publishing Ltd

LaVergne, TN USA
14 April 2010
179293LV00001B/56/P